NORTHERN FRIGHTS

NORTHERN FRIGHTS

DRAUGR

THE HAUNTING OF DRANG ISLAND

THE LOKI WOLF

ARTHUR SLADE

Harper*Trophy*Canada™
An imprint of HarperCollins*Publishers*Ltd

Northern Frights
Copyright © 2014 by Arthur Slade. All rights reserved.

Published by Harper*Trophy*Canada, an imprint of
HarperCollins Publishers Ltd

First Edition

Draugr
Copyright © 1997 by Arthur G. Slade.
Originally published by Orca Book Publishers: 1997

The Haunting of Drang Island
Copyright © 1998 by Arthur G. Slade.
Originally published by Orca Book Publishers: 1998

The Loki Wolf
Copyright © 2000 by Arthur G. Slade.
Originally published by Orca Book Publishers: 2000

No part of this book may be used or reproduced in any manner
whatsoever without the prior written permission of the publisher,
except in the case of brief quotations embodied in reviews.

HarperCollins books may be purchased for educational, business, or
sales promotional use through our Special Markets Department.

HarperCollins Publishers Ltd., 2 Bloor Street East, 20th Floor,
Toronto, Ontario, Canada, M4W 1A8

www.harpercollins.ca

ISBN 978-1-44343-140-8

Printed and bound in the United States
RRD 9 8 7 6 5 4 3 2 1

CONTENTS

DRAUGR

This novel is dedicated with love to my parents, Robert and Anne Slade. I owe you so much more than I can ever repay.

I also want to extend my gratitude to Emily, the town librarian. Thanks for lifting those heavy books on Norse mythology and passing them down to me when I was a little boy.

And my apologies to the wonderful inhabitants of Gimli, Manitoba. In the course of writing this novel I may have accidentally moved around an ice cream shop, a graveyard, and a few other things. I promise to put them back when I'm done with them.

Draugr *(draw-gur) m. 'undead' man, ghost*

—Definition taken from

E.V. Gordon's *An Introduction to Old Norse*

1

Grandpa was going to murder us.

Not with an axe. Not with a shovel. But with words.

"Sarah sit down," Grandpa said softly to me. "I haven't even started my story."

"But I'm scared already." I'm young, I'm fourteen, and I have my limits. His last tale ended with a headless woman searching through the streets for her head every Halloween. I wasn't going to sleep tonight. Why did Mom and Dad send me here every summer?

Grandpa rubbed his big, rough hands together. He was tall and even though he was in his late seventies, he had the energy of a man half his age. "This is my last yarn for tonight. I promise. And it's my best one."

I sat down. At the bottom of my beating heart, I really did like his stories. So did Michael, my twin brother, and my cousin Angie, who were both hugging pillows, waiting for Grandpa to begin. Michael and I looked nearly the same, with blue eyes and dark hair. Except, of course, he was a boy and about half as smart as me. Angie was our opposite, with bright red hair and green eyes. This was one of the few times that she was actually quiet.

Grandpa smiled and his face creased into a thousand wrinkles. "The difference between this story and the others is this one is true. Every word of it. I do want to ask you a question before I begin though . . . are you afraid of death?"

"Well . . ." I started. "Uh . . . I haven't really thought about it."

"That's alright, Sarah," Grandpa said softly. In the dim light he looked suddenly older and tired, as if just voicing that question had taken years from his life. He cleared his throat. "I have an even more important thing to ask you. Are you afraid of the dead?"

How do you answer something like that? What do you say? "No," I lied. Michael and Angie shook their heads. This was becoming a little too weird, even for me.

Grandpa stared, those blue haunted eyes of his looking right through me. He seemed to be in a trance.

"Yoo-hoo, Grandpa!" Michael called. He snapped his fingers. Once. Twice.

No reaction.

"Are you okay?" I whispered. "Grandpa?"

Grandpa shook his head. *"Draugr,"* he whispered as he crossed himself. The name echoed through the room and though I didn't know its meaning, I felt it. There in the quivering of my stomach, in the dryness of my throat. The name.

Grandpa was still staring. I whispered to him, but he didn't seem to hear me. Finally he looked directly into my eyes. "Long ago," he said, his voice even and controlled, "when I was quite young and I still lived in Iceland, I had an evil cousin, evil in the way only men can be evil. He respected no one, not his parents, not his kinsmen. No one. He complained about the work he had to do, about the way others did their work. He had venom in his blood and his tongue was like a serpent's—he spit only insults at the world and defied everything. His name was Borth."

Grandpa paused. He closed his eyes and I imagined him looking back in time, seeing his cousin standing amidst snow-covered hills in Iceland.

Grandpa opened his eyes again, still staring into the distance. "Borth was a strong youth, he could outwrestle many of the men in the valley and he loved fighting. His mother died giving birth to him and from that day forward he carried *ólán*—bad luck. If he walked by your house, your cows would run loose, your food would burn in the oven; women would prick their thumbs if he entered a room as they were sewing. He used to hit me as if I were nothing more than a bag of flour. No one had any love for Borth.

"One day in December I murdered him. Not by myself, I had help, but I *murdered* him. I know I am old and harmless now, but then I was beaten, a beast, a dog. I had been kicked by my cousin too often and finally a time came when I could take my revenge. A group of us, my kinsmen and friends who had all been violated in one way or another by Borth, made a pact to teach him a lesson. We were just children, that's all. Children, hardly even as old as you three. I was the eldest though, and they all followed me.

"We hid in the pass at Ogen's valley, all six or seven of us, on a night when there was a full moon. We knew Borth would cut through the valley on his way into the village. We had dressed in rags and made masks of wood and feathers, so that we looked like mound dwellers. Some of us had even grabbed stones to throw at him. Just to scare Borth, that's all we wanted, to run around and poke him with sticks, to yell his name, and then run away. It was supposed to be a trick, a warning, nothing more.

"Borth rode up a little after dark. The clomping of his horse, a beast as huge and evil as him, echoed in our ears. I glanced and saw that my companions were frozen with fright, hypnotized by that sound and the sight of Borth. He looked so big in the saddle, his shoulders as gigantic as a troll's, his long cloak flowing down behind him.

"I knew nobody would move unless I did, that we would sit there and he would pass. Our moment would pass. So right before he arrived, I threw myself onto the path in front of him and screamed, waving my arms and launching a handful of dirt. Everyone else followed me, yelling and hooting around the horse, slapping its legs with their sticks. We were like little dwarves up from out of the ground, finally getting our revenge. His mount reared up, its giant hooves sliced the air above us. It neighed in anger, nostrils flaring. But we weren't frightened; we felt strong then, all of us, powerful with vengeance. We continued our attacks. The horse reared again and Borth shouted in anger, yanking with all his strength on the reins. One rein snapped and he tumbled from the saddle, still yelling.

"The path was very rocky. Even above the ruckus we were making, I heard a soft thud when his head struck a stone. His horse bolted and we surrounded Borth, poking him with sticks and kicking at him, screaming his name in our lust for vengeance. Then as one, realizing something was wrong, we stopped. Borth didn't move. We all looked at each other, but no one said anything. We knew he was dead.

"I don't know who ran first, one of us did, and then we all followed, just running and running down the pass and across the fields, away from Borth's body.

"One of the villagers found him the next morning in a pool of frozen blood. We buried him three days later in the family cemetery. It was a strange funeral. No one cried. No one could.

"I returned to my daily work, not able to tell anyone my story. And I prayed nobody would discover what we had done. Then one morning, about two weeks after his death, I went into my family's hen house and found one of our chickens dead on the floor. It had been strangled. There were no tooth marks, so I knew it hadn't been killed by an animal. I figured one of the children from the village was just playing games and I forgot about it. But when I came back the next morning, another chicken was dead. This time its legs and head had been severed and placed beside its body. It made me sick to see, sick and very angry that someone would do this to our livestock. So I decided to catch whoever it was.

"That night I took my pitchfork with me and I stayed in the coop. I leaned up against the far wall. The coop was small. I could almost reach the door from where I was standing. It was warm too and I was dressed in a thick coat, so I soon sat down in the hay on the floor and fell asleep. I dreamed of a river filled with acid and blood that was slowly overflowing its banks. There were snakes in that river, huge snakes, the sons of Jormungand. Fire burned along the far bank. It was a strange, powerful dream, a dream from the old times.

"Then a noise woke me. The hens were moving around restlessly in the same way they do on the day I take them to the block. I stood up, still tired, the dream making my thoughts

11

slow. I could sense the same thing as the chickens. The feeling that Death was floating through the air, searching. I wanted to get in a corner, to hide, but there was nowhere to go. I waited.

"At first nothing happened, then I heard a noise like something being slowly dragged across the ground outside the coop. The sound would stop, then start again. There was this growling too. The noises ended before I could really be sure I heard them. I breathed in, relieved, then the door to the coop creaked inwards against the wooden bolt. A scratching sound filled my ears, as if a huge nail were being slowly drawn from the top of the door to the bottom. I froze, my breath caught in my mouth. The chickens had stopped moving. Everything was completely silent.

"Then again came the scratching, this time louder, harder, so it seemed a groove was being dug into the wood. The door began to rattle, the whole coop creaked as if a giant hand were pushing on its side. I felt suddenly cold. The scratching started for a third time; one of the planks on the door snapped, and splinters and wood fell in on me.

"I could wait no longer. I grabbed my pitchfork, stepped forward, and yanked the shaking door open. An icy wind swept straight into my eyes and I had to squint against it. Before me, with one arm raised, was a huge shadowy man, misshapen in the moonlight. He took a shambling step towards me and became clearer so that I saw he was covered with dirt. Grass was stuck in his frozen, messy hair. He stepped again, moving as if his legs were made of wood. I realized his head was not frozen with water but with black blood. His eyes glowed.

"'*Cousin,*' he rasped. He stepped again. '*I hate you.*'

"A huge white hand reached towards me. I stepped back,

slipped, and struck my head on the hen's loft. I fell unconscious to the floor. There I slept as if dead.

"When I awoke, hours later, I was sore and stiff and there was a dirty palm print on my jacket.

"I knew what had happened to Borth. He was a *draugr*, a revenant. My cousin was so full of hate he had become the walking dead. I did not know what I should do. The next time he returned he would drag me to his lair and tear me limb from limb. So I went home, took the silver cross my mother had given me, and I walked to the cemetery and buried that holy symbol in the soft dirt of his grave.

"He has not come back, but he is not gone. He waits underneath that earth. The dead know who killed them, they know, and if they hate enough—if they hate enough—they'll find a way back. Sometimes I can hear him screaming in the wind. And I wonder what will happen if someone goes to his grave and removes the cross?"

Grandpa leaned back in his chair. He looked very serious. Once or twice I caught him staring at the door as if he thought something might be lurking outside.

We sat there silently for a few minutes.

Grandpa clapped his hands, startling all of us. "Bed time," he said. "Hope you have a great sleep."

We slowly got up and prepared for bed. When I came out of the bathroom, most of the lights were off and Michael and Angie had gone to their rooms. Grandpa was sitting in his reading chair, squinting at an old book. A full moon shone through the window, giving him a pale, eerie look.

"Grandpa," I whispered, "how come the moon's so bright tonight?"

He looked up, seemed a little surprised to see me. "Oh," he said, "it's just a full moon—the *Hagalaz* moon. The kind of moon that makes hair grow on werewolves."

"*What?*"

He winked. "I'm kidding. It's just your everyday, normal moon. Nighty-night."

I went to bed. It took me quite a while to fall asleep.

2

For the last two summers my mom and dad sent Michael and me to visit Grandpa Thursten for two weeks. We'd catch the bus in Chillicothe, Missouri, and head north to Canada, to the small town of Gimli, Manitoba. It's next to a huge lake, and Grandpa lives in a six-room log cabin in the trees there.

Grandma Gunnora, his wife, used to live there too, but she died four years ago. I think that's one of the reasons Mom and Dad want us to come here—to keep Grandpa company. The other reason is they want to get us out of the house. We tend to get a little crazy when school's out.

This year Angie, my favorite cousin, was allowed to go with us and I was really looking forward to all the fun we'd have. Angie's not only my cousin, but she's one of my best friends too. I usually get to see her three or four times a year . . . but never for two weeks in a row.

It was our first morning at Grandpa's and the first full day of our vacation.

"Let's go for a walk," Angie suggested after we were finished breakfast. She was wearing a plaid shirt and had tied her red hair in a long ponytail. She'd been bouncing around the kitchen, putting away dishes and humming for the last ten minutes.

Like her whole family, Angie was a cheery morning person. I always found it a little revolting. She slid the last dish into the cupboard and rubbed her hands together, giving me a mischievous smile. "We might meet some of the locals. Maybe you'll finally find someone desperate enough to date you, Sarah."

"You take that back!" I demanded, but Angie just laughed and soon I couldn't help but chuckle too. She was right, I wasn't really lucky in the guy department. "I'll tell Grandpa."

I went into the living room where Grandpa was sitting with his cup of coffee in one hand and the same old book in the other. He hooked a finger around his reading glasses, slid them down his nose a little and looked up at me. "You're going to go for a walk. I know. I heard Miss Bright Eyes announce it to the world." He motioned me closer and asked quietly, "Does she have a volume knob?" I shook my head, laughing. Grandpa, like me, was definitely not a morning person. "Well," he shrugged, "it would be nice to have you kids out of my hair—I mean, have a pleasant walk. And don't fall down any holes. You might meet a rabbit you don't like."

He was always saying things like that. I'd probably find them funny if I could understand them.

Michael was out on the porch, sitting in Grandpa's rocking chair, catching the first warm rays of the sun. He looked like he was asleep.

Angie and I tried to tiptoe past, but the moment we got to the steps, he announced, "I'm coming too!"

We rolled our eyes and pretended to be upset.

"You two would get lost without me." Michael was grinning now and walking towards us.

He's not my identical twin, by the way, but we do look quite a bit alike. The only difference is in our mouths. His tends to open up and tell stupid jokes constantly—I tend to be silent and tasteful.

But I will admit that Michael is my other best friend. We're the same age—we've been through so much together. Always in the same classrooms, hanging out with the same friends, playing on the same teams. I don't know what I would do without him.

We headed out of the yard. A few minutes later all three of us were walking north down the road, away from Grandpa's cabin. We soon came to the lake and decided to follow the shore, kicking at driftwood and passing by all the other cabins. I could hear a chainsaw growling in the distance and I imagined there were a lot of sleepy neighbors cursing that noise.

Not too many people were up yet. We went by a cabin where a middle-aged, sour-faced man stared at us like we were aliens. "Morning!" I said, waving, but he continued to glare. We hurried past. Were all the locals like this?

"I shoulda mooned him," Michael said when the cabin was out of sight. "That woulda given him something to stare at."

Angie laughed. "Or scared him back into his home, at least."

"Hey!" Michael gave her a friendly shove. "It's an honor to see my bare—"

"I don't want to hear this!" I interrupted. "There are some things I just don't want to picture."

Both Angie and Michael started chuckling. "Okay, okay," Michael said finally, "no more butt jokes for the rest of our holiday."

I sighed. We continued on, going past more cabins, some of them huge, with three levels and three-car garages. But the farther we went, the smaller and older the buildings seemed to get, until we passed two or three in a row with broken windows and lopsided doors and no sign of anyone living inside.

A few steps farther and we found a group of cabins whose roofs had collapsed. There was a swampy smell surrounding them and it was darker here, as if the light couldn't quite reach this place. I was starting to feel a little edgy. It looked like this part of the lake had been abandoned.

We kept walking. Soon we found ourselves away from the lake in a little clearing with a small stream. There were no footprints, paths, or signs of buildings. It was warm and muggy, even though the trees were now casting thick shadows across us. I heard frogs croaking up a storm, but they clammed up as we approached.

We wandered farther into the clearing. Feeling like a rest, Angie and I sat on a log and stretched our legs.

"I'm going to catch a Kermit." Michael rubbed his hands together. "Maybe we can have frog legs soup for lunch."

"Oh, gross," I said.

"I hear it tastes like chicken," Michael said over his shoulder and went wandering off.

"His brain gets smaller every day," Angie pointed out.

I laughed. "Yeah, sometimes it's hard to believe we're related." Angie smiled.

I couldn't. Because I suddenly had this strong feeling that something was wrong here. That we were in danger.

A moment later Angie gave me a funny look. "You sick?" she asked. "How come your face is so pale?"

"I . . . I don't know," I said, looking around the clearing. Everything looked normal. "No reason, I guess."

A second later, Michael called out, "Hey, get off your butts and get over here. I found something cool."

"I'm kinda frightened to see what he thinks is cool," Angie whispered. She got up and started on the way to where Michael was standing. It took me a moment to stand; the effort left me exhausted. I had to struggle to catch up with Angie.

"It's a path," Michael announced when we got there.

"I can see that, Sherlock," Angie answered. She was bent over, tightening the laces on her boots. "The question is . . . where does it go to?"

"I don't know if we should . . ." I started. ". . . uh, guys."

They were already heading down the path. I followed. At first the trail was straight and easy, but within a few hundred yards it twisted around the hills and led deeper into the trees. I was pretty sure I could find my way back, but I wished I had a long spool of string to trail behind us like they did in all the fairy stories.

"I'm glad I brought my hiking boots," Angie said.

"Me too," I answered. My feet felt safe in the big, thick Hi-Techs. Like I could climb anything.

The trees became wider and taller so that they blocked out most of the light.

"We probably won't find any new friends here." Angie was looking around. I wondered if she was feeling the same uneasiness as me.

"HELLO, NEW FRIENDS!" I yelled, to show I wasn't frightened. Angie's back straightened and I realized I had startled her. She frowned at me. I shrugged. "I don't think there's a soul around. It doesn't seem like anyone's been out here for years."

Michael had jogged ahead and had almost disappeared around a corner. He certainly seemed to be in a hurry to go nowhere. Angie and I doubled our pace until we caught up with him.

Now the trees were definitely bigger and older, their thick, dark roots creeping over the path. Twice I almost tripped. I was starting to get a little tired and hungry. I wondered how long we had been out here. I looked at my wrist but it was bare.

"What time is it?" I asked.

Both Michael and Angie stared at their bare wrists. They had forgotten their watches too.

Michael looked at his other wrist. "I swear I put mine on this morning. I remember taking it off the dresser next to the bed."

"I wonder if we should go back?" Angie whispered. She looked a little pale.

"Grandpa's probably getting worried about us," I added. "We've been gone for hours, I bet. It might even be lunch time."

Michael shook his head. His dark hair had flipped over one eye. "Let's just explore a little farther. This has to go somewhere."

"Well . . . okay," I agreed. Angie nodded but didn't meet my eyes. We went ahead.

The path grew narrower and now the trees seemed to be leaning over us. We were in a world that was part shadows and part light. And it was cold. Some of the winter air still clung to these trees.

"I see something—someone," Michael said a second later. He was a few yards ahead of us again.

"What is it?" I strained my eyes.

"A little kid, I think."

We came over a rise and into a dimly lit clearing. Michael was right. There, standing next to a dying tree, was a young boy, maybe five years old. His clothes were ragged and torn. He was shimmering and hard to see.

"*Go away,*" he moaned. "*Go away. Bad here.*"

3

"Do you think he's sick?" I asked. He certainly seemed unhealthy, all pale and thin. He leaned against the tree. His mouth was still moving, but no sounds were coming out now. We walked slowly towards him.

"It looks like there's something wrong with him . . . like he's lost," Angie said. "But how come we can't get near him?" The closer we came, the farther away the boy seemed to get, moving from tree to tree. But he still stared at us, holding one hand out as a warning.

His mouth opened and closed. A second later I heard the words as if they were being carried on the wind. *"Go away!"*

We edged closer. He retreated backwards, but I couldn't see his feet move. He seemed to be drifting away from us.

"I'm going to run," Michael announced.

"I don't think that's—" I started to say, but Michael had already dashed off. He pushed branches aside and hopped over fallen logs. He was halfway to the little boy when I got a strong feeling in my gut that something terrible was going to happen.

"Michael! Michael!" I screamed but my voice was a whisper

now, like I was yelling into a great big empty space. I looked at Angie. All the blood had drained from her face.

I squinted into the distance. The boy's mouth was moving faster, his eyes wide. *"Bad here! Bad!"*

Michael tripped once and got up, brushed himself off, and kept running. Finally he was right in front of the kid. Michael seemed to be shimmering too.

"Evil!" The child yelled. *"Evil!"*

Michael reached out a hand.

The boy vanished.

Michael patted around, looking this way and that, then turned to us. "Do you see him? Do you see him?" he yelled.

"No," Angie answered. It took us a few seconds to get down to where Michael was standing. It was chillier there and the air seemed very still. It smelled a little like smoke, as if some of the trees had been struck by bolts of lightning a long time ago and were still smoldering.

There was no one to be seen at all.

"Where . . . where could he go?" I asked. "There weren't any holes for him to fall into." We searched around. I thought I heard a whisper for a second or the sound of crying, but when I held myself perfectly still and listened, I heard nothing.

We split up and looked around. I made sure that the other two were always in my sight. After about ten minutes we met back where we had originally seen the boy.

"We better get home," I suggested.

"We can't just leave him," Angie said.

Michael examined the palm of his hand. "I don't think he was really here."

We both stared at him.

"I'll explain later. Let's start walking first."

We agreed and began heading back down the path.

It seemed to take years to get to Grandpa's cabin.

4

It wasn't until after we had eaten Grandpa's chicken soup and sandwiches and done dishes that Michael finally told us about the boy. We were in the living room. Angie had a blanket around her shoulders, though it wasn't really that cold. Grandpa was on the deck.

"When I touched him . . ." Michael started to explain. ". . . well, I really didn't touch him."

"What do you mean?" I asked. Michael's blue eyes, so like my own, looked troubled.

"My hand went right into him." He held out his hand, re-enacting the event. "He was—he was made of mist. And it was really, really cold. It was as if he was a ghost or something."

"There's no such thing as ghosts," Angie said.

"I know that," Michael huffed. "But there was something really strange about this boy."

"He probably just lives nearby," Angie suggested. "In a farmhouse or something."

"But he disappeared. Right in front of me. He couldn't have gone anywhere or run away. He just wasn't there anymore."

Angie shivered under her blanket. "A trick of the light. It was kinda dark in there."

"I don't know," I said finally. "Maybe we should tell Grandpa."

They both looked at me. A moment of silence passed.

"At supper time," Michael answered. "I . . . I want to think about it more. He might believe all his stories went to our heads."

"Yeah, I want to go into town," Angie said, throwing off her blanket and getting up. "Walk around and see the sights—if there are any. Get away from all these trees and things. Maybe there's something fun going on. C'mon."

We followed her out the front door. I was quite happy to not think about the boy any longer. I needed time to clear my head.

Grandpa was sitting in his rocking chair, whittling. "Yeah, yeah, I know you're going to town. I heard Miss Loudspeaker announce it. I bet even my neighbors heard it." He flicked his knife and a long sliver of wood came off. I wondered what else he had heard. If he did know more, he didn't show it. "You three blurs don't slow down for a second, do you? It makes me tired just looking at you." He sent another chip skyward. I couldn't tell what he was carving. "Since you're going that way, would you mind picking me up a copy of this week's paper? Your ol' Grandpa Thursten would love that."

We agreed to do that and just as we were heading out of the yard, Grandpa yelled, "Don't fall in any holes—"

"—you might meet a rabbit you don't like." We finished it for him.

"Oh, you heard that one before."

We all laughed, then followed the road into Gimli.

"Grandpa sure hears a lot," Angie said when we were a safe distance from the house. "Doesn't he know old people are supposed to be deaf?"

"He can probably hear you right now," I said.

"No. He couldn't . . . could he?" Angie looked back. The cabin was quite far behind us.

"Well, the way you shout everything he could." Michael was grinning.

"I don't shout. I speak calmly and clearly."

"And loudly," I added.

Angie fumed. I knew she was searching for a perfect comeback, but her moment had passed. "You're both just jealous," she mumbled. We all chuckled for a second and continued onwards.

It took around forty-five minutes to walk into Gimli, past houses, cabins, trees, and more trees. Finally, we came over a small rise and there was the town itself laid out before us. It was really quite small compared to most towns in the U.S. And from this distance it appeared there wasn't very much going on.

But Michael and I had learned the previous year that looks could be deceiving. We'd found more than enough things to keep us entertained through our whole vacation.

The sun was warm and we strolled up and down the streets, looking in store windows and getting a feel for the place. A few people stared at us like we were escapees from an asylum. One old woman even looked up, saw us, then hobbled across to the other side of the street.

"Sarah," Michael said, "take a look at my forehead."

"Why?" I asked.

"Because I think there's a sign that says *Danger: American kids approaching.*"

We giggled and guffawed so hard we had to stop walking. This made a few more people stare at us. We noticed and started laughing some more. Then we headed down the street, holding our sides.

Already the events of the morning seemed far behind us, maybe even a daydream. We scouted around for an arcade or a park, but didn't have any luck, and I discovered I couldn't remember where anything was . . . almost as if the whole town had changed since last summer.

"What kind of place is this?" Angie asked. "It's as dull as math class. Is it against the law to have fun in Canada? And what kind of name is Gimli anyway?"

"Well . . ." I said, giving a long, dramatic pause, ". . . I happen to know the answer to that. Grandpa told me this town is named after a gigantic hall where the old Viking gods would stay after the world ended. Kind of like a hotel for the big shots."

"Well, how come everyone's staring at us?" she asked.

"'Cause they're Icelandic . . . just like us," I answered. "They like to stare and they like to tell long stories. Grandpa warned us about that last summer."

"So whatdaya think people from Gimli call themselves?" Michael asked.

"What do you mean?" Angie responded.

"Well, are they Gimli-ers and Gimli-ettes, or just plain Gimli-ites?"

"Michael, you're just plain stupid," I said.

"Just curious, that's all. Just using the scientific part of my mind."

"What mind?" Angie teased.

Michael rolled his eyes. "Just trying to teach you two how to think."

"Hey, look," I said. "Books."

We had come to a plain-looking bookstore at the end of an unremarkable street. The sign on the front said: *Odin's Eye Books.*

"I have a feeling I'm going to like this place," Michael said. We followed him inside.

The store was small, hot, cramped, and smelled like books. I loved it right away. The old woman at the till, who was half hidden in shadows, smiled at us and I felt instantly welcome. We rummaged around for a while, pulling out novels, reading the back covers, then putting them back. Angie went straight to the romance section. I discovered a fantasy work I had been looking for and made my way to the front. I also picked up a copy of *The Interlake Spectator* from the pile that sat on the counter.

"That's a good book," the woman said softly. I looked up at her and almost dropped my money on the floor.

She only had one eye.

Her good eye was a swirling color of gray and I knew she could see right into my thoughts, right into the very center of my spirit. Her left eye was covered by a patch. She was in her sixties, her hair gray and tied in a bun, and she wore brown clothes.

"Uh . . ." I said.

She grinned. Wrinkles formed around her eyes, made deep from years of smiling. "Don't worry. I know I look a little . . . unique. I lost my eye a long time ago."

"Uh . . . sorry."

She shrugged; her shoulders were wide. It seemed like she was made out of earth. "I see a lot more with one eye than I ever did with two. I guarantee it. By the way . . . what's your name?"

"Sarah."

"Sarah who?"

"Sarah Asmundson."

She nodded for a moment. It was as if I had answered an unspoken question. "You've got Grettir's blood in your veins."

"Oh . . . do I? Uh . . . good."

"Here's your change." She opened a wrinkled hand. Coins seemed to appear magically in her palm. Had she even opened the till?

I took the quarters with shaky hands. They were warm.

"If you ever have any questions about anything in town . . . just ask me," she said. "I'm Althea, Gimli's answer lady."

"Sh–sure . . . see ya." Then I turned and went out the door, my brother and Angie following.

"Whoa—she was big time weird!" Angie exclaimed when we were a few blocks away. "The way her one eye just kinda glowed. Bizarre woman, that's for sure."

"You don't even know her!" I felt a little angry, but didn't know why.

"I could tell just by looking."

I fumed.

"Wake me when you kids are done fighting." Michael took *The Interlake Spectator* from me. "Let's see what's happening in this burg."

He made a show of opening the paper. We all looked at it.

DRAUGR

The headline read: MYSTERIOUS DISAPPEARANCE RECALLED.

The picture beside the headline was of the boy we had seen that morning.

5

"I . . . I don't believe it," Angie whispered.

"It's him. It has to be." Michael was pointing at the boy's picture. "He's a dead ringer."

"I have to sit down," I said. Which was true. My legs felt like they were suddenly transformed into wet clay. We went ahead to a small park and collapsed on a bench. Three pine trees cast three shadows across us and I shivered.

We read the article silently.

> In the spring of 1941 young Eric Bardarson disappeared. The Bardarson family had been picnicking north of town. When they went to leave, their son had vanished. A search party was organized and though they spent the next few days searching, no trace of the boy was ever found. Donations to the Eric Bardarson Arts Scholarship are gratefully accepted.

"I told you he was a ghost," Michael said. "He has to be."

"It could still be some kind of trick." Angie didn't sound very sure of herself. "Couldn't it?"

"I don't know." I examined the picture of Eric. He was wearing what looked like a school uniform: a tie, a shirt and suit jacket, shorts, long socks, and black shoes. He looked exactly like the boy we had seen. The only difference was that he was smiling in the picture.

Staring at the photo made me feel uncomfortable. In it he was a happy, young kid who was probably thinking about playing baseball or riding his bike; he had no idea that in a few days he would disappear forever.

Well, not exactly forever. If he was some sort of spirit.

I glanced at the rest of the front page. There was something about city taxes and a festival named *Islendingadagurinn* and at the bottom of the page was a grainy picture of a dead cow. The article below it explained that this cow, like several others recently, had been killed and had all its blood sucked out.

What kind of town was this?

I got off the bench, stepped out into the sunlight. I didn't want to be cold anymore. "This is all way, way too weird."

Both Angie and Michael stood too. Michael folded up the paper. "Yeah, I'll say. Last year all we did was suntan, roller blade, and go fishing. And listen to Grandpa's stories."

I crossed my arms. "We had better tell Grandpa tonight, for sure. Even if he thinks we're just being stupid, crazy kids."

Michael and Angie nodded in agreement. They followed me down the sidewalk and we started trying to find our way out of town.

"Hey! Hello there!" someone yelled from behind us.

We turned around. Standing by the bench we were just on, waving a plastic bag, was a blonde-haired guy who looked about fifteen. He was wearing a black T-shirt and blue-jean shorts. He was as tall as Michael but very stocky.

"Hey!" he repeated.

It took me a moment to realize the bag he was holding was mine. With the book I had just bought. He started coming towards us.

"You forgot this," he said when we were face to face. He had blue eyes and was grinning. His face was tanned.

"Oh . . . thanks," I answered as I took the bag. "I'd have been mad at myself if I lost it—hey, how'd you know it was my book?"

"You look like the bookish type." His grin got even bigger, revealing straight white teeth.

I wasn't sure if that was a compliment or not.

"I mean it in the nicest way possible." Was he reading my mind? I noticed that his hair was shaved at the sides like a skate boarder's. He looked familiar, almost like someone I had seen on TV. "You three are new in town, aren't you?"

"How could you tell?" Michael asked. "Is it stamped on our foreheads?"

"No. I know most everyone around here who's my age. This place fills up with tourists and visitors in the summer. Besides, your shirt has the Dallas Cowboys on it . . . we're all Blue Bomber fans here."

"Who?" Michael's face became a living question mark.

"Winnipeg's football team."

"I've heard of them," I said, even though I hadn't. I just wanted him to look at me. "We're from Missouri."

"Missouri? How come you don't have accents? Why don't you say *Y'all* and all that stuff?"

"Why don't you say *eh* all the time?" Michael asked.

"Uh . . ." he paused, still grinning. "I see what you mean."

"We grew up in Montana," I explained.

"*They* grew up in Montana," Angie added. "I'm from North Dakota."

He looked at her and I felt a twinge of jealousy. "My name's Brand." This time when he smiled, dimples formed in his cheeks.

We all introduced ourselves and Brand shook everyone's hand. He had a firm, warm shake and I didn't want to let go. Angie winked at me when Brand wasn't looking and I almost blushed.

"So where you guys staying?" Brand asked.

"With our Grandpa, Thursten," Michael answered.

Brand laughed. "Ol' Thursten. Does he still tell that story about the headless barmaid?"

"Yes," I answered. "Do you know Grandpa?"

"He used to recite stories to us kids at school. We'd all have nightmares later. He's really good friends with my grandmother. They sit and talk Icelandic to each other. Can't understand a word they say . . . except when they point at me and say *eykom* every once in a while."

"Akarn?" Michael asked.

"Little acorn. That's what they call me. He's a fun old guy."

There was silence for a moment. Brand kept grinning through it all. He ran his hand through his hair. It went back to its original position. "Well, I have to go. If you guys come into town and want me to show you around, you can find me at *Ye Ol' Ice Cream Shoppe.* I work there most days."

"We will," I said, maybe a little too enthusiastically.

Then he turned and was gone, striding down the street.

Angie looked at me and raised her eyebrows. "Well, well, well . . . I think I sense a crush coming up."

"Oh, c'mon," I answered. "We just met him."

"And?"

"And . . . and we better get back to Grandpa's."

Angie laughed. I knew it wouldn't be the last time she would tease me about Brand. We started walking out of town.

6

When we got back to the cabin, Grandpa wasn't on the deck. There were lots of wood chips so he'd obviously been busy. We went through the front door.

"Grandpa, we're home!" Michael announced.

No answer.

"Maybe you should yell, Angie," he suggested. "He always hears you."

Angie frowned. "Ha. Ha. Ha."

We poked our heads into each room, called out his name. Still nothing. It was almost funny, each of us following the others around like three miniature stooges, opening doors, yelling, closing doors. Except I was beginning to get a little worried. Grandpa hadn't said anything about going anywhere.

"Oh great, we've lost him," Angie exclaimed, collapsing into a sofa chair. "How are we going to explain this to our parents? We lost Grandpa . . . but we had a great holiday."

"I told you a bizillion times, don't exaggerate!" Michael stretched out on the couch and yawned; his mouth became a gaping O. "He's got to be around here somewhere. He likely stepped out with one of his friends. They're telling each other big long stories about giant snakes or dead people right now. That's all they seem to talk about around here."

I sat in the other chair. "You're probably right." I covered my mouth as I yawned. It had been a long day already. I settled myself down, relaxing my body. I glanced at Michael and Angie; both had their eyes closed. We all deserved a nap, I figured. I let my eyelids slowly slide together.

I drifted into a vast, warm darkness. A moment later a dream worked its way into that black space. I was suddenly stumbling through a thick forest of trees at twilight. Ghostly wisps of fog drifted ahead of me, catching the light of the moon. I wandered for a time, shivering and looking ahead. I wanted to go back, to get out of the trees, but something was pulling me forward, one step at a time.

I saw a figure in the distance and so I headed towards it. With each movement I was growing lighter, until my feet were no longer touching the ground. A wind had come up, pulling me a few feet above the earth and making me float.

I came closer, moving faster now. The figure was the boy: Eric. *Go away!* he was waving his hand at me. *Bad here! Go away!*

He motioned harder; now he was yelling but I couldn't hear him. He looked very frightened. As I passed him I could see tears in his eyes.

Big, ghostly tears.

And I knew he was crying for me. Crying because he must know what lay ahead, where I was going. How bad can it be when a ghost is weeping for you?

I floated past and I couldn't even turn my head to look behind me.

A few seconds later I saw it.

A cabin. A very old cabin. Maybe one of the first ones built in this area. All logs and a sod roof, but the floor had sunk in on one side so it leaned crazily, the door at an odd angle. I knew there was darkness inside those four walls, that every nightmare I'd ever had was nothing compared to what waited through that doorway. I kept coming, heading straight at the door, gaining speed.

It opened.

And I was swept inside, into pitch blackness. Cold, smelly air surrounded me. The door slammed shut and I fell to a soggy floor. I pushed myself up and something wet squished below my hands. I sucked in my breath, felt my lungs tighten.

I couldn't breathe. I was suffocating.

Then something started to slam on the door.

And I knew the dark evil thing was outside, wanting to get back in. Into its own home.

It banged against the door. Harder.

And harder.

The wood splintered into pieces. Then there was a dark blur of motion, two eyes glowing, two arms reaching for me.

Then I found air, snapped awake.

I was up out of the chair and standing on the floor. Alive. Heart beating. Breathing. In and out, like they were my first breaths ever. Once. Twice. Three times.

My heart wouldn't slow down.

Both Michael and Angie were still asleep. I looked around. I was okay, everything was going to be alright.

This was the real world.

The door to Grandpa's house swung open and banged against the wall.

A wolf was standing there, its gray, soulless eyes staring right into mine.

7

I screamed. Michael shot straight up into the air. So did Angie.

"What! What! What is it?" Michael asked, squinting at me, sleepy and angry at the same time. Then he saw the animal, its mouth open showing huge, glistening teeth. Michael jumped off the couch and backed away. "Nice puppy . . . *nice puppy.*" It looked from me to Michael to Angie, trying to decide which one it was going to swallow whole first.

I held myself completely still.

"Who in the blazes is doing all the screaming?" asked the wolf.

I shook my head. Was I still dreaming?

Grandpa stepped into the doorway, standing behind the creature. He was carrying a shotgun. "Somebody answer me! Who is yelling to wake the dead? Was it you, Angie?" He reached down and patted the wolf's head. It arched its neck to give him a better angle.

Grandpa walked inside the house. "Well?"

"Uh . . ." I started. "It was me. I . . . uh . . . was dreaming and the . . . the wolf was just there and so . . ."

"Wolf?" He scratched his head. "Oh, Hugin here. He's only part wolf. He's half German shepherd too. Scared you, did he?"

"Y-yes."

"Well . . . it's good to be scared. Lets you know you're alive. Bet your heart's beating like crazy now."

It was. I was going to wear it out before I turned sixteen.

Grandpa went to the closet and put his shotgun away. He locked the door, put the key in his pocket, and turned back to us.

"What were you doing?" I asked.

"Just poking around in the bushes. Thought I heard something out there this afternoon. So I borrowed Hugin here from a friend of mine and we went out tracking."

"Did you find anything?" Michael asked. His voice sounded squeaky. Like he couldn't catch his breath.

"I think you need a drink of water, son." Grandpa cocked one eyebrow. "Or has your voice always been so high pitched?"

"No—" Michael squeaked, then paused to cough. "No," he said in a deeper tone.

Grandpa nodded. "That's better. Now what was the question . . . oh yeah. I didn't find anything. Just a few broken branches and what looked like tracks."

"Tracks for what?" Angie was still watching the dog.

"I couldn't tell. I tried to follow them, and I thought Hugin had the scent, but, after bumping through the bush for a few hundred yards, he just turned and looked at me, barked a couple times like he was reciting the dog alphabet, then he ran straight home. So I followed."

Michael sat down. "Did something spook him?"

"No. There's nothing in that big ol' world out there that will spook Hugin. I think he came back to the house 'cause he thought it would be safer for me. Guess we'll never know what was out there. A bear, most likely."

Hugin padded across the floor and sniffed at my feet. "Does he bite?" I asked.

"He hasn't bit anyone this week as far as I know. Though he ate a kid whole last week. The kid was trespassing, though." Grandpa went into the kitchen. Why couldn't he just answer questions with yes or no? He was worse than us teenagers.

I reached down and patted Hugin's head. It seemed about ten times as big as my hand, hard and padded with thick fur. I got down and looked eye to eye with him and he licked my face. It didn't take me long to realize that I liked this dog. My father made his living training bird dogs, so I knew a good dog when I saw one.

Even one that was part wolf.

I could tell Hugin was more than just a normal canine. He was a king: noble, strong, and proud. The type of dog who'd drag you out of an avalanche or a burning building.

I sat back on the couch and Hugin nuzzled against my legs, pinning me there, forcing me to pat him. Angie joined me and Hugin began wagging his thick gray-and-black tail, quite happy to have so much attention.

I could hear Grandpa banging around the kitchen, glass clinking. He came out a few minutes later, a pot of tea in one hand and cups in the other.

"Who's Grettir?" I asked as he set the tea on the coffee table.

"Grettir? Why?"

"That old lady at the bookstore said I had Grettir's blood in my veins."

"Oh . . . Althea." He shook a finger at me. "I warned you

about the folks in Gimli. They'll talk your ear off if you give them half a chance. Then they'll move to the other one. And she's the worst of them all." He lifted up the tea pot, motioned with it. "Hugin here belongs to her. She named him after one of Odin's ravens. It means thought—he's supposed to be faster than the speed of thought. Which isn't very fast in your case, Michael."

"Geez! Thanks, Grandpa!" Michael crossed his arms.

"Nice comeback, kiddo." Grandpa began pouring tea into a cup. "Anyone else?" he asked when he was finished. I can't say I much like tea, but a warm drink was exactly what I needed.

"Sure," I said.

"Well, pour it yourself." He laughed and sat back. "Grettir, Grettir, Grettir." He took a sip from his tea cup. "She's picked an old name . . . he might even be an ancestor of ours. Grettir Asmundson he was called or Grettir the Strong."

"When did he live?" I was pouring my own tea. Hugin had abandoned Angie and me for Michael's attention.

"I don't know exactly. The stories written about him date back to the 1300s, but he lived long before then. He was supposed to be one of the strongest men in Iceland. As far as I can remember, he just fought most of his life, recklessly. Though he was supposed to be a nice guy too—well, nice in a Viking kind of way. He even battled mound dwellers and supernatural monsters because human foes weren't tough enough for him. But that proved his undoing because one day he locked horns with a monster who was too much for him."

"You mean he lost?" Angie asked.

"No, not exactly. You see, he decided to try and wrestle a particularly mean thrall."

"Thrall?" I asked.

"An undead man. This happened a lot in Iceland in the old days. People just didn't seem to want to stay dead. They hung around and made a lot of noise and broke things. This thrall was a cruel, bitter sheep herder who had died mysteriously the night before Christmas—I think his name was Glam. He came back from the dead and started haunting the farmer he had been working for.

"Anyway, Grettir had heard about him and decided to spend a night at the farmhouse. He hid in a big fur blanket and waited. After about a third of the night had passed, something huge banged on the roof, then kicked in the door. It stomped across the floor and grabbed the fur. Grettir held on and the blanket ripped in two between them. Then they wrestled with each other so hard that they broke the door frame and the roof of the house and rolled outside, under the moon. Grettir was stronger and he overpowered the thrall and knelt on his chest. With his last bit of strength, Glam put a curse on Grettir so that from that point on, anything Grettir did with his strength would only lead to bad luck. Then Grettir lopped off his head . . . kind of messy but it's the only way to kill these thralls, I guess. Grettir later was outlawed as a murderer and had to spend his last days on Drang Isle, a cold, desolate place. I think there was a price on his head and someone finally murdered him, even cut off his hand after he was dead. Just to get him to release his sword."

"That doesn't sound like a very happy ending," Angie said.

"It was his life. The old sagas aren't Hollywood movies. They're gritty. Full of blood and smoke and tough characters. Kind of like the people who settled Iceland. And Gimli, come to think of it."

"So we're supposed to be related to this Grettir?" I asked.

"There's a good chance we are. I'll have to go back to the homeland sometime and look up our family trees. Maybe at the next big Asmundson reunion."

"We are related to him," I said suddenly.

Grandpa looked at me. "Why do you say that?"

"Uh . . ." I hesitated, trying to understand what I had meant. "It's just a gut feeling. When you told the story, I felt like I was there . . . with him."

Everyone stared at me. Grandpa smiled. "You may be right," he said. "Do you ever get any other gut feelings that come true?"

"Um . . . no," I said. I wasn't quite sure what he meant. "I don't think so."

He stared at me for a long moment then nodded to himself. What had he figured out? He set down his cup. "Did any of you three happen to pick up a paper for me?"

"Uh . . ." Michael started.

Grandpa looked at him. "Uh . . . did you, or didn't you?"

"We did," Michael continued. He got the paper and handed it to Grandpa. "But before you read it there's something we have to tell you."

8

"Actually," Michael said a second later, "maybe you should take a look at the paper first."

Grandpa shook his head. Clearly he didn't have a clue what we were talking about. "Open the paper, close the paper— what's going on here? All three of you look like you just missed being run over by a big semi."

"Please," I asked.

He must have heard the frightened tone of my voice. He opened *The Interlake Spectator* and looked at it for some time. Then he glanced at us. "Is it the dead cow story? Don't tell me you guys really did it. Here I thought it was just aliens." He laughed.

"No . . . see the boy there." Michael pointed.

"Yes."

"We saw him this morning."

Grandpa's face hardened. "You what?"

"Well . . ." Michael began, then he explained how we had wandered into the trees and everything that had happened to us after that. Grandpa looked serious but didn't speak a word until Michael was finished. He set the paper down, rose slowly from the chair as if some of his strength had been sapped. He went to the back door, pulled the curtain aside, and stared out. He stayed that way for a full minute.

Michael, Angie, and I looked quizzically at each other. "What—" I started to ask.

Grandpa turned towards us. His eyes were cold and very serious. "You're going home tomorrow," he announced.

"What?" we exclaimed in unison.

He came a few steps closer. "I said, you're going home tomorrow. I'll call your parents tonight. Till then, no one leaves this house. Do you understand?"

"No, I don't understand," I said. "Why are you sending us home? What did we do?"

"You didn't do anything. It's just that . . . business has come up. I can't look after you anymore."

"What business?" Michael asked. His frown mirrored my own.

"I have to go away for a few days. Look after some things. Old unfinished things. So you three will be heading home."

"But—" I started.

"No buts. This is the way it has to be. I'm sorry, but I forgot about this . . . business." His face softened. He spoke gently. "You can stay even longer next summer. Okay? All summer if you want. We'll have twice as much fun."

It sounded like he was trying to bribe us.

"Okay?" He repeated.

We were all in shock. "Uh . . . sure," Michael answered. What could we do?

"It's settled, then." Grandpa smiled. "I really am sorry,

believe me." He leaned over, picked up the tea pot and the empty cups, and started back towards the kitchen. Hugin padded after him, then Grandpa whispered a few words in another language. The dog obediently turned around and sat in the middle of the room.

Almost as if he was told to keep an eye on us.

Angie looked quite upset. I was about to say something to her when Grandpa came back into the room. "I have to go out for a few minutes." He was putting his hat on—a Toronto Blue Jays cap. "Will you three do me a favor? Will you just stay in the house? I . . . I think it might have been a bear I heard this afternoon."

We nodded. Grandpa said something else to Hugin. The dog looked at him, then back at us. Then the door closed softly behind Grandpa.

Michael crossed his arms. "Well, that was very, ultra bizarre."

"That's for sure." Angie had her arms crossed too and seemed to be shivering. "I've never seen him like this before. What did we do to get sent home?"

I just couldn't stand to sit anymore. I got up and paced the floor. "I don't think we did anything. I think . . . well . . . I don't know. That he's trying to protect us," I said.

Michael motioned and Hugin padded over to him. The dog rubbed up against his knees. "I have a feeling you're right. There's something wrong. The fact that we saw that gho— that kid really bothered him."

"And what was he out looking for today?" Angie had her feet up on the couch now and was hugging her knees. "Was it really a bear?"

"And why is this dog so smart?" I asked. I noticed that Hugin was turning his head as each of us spoke, as if he understood every word. He looked at me and it seemed like he was smiling.

"Well, I don't want to go home," Michael announced. "We just got here. I am not going to take another long, stupid bus ride. It's not fair."

"I don't know if we have a choice," I said. I leaned against the wall next to the mantel. At eye level was a picture of Grandma and Grandpa, both in fishing gear. Maybe if she were still alive she'd explain what was going on. She was always so good to us kids.

"Maybe we can talk to him," Angie suggested.

I shook my head. "I don't think so. You saw the look on his face. It was almost as if he was frightened."

Hugin's ears perked up. He rose and walked past me, brushing my legs.

"Grandpa doesn't get frightened—nothing scares Grandpa," Angie said.

"I know . . . but . . . he just seemed that way. For a second. Maybe just frightened for us is what I mean."

"You know—" Michael started.

He stopped. Hugin was barking, loud and strong, at the back door.

9

"What's up, Dog?" Michael asked. He had walked over to Hugin and was looking out the window in the door. Hugin's hackles were raised and he had pulled back his lips, showing long white canine teeth. I knew this was an animal I would never ever want mad at me. "What is it, boy? What do you hear?" Michael reached for the door.

"Don't open that!" I yelled.

Michael frowned. "Why?"

"Grandpa said we're supposed to stay inside. And because . . . because you don't know what's out there."

Michael rolled his eyes. "I looked out the window. There's nothing in the backyard, Sis. The dog probably hears a raccoon or something. They have raccoons here, don't they?" Michael turned the knob and slowly pulled the door open.

"Don't!" This time it was Angie.

Michael ignored us both and stepped into the doorway. Hugin stood beside him, barking even harder, so his whole body seemed to shake. Then he switched to a low, angry growl. "I . . . I don't believe it . . . it's . . . gigantic," Michael exclaimed.

His eyes were wide and frightened. He stepped out the door. Hugin followed. "It's . . . oh no. OH NO! IT'S GOT A HOLD OF ME!"

"Michael!" I ran to the door. "Michael!"

He was gone. Hugin was about halfway across the yard, snarling at the trees. "Michael!" I yelled. Angie had joined me. "Where—"

"Surprise!" Michael popped up from a bush beside us. We screamed in unison and Michael rolled on the ground laughing. "Got you! Got you!"

"That's not funny!" I yelled when I had caught my breath.

"It was to me." Michael was standing now, holding his side. "We all needed a good laugh."

"Neither of us laughed." Angie had one hand on her hip.

"Well, I sure did." Michael was brushing the grass off his pants. "I got a big hardy-har-har out of it."

"Look at Hugin." I pointed. He was at the edge of Grandpa's yard, where the grass gave way to huge pine trees. He was barking and growling crazily. I noticed the fence gate was open. "Something really is out there."

Michael looked. "Bah. It's probably nothing. Though he's sure barking a lot."

"C'mere, Hugin," I called. The dog looked my way, then continued growling. "Come on, boy." He ignored me.

I took a deep breath and started walking towards him.

"Sarah, what are you doing?" Angie asked.

"Just getting the dog," I answered, but my voice was so hoarse that I don't know if she heard me. Each step was impossible to take, but I pushed myself ahead. Some part of me refused to be scared.

I stared at the open gate. Beyond the tall fence was thick underbrush and more trees, all darkened by afternoon shadows. Anything could be in there, I realized.

Sarah, don't be stupid, I told myself. Turn around and go back to the house.

But I couldn't. Not without Hugin.

A few steps later I was beside him. He was growling even louder as if trying to ward something away.

I trudged past him. Closer to the gate, closer. I couldn't seem to stop myself.

"Sarah!" This time it was Michael. But he sounded so far away, like he was yelling from the end of a long tunnel. I could barely hear him.

Hugin stayed behind me. Barking now, maybe trying to warn me. Was he frozen to the spot?

I felt a chill. The temperature was plunging to the freezing mark here at this end of the yard. Even my bones were getting cold.

Still I carried on. The gate loomed in front of me. I had this awful fear that I was going to walk right through it, out into the wilderness, and never return again. There was a whispering sound just beyond the fence. Almost like breathing.

Or was someone calling my name? An ancient, raspy voice.

Hugin stopped barking. Or maybe I couldn't hear him anymore.

I reached the gate. It took all my will to stop my feet from moving. I extended my arm, my fingers dull and cold.

With all the strength I could muster, I pulled on the gate. It closed slowly, squeaking and whining. For a moment I thought I saw a dark, rustling shape moving outside, then with a *click* the gate was shut.

I stepped back. There was dirt on the top part of the gate. It almost looked like a handprint.

I took another step back. Hugin renewed his barking, ran up to me, and leaned against me, growling. Something in the solidness of his body gave me strength. I turned around.

Both Angie and Michael were standing there, staring at me. I walked towards them.

"What were you doing?" Michael asked when I got closer.

"I—I just had to close it," I said. "If I didn't . . . well, I don't know . . ."

I kept going towards the cabin. "Let's go inside," I said. "I've had enough excitement for one day."

I called once from the doorway and Hugin came running. I felt relieved when all of us were inside. Michael and Angie sat down, but I couldn't take my eyes away from the window. Hugin stayed by the closed door, no longer growling. He just seemed to be waiting.

A few minutes later Grandpa came through the front door, hugging a bulging bag of groceries. Celery stalks peeked out the top. "You three weren't going anywhere were you?" he asked when he saw me by the back door.

"Uh . . . no," I answered.

Hugin barked once and Grandpa walked over to him. He said a few soothing words in Icelandic, then patted the dog on its head. Hugin wagged his tail and settled down by the back door.

Grandpa winked at us. "Well . . . I got the fixings for a wonderful meal. I'd appreciate some help in the kitchen."

And so we helped cook supper, slicing carrots, celery, and onions for a beef stew. I found I was glad to be doing something to take my mind away from the fact that we would be leaving tomorrow. The kitchen filled with the smells of cooking food, aromas that reminded me of being at home with my parents on those cool winter nights in Missouri.

None of us spoke while we made supper. Even Grandpa was quiet, he only opened his mouth to say, "Cut enough carrots for a hundred rabbits. You guys will have the best eyesight in all America." I set the table, trying not to let the cutlery clink. It was almost as if there was someone in the other room whom we didn't want to wake up.

Once Hugin made a whining sound then stopped. I glanced and saw that he was resting his head on the floor. But his eyes were still sharply fixed on the door.

We sat down to eat a few minutes later. The stew was wonderful, with thick gravy, tender meat, a layer of dumplings, and more vegetables than I could care to count. It was like the first time I had ever tasted stew—as if everything was brand new.

"This is very, very good," Angie said. I guess I wasn't the only one enjoying the meal.

"Yeah, it is," Michael agreed. "But there's enough garlic in here to knock out a vampire."

Grandpa narrowed his eyes, looking serious. "Just eat it all up," he commanded gruffly. "Okay?"

"Uh . . . sure." Michael was scooping up another forkful. "I—actually like garlic, Grandpa."

"Good boy. Good for you." Grandpa was smiling again. "It's good for your health . . . but bad for your breath."

We chuckled half-heartedly. Angie shot me a quick look that seemed to say: *Has Grandpa gone bonkers?*

When we were finished eating, Grandpa cleared his throat. "Tonight you're all going to sleep in the main guest room."

"What?" I set down my glass. "We can't sleep in the same room as Michael."

Grandpa smiled. "You're going to have to put up with his snoring for one night."

"I don't snore!"

"Why do we have to sleep together?" Angie asked.

"I need the other spare room. There's work I have to do."

"Why do we have to go home?" I asked.

"Because there's business I forgot. I can't look after you and do it too."

"What business?"

"My business," he said with finality. "Will you three do dishes? I have to make a few phone calls."

Grandpa got up and went to the phone hanging on the living room wall. We went into the kitchen. Michael washed while Angie and I dried. From where I was standing I could hear Grandpa on the phone. I moved a little closer.

I caught the tail end of the conversation. "No. I can't explain. You'll have to take my word for it, Robert." Then he hung up. He had obviously been talking to Mom and Dad. I wished I had been listening a little earlier.

He picked up the phone and dialed again. I edged closer to the wall.

"It's taking you a long time to dry that dish," Michael said.

I motioned him to be quiet.

He turned back to the sink, muttering, "If you want to be lazy, go ahead."

I strained my ears. Grandpa was talking in another language on the phone. Icelandic, I assumed, because every second word had a *th* or a *grr* sound. I could tell by the tone of his voice that he was upset. He had taught me a few Icelandic words, mostly put-downs, but I couldn't pick anything out of what he was saying. He paused for a second and I assumed he was listening to whoever was on the other end of the line.

"*Nei,*" he said suddenly. "*Draugr.*"

I caught my breath.

"*Draugr,*" he repeated. Hugin pricked up his ears.

I knew that word. Why was Grandpa saying it?

He started whispering now and no matter how hard I tried, I couldn't hear what he was saying. A moment later he hung up the phone and I quickly went to the sink, picked up a dish, and started drying.

"Aren't you done yet?" Grandpa asked. He was in the doorway, smiling.

"We would be but Sarah's too slow," Michael said.

I kicked him.

"She's just careful that's all." Grandpa was still smiling. It seemed a little unreal—he was forcing himself to look happy. I thought I could see something in his eyes though, a kind of haggard look. Like he was very tired but just putting on a nice face for the company. "It's all set up. Your mom and dad will pick you up from the bus back at home."

"Oh . . . good," I said.

"Yes, it is. I really am sorry things worked out this way, kids. I was looking forward to having you three around." He turned. "Now if you'll excuse me, I've got a few things to do."

He left. When we finished the dishes we went out to the front room. Grandpa must have been in the back room. It sounded like he was banging on something metal. Occasionally I caught the smell of burning wood.

"What's he doing?" Angie asked.

"Who knows." Michael sat back. "I think he's gone a little loco."

"It's hard to believe our holiday will be over tomorrow." Angie was looking down. "Over even before it started."

We were all quiet. Grandpa was silent too. Whatever he'd been doing was done. He came walking out carrying Michael's suitcase. "I got your stuff here, Michael." He set it down. "Well," he announced. "It's bed time."

"Bed time? It's only eight o'clock!" Michael exclaimed.

"Eight fifteen, actually. And you've got to get on the bus early. You don't want to argue with ol' Gramps on your last night here, do you?"

I did. But I kept my mouth closed.

"We're all going to need a good sleep tonight," Grandpa added.

I changed into my nightgown in the bathroom. About fifteen minutes later we were all settled in our beds; Angie and I in one, Michael in the other next to the small window.

Grandpa knocked on the door then poked his head in. "Lock this tonight, will you? And if you hear anything . . . whatever it is . . . don't leave this room." He paused. "Good night."

He closed the door.

10

"What on earth was that all about?" Angie asked. She was hugging her pillow. "I'm starting to get freaked out."

"You're not the only one—but I am going to lock the door." I rolled out of bed and twisted the key in the door, then turned the handle and pulled to be sure it was locked. I tugged the old iron key out of the keyhole. It was about six inches long and heavy. I set it on the bedside table and crawled back under the blankets. "Maybe we should board up the window too."

"There's something really wrong here." Michael was sitting up in the other bed. "Grandpa's just not acting like himself." He flipped his hair back out of his eyes. "I wonder if . . . like . . . he's getting senile or something? Or Alzheimer's?"

"Alzheimer's is when you forget things," Angie said.

"You know what I mean. Maybe he's sick."

"I don't think so." I paused, trying to find the right words. "I think it's something worse. Well, this may be nothing, but after he phoned Mom and Dad he called someone else and talked in Icelandic. The only word I understood was *draugr*."

"You mean . . . like . . . from his story?" Angie was squeezing the pillow even closer.

"Yeah, that same word. It might not mean anything. And I might have heard it wrong . . . but I don't think so."

Michael looked right at me. "Sarah, you don't really believe that story was true, do you?"

"No . . . but Grandpa thinks something's going on like that story or that involves it. I don't know. It's all a little confusing. He is scared of something, though."

"What can we do?" Angie asked.

I shrugged. "Wait until morning, I guess. What do you think, Michael?"

"You're right. That's all we can do." He settled himself below the covers. "I know one thing . . . it's going to be hard to go to sleep tonight. Mega hard."

"Should we . . . should we leave the light on?" I asked. They both looked at me, their faces pale.

"No," Michael said finally. "I'd feel like a little kid." He reached over and clicked it off.

The room went completely black. "Uh . . . good night every-one," I whispered.

"Good night," they echoed.

Hope I see you in the morning, I thought to myself.

It took a moment for my eyes to adjust to the darkness. A silver beam of moonlight came in through the thin curtains, projecting an image of the window on my wall. It was obviously a full moon tonight.

Which didn't make me feel good at all.

I couldn't relax. I kept glancing back and forth, back and

forth, from one side of the room to the other. I'm not sure what I was looking for.

But at some point my eyes must have gotten tired, because I fell asleep. And this time I didn't dream. There was only darkness within deeper darkness.

I awoke suddenly. It took me a moment to remember where I was and that in a few short hours I'd be on a bus heading home. How much time had passed? Was it midnight yet?

I saw that the moonlight had moved farther down the wall. It seemed brighter and the shadow of the window was larger. Was the moon coming closer to the earth?

I could hear Angie's soft, rhythmic breathing beside me.

Michael was snoring.

I laughed quietly to myself. A low, nasally, grumbling sound came from his side of the room like low thunder. Poor Michael, he always thought he was so perfect. Now I finally had something to tease him about. All the way home I could imitate his buzzsaw snoring. That would help the trip go faster.

His wheezy inhalations got worse, became thicker and deeper like he had suddenly developed a really bad cold. He wasn't going to choke was he? Didn't some people die from snoring too loud? Or too long?

Or was it they forgot to breathe?

Gradually I realized the snoring sounded more like deep, throaty growling.

Not coming from Michael at all. But beyond him.

Outside the window.

A dark shadow was creeping slowly across the wall. A twisted, bulky shape edged up to the windowpane, blocking the moonlight. The silhouette grew larger. I tried to move my neck, to look towards the window, but all the strength had been drained from my body.

Boards moaned as if something huge had leaned its weight on the outside wall, trying to get closer.

To see what was inside.

Then I heard a sharp scraping noise like a nail being drawn against glass. Digging a deep groove.

I still couldn't budge. A cold Arctic mass of air crept into the room and was freezing me in place, slowing the blood in my veins, the thoughts in my head. I was trapped, helpless. I just stared at the shadow on the wall.

Angie wasn't breathing anymore. At least I couldn't hear her.

"Angie?" I whispered, my voice hoarse, my lips sluggish. It was hard to find the air to speak. "Michael?"

They didn't answer. I tried to move my arm, to jostle Angie awake. I could only edge it slowly towards her, an inch at a time. It was becoming very hard to concentrate. I felt, oddly enough, like sleeping—that all I really needed to do was close my eyes and rest and everything would go away.

I knew I couldn't surrender to this drowsiness. It was a sleep that would leave me in darkness forever.

My heartbeat slowed. My eyelids grew heavier. I didn't seem to have the energy to stop them from sliding shut.

The house creaked. Even more weight was leaning on it now. The low rumbling outside the window grew louder.

With a huge effort I moved my hand an inch to my left and touched Angie's arm.

She was ice cold.

"Angie," I whispered. *"Angie, wake up."*

No reaction. Not even a whisper. And I couldn't find enough strength to shake her. It was getting harder and harder to stay awake. I blinked and my heavy, tired eyes stayed closed for what must have been a minute.

When I opened them again I could hear a soft sliding sound.

The window was being opened! I was sure of it. Slowly, quietly opened.

Then came a wet, hollow breathing. My limbs, my chest, everything had stopped working. I couldn't even feel really frightened except inside my head. I had to keep myself awake. Somehow.

The window slid higher, letting in a chilling breeze.

And with it came colder and colder air. Not outside air, but something far different, from another age, another place. Air from cellars a hundred years old. From dark caves. From the deep, undisturbed chambers inside burial mounds. Heavy with the scent of dirt. It spilled into our room.

Every time I inhaled, my lungs grew emptier so that I needed more air.

My breathing slowed.

My eyes closed again.

It took all my willpower to open them, to stop the sleep from settling in on me.

Now there was no moonlight Only darkness. Whatever was outside the window had blocked it completely. It must be huge.

Then came a cracking sound of boards slowly being broken as the window frame was tested. The shadowy shape was too big to fit through that space. And yet it was forcing itself inside.

I knew the boards wouldn't hold for long.

I moved my arm closer to Angie, found her hand. It was frozen, each finger made of ice. I imagined mine felt the same. But one of those icicles seemed to move. Was she awake too? Lying as paralyzed as me?

Maybe together, somehow, we could get out of this. Even if we could scream, that would be something.

I tried to open my mouth, to whisper to her, but my lips wouldn't budge. I concentrated on squeezing her hand, but my fingers hardly moved at all.

A board snapped and part of the house surrendered to this outside force. Glass shattered, slowly. I could hear each creaking, cracking sound like ice breaking up in spring, then the tinkling sound of the glass hitting the floor piece by piece.

I had stopped breathing ages ago.

Another huge wooden crack was followed by a third one. Bits of plaster fell down. Then a fourth crack and a fifth. And I knew it was almost in the room, it was succeeding.

A smell floated into my nostrils, a stench of rotting meat and spoiled milk, of old urine and smoke. Inescapable and heavy.

The intruder was sniffing now, probably at the edge of Michael's bed. It paused only to growl. I knew it was searching, that it couldn't quite see us. The window was still creaking and cracking, so it wasn't all the way in the room yet.

A window smashed in some distant part of the cabin.

I thought I heard Michael moan in pain.

Then Hugin started barking, outside. The deep sound of his warning brought me further away from sleep. I tried to move, but failed.

There was a loud growl in our room, low, angry, and threatening. The boards smashed and cracked. Plaster fell in on me from the ceiling.

Doors slammed here and there inside the house—Grandpa! He yelled something I couldn't understand. A name. Or was he swearing?

He knocked over a table. Glass shattered. Then he slammed another door. He seemed to be desperately searching for something.

Hugin was closer now. His snarling sounded muffled. Did he have a hold of something?

There was a final crack of wood, a retreating throaty roar, and the remains of the window slammed shut, echoing through the room.

The thing was gone. I couldn't turn my head, but I knew it had turned away from us to face the dog.

Hugin was struggling with something—someone—just outside our room.

I found I could move my eyes slightly, but my head refused to budge. From the angle where I was lying I could see the edge of the window and not much more. Half the curtains were off, had been knocked to the ground. It looked like the window had been broken along with a lot of the wall around it.

The back door slammed. Grandpa wasn't going outside was he?

Grandpa! Don't! I wanted to yell. Instead I just mouthed the words. My lips were too cold to move.

But the room seemed to get warmer. Or my body was. I could move slowly. I squeezed Angie's hand.

She squeezed back, weakly.

Something huge slammed into the side of the house. Boards crashed, our wall shook and threatened to topple in.

My heart started beating again. I could breathe, too.

Grandpa started yelling again. In Icelandic. Short, harsh words. He *was* outside. What was he doing out there?

I discovered I could move my neck now and I turned. The window had been smashed in, the remaining torn, dirty curtains were fluttering in the breeze. I couldn't see outside. Both Angie and Michael were lying with their eyes open, their faces pale.

"Guys . . ." my voice was a hoarse whisper, my throat dry, "can you hear me?"

Angie gave me a muffled, *"Yes."*

"I . . . I can't move," Michael whispered. "Sarah, why . . . can't I move?"

"I don't know," I answered. "But I think Grandpa needs our help."

"I dreamed something had a hold of my leg," Michael said. I could see dark blotches of dirt on his bed. "It was a dream . . . wasn't it?"

The shotgun fired.

Something struck the cabin wall with the weight of a two-ton truck. Glass shattered.

"What was that?" Angie asked, frightened.

Before I could answer I heard Hugin just outside our window, growling low and hard as if he had a grip on some animal that he wouldn't let go. Grandpa screamed. Hugin struggled, roaring and growling. Then he made a *yipping*, almost human, cry of pain.

An object hit the house. Smaller than the first time.

The shotgun fired again.

"What's going on?" Michael asked.

I was trying to sit up. Unsuccessfully. "I don't know. But I have to find—"

I was cut off by a scream.

Grandpa was crying out, a long and painful wail that suddenly died. This was followed by a roar I knew wasn't a dog or a man.

I found I could move. I grabbed for the key to the door, knocking it to the floor.

I saw Michael stand up. He struggled to take the few steps to the window.

"Don't!" I yelled.

He looked at me.

"You don't know what's out there," I said, then I scooped up the key and went to the door. "We . . . we need to arm ourselves. We need something to protect us."

It took a moment of fumbling to place the key in the lock. Then it wouldn't budge. "Oh no . . . oh no," I whispered.

I twisted and twisted.

With a clicking sound the key turned. I quickly rotated the knob and threw open the door.

Michael and Angie followed me into the darkened living room.

"What's out there?" Michael asked. "Was it a bear? Did you see it?"

"No," I answered. "But I think whatever—whoever—it is, it's really big."

I found it hard to move. My body was still clumsy. My legs and arms were tingling.

Michael went to the closet and found a bat. I took the hockey stick that was above the mantel and gave a steel poker to Angie. The stick felt too small in my hands. Who'd be scared of me?

We went to the back door, stopped, and looked at each other. I breathed in, my first good breath of air. "Let's do it," I said.

Michael turned the knob.

11

There was one light in the backyard, high on a pole. It seemed to have only about forty watts of power, just enough brightness to turn everything into shadows. We took a few tentative steps outside.

What I saw was enough to frighten me.

A large section of the fence was broken; long, thick slabs of wood looked as if they had been snapped like toothpicks. Grass was uprooted all across the yard. Then I looked to my left. Part of the cabin was caved in, boards stuck out like broken bones. It was the spare room—where we had slept. And it looked like there was blood on the wall. A large, spattered, black pool.

"It's a battlefield!" Michael exclaimed. "What happened?"

"I don't know. But we have to find Grandpa." I clutched my hockey stick tighter and started out into the yard.

"Grandpa! Grandpa!" we yelled.

It was hard to make sense of the shapes around me. There was too much gloom and darkness. I squinted, wondering if I should take the time to find a flashlight. There had to be one in the house somewhere. But what if Grandpa was just a few feet away, lying on the ground?

I stumbled across a groove in Grandfather's tiny garden. It was as if something had been dragged along the earth, through the carrots and pea plants. Part of Grandpa's plaid shirt was stuck to a rake.

I picked up the tattered cloth. It was stained with a dark wet spot. I wasn't sure if it was blood.

My heart sped up. I followed the track, coming closer to the end of the yard.

A few steps later I found his shotgun. The double barrel was bent upwards.

Then I came to the edge of the fence. Boards and posts and wire were all broken and snapped, pointing inwards, like a bull-dozer had slammed through it all. Just past that were trees and underbrush.

I thought I could hear a rustling sound.

"Grandpa?" I whispered. I couldn't take another step. I felt safe in the yard, in the dim light. "Grandpa?"

The bushes moved. A twig snapped.

I moved backwards. Could I hear breathing? Deep, animal-like inhalations?

"Do you see something?" Michael asked.

It took me a second to find my voice. "Y-yes. We better call the police."

I was still stepping backwards but looking ahead. Finally I turned and started running quickly towards the cabin.

Angie and Michael followed.

Michael slammed the door behind us and put his weight against it.

Angie was standing behind him, her hands tight on her steel poker. "Phone the cops!" she yelled. "Phone the cops!"

I dialed 911, hoping emergency numbers were the same in Canada as they were at home. An operator answered and I quickly told her what had happened, trying not to sound panicked. I must have spoken too fast because she commanded me to calm down and repeat everything slowly, which I did. "Make sure you stay in the house," she said before she hung up.

Michael was staring out the door's window. "I don't see anything," he said. "Do you know what you saw?"

"I . . . I didn't really see anything. I just . . . thought I heard breathing." I paused. "I could just feel it there . . . looking at me."

"Maybe it was Grandpa," Angie suggested.

"No. It was like an animal or something."

I went to the living room window. The yard was still.

"Oh . . . geez," Michael exclaimed.

"What?" I asked.

He was gawking down at his sleeve. There was a small gash on his upper right arm. "I must have cut myself. Not too deep but it's bleeding."

I stayed at the back door while Angie helped him wash the wound and wrapped a handkerchief around it. I noticed Michael was limping when he returned.

A few minutes later I could hear a siren. We went out the front door and huddled together on the driveway, holding our weapons. We looked like rejects from some sports team.

I imagined lights flicking on and people looking out their windows as the cop car zoomed past. The whole neighborhood was probably waking up.

A police cruiser turned into the driveway and came skidding to a halt on the gravel. The siren stopped, but they left the flashing lights on. Two officers got out at the same time, both tall, wearing dark uniforms.

The driver introduced himself. "I'm Sergeant Roberts." He had a mustache and serious dark eyes. "Is the intruder still here?"

"No," Michael said. "At least we don't think so."

Then I explained quickly what had happened, adding that I thought I heard an animal just outside the fence.

"Show me to the backyard," Roberts commanded.

They followed us through the house and outside again. Sergeant Roberts and his partner looked around with their flashlights.

The other officer pointed his light at the wall. It *was* a splash of blood. He moved a few steps closer and examined it. "There's pellet shots here from a shotgun," he said.

Sergeant Roberts was walking around shining his flashlight in different areas of the yard. He bent over and eyeballed the shotgun. Then he walked to the edge of the fence. I watched, holding my breath, wanting to tell him not to go too far.

He stepped past the fence line. Into the underbrush. He was shining his light there.

"Oh dear," he said suddenly. "Oh no."

Something in the tone of his voice frightened me. I had to see what he was looking at. I took a few steps towards him. He was pointing his light on a pile of grass and upturned dirt. I glimpsed a gray shape—but it seemed so far away—it looked like the mangled form of an animal.

A dog. Hugin. Legs and head at crazy angles.

Was it his breathing I had heard?

Sergeant Roberts pointed the flashlight back at us. Blinding me. "Sandowski, you better radio for backup. We'll need some search equipment and a few more pairs of eyes. And get those kids inside."

Officer Sandowski led us into the house and got us to sit down. "Don't move, please," he said. Angie was shaking, so he picked up a blanket and gave it to her. Then he went out to the car.

None of us spoke. I couldn't even think straight anymore.

A moment later Sandowski returned. "Do you three have anyplace you can stay tonight? Any other relatives close by?"

"No," Michael answered. "We just know Grandpa. We're here for a holiday."

"Well, I'll have to arrange for someone to come—"

There was a sudden loud knock at the door.

He turned, confused. He went to the front door and opened it, his hand on his holster.

Althea, the woman from the bookstore, was standing there.

12

"I will look after them," she said. Althea stepped past the officer and into the house. She was wrapped up in a thick, gray
shawl. She seemed to be glaring with her one good eye.

Sandowski stepped back. "But . . . Mrs. Thorhall. Did they
phone you? I don't understand. How did you know to come
here?"

"I heard you go past my house. I live a little less than a mile
away. I knew something bad had happened. Thursten asked
me to take care of the children if anything went wrong." She
turned towards us, squinting. "Are all of you alright?"

I nodded. So did Michael and Angie.

"Did Mr. Asmundson expect trouble?" Sandowski asked.

"He said he saw a large animal earlier this afternoon. He
thought that it might be a bear. He borrowed my dog to help
him track it."

"I don't think a bear could make that much . . ." He paused,
looked at us then back at Althea. "Anything you could tell me
would help."

"Why don't we go in the yard for a second?" Althea suggested. "You three sit tight."

Althea and the officer went out the back door. I could hear her talking to him, but none of the words were loud enough to comprehend. A third voice joined in: Sergeant Roberts.

"What's going on?" Angie asked. "Does she know something?"

I shrugged. "If she does, she doesn't want us to hear it."

A moment later I heard Althea say, *"Oh no . . . oh no . . . no . . . not him."*

I realized they had probably told her about Hugin. There was a long period of silence, then they began talking again.

"We're being left in the dark," Michael said. "Just because we're kids."

The door opened. Althea came in, both officers a step behind. "That's all I really know. If you need any help, please call me."

"We will," Sergeant Roberts promised.

Althea gathered her shawl tighter around her shoulders. "All that's important is to get the children out of this house . . . now. To let you do your work."

"Yes," he agreed. "If you can take them that would be a big help."

Althea turned to us. "I know this is all a little rushed, but please grab your clothes and come with me. Your grandfather phoned me earlier and asked me to look after you. Apparently you have a bus to catch tomorrow morning."

"I'm not going on that bus," Michael said.

Althea looked at him, calmly. "I understand. We can talk about that in the morning. Everything will make a lot more sense then. Please, we must go."

Something in the tone of her voice made me believe her, made me hurry. I went to the bathroom and changed into jeans and a sweatshirt. A few minutes later we were at the door, ready to go, our suitcases in hand.

Sergeant Roberts was there. "Your grandfather will be just fine," he promised. He didn't seem to believe what he was saying—he was just repeating a line he had practiced again and again in some police drill.

"I hope so," I answered.

We followed Althea to her green truck, walking in a dream. It was a big old monster of a vehicle with an extended cab. Michael had to tug pretty hard to open the passenger door. We slid in silently.

Everything was happening too fast. I wanted to somehow slow it all down so that my thoughts could catch up.

"Close the door tight," Althea said.

Michael slammed the door and a moment later we were on the dark road, dim lights shining ahead of us. Two police cruisers passed by, heading towards Grandpa's cabin.

I almost started crying.

"It's all going to work out," Althea said, she touched my shoulder. I glanced at her. The dash lights cast dark shadows in her wrinkles, making her look even older.

I couldn't think of anything to say, so I just stared down. We traveled the rest of the way in silence. Soon she pulled up to her house, an old, white, two-story building with a bright yard light.

We all got out and followed her inside. Her home was warm and inviting.

"Would you like anything?" she asked. "Tea? Hot chocolate?"

We shook our heads. I was too tired to even yawn. I glanced at Michael and Angie. They could barely keep their eyes open. "I think we just need to sleep," I said.

Althea showed us to our room on the second floor. Two beds covered with huge quilts. A small window. An old radiator in the corner. It felt cozy and safe.

Althea said good night and we slipped into our beds. I wanted to say something to the others . . . even good night . . . but I was just too exhausted. Too much had happened and my body felt heavy.

The quilts were warm and thick.

I fell asleep.

13

I woke up to bright morning light streaming into the bedroom and to the smell of bacon. A moment later Althea knocked gently on our door.

"Good morning," she said. "Breakfast is ready."

I mumbled thanks, slid out of bed, and gathered up my clothes.

"It just doesn't seem real," Angie said.

"What doesn't?"

"This room. All the sunlight. It's like nothing happened last night. Like it was all a dream."

Michael gently removed the handkerchief on his arm. The wound was thin and dark. "Everything happened alright. My arm hurts and my leg feels like it was squeezed in a pair of vise grips." He lifted the leg of his pajamas. A purple, circular bruise colored his ankle. "I really would like to know how that happened."

I thought I knew, but I kept my mouth shut. It just seemed too early in the morning to start thinking about things like that. I went to the bathroom and changed into jeans and a

T-shirt. It's funny, my ankle seemed to hurt too. I looked at it, but there was nothing wrong. I guess I was just feeling sympathy pains for Michael.

I needed to have a bath. There was a huge bathtub in one corner, with legs shaped like tigers' paws. It would be so nice to take a long soak, to get all the stiffness out of my muscles. But I didn't have time.

I wandered downstairs, following the smell of bacon and coffee to the kitchen. I passed through a hallway and stopped in the living room. There were hundreds of books on a bookshelf that went from the floor to the ceiling, all neatly stacked and ancient looking. No Danielle Steele or Stephen King books here. Most of them were in other languages, Old Icelandic I guessed—with names like *Volsunga Saga* and *Ari's Libellus Islandorum*. I touched the jacket of one of them and tiny pieces came off on my fingers. I wouldn't have been surprised if some of these books were the only copies in the world.

Three books lay open on the coffee table.

What would Althea be reading?

I heard the clinking of cutlery in the kitchen; she was obviously busy. I padded over to the table and looked at the first one. It was as aged as all the others, a book that looked like it had been brought over here on a Viking ship and carried across the land in a treasure chest.

It was open to a dark ink drawing of a huge man in a tattered tunic with a fur vest. His arms were bare and bulging with muscles. He was kneeling on a giant, ugly, black shape that could barely be called human looking. He seemed to be holding the creature down. The thing's eyes were glowing in a frightening way. And the moon was shining on them both.

Not exactly what I wanted to see first thing in the morning.

I carefully turned the book over, afraid it would fall apart, and saw that it was titled *Grettis Saga*. It was the story of Grettir, the man whom Althea said was our ancestor.

I set it down. I glanced at the other two books and realized they were journals. I peered at the writing inside the one on top. It was all scribbled, written by someone in a hurry.

The smell of bacon finally drew me towards the kitchen.

"Sarah, you're up!" Althea was standing by the stove, scraping a huge pile of scrambled eggs from a black iron pan into a bowl. She was wearing a dark brown dress that reminded me of an oversized potato sack. Except it looked really comfortable. "I thought I'd have to bang on your door with a hammer." She smiled and winked with her good eye.

"Uh . . . no you wouldn't have to do—" I started and before I could say anything else, Michael and Angie stumbled into the room behind me, rubbing the sleep out of their eyes.

"You're all awake. Good." Althea was still smiling, though I noticed now that she looked tired and strained, like she hadn't slept for ages. Had she been reading all through the night?

"Did you hear anything about Grandpa?" Michael asked.

Althea nodded. "I talked to the police this morning. They . . . they haven't found him yet. They're going to continue looking today. They're organizing a search party."

"Do they know what . . . who he was fighting with?" I asked.

"No," Althea answered. "But they probably didn't tell me everything. That's the way the police do things."

"What can we do to help?" Angie's voice sounded as worried as I felt.

"I don't think you can really do very much. I'm sorry but

that's the truth. It's in the hands of the RCMP now—they'll take care of everything." She came over with a plate of fluffy yellow scrambled eggs and bacon. "I know this is bad for your arteries, but eat up. You have a long day ahead of you."

We ate. And despite my mood, the food tasted delicious. The bacon crispy and perfect. I followed it all with a small glass of orange juice. When we were finished, Althea looked at us. "Just leave the dishes. I'll get them later. You better hurry, we have to get to the bus depot in the next hour. The bus leaves at 10 AM sharp. And they don't wait for anyone."

"We can't go," Michael said.

Althea looked down. She spoke softly, her voice persuasive. "I understand, Michael. You're worried about your grandfather. That's only natural. But what do you expect to do? Help the police? They know what they're doing. It will be better if you three go home, to your parents."

"And wait?" I asked.

"Yes. Wait. That's all we can do now," she answered.

"But—" Michael started.

Althea still spoke softly. "No, Michael. I promised your grandfather I would send you home. That's what I intend to do. You'll be safer there."

"Safer?" I asked. "What do you—"

Althea shook her head. "It will be better for you, is what I meant. Better for all of you. Now, please, go and get ready. I'll take you into town in twenty minutes."

We left the table and went to our room.

"This is stupid," Michael said as he zipped his overnight bag closed. "We can't just leave Grandpa here. Not without knowing what happened to him."

"We don't really have much choice," Angie said. "Grandpa wanted us to go home. Althea wants us to go. What can we do?"

I sat on the bed. "It just seems like something's going on and no one's explaining it to us because they don't think we can handle it."

"I agree," Michael said. "Althea and Grandpa are both keeping secrets."

I was starting to feel a little angry. "We have to find—"

"Are you ready?" Althea asked through the half-open door. I nearly jumped out of my skin. I hadn't heard her come upstairs. "I have the dishes done and the truck running."

"Uh . . ." Michael paused. "Uh . . . yeah."

The door swung open. She was smiling. "Then come on. Let's pile in and head to town." Her voice had that fake cheeriness that sometimes crept into my parents' voices when they were trying to get me to do something I didn't want to do.

We followed her downstairs and out into the driveway. It was a warm, perfect day, already starting to get a little hot. All across Gimli, families would be heading out their doors to go suntanning and boating. But we were on our way to a bus and home.

We got into the truck. Michael sat in the tiny seat in the back. Althea looked around, left then right, as if she was afraid of running over something. Then she sighed and I thought I could hear real sadness in her voice. I glanced at her.

"I was looking for Hugin," she explained. "He usually comes with me when I go to town."

She took a deep breath and put the truck in reverse, turned around, and headed out onto the paved road. She went left, away from Grandpa's cabin and towards town. She drove slowly.

Somewhere behind us in the trees there were police officers calling for Grandpa, looking for prints, their German shepherds following scent trails that no one else could see. Would they find anything?

I didn't think so. I just knew it in my gut.

We drove on. After a few minutes I remembered what I had discovered in the living room. "Althea?"

"Yes?" she answered.

"I—I noticed some books in your study. This morning. One of them was Grettir's saga."

"Oh yes. I was reading it last night."

"It was open to a battle scene. Is that where Grettir fights that . . . that . . ." what was the word Grandpa used? ". . . *thrall?*"

"You know about Grettir and Glam?"

"Yes."

"That's the point where Grettir is cursed by Glam. He says he will always see Glam's glowing eyes before him, whenever it is dark or he is alone. So he will never be at peace."

"Why were you reading it last night?" I asked sharply.

"I . . ." She paused. "I was reading it because after I met you in my store, it reminded me that it had been a long time since I'd looked it over."

"Oh," I said. I wasn't sure why I had asked her. "What were the other books?"

"You're certainly inquisitive, aren't you? Your grandpa said you were pretty sharp." She glanced at me, smiling slightly, then looked back at the road. "They were old family histories. Just reading about my relatives and such. Nothing more than that."

I nodded. I wanted to ask her another question, but couldn't think of anything that didn't sound stupid. I was missing something somewhere.

We passed the sign that said: "GIMLI 1 KILOMETRE." The morning sun erased all the shadows and seemed to have polished up the town, making it look clean and perfect.

A short while later we pulled up at the bus depot. Two cars and a pickup truck were parked in front. There was a coffee shop right there and a laundromat. Neither seemed very busy. A Grey Goose bus sped past us, momentarily blocking the sunlight.

"Is this where we catch the bus?" Angie asked once we had parked. "It looks different in the day."

"This is it." Althea opened her door. "I'll go inside and get your tickets. It's plenty hot out, so why don't you three have a seat over there?" She pointed at a bench next to the depot. "The bus should be here in about ten minutes."

We got out of the truck, our suitcases and overnight bags in hand. My luggage felt like someone had stuffed twenty bricks inside. We trudged over and collapsed onto the bench. Althea disappeared into the station. The door squealed as it closed.

"This sucks," Michael announced. "It's just completely wrong."

I agreed with him. But I had no will to move or to say anything else. I felt sapped of my strength. Empty and tired.

A hot, dry wind came up, twirling with dust and scraps of paper. It twisted its way against the side of the building and right over us and seemed to hover there. I coughed, rubbed at my eyes. A second later the mini-tornado was gone, but I was still trying to clear my throat. A pound of dirt had found its way onto my face and into my hair.

I heard the door squeak open again.

"Are you alright?" Althea asked. Her voice sounded muffled. Were my ears filled with dust? She had three tickets in her hand. "You sound like you have something stuck in your throat."

"The . . . wind," I answered. Then coughed again before I could say any more.

"Maybe I'll get you all a drink before you go." She turned and went back into the depot.

At the same moment I heard a screeching, scraping noise that sounded like metal being twisted and torn in two. The bus was here, slamming on its brakes, bringing another cloud of dust with it. My coughing doubled. The bus went by only a few feet away from us and I glimpsed tinted windows and a bus driver with sunglasses. I knew already that I was doomed to sit beside the most boring person in North America and listen to his or her stories about what it was like to be a kid.

For hours on end.

I stood, choking now.

"Sarah?" Angie asked. "You gonna be okay?"

"No . . ." I mumbled. The dirt was clinging to the inside of my throat. "Just gonna go . . . to the bathroom. Wash my face. Gargle water too."

I stumbled away from the bench and into the coffee shop. I pushed open the door into the ladies' room. There I twisted on the taps and wet my face with cold water. Then I bent down and gulped a few mouthfuls of icy, bland-tasting water. It woke me up and my coughing slowly died. I ripped off a paper towel and dabbed at the excess water. It was like drying my face with sandpaper.

When I looked in the mirror, I almost scared myself. My hair was wild. There were black bags hanging below my eyes. The stress of the night before had worn lines in my face, deep creases. I looked like one of those old rock stars who should have settled down years ago. Was my face going to stay this way?

But there was something else I hadn't seen before in any of my family pictures. A hardness. A strength. It was revealed in the shape of my jaw, in the steadiness of my eyes—a look that reminded me of my grandfather. A similarity. Passed down through the ages.

Blood of my blood. That's what he was. And he was in danger . . . a danger I was beginning to realize even the police couldn't save him from.

I drew in my breath. Straightened my back, heard it crack.

I looked around, not sure why—like there was something in the bathroom that I needed to find.

The window was set low in the wall, open to let in the summer air. I went over to it, yanked it all the way up. I knew I could fit through if I stood on the toilet.

And if I went out the front, Althea would see me.

I climbed on the back of the toilet, stood, and pulled myself out. I scraped my knee on some metal part of the window, but didn't really feel it. Then I lowered myself onto the ground and glanced around. I was at the back of the bus depot. Gimli was in front of me. Houses and more houses.

It was only a short dash to the alley. Beyond that was a park.

I was overcome by a burst of new energy. I was taking action, doing something.

I started running.

14

Not once did I think of Angie or Michael in those first few minutes. I just knew that I had to get away from Althea, from the bus that would swallow me up and take me home. I sped through the park and up another back alley, not sure where to go. I stayed away from main streets, afraid Althea would be searching through them. I knew that, even with one eye, Althea would be able to see much farther than most people. Maybe even into the future or the spirit world.

I realized that by running I would attract the townspeople's attention, so I slowed to a quick walk. I must have gone down every back alley in Gimli. Finally I found a brick school that was large enough to be a fortress. It seemed quite old, maybe even as old as Grandpa. It was surrounded by a big yard and walled in by a carefully trimmed hedge. I wandered around back and found a hiding place in the bushes. I had this fear that Althea could sense where I was, just like those people who point and find water, so I snuggled deeper into the branches.

I had no idea what I was going to do next or where I would go—just that I had to stay here in Gimli. I hugged my knees.

Some of the strength I felt only an hour or two ago was slipping away now that I had stopped moving.

What could I do here? What had happened to Grandpa? I felt small and too young to be trying to do something on my own. And most of all, I felt alone.

Right at this moment, Angie and Michael were riding a bus, miles from Gimli, wondering what had happened to me. I probably should have told them, but I couldn't without getting caught. They'd just have to tell Mom and Dad: "We had a great time, but we lost Sarah. Is that okay?"

A group of crows landed in the grass a few yards away. They pecked at the ground. One of them watched me, showing no interest in worms or bits of garbage at all.

Was every animal in Gimli extraordinarily intelligent?

Grandpa used to say crows were the smartest of all birds and they watched everything and reported back to their master, one-eyed Odin.

Maybe they would lead one-eyed Althea to me. I grabbed a few pebbles and tossed them at the birds. They all took off, cawing and flapping their wings.

Except the largest one. He continued to stare at me.

"Go away," I whispered. "Go back to your nest."

He *cawed*. A loud, startling cry.

"Beat it! Go on!"

He made three more loud *caws*, then with a majestic movement, unfurled his wings. He was even larger than I had first thought. With the easiest of motions he was suddenly in the air. He circled around the bushes three times, then flew off.

Grandpa had also told me that crows were messengers. That often they brought tidings from loved ones.

Was it trying to pass on a message about Grandpa to me?

I shook my head. *Sarah. Sarah. Sarah. This town is getting to you. Now you're starting to think like them.*

I sat for at least another hour, then finally decided it was time to wander again. I got up, dusted myself off, walked out of the school yard, and headed downtown.

I intentionally stayed away from the bookstore. I meandered quickly up and down the streets, not sure what I hoped to find. Finally I saw a sign that said *Ye Ol' Ice Cream Shoppe.* Luckily I had my wallet in my pocket.

I knew exactly what I should do.

I went inside the air-conditioned store. It was small. The whole counter was see-through glass with pail after pail of multicolored ice cream behind it.

"Hello there," an old man said. He had a white cap on and his shirt was like a hockey referee's. It said *Mr. Scoop* on the front. "What flavor can I do for you today?"

I shrugged. Looked through the glass.

"There are so many choices." It was ice cream heaven.

"I'd recommend Tiger, Tiger," he said. "It's the perfect taste for this kind of day."

Immediately I started to salivate. I hadn't eaten anything for hours. "Yes, please. Just a small cone."

He grabbed a cone and started scooping up the ice cream. When he was finished he stood and handed a heaping orange-and-black mass of Tiger, Tiger to me.

"That's as small as we go here," he explained.

I smiled and slid a dollar coin and two quarters over to him. I licked the cone. It tasted perfect. "Uh . . . is . . . Brand around?"

"Brand?" He raised one eyebrow and winked at me. I didn't get the joke. "Brand's just finishing up in the back."

As if on cue, Brand came out. "All done," he announced. Then he looked at me, smiled. "Hey . . . hi! It's Sarah, right?"

"Yes. I . . ." I paused. Was I blushing? "I came to take you up on your offer . . . to . . . uh . . . show me around."

"Good." He waved at the man. "See you, Scoop."

We went outside, down the sidewalk.

"You know," he said softly, "I heard about your grandfather. I just want to say I hope he's okay."

"Me too," I answered. "How did you hear?"

"My best friend's dad is on the force. Derrick Roberts."

"Oh . . . Sergeant Roberts . . . I met him." I paused. "Did your friend know anything about what's going on?"

"Just that they were still looking. That's all he told me."

We walked a little ways in silence.

"He's a tough old guy," Brand said, "He'll pull through."

I nodded, but I couldn't take comfort in his words. Because something had entered my room last night that I had never seen or felt before. If it could tear holes in the cabin and kill Hugin like snapping a toothpick, what chance did Grandpa have? I shivered.

Brand pointed at a long narrow street to our right. "Why don't we walk up this way—we can see the lake then. Boardwalk is just up here."

"Sure."

We changed direction. I finished the last of my cone. The center of my stomach felt cold, as if the ice cream refused to melt.

"So where are your two friends?" Brand asked.

"Uh . . . Michael and Angie went home. They had to get back to do some . . . stuff. They're not my friends though . . . Michael's my brother and Angie's my cousin. But I like them just as much as friends. Most of the time, that is."

"I thought you all looked alike, especially you and Michael."

"He's my *tvinnr.*"

"Your what?"

I shook my head. Why was I suddenly speaking another language? "My twin, sorry. *Tvinnr* is an Old Icelandic word that Grandpa says is the origin of the English word twin. But yeah, we're twins. Not identical twins, of course."

"Twins! That's cool! You guys ever have any of those twin things happen? You know, he stubs his toe and your toe feels sore . . . that kind of thing?"

"Well . . . I'm not sure," I answered. My right ankle suddenly tingled with pain—the same ankle Michael had hurt. Could there be a connection? I wondered.

Brand was staring at me. I blushed. "Uh . . . sometimes I know when he's just about to make a bad joke."

"I guess that's the same thing." Brand paused. "So you're here by yourself then. Where are you staying?"

"Um . . ." For some reason I didn't want to mention Althea's name, almost as if she might hear me and come running. "At a woman's place. A friend of Grandpa's. Andrea."

"Andrea who?"

"I can't remember her last name. She lives just past Grandpa's house."

"East, west, north, or south?"

"I'm not sure."

Brand nodded. He was staring at me, almost as if he didn't

believe anything I was saying. "I thought I knew most every-one up that way. I guess I don't."

"I think she just moved into her house recently." Now I was outright lying to him. I had to change the topic. "How far is it to the lake?"

"We're almost there." A few steps later he cleared his throat as if getting ready to say something important. Was he going to call me an out-and-out liar? He turned to me, a worried look on his face. "You know . . . I don't want you to take this in a mean way but . . . you look really bad."

I had a sudden flash image of how I had appeared in the bath-room mirror, hair pointing in all directions. I didn't imagine I had gotten any prettier, though. I wanted to be at my best around him. "It's . . . I've been through a lot . . . that's all."

"Well, we don't have to walk any farther . . . we can just go sit somewhere."

"I—I actually don't mind walking. It'll help keep me awake. And . . . uh . . . I like talking to you too."

He smiled. A very handsome smile. A moment later we went past the last building. We were on Gimli's boardwalk and the lake now appeared in front of us. Brand spread out his arms, sound-ing like a circus announcer. "Here's the wonderful wacky world of Lake Winnipeg." There were a few motorboats out, one or two sailboats. Seagulls were darting through the air. I suddenly realized that even though my life had been turned upside down and inside out, the rest of the world carried on as it always had.

There were a few clouds forming in the distance. But here we were splashed with bright, warm sunlight. I still felt cold though, as if nothing could heat up my bones after the night before.

"I spend a lot of time here in the summer," Brand was saying. "Water-skiing and fishing and stuff. Have you ever tried tubing? You know—where they drag a tire tube behind a boat. Do they have that in the States?"

"Yes, of course! But I haven't tried it yet."

He smiled. Ran a hand through his short hair. "It's absolutely wild."

We went a bit farther down the walkway. Brand waved at some kids our age out on a motorboat, and they waved back, then made a sharp turn, sending a huge wave rolling our way. I could hear them hooting with joy. That was the kind of fun I wanted to be having right now.

"This lake is huge," I said.

Brand nodded. "I know. My grandma and grandpa used to bring me out here when I was a kid and tell me stories about the lake. It was even bigger during the ice age; it covered most of this part of the province . . . it was called Lake Agassiz or something like that. Kinda makes you realize how old this place is."

We walked by a giant statue of a Viking. I couldn't help thinking of all the Icelandic people who had settled here. Including my ancestors. I could use their strength and help right now.

"Are your grandparents still around?" I asked.

"Uh . . . Grandpa died last year. But Grandma's still here. The only person I know who could tell stories as good or better was your grandpa—is something wrong, Sarah?"

"I . . ." I held my stomach. "I just feel sick suddenly." I knew what it was—just mentioning Grandpa was affecting me. Making my stomach turn with fright.

Then a second wave of nausea swept over me and I felt as

if I would black out. The bright sky disappeared, the clouds swirled around me. I knew I was hallucinating. I was buried in dirt and I couldn't move my limbs. I smelled smoke and for one brief moment a face hung in front of me, with a twisted mouth and large, moon-colored eyes. Then I heard a pounding sound, the creaking of wood. A snap.

A moment later it all disappeared. The sky was blue. Brand was saying something I couldn't understand and my knees were shaking.

"Can . . . can we sit down?" I asked.

He helped me to a bench and we sat. I breathed in and out slowly; trying to steady myself. Finally my stomach returned to normal.

"What was that all about? Your eyes rolled back into your head. I thought you were going to pass out."

"I just got a very powerful feeling of Grandpa. He's in trouble."

"What do you mean?"

"I . . . I don't know. Just a gut feeling, I guess. Like Grandpa was buried or something."

"Really?"

"Yes . . . really." I decided it was time for me to take a chance. "Uh . . . have you ever noticed how . . . weird this town is?"

Brand laughed. "Weird? Of course, it's what makes us such a great tourist attraction."

"I mean really weird. Scary weird."

He looked suddenly serious. "What do you mean? Did something happen?"

Then I just started talking, not caring if he thought I was some crazy American girl. I described the little boy in the trees and explained how something had broken the window in the cabin. I spoke until I was tired, describing as much as I could. Brand stared seriously at me through all of this, his jaw muscles clenched.

When I was finished he took my arm. "C'mon," he said.

"Where to? The loony bin?"

"No," he said. "I know what we have to do."

15

Brand wouldn't tell me where we were going. He led me back into town and I followed him like a zombie.

He pulled me into an old restaurant with a jukebox and black-and-white pictures of hot rod cars on the wall. He guided me to a booth and sat on the other side. Before I could even open my mouth to ask him a question, the waitress popped up in front of us as if she had just risen through a trapdoor. Her blonde hair was in a ponytail—she looked like a character from an Archie Andrews comic.

"Whattya want?" she asked.

"Coke, please," Brand said.

"Hot chocolate," I answered.

She narrowed her eyes. "Hot chocolate? It's twenty some degrees out there, dear."

"Please," I said.

She smiled. Shrugged. "Sure thing. You kids are into the weirdest stuff these days."

After she left, Brand said, "Just sit here, okay. I'll be back in a second."

"Uh . . . sure."

He stood up and went outside. I watched him walk past the front of the restaurant. He waved and gave me a quick smile. I leaned closer to the window and twisted my neck to see where he was going. He went a little farther down the sidewalk and stopped at a pay phone. What was he doing?

The woman appeared with the hot chocolate. I drank, feeling it heat up my stomach. I took another sip and another.

Brand returned a few minutes later.

"Is it helping?" he asked.

"Is what helping?"

"The hot chocolate? Do you feel any better?"

"Yes." I finished off the rest. "It's a lot better now."

"Do you think you really felt what was happening to your grandpa or was it your imagination?"

I paused. The answer came from deep inside me. "No. For a second I was seeing what he saw. Don't you find that a little crazy?"

Brand shook his head. "No. I . . . uh . . . when my grandfather died, I saw his spirit. Just kind of floating in front of me. And he said something, then smiled and was gone."

"What did he say?"

"He told me to get good grades."

"What! You're kidding."

"No. He used to say that to me all the time. He wanted me to become a history professor someday."

"Are you saying that was Grandpa's ghost I saw?"

"No. I just think that we are all connected in some mysterious ways. Especially with our own kin."

"So do you mean Grandpa was sending me a message?" I asked.

Brand sipped from his Coke. "Yeah . . . kind of, I guess. I don't know. This just means he's alright."

"For now," I added, and once I said it I realized Grandpa wouldn't be alright for long. He was in danger.

Something else was bothering me. "Who were you talking to on the phone?"

"The phone?" He paused. "Oh . . . yeah . . . there's—"

Just at that moment the door to the cafe swung open. Althea swept in, her face set in grim lines.

"—someone I want you to meet."

Althea pointed at me like she'd just caught a jewel thief. "I've been looking for you, Sarah."

16

"Oh . . . you two know each other." Brand seemed worried. "You didn't tell me that, Grandma."

"I didn't want you to inform her I was on my way." Althea still looked like she was about to explode. She loomed closer to me. "You shouldn't have run away, Sarah."

"I'm not going home," I said, surprised at the serious tone of my voice. Almost as if someone else were speaking through me.

"Not today, you're not . . . the bus is gone." She was now right in front of me, glaring down. "But you will tomorrow. I made a promise to your grandfather and I'm going to keep it."

"But—" I started.

"Don't argue with me, Sarah." I knew she wasn't making a request. "You and Brand will come with me now."

I sighed. Everyone was pushing me one way, pulling me another. How much more of this could I take? I left money on the table and we followed Althea. Once outside, Brand turned to me. "I didn't know you knew Grandma. I didn't mean to get you into trouble."

"I'm sorry," I said quickly, "I didn't tell you everything. I should have."

We got into Althea's truck and she started it up. "Where are we going?" I asked.

"Home. Where I can keep a close eye on you. I might even be tempted to tie you up."

It didn't sound like she was joking.

With that Althea was silent and we drove all the way to her home without speaking another word. We pulled into the yard, parked in her driveway, got out, and followed her into the house. "You might as well head straight into the backyard." Althea motioned towards the patio. "Just don't run away."

I walked solemnly through the living room, slid the door open.

Sitting on lawn chairs, in sunglasses, T-shirts, and shorts, were Angie and Michael. Michael sat up when he saw me. "Hey, Sis!"

"What are you guys doing here?"

Michael smiled. "Just wondering if we should be mad at you or not."

"Mad at me, for what?"

"For leaving us at the bus depot," Angie cut in. "For not telling us your getaway plan. Nice cousin you are."

"Well . . ." I paused. "I'm sorry. It just kinda happened. I really should have somehow told you guys."

Michael shrugged. "It's okay. Once we figured out you were gone Althea changed our tickets to tomorrow, so we get to stay an extra day. Of course we aren't supposed to take a step outside this yard." He paused. "She was a little P.O.'d at you."

"I figured that out." I sat on the edge of a weathered bench.

"She'll get over it," Brand said, settling himself on a lawn chair next to me. "She forgives and forgets pretty fast. It's part of being a grandma."

"I heard that!" Althea was standing at the door, right behind us. I turned. She had a container of iced tea in one hand and several glasses in the other. "I forgive people, Brand. But I've got the memory of an elephant. You should know that by now. Remember when you broke my favorite dish because you thought it would make a great Frisbee?"

Brand looked a little sheepish. "Uh . . . sorry, Grandma," he said.

"It's alright, I forgive you." She came out and set the container and glasses on the round wooden picnic table. She sat down and stared at us. "I think it's time we all had a little talk."

"About what?" I asked.

"I want you to tell me everything you saw and heard last night. Everything. Even if you think it's strange."

"And . . ." I started, not sure if I had the guts to pull it off, ". . . what do we get in return?"

Althea narrowed her good eye, gave me a piercing look. I stared back. "What do you mean?" she asked after a few moments.

I couldn't hold her stare. I glanced down, then back up at her. "I . . . uh . . . we want to know what's happening. There are things Grandpa didn't tell us—that you aren't telling us. And we want to know what they are. You can't just keep secrets from us because we're young. We're old enough to handle it."

"She's right," Michael added. "We want the truth."

Althea sat brooding for a moment, then she looked directly at me. "You do have Grettir's blood."

I didn't know exactly what she was talking about, but I nodded as if I understood.

Althea looked me up and down. Then stared at Angie and Michael. "Perhaps I've underestimated you. All of you. Maybe it would have been better if I'd told you the truth from the beginning." She paused for another second. "Alright," she said, "I'll tell you everything I know, and you can deal with the nightmares and the possibilities—it's a deal. But first each of you give me your version of what happened. And don't leave out the smallest detail."

Again we spoke about seeing the little boy in the forest and how he had disappeared. Then we all recounted what we could remember about Grandpa's disappearance. Althea nodded and listened closely, asking very few questions. When we were done she sat back. She seemed to believe every word.

"Were any of you hurt or bruised or touched by this visitor?" she asked.

"Yes," Michael said. He moved his legs, displaying the circular purple bruise around his ankle. It looked even worse than this morning. "I don't remember exactly how this happened, but I know it was last night while I was dreaming."

Althea examined his ankle closely. "It's very deep bruising. Does it hurt?" she asked.

"A little, yes," Michael answered. "It's just kind of numb."

Althea rose slowly and went into the house. We were all silent. I looked around the back yard. There was a garden growing there, corn stalks stood straight and tall. There was also a red truck next to a small shop.

Althea came back a few seconds later with a white plastic jar. She dipped her hand in and pulled out a wad of greenish lotion, then rubbed it around Michael's ankle. Once finished she sat back and tightened the lid on the jar. "How does that feel?"

"Much better." Michael was staring at his ankle, a look of awe on his face. "It's tingling and it feels . . . alive, I guess."

The bruise already appeared to be fading.

Brand gently touched my shoulder. "You should probably tell her about how cold you've been."

"Cold?" Althea was looking at me. "Is this true?"

"Yes." I shivered. "I just can't seem to warm up. And . . . I forgot to mention . . . I . . . uh . . . saw an image of Grandpa."

"What kind of image?"

"Well, it was more like a feeling that he was buried."

"Hmm," she said. "Hmm. This is all making sense. I should have told you from the beginning. Yes, I should have." She stood up. "Just wait here. There are a few things I want to show all of you."

Then she disappeared into the house.

17

"What's she doing?" Angie asked.

We could hear Althea banging around inside, closing and opening doors, dropping things.

"It sounds like she's remodeling the living room," Michael said.

"My guess is Grandma's setting something up for us." Brand was sipping from his iced tea. "I'm not sure if I want to know what it is."

I sat back. The sun's rays couldn't even warm the top layer of my skin. I wanted to find a parka, a pile of blankets, or a roaring fire, but I knew none of these things would be enough to heat me up.

"We talked to Mom and Dad," Michael said to me.

"What did they say?"

"They want us to get home at once—Angie is supposed to come all the way to Missouri since her parents are still in Europe. Dad was quite upset that we couldn't take another bus today."

"Were they upset about Grandpa too?"

Michael nodded. "Yeah, really shaken up. Mom started crying. Dad was asking me all these questions—and I didn't have any answers. Dad's going to fly out here, but he can't get away until tomorrow."

"Well, why don't we wait till he gets here?"

Michael shook his head. "No. He made me promise I would go home tomorrow. That all of us would go."

I sat back. So we would have to leave in the morning, no doubts about it. Had I run away just to delay something that was going to happen anyway?

"Hey," Michael said suddenly, "did you know Dad speaks Icelandic?"

"A little. I didn't think he knew too much, though."

"He and Althea talked for at least five minutes in Icelandic . . . I don't think she wanted us to know what they were talking about."

"Did you understand anything they said?" I asked.

"I heard them mention Thursten once," Angie answered.

"Me too," Michael said, "and another name . . . Kormak or something. But other than that it was all noise. I couldn't make any sense of it, other than it sounded serious."

"I'll tell you what it was about." Althea was standing at the door. "But not right now. Come into the house. I have a few things to show you."

I stood up, shaky. I was beginning to feel like I had just finished a marathon. We all made our way through the sliding door into the living room. The coffee table had three old books on it. I recognized them as the ones I had glanced at in the morning. There was also a metal vial and a huge, heavy-looking iron cross. Beside them was a pot of tea and five cups.

"Have a seat," Althea motioned and we sat down. Me on the couch beside Brand. Angie and Michael in separate chairs. I shivered. Now that I was out of the sun, I felt even colder. "All of you should drink some of that tea. Especially you, Sarah. It'll warm you up."

I doubted this. I poured myself a cup, sipped it. It had a sharp taste, a tangy lemony scent. I can't say it was good, but I felt it burst against my tongue, down my throat, and spread throughout my body as if it were entering my bloodstream and heating it up. I took another sip. "It works," I said, astonished.

"Yes. But don't drink more than one cup." Althea was sitting across from all of us, near the tea table. "It'll burn some of your inner energy."

She paused. Moved the cross, held it in her right hand.

"I guess I'll start at the very beginning." Her tone was solemn. She wasn't looking at us, but at the cross. Her face seemed more wrinkled, as if just the act of telling this story was draining her. "I'll start with the death of Eric Bardarson. I remember when it happened . . . I was in my early twenties. I was one of his teachers at the time. He was in grade two, if I remember correctly, and he was really a gentle, lovable kid. Always dreaming. Always happy. It was a pleasure to teach him.

"It had been a very wet spring. There were heavy snows all winter, and the moment it started to warm up enough to melt, the sky darkened and the rain fell. And it kept pouring for weeks on end, so much rain and cloudy weather you could feel it in your bones. It made everyone upset, less likely to say good morning. Some of the older people just gave up—the winter and a hard spring was too much. Needless to say, we all wanted a break.

"It came somewhere in the middle of May. The sun was out one morning and stayed all day, burning away the water. Everyone wandered outside to look, to laugh, to smile. Some of the kids even wore shorts to school, which was against the rules, but we teachers didn't care.

"When the weekend arrived, the earth was getting dry and a lot of families headed out along the lake or up to Camp Morton to have picnics and play games and visit all their friends whom they hadn't seen all winter. The Bardarsons were one of these families. But unlike everyone else, they went into the woods. You had to walk a long way to get to Thor's Shoulder, a clearing on a giant hill. You could look down on all of Gimli and see the lake. It really was quite beautiful.

"And I guess they had a wonderful picnic. Besides Eric, the Bardarsons also had a boy and a girl a grade or two ahead of Eric. They spent the whole day with each other. Eating and playing games. They let the kids wander around as long as they didn't go too far.

"When it came time for them to leave, Eric had disappeared. His brother and sister said he was right behind them, but when they turned he was gone. The family frantically searched for him for hours, but there was no trace. It was growing dark so the father sent his wife and children to get help and he stayed there calling out Eric's name. He finally grew tired and leaned against a tree. He lit a fire hoping to attract his son. He said he heard many strange sounds that night, howling and voices, but saw nothing of Eric.

"The next morning, and for days after, the search party tramped around the area. They couldn't even turn up a scrap of clothing. It was decided the heavy rains had softened the earth so much that the boy must have fallen into a bog and smothered to death. Others said wolves may have gotten him, but this seemed unlikely because even wolves leave remains.

"There was only one person who lived in that area—old man Kormak. He had a cabin and he survived by trapping animals for his own food and gathering berries and edible plants from the brush. The police did ask him if he knew anything, but they could make no sense of what he said. The rumor was that all the rain pounding on his cabin had driven him insane. I only saw Kormak three times while he was alive. And each time he looked the same: he was a big-boned man, with wild hair and a thick beard. He wore animal skins with the heads still attached. And he never bathed.

"There were rumors that he had something to do with Eric's disappearance. People also whispered that Kormak liked to spend time at graveyards and such . . . but no one could prove anything. Finally, the search was given up. Every couple of years there's something in the paper about the boy—it's one of the biggest tragedies to hit Gimli."

Althea paused. She reached slowly down to her cup of tea, grasped it, and took a sip.

"What happened to this Kormak guy?" Angie asked.

Althea set down her cup. "He died about five years later."

"Well," I said, "if this boy and Eric are the same person— then why? I mean, what was he doing out there?"

"Let me begin by saying that I've seen him too."

"You have?" Michael asked.

"Yes." Althea nodded. "About four years ago this summer I was on my way north to a reading by a writer friend of mine. I had agreed to set up a display of his work. It was late and I was driving not too far from where you three were walking. All of a sudden there was this little glowing figure on the road—he just appeared out of nowhere. I slammed on my brakes, swerved to miss him, and he vanished. At the same time I came over the rise of a hill and a deer was in the middle of the highway, staring at me. I would have never been able to stop in time. I got out and looked for the boy but he had disappeared."

"You mean he warned you?" Brand asked.

"Yes. I think so. I don't know exactly how he died, but I think his spirit is here as an omen of sorts—a good omen. I know Eric is more likely to appear in the early summer—it's near the anniversary of his death. Powerful things happen around the anniversary of anyone's death, sometimes good, sometimes bad. I have met a few other people who've seen him. One was a woman hiker who would have fallen into an old well if he hadn't attracted her attention. I think he's there to try and stop more bad things from happening."

"That's awful," Angie said.

"What do you mean?" I asked.

She looked a little sad. "That this poor boy has to wander around, warning people. Never doing whatever little boys get to do in heaven."

Althea nodded. "It does seem unfair, doesn't it? But we don't know what happens next. I don't think time is the same to him. Maybe he drifts from here to a better place and back. Who knows."

"It doesn't sound like much of an afterlife." Angie was frowning now.

"It's not for us to judge," Althea said finally.

I sat back. "What do you think the boy was warning us about?"

"I can't really say for sure. Just that something bad was going to happen. And obviously it did."

"Was he—" I swallowed. "Was he warning us about a *draugr?*"

Althea laughed, so loudly and forcefully that I was shocked. "Heavens no! Thursten's been filling your head full of stories. I'll tell you what I believe happened last night. It's exactly what I told the police."

18

Althea reached for the largest of the books on the table, a tattered and stained journal. It looked like it had been through the wringer a hundred times over. I remembered that it had scribbled handwriting inside.

Althea opened the cover carefully. "Last winter I found a large, brown package waiting for me at the post office—it was this book. It had been sent to me by members of Kormak's family. They still own the land he dwelled on, and one of them had made the journey to the cabin and found this. They kept it at their home in Iceland for a few years, unopened. Then they heard I was writing a history of Gimli, so they sent it to me. It's Kormak's old journals."

"What does a man who died years ago have to do with Grandpa?" Michael asked.

"I'll get to that. Just give me a second." She flipped through a few pages, read a bit to herself, then flipped ahead some more. All the paper was yellow and the book looked like it would fall apart. "Ah, here's something." She pointed at the page. "'*And I can feel the hatred boil up, a living thing inside me. Every time I see his face, hear his voice . . . I know he is my born enemy. I loathed his father . . . I loathe him. This Thursten from the valley, son of Thorgeir.'* Then Kormak writes *blóth* about twenty times in a row."

"What's that mean?" I asked.

"Blood. He seemed pretty obsessed with blood."

"Was it Grandpa he hated so much?" Angie had her arms crossed.

"Yes," Althea answered. "It was. About the time this was written, your grandfather had just arrived here from the old country. By talking to him and by doing research on my own, I discovered Kormak was one of the Grotsons, a family that had a long-standing grievance with the Asmundsons, your family. He had moved here and brought the feud with him."

"What was the feud over?" I asked.

"Well, about seventy years ago, Kormak's father accused your great-grandfather of stealing one of his cows. It even went through the courts and Thorgeir was declared innocent. But there was a rumor that the old farmer actually was in love with your great-grandmother . . . though she'd never had anything to do with him. Apparently he passed this hatred down to Kormak."

"Did he ever do anything to Grandpa?" Angie asked.

Althea shook her head. "No. Just wrote in this book. Kormak was a little bit bothered in the head. Pretty well everyone whom he had cross words with—and that was a lot of people for a hermit—ended up in this journal. But most of the entries were about Thursten."

"Okay," Michael said, "so this Kormak guy didn't like Grandpa and he wrote a bunch of mean stuff, then he kicked off. What's this have to do with today?"

"Well . . ." Althea flipped ahead a few pages. "Right here is Kormak's last entry, presumably written only a few hours before he died. It says, *'Revenge will be mine after night, after death, after everything. The light will not claim me.'* It's dated the same day he collapsed in his front yard with a failed heart: June 30th, 1945."

Althea flipped ahead another page or two. "And right here the strangest thing happens. There are new entries written after Kormak's death. With dates sometime in the last five years, if they can be believed."

My heart had skipped a beat. "New entries?"

"Yes, written in a similar hand as before . . . but forty-five years later. Here, I'll read you one." She ran her finger down the page, stopped. *"'Darkness and fog and cold creep through my bones. I have had dreams and heard crowing voices, twice now the wolves and rats and all the dark creatures have come knocking at the door. The third time will be the last.'"*

"It doesn't make any sense," Brand said.

"No," Althea answered. "Not at first. But when you read more it starts to make a certain crazy semblance of sense. Here's another one. *'And I feel the hatred wrap around my flesh and sink its fangs into my heart. It is eating at me like the snake Jormungand who bites his own tail. It is an old, old hatred passed down through my flesh, my spirit, my bones—from father to son to son. A hatred for one man, one name: Thursten.'* This entry is dated only three years ago.

"I'll read you the very last one. It's the worst. *'Blood. Dead. Flesh. I am returned from the dirt, up from the ground. Draugr . . . Draugr . . . Draugr . . .'"*

"Did Kormak write this?" I asked.

"No. Kormak was long, long dead and buried. His son wrote it."

"Son?" I had finished the last of my tea and was beginning to feel the coldness creep into my system once again. "His son?"

Althea nodded. "Well, I did a little research on this—I don't think his family read all the book. They just saw it was old and sent it to me—I'm good friends with Kormak's first cousin. I got the impression they weren't too proud about Kormak's branch of their family tree—but they did find him interesting.

"After I read the journal I wrote to the Grotsons about the new entries. They sent back a letter saying they didn't know anything about them. But they included a piece of information that made me think quite a bit. They said Kormak had married only a year or so before he left for Gimli. His wife was quite young and many believed it was an ill match and that he had somehow bewitched her. Anyway, he left her with child and vanished to Canada. He apparently never saw his first and only offspring—a boy.

"They told me his son was *rotinn*—rotten inside. His mother had a hard time raising him, it took years from her life. Apparently her hair went gray and her skin wrinkled up by the time she was twenty-five. He fought with everyone, was kicked out of school, and spent time in jail. But all this time his mother told him what a great father he'd had. She died, presumably of exhaustion, when she was thirty-four. Some of the relatives tried to care for the boy, but within six months he had disappeared. No one heard about him again for years. He just wandered around Iceland and Norway, wherever he could find trouble."

"What was his name?" Michael asked.

"Kar. About five or six years ago, people who knew of him thought they had seen him passing through Gimli. He looks just like his father, sallow sunken eyes and heavy cheekbones. The people who saw him went to church that night to pray for the town. They said looking into his eyes was like looking into the burning orbs of the Devil.

"A few days later I was down having coffee at a restaurant and I heard that hunters had seen lights in Kormak's cabin. Of course, no one dared to go near it. Even fifty years later, no one wants to have anything to do with Kormak."

"So you think this Kar wrote in the journal?" I was starting to understand what Althea was getting at.

"Yes, he might have stayed at the cabin and later his family members, not knowing he had lived there or was still there, took this from the table. I think Kar read it, then started to hate your grandfather just like his father did. His side of the Grotson family is known to be a little . . . mad. And the stories of people coming back from the dead are pretty common in the old land. He probably made himself believe he was actually undead. And he's been planning his revenge for years. This is what I told the police and they're looking for him now."

"But he couldn't have done all the damage to the house," I said, "one man couldn't have."

Althea narrowed her eyes. "I haven't seen the cabin in daylight yet, but I do know that it was dark and all of you were in a state of fear and worry, and sometimes your imagination makes your memories bigger than what you actually saw."

"But—" I started.

"You would also be surprised how much destruction a deranged Icelandic man can do."

I fell silent. I wasn't sure what was right. Maybe it only was a few broken windows and boards magnified by my frightened mind.

"There's one more thing you should know." Althea looked seriously at us all. "Your grandfather and I traced your family lines back. And this Kar is actually related to you—a third cousin."

"We're related to this crazy guy!" Michael exclaimed. "Great gene pool we come from."

Althea spoke slowly. "This is what I believe happened. You're old enough that I can tell you the truth. I think Kar has probably dragged Thursten away and buried him . . . but kept him alive. *Draugrs* were known to do this to their victims as a sort of slow revenge. That means your grandfather is most likely still alive."

"For now," Michael whispered.

We were silent.

"What can we do?" I asked finally.

"Pray," Althea answered. "Tonight—"

The phone buzzed. It was sitting on a small desk and looked like it was a fax machine too.

Althea went to it and picked up the receiver. "Hello."

She paused for a moment. Her face became set in stone.

"I understand. Yes, I will be there shortly."

She set down the phone and turned to face us. "The police are having difficulty locating Kar's cabin. Even their dogs seem to lose their sense of direction. I'm going to go out and help them."

"Why you?" Brand asked, clearly concerned about his grandmother.

"Because I know those woods better than anyone. I'll be

safe. There will be six officers with me." She smiled. "It's not every day I get to be around six handsome men in uniform."

A minute later she was at the door, workboots on, her shawl around her shoulders. "Brand, there are leftovers in the fridge. Please, feed our guests." She turned to us, her one gray eye serious. "We will find your grandfather," she promised.

Then she was out the door and gone.

19

"We're not just gonna wait here, are we?" Angie asked.

"What else can we do?" Michael flipped his hair out of his eyes. "We have to sit right here. But I don't know if I'll be able to stand it."

"Grandma knows what she's doing," Brand said. "She's worked with the police before—she helps them quite a bit. And if anyone can find your grandfather, she can. She has a gift for those kinds of things."

"You mean she's done this before?" I asked.

"No . . . not exactly," Brand answered. "She just has a knack for finding things, including people. Once when I was a kid I ran away from home and, to make a long story short, I got lost in the dark. For hours. She was the one who found me. She just knew exactly where I was."

"Yeah . . . you're right," I said. "She seems like she's capable of anything." The noose in my stomach was loosening. I sighed. "The police are trained for this kind of thing too. Everything will work out."

"The Mounties always get their man," Brand said, a little

flippantly. He was smiling. "It's what they're known for." He stood up. "You know what we need right now is a little grub. How about leftovers?"

"I'll help," I said a little too quickly. Angie gave me a quick wink. "That is, if you need help."

Brand motioned with his hand. "Sure. The more the merrier." Then he headed for the kitchen.

I ran a hand through my hair and my fingers got stuck in the knots. "I have to go to the washroom first," I said. I turned left and went up the stairs. I thought I could hear Angie and Michael laughing behind me.

Once in the bathroom, I looked in the mirror. There was dirt on my face, my hair looked even worse than it had in the morning. Oh no! My heart sank. I had looked like this all day. I found a brush and quickly brushed out the knots, practically pulling my hair out. When I was done, I pulled it back and tied it with a barrette I found on the counter.

Then I laughed at myself. Here I was worried about my looks on probably one of the worst days of my life. It was silly.

I did take the time to wash my face.

Just before I left I stared at myself.

That hard look I had seen before was still there. A feeling of strength.

I wished I could understand where it was coming from.

I found Brand in the kitchen, opening the oven door. A turkey pie was in his right hand. He slid it into the oven. "This'll be perfect," he said to me. "You got here just in time . . . what temp should it be?"

I turned the knob to 375 degrees. "It'll probably take at least twenty minutes."

I glanced up. Brand was staring at me, a look of caring in his eyes. "How are you feeling?" he asked quietly.

"Uh . . . good," I answered, suddenly feeling queasy. "Better, I guess, now that I know Althea is going to help in the search."

"All three of you should get medals. You've held up really well." He paused. "In fact, you deserve a medal for getting away from Grandma. I would have thought it impossible."

I smiled. "It already seems like it was years ago."

Brand put his hand on my shoulder and squeezed lightly. "Your grandfather has probably whipped this Kar into shape and is just waiting for the cops to show."

I smiled. "Yeah. I hope so."

Brand opened his mouth to say something else and at that moment the phone buzzed twice. He shrugged, went over, and put the receiver to his ear. Instead of saying hello, he reached down and pressed a button. The phone made a squealing noise, then I heard a humming sound.

"A fax is coming through," Brand explained. "It's probably from one of Grandma's writing friends—they're always faxing each other about Viking myths."

Brand watched the paper come out the top. "Wait a second—" he paused, "it's from the Mounties."

He watched until it was completely printed. Then read it over. "Oh my . . ." he whispered.

"What is it?" Michael asked.

Brand looked up, his face suddenly serious. "It's from one of Grandma's friends in the RCMP detachment. Grandma must have asked her to look up the records on Kar. Apparently there was some kind of computer problem, so they couldn't get the information right away. But it says this Kar guy died three years ago. Someone found him dead up in the trees—he had been attacked by an animal of some sort. He was buried in the Gimli cemetery." He paused. "They're going to concentrate on a few other leads. They brought park officials in to help them track a bear."

"A bear?" Michael asked. "Do they believe it's a bear now?"

Brand shrugged. "I don't think they really know."

"Let's go for a drive," I blurted.

"A drive?" Brand looked at me like I'd turned into an alien. "Grandma should be back soon. Besides, I only have my learner's license."

"Where do you want to go?" Michael asked. Was he thinking along the same lines as me? I glanced at him, saw a look of concern.

"Well . . ." I paused. I suddenly realized how bizarre my idea sounded. I realized I had to say it anyway. "I want to go to the graveyard."

"The graveyard?" Brand exclaimed. "Are you crazy? Why do you want to go there?"

"I just have a hunch that's all. About Kar."

"Which is?"

"I'll know when we get there. That some kind of clue about Grandpa will be waiting at the cemetery."

"I think she's right," Michael said. He still had that same concerned look. "Let's go."

"Yes, let's go," Angie echoed. She too seemed very serious. Was it some kind of family ESP? Did they have the same hunch as me? All three of us had gathered around Brand.

"We can't just go." He took a step back. "I can't drive without an adult."

"We'll be okay as long as you drive safe," Angie said. "Besides, if you add all of our ages together—we're in our thirties."

"Forties, actually," Michael added. "Forty-two to be exact."

Brand took another step back. "But it'll be dark soon."

"We'll take flashlights," I answered. All three of us moved closer.

"You Americans are crazy. Grandma will kill me."

Angie put her hand on his shoulder. "We'll be gone tomorrow. We won't be any more trouble after that."

Brand paused. He looked at us, shaking his head and grinning. "Oh . . . okay. You win. If we hurry we can get back before Grandma returns."

We cheered. Michael punched Brand playfully on the shoulder. "It'll be wild."

"It better be. 'Cause I'll be spending the rest of the summer in the dog house."

Brand went to the broom closet and dug out two huge, black, metal flashlights. They were the kind the police usually carried. I turned the oven off, put the turkey pie back in the fridge. Within a minute we were all ready to go.

Brand handed a flashlight to Angie and one to me. "We can take my grandpa's truck. It's out behind the house. I don't think it's been driven for a couple years, so we might be hoofing our way back."

"Let's hurry," I said. "Please."

Brand looked at me. His face was solemn. "Okay, for you I will."

Then we followed him through the patio doors and into the backyard.

20

The truck was the one I had spotted before—an old red Chevy with big tires, rectangular windows, and curved metal fenders. It gleamed in the sunlight.

"Is this a '57?" Michael asked.

"It sure is," Brand answered. "Grandma said she'd give it to me when I turn sixteen. She'll probably change her mind after tonight."

We piled into the truck and slammed the doors. Brand found the keys under the floormat. "Cross your fingers everyone." He gently pushed the keys into the ignition and pressed in the clutch. "It's been a long, long time since this baby's been started." He turned his hand.

The truck roared to life like it had been waiting years for this one moment. The loud rapping of the mufflers echoed all around us. Brand removed his foot from the gas and it idled evenly. "Well, I'll be damned."

I saw that the gearshift was on the steering column. "Is that a three on a tree shifter?" I asked.

"Yes." Brand gave me a bewildered look. "I'm surprised you know about it."

I shrugged. "One of our neighbors had an old truck like this. He let me drive it once. For about ten yards. It was weird not to have the shifter on the floor."

"You're full of surprises, Sarah," Brand said. Angie nudged me hard, so that I was sitting right next to Brand. Then she moved over so that I couldn't move back.

I didn't try anyway. I was right against Brand.

Brand pulled the truck into reverse and started backing up. A moment later we were around the front of the house and turning onto the road. "Scream if you see Grandma," Brand said, half serious, half joking.

We turned left, heading for Gimli.

The truck purred along the highway, rumbling melodically. It rode smooth and perfect. Brand drove the speed limit, scanning for potholes and deer.

The setting sun turned the rearview mirror red.

"Hurry, please," I said. I was beginning to get a feeling of urgency. "Hurry!"

"I'm going as fast as I dare," Brand said. "I don't want to attract any attention."

About a mile later we turned off the road and went along the outskirts of town. Shortly after that we pulled up to the Gimli Cemetery. The main gates were made of iron, at least fifteen feet high, and set in two pillars. A stone wall surrounded the whole graveyard.

"It looks like a jail," Michael said.

"Yeah," Angie agreed. "It's almost like they don't want anything to get out."

We putted through the gates; the rumbling of the truck was twice as loud here. There was no sign of life, just row after row of headstones, some huge and obviously expensive, others as small as dinner plates.

"I had no idea there'd be so many graves," Angie said. "There are more graves than there are townspeople."

Brand switched the lights to bright. "I wonder where we'll find this Kar's grave? Any ideas?"

"It's only a couple years old," I said, "so it's probably farther back."

We rolled down the road, passing columns of headstones until we were three-quarters of the way through the cemetery.

The sun was falling off the edge of the world. Soon we would have no light at all.

Michael pointed. "That grave was from two years ago."

"Let's stop," I suggested. "We'll have a better chance of finding it on foot. And we might as well split up."

Brand pressed on the brakes, halting the truck. We piled out. Angie turned on her flashlight and she and Michael went one way, Brand and I the other. "Holler if you find the grave," I yelled. "Scream if you see anything weird."

Michael shrieked. It echoed through the graveyard. "Just practicing," he said.

"You're not funny, Michael." Angie pushed him ahead. "Let's get going."

I clicked the light on my flashlight, finding it quite bright. We started walking past headstones. Some for children, some for adults. We were careful not to tread on any graves.

"How will you know it?" Brand asked after a few minutes. "It might not even have a marker."

"I'll know it when I see it," I said with certainty. It was the grave of my grandfather's enemy. All of Kar's anger would still be waiting there, radiating from under the dirt, making the hairs on the back of my neck tingle.

We walked on, keeping a quick, careful pace. The lights of Gimli were twinkling to my right but they didn't cast any brightness our way. It seemed we were in a twilight world of dark shapes and gray shadows.

Moments later the world turned completely black. Thick gray clouds had blotted out the last rays of the sinking sun. My flashlight wasn't very bright anymore. It flickered occasionally and when it worked it cast a dull yellow beam.

"I hope these batteries don't die," I whispered.

"They shouldn't," Brand said. "I've used the flashlight a thousand times. It should work for at least another hour."

I glanced over my shoulder and couldn't see Angie or Michael. "I wonder if they're okay," I worried.

"I'm sure they're fine," Brand answered. "Your brother and Angie seem to be just as capable as you."

I walked on, letting the compliment sink in. He thought I was capable. I'd always felt a little disorganized in my life, like I wasn't doing things right.

He thought I was capable!

"I do wonder," Brand asked, "what exactly you expect to find here?"

"It's . . . it's just a gut feeling I have. It might be nothing. But I need to look."

"Well, Grandma always says to trust your guts . . . I thought she was talking about cooking."

I snickered, glad to be able to laugh a little. We continued looking. I flashed my light at stone after stone, reading each name and forgetting it a moment later. Was that all there was to our lives? Would I one day just be a name on a stone, for strangers to pass by?

I felt an icy chill run up my spine.

A dog barked in the distance. Was it barking at us? Or was it a warning?

It stopped after a few seconds.

"Did you get to meet Hugin?" Brand asked.

"Yes."

"Something about that dog just barking there sounded a little like him. It couldn't be, of course . . . could it?" Brand paused. "He was a really good dog."

"I know. He amazed me."

"My friend overheard his dad talking about how Hugin died. I guess his back was broken and his legs too. And he still crawled after your grandfather, trying to save him." Brand drew in his breath. His face became hard and angry. "I really want to help get whoever did that to Hugin. That's one of the reasons I brought you guys out here. Just in case there is some kind of answer. Something I can do."

I shone my light on the next gravestone. The words were worn by wind and rain, but I could read: *Kormak Grotson. December 6th, 1894–June 30th, 1945.* "I think there is."

We shuffled closer, careful not to step on the grave. I was afraid my feet would sink down and I would be trapped. Or a hand would come up.

"It's his father's grave," Brand said. "Why didn't I think of that? Kar's final resting place is probably right around here."

"I'll tell the others," I said. I took a step to the side and started to yell, but in that same moment my footing crumbled below me. The flashlight flew from my hand and I found myself tumbling down, down a long slope into wet, dark earth.

I hit something hard and came to a stop.

It took me a moment to regain my senses. There were dark walls of earth all around me and a sore spot on my head. I inhaled a deep breath and smelled the rotten smell of decaying flesh.

I was surrounded by loose dirt. It could fall in at any time.

Panic bubbled up inside me. I pounded away at the ground, feeling trapped.

"Sarah!" Brand called from somewhere above me. "Are you alright?"

"Yes," I said. I stopped flailing. "I've fallen down a hole or something."

I noticed that the flashlight was only a foot away, so I grabbed it and pointed it down.

I saw wet, cool earth, broken boards, and tattered pieces of clothing. I was standing on top of a casket.

It was empty.

I caught my breath. I was in a grave.

"Keep cool. Keep cool," I repeated.

"What?" Brand said. "Did you say something?"

I shone the light up. I was only a few feet from the ground. It wasn't that deep after all. I saw Brand's face floating in the air. His hand extended towards me out of darkness.

Then my light hit a small grave marker above me. It read: *Kar Grotson. April 16th, 1942–June 30th, 1993.*

I was standing on Kar's casket.

Suddenly I remembered where I'd smelled the familiar

earthy smell. In my room at Grandpa's, the night before. Right after the window was broken.

"Get me up! Get me up!" I yelled. "Now!"

I grabbed Brand's right hand. He held on tightly. With him pulling and me desperately digging into the earth I made it to the top in record time. I lay there for a second, breathing hard.

"You gonna be okay?" Brand was leaning over me.

"I—I think so." I paused. "I want to get out of here, though. Now."

I heard running footsteps, saw a bobbing light. Michael and Angie came up. "What's going on?" Michael asked. "We thought we heard screaming."

By this time I had sat up. "We found his grave."

Michael pointed his light down. "It's empty."

"I know." I stood, looked over the edge.

"Well, where is he?" Angie asked. They peeked down as if afraid something would grab them.

"I don't know," I answered. It took all my will to just glance at the casket again. "But look at the boards. They're pointing upwards as if they were broken from the inside."

21

My own words echoed around us. We stared at the open grave, two flashlights trained on an empty casket and a hole half filled with wet, loose earth.

On impulse I pointed my light at the gravestone. Then I pointed it at Kormak's.

"It's the same day," I whispered. My knees felt like they would give out.

"What?" Brand asked. He held my arm, steadied me.

"They died on the same day," I said. "June 30th. Different years but the same day."

"Wasn't it June 30th just a few days ago?" Angie asked.

"The day before we arrived," Michael added.

"And didn't Althea say there was something powerful about the anniversary of someone's death?" I asked.

We were silent.

"Let's get out of here," Michael said. "I've seen enough. I don't feel safe any longer."

We raced back to the truck, tripping over stones and flower arrangements. I think we might have even trampled across a few graves, but I didn't care. I just had to get out of there. Once inside the vehicle we slammed the doors shut.

We all tried to catch our breath.

"He . . . he can't be . . ." Angie trailed off.

I shrugged, tired. "All I know is what I saw."

Brand started the truck, flicked on the lights. Two beams illuminated an army of headstones. My sense of direction was gone. For a moment I wondered if Brand knew the way out.

I didn't want to get lost here. Not in a place where the dead sleep.

Brand pulled the Chevy into gear, turned left, and headed down the road. "Someone could have dug it up," he said. "Broke the casket. And pulled the boards back towards them."

"Why?" I asked. "What would be in there?"

Brand shrugged. "You never know what people are looking for or why they do things. Specially around here."

We headed through the main gate and onto the highway. I sighed quietly. I would feel a lot better with the graveyard behind us.

No one spoke until we reached Althea's house. The porch light was on, but her truck wasn't there.

"Grandma's not home," Brand said, "that's really weird." He pulled up the front driveway and parked. We piled out and headed into the house.

It was exactly as we had left it.

"It doesn't look like she's been here at all." Brand turned on the light to the living room. "I wonder what's taking so long?"

"Maybe we should phone the police," Angie suggested. "They might know where she is."

"It can't hurt," Brand agreed. "I'm starting to get worried."

He dialed the phone. I went into the living room and paged through Althea's books, which were still sitting on the coffee table. I stopped at the etching of Glam and Grettir battling each other. I looked at it and I knew the person who had drawn this picture had captured something real.

How could Grettir have beaten a creature as huge and full of hate as Glam? It was impossible. And yet he had done it.

We needed someone like Grettir now.

I touched the metal cross beside the books. It was cold and plain. I lifted it and was surprised at its weight. Then for no reason I could understand, an image appeared in my mind. Of Grandpa on the porch, whittling with his knife. And smiling.

What did it mean?

"They said she didn't show up," I heard Brand say. I set down the cross and wandered back to the main room in a trance. "They said they'd send a cruiser up to where she was supposed to meet them."

Brand's words echoed from wall to wall. The room went in and out of focus. I stepped in front of everyone and they all looked at me.

"We have to go to Grandpa's cabin," I said, holding my head.

Brand's eyes widened. "What! First the graveyard and now the cabin! What for?"

"My grandfather was carving something. I want to see what it was."

"No. No. No." Brand held up his hand like a school crossing guard telling a car to stop. "There are cops everywhere. I can't just go driving again. We got lucky last time."

"Brand—we have to go," I said. I straightened my back, felt taller suddenly. "Believe me. It's the only way to get anything done. We've been waiting for everyone else to solve this. We have to take matters into our own hands."

"She's right," Angie said. Just her words seemed to make me stronger. "We have to see what we can find there."

Brand shook his head. "I don't know what they put in Missouri water, but I don't ever want to drink it." With that he spun around and headed for the door. "C'mon, we might as well get going. Just be ready to spend the night in jail."

We followed him back out to the truck. This time he had a problem starting it; the engine turned over and over. "It just doesn't seem to want to catch," Brand said. He stopped, tried again, and it roared.

A moment later we were on the road, heading to the highway. Brand turned right, his foot heavy on the gas. The tires spun in the dirt and squealed when we hit the pavement. "Oops," Brand said.

"I thought we were trying to avoid getting caught," Michael said.

"We are." Brand patted the dashboard. "I sometimes forget how much power this baby has."

We sped down the highway. The sky was completely black; I couldn't see any stars—even the moon's brightness had been cloaked by trees. It only took a few moments to get to Grandpa's cabin. We pulled up the driveway, parked out front. None of the lights were on, so Brand left the truck running with its headlights flicked to bright.

No one moved. We stared out, safe behind our windshield.

The place looked like it had been deserted for a hundred years. The police had placed yellow plastic ribbon around the cabin, marked with the warning: CRIME SCENE DO NOT ENTER.

The bushes around the yard seemed to have moved closer to Grandpa's home. I wondered what could be hiding there?

No one said anything. Finally I grabbed the door handle and pushed the door open. It took all my willpower to step outside.

I took another step or two and was relieved to hear Brand's door open. I led everyone up to the cabin. "Here goes nothing," I said, then I ducked under the ribbon and opened the door. I flicked on the light.

The living room looked like someone had swung a wrecking ball through it. The table and couch were overturned, there were books scattered on the floor beside cushions and drawers. Most of the closet doors were open.

"The police must have been looking for clues," I said.

"I wonder if they have a special task force that cleans up after them?" Michael asked.

Brand picked up an overturned lamp and set it on the floor. "It seems like I've asked you this a couple of times tonight— what are we looking for?"

"I don't know," I answered. "Something that Grandpa was carving or making. I think you'll just know when you see it."

"Could you be more specific?" Michael asked.

"That's all I know," I said. I started searching around the main room, grabbing books and turning over cushions. After a few minutes I realized it didn't seem like the right place to find anything.

I went into the room Michael, Angie, and I had shared just the night before. The light wouldn't go on. I could see the remaining curtains moving in the breeze. There were thick pieces of splintered wood on the floor. Shattered glass glittered with moonlight.

In the center of the wall, where the window used to be, was a huge, gaping hole. Only part of the frame was still there.

No man could have done that.

Michael and Angie were peering over my shoulder. "I don't remember that much destruction," Michael whispered.

"I do," I said.

"Maybe the cops somehow made it bigger." Angie paused. "Like when they were looking for stuff or something."

I shook my head. "I don't think so." Then I stepped past them and out of the room.

A thought struck me. "Do you remember Grandpa going into the guest room to work on something? I think there was a reason why he had you sleep in the same room as us."

"So we'd be safer?" Michael asked.

"That was one reason. But I don't think he wanted us to see what he was doing."

I went down the hall to the spare room and flicked on the light, surprised that it worked. There was a small bed in one corner, a workbench on the other side, and a number of carving tools on top of a cupboard. A few of Grandpa's wood-burning drawings hung on the wall: a bear, a hawk, and a wolf. They looked so real that their eyes followed me when I moved.

Grandpa had left a book open on the bench. Beside it was a small object. When I got closer I saw that it was a wooden cross. He had been burning symbols into it. In the book there was an image of the cross, drawn in ink. Grandpa had about three-quarters of the runes from the picture burned into the cross. It looked beautiful. Next to the cross was a wineskin with a sticky note on it that said: *do not drink . . . consecrated water.*

I looked at the front cover of the book. It was hard and black, but there was no title. The words inside were Icelandic, of course.

"Did you find something?" Michael asked. He, Brand, and Angie had piled in behind me.

"I think so." I showed them the book. They examined it. "Grandpa seemed to be working on this cross, but it doesn't look like he was finished what he wanted to get done."

"Do you think it was to ward something away?" Angie asked.

"Probably. But he had this water too. What was he doing?" I asked.

"Getting ready for something, I'd say." Brand was touching the wineskin. "Is consecrated water the same as holy water?"

"I think so," I answered.

"And don't they use it on vampires?" He continued.

We were all silent.

I ran my hand across the cross. It felt warm, as if heated from the inside. I held it, found that it was only a little bit larger than my hand. On impulse I stuffed it into my jacket pocket. It was a tight fit, but I was able to get the cross in. Then I reached for the wineskin.

"What are you doing?" Michael asked.

"Taking this stuff with us. I just feel safer with it." I looped the strap over my shoulder. "Did you guys find anything else?"

"Nothing," Angie said. "The place is a real mess."

"So what do we do now?" Brand asked.

I looked around. They were all staring at me, expecting an answer. "Do you know where your grandmother was going to meet the police?"

"Yeah," Brand said. "It's only a little ways up the road."

"Why don't we go check just to be sure she isn't still waiting there?" I suggested.

"Well . . ." Brand said. "If she is there and she sees me in Grandpa's truck, she'll be pretty mad." He paused. "But I do want to make sure she's alright. She'll understand."

"Then let's go," Angie said.

We made our way out of the house.

22

"It's just a little bit farther on," Brand said.

We had turned off the highway and had been traveling down a gravel road for about ten minutes. The truck's headlights only made a slight glowing dent in the darkness. Trees crowded around us. Little wisps of fog drifted here and there. "I'm sure it is. Just keep your eyes peeled."

I was beginning to feel that familiar cold again. Right down to my bones.

"Is there any heat in this truck?" Michael asked. So I wasn't the only one who was freezing.

Brand cranked on the heater. "It'll take a while for it to warm up. I can't believe how much the temperature has dropped."

The fog was getting thicker. Our lights seemed to be fading, not even close to casting brightness as far as they had before.

We crawled ahead. The truck didn't get any warmer.

"I think that's it, coming up." Brand pointed. "I'm sure of it."

I could see a turnoff ahead that led onto a flat, open area. As we got closer I saw that it was a rest stop in the middle of nowhere. "This is where a lot of the hunters park when they go hunting," Brand explained. We turned off the road. The clearing ended suddenly, surrounded by a wall of trees and underbrush. It was obviously empty.

"Well, she's not here," Brand said. "We must have missed her, somehow." He stepped on the gas, began doing a U-turn.

I saw a glint of metal in the trees as the truck's lights swept the area. "Wait a second," I said.

"What is it?" Brand stepped on the brakes.

"I thought I saw something reflect the lights out there." He backed up and swung the truck the other way.

"There!" I pointed my finger when the light glinted again. "Right there!"

"I see it," Michael said.

Brand pulled straight ahead. A few of the trees were broken and bent over as if something big had been dragged across them. "I can't see anything through all this underbrush. We'll have to take a closer look on foot."

"Go outside?" Angie asked.

"It'll be okay," I said, flicking on my flashlight. "We won't be too far from the truck."

Brand left the Chevy running. We got out and made our way to the underbrush. I ducked and fought my way through thorn trees that poked at me. Whatever was out there was still too far away to see. I could just barely make out a large shape.

"That's weird," Michael said. He stopped for a second, bent over, and rubbed at his ankle.

"What is?" I asked.

"Well, you know that bruise I got last night? It's aching like crazy. I can hardly put any weight on it. And my cut hurts too. The farther we get into this bush . . . the more it hurts."

"Do you want to go back to the truck?" Brand asked.

Michael stood up. "No. I'll be okay. It's not too far away."

We carried on, forcing our way through the underbrush until we came into a clearing. I pointed my light, Angie pointed hers.

I drew in my breath.

It was Althea's truck.

23

All the windows had been smashed and the tires flattened.

"Grandma!" Brand yelled, and before I could say anything he went running to the truck. I followed, the light from my flashlight bobbing and jumping with each motion. I could barely see where I was going.

I reached the truck a step behind Brand. He yanked open the door and glass rained down onto the ground. "Grandma! Where are you?"

I pointed the light inside the cab, over Brand's shoulder. It was empty. Broken glass was scattered across the seat. Brand backed out, went around the other side yelling.

Angie and Michael joined us. "What happened?" Angie asked.

"I don't know—an accident I guess." All I could see was glass and twisted metal. The door looked bent. Had Brand done that? I shone my light along the side. "Do you remember these dents?" I asked.

"No," Michael answered. "It was in rough shape, but I don't remember anything like that."

"Get a light over here!" Brand yelled. He sounded desperate. We ran around to the other side of the truck, both pointing our flashlights. Brand was down on one knee, examining something. "Closer! Closer!"

I ran up. On the ground in front of Brand was Althea's shawl. Or half of it at least. It had been torn in two. Brand was gripping it tightly. "Whoever did this is going to pay." He stood up, the shawl in his hand. His face was pale and his jaw muscles tight. "Someone's dragged her away."

I pointed my flashlight just past him, illuminating a trail of broken branches and turned-up dirt. "You're right . . . it looks like they went that way."

Brand handed her shawl to me. "I'm going to find her."

"Wait," I said, "we should go back to Grandpa's and call the police. Then we can start looking."

Brand shook his head. "No." He reached out and took the flashlight from Angie's hands. "You three take the truck and head back there. I'm going to look for Grandma." Then he turned on his heel and started running through the trees.

"But we shouldn't split up!" I yelled.

He was already gone. A small blur in the distance, flashlight bobbing like a firefly.

I looked at the other two.

"Now what?" Michael asked.

I shrugged. "Let's hurry back to Grandpa's and phone the RCMP. Then we'll double back here and help him look."

They agreed. We turned and forced our way through the underbrush, heading for the truck. Its lights were a beacon to guide us. A thorn scratched a line across my forehead. When we got closer, I realized something was wrong, there was a sound I couldn't hear. I made it through the last branches into the open.

"Didn't Brand leave the truck running?" I asked.

"I . . . I can't remember." Angie was silhouetted in the lights, squinting. "I hope the battery didn't die."

I got in the driver's side, found the keys. They were in the on position. Michael and Angie jumped in the passenger side. I took a deep breath, pushed in the clutch, and turned the key.

Nothing.

I tried again.

Nothing.

"Oh no," Angie whispered. "This is bad."

"Hurry. Hit the dash or spin the steering wheel or something," Michael suggested. "Maybe it's just some kind of loose wire." I did those things, moving the wheel and twisting the key as hard as I could.

Just when I was about to give up, the motor began to turn. And turn and turn, slower and slower, like it was losing power. "C'mon," Michael said, slamming his fist on the dash.

I thought I could hear a ghost of a sound, like someone yelling in the distance, maybe even calling my name, then the truck roared and I stomped on the gas a few times. "It started! It started!" I exclaimed.

It took me a moment to find reverse. The gears ground. I pressed the gas too hard and we shot backwards, a cloud of dust filling our headlights. I slammed on the brakes and we skidded in a half circle. When we came to a stop I realized we were on the road, pointing towards the highway.

"Great driving, Sis," Michael said. I didn't know if he was being sarcastic or not.

I found another gear, stepped on the accelerator, and the truck rocketed forward into the mist. "Not so fast," Angie said. "We can hardly see two feet in front of us."

It was true. The fog had grown grayer and thicker. Our light seemed to bounce off it. But I had to hurry. Brand was out there all alone.

And Grandpa and Althea.

"The cops must have been here and not seen her truck," Angie said.

"Probably," I agreed. "It was pretty far in the trees."

"Yeah, but how did it get there?" Michael asked. "She wouldn't have accidentally driven it into the trees."

"Maybe she was trying to hit something," Angie suggested.

"Or it got dragged in there," I added.

"By what? What could drag it in there?" Michael asked.

"The same thing that put the hole in Grandpa's cabin."

We were silent for a moment. No one seemed to want to argue with me.

The fog was clearing a little, so I sped up.

Angie screamed. A moment later I saw why. A figure was on the road in front of us.

The little boy. The ghost boy. Holding out his hands, warning us to stop.

I slammed on the brakes, but it was too late—we were heading right through him. He turned into mist and we came over a small rise into clear air, the truck skidding on gravel.

There in front of us, illuminated for a second, was a half man, half monster, his mouth open in a growl.

24

I yanked on the wheel.

I had a moment to see him clearly as we passed right by, his eyes huge and glowing, his dirty, lumpy hair blowing in the wind. We were so close he could have reached in the driver's window with his enormous arms and yanked me out.

The truck fishtailed past.

The wheel spun, I lost control, and we shot into the ditch and up an embankment, saplings snapping in front of us. It didn't seem like we were going very fast anymore, or perhaps my mind was slowing everything down.

We piled into an old, giant pine tree. I was thrown forward, my head bashed into the steering wheel, and I rolled down to the floor.

Then there was only blackness.

For a few moments I thought I heard voices all around me telling me to wake up, that it was time to move, to go. They sounded so familiar. They gave me the courage to open my eyes.

I couldn't see anything. I heard moaning though. I wasn't

sure if it was coming from me or not. I tried to move and found my body wouldn't respond. Had I broken any bones? Why hadn't I put on my seat belt? I was in too much of a hurry, I had forgotten it.

I realized it wasn't me who was moaning. It was Michael or Angie. They must have been hurt bad. I twisted my head to look but this sent a sharp signal of pain to my brain.

I wasn't going to do that again for a while. I hoped nothing was wrong with my spine.

There was a noise, a small cracking sound outside the truck.

This was followed by the sound of wrenching metal. Something was trying to yank the passenger door from its hinges. A cold blast of air came in.

"Help me," Angie was whispering. *"Help . . . me."*

I could hear her sliding on the seat. I tried to move but couldn't. She started to scream, then was suddenly muffled as if a hand had covered her mouth.

I heard a thump.

Then silence.

The crack of snapping twigs was followed by the sound of sniffing. The smell of old graveyard earth—a dark, dank scent, rotten and sweet at the same time—rolled into the truck.

This time Michael moaned, then yelled in panic, *"Hhhhey . . . let—"*

He fell silent. Something else cracked. Not a twig.

Was it a bone? Michael's neck?

I still couldn't turn my head or move.

The familiar cold had stolen the strength from my limbs.

But not all of the feeling.

Because something rough and strong was wrapping itself

around my ankle. It felt like the gnarled roots of a tree in the shape of a hand. The grip grew tighter and tighter so that I almost cried out in pain.

Then it began to pull. I slid towards the other door, helplessly dragged across the floormats. I latched onto the brake pedal with my left hand.

With my right I grabbed the gas pedal.

Now I heard grunting, a wet, monstrous roar, as it exerted more strength, trying to get me loose. I held tight, feeling the muscles in my arms and my legs stretching. I heard a popping sound as the vertebrae in my back straightened.

"No. No," I whispered through clenched teeth. *"You can't have me."*

This seemed to anger it. The grip on my ankle doubled, threatening to crush my bones. It roared, pulling so hard that I felt like any moment now I would snap in two.

My fingers started slipping. Bit by bit. I didn't have near enough strength to hold on. Whatever had a hold of me was too strong.

I kicked my free foot in the air, but couldn't hit anything. Then I slid it to the side and propped it against the seat, finding even more leverage.

"You can't have me," I repeated. *"Let me go!"*

Again came the rumbling growling sound, like a dog but larger, wilder. It breathed out. And yanked harder.

My shoe came off, the thing's grip slipped.

I heard a *whomp* as something huge hit the ground. I knew I would only have a second. I let go of the pedals, scrambled onto the seat, and reached out into the cold air to grab the open door.

It wouldn't budge. The door was bent open. There was a blur in my vision to the right of me, moving fast.

Coming straight for me.

I tugged hard, getting my whole body into it. The truck's door screeched and scraped shut with a bang.

A second later the whole truck shook as a heavy weight plowed into its side. I tried to roll up the window, but realized suddenly the glass was gone.

A giant fist struck the door. The metal bent inwards. I quickly backed away. A second blow bubbled the door, spraying me with bits of metal and glass. I snapped my eyes shut and held up my hands.

When I opened them again I could see two glowing pools of light—eyes peering in at me. A huge, dark, hairy arm the size of a boa constrictor reached in, fingers spread wide. The truck groaned.

I pushed back against the driver's side, tucking my legs under me. I tried to open the door, but the handle wouldn't budge.

The hand came closer, the face pressed in the window. Eyes glowering.

I reached around for something to hit it with. My hand bumped a solid, small weight in my jacket pocket.

I unzipped the pocket and grabbed the cross my grandfather had carved.

It felt hot. I held it out in front of me and the cross glowed dull blue. I knew it wasn't moonlight.

The monster paused. He pulled back slightly but not out of the window. It was like he was deciding what to do next.

"Get back!" I hissed, surprised at how solid my voice sounded. "Get out!"

The eyes blinked. Still it didn't move.

"You're Kar, aren't you?" I said. "Kar. You were a man once, weren't you?"

It breathed out, a slow sighing movement. The snakelike pupils went from my face to the cross then back to my face.

"Do you remember?" I asked. "Once you were a man."

The yellow eyes blinked.

"I'm Sarah Asmundson," I said, not sure why. I wanted it to know that I was a person. Maybe somewhere inside him there was still something human. "You have my grandfather . . . Thursten. You—"

It was the wrong thing to say. The pupils suddenly glowed, his eyes narrowed. With a hiss he pressed against the truck and leaned in, extending his arm to full length.

He grabbed at the cross.

There was a blinding flash of light. A smell of burning flesh. Kar screamed and fell back. I was hit by a shock wave that drove my head into the door.

I saw bright, swirling lights.

Then darkness.

25

I opened my eyes, turned my groggy head. I had no idea how long I was out. My skull ached, my ankle, my arms—my whole body felt like a herd of buffalo had stampeded across it twice. The interior of the truck smelled like smoke and burnt flesh. I felt my hair; some of it came away in my hands.

What had happened?

I inhaled and held my breath. Listening. There was nothing. Just silence. I looked, but everywhere was inky darkness. I couldn't see a thing through the windows.

I peeked my head up a little higher and stared out the back. By squinting I could make out a huge, lumpy shape moving on two feet. It disappeared into the bushes.

It looked like it was carrying two sacks of potatoes.

Michael and Angie. Kar was taking them away.

I had to do something. I had to.

But what? I scrambled around the truck, searching for the flashlight. It was like one of those nightmares where you need something really bad but it just keeps slipping out of your

grasp. It could have gone anywhere when the truck went off
the road. Even been thrown out.

My hand felt something hard and round under the seat. I
pulled.

The flashlight.

I pushed the switch forward. No light. Nothing.

I slapped the flashlight in my other hand, a movement I'd
seen my father do a hundred times before when he was going
out in the night to check the dogs. That moved the batteries
around and suddenly the flashlight grew bright, shrinking my
pupils.

I pointed it down.

The cross was on the seat. Broken in two.

The wood was still smoldering. I touched it and burned my
hand.

I knew it wouldn't be any help anymore.

I climbed out of the truck. I felt on my back. I still had the
wineskin. I had no idea whether it would do me any good.

I took a deep breath and started in the direction I'd last seen
Kar. My ankle almost collapsed beneath my weight, but I carried on, pushing into the underbrush, branches slapping at my
face. Even in the dull light, his trail was easy to follow. Broken
bushes, bent saplings, and huge prints in the soft earth.

I charged on, deeper into the woods, running past trees, tripping over roots. Getting up and running again.

No one's going to find us, I thought. All of us could die out
here, lost in the trees.

I should have phoned the police.

A few steps later it dawned on me that they were probably

patrolling the area. They'd see the truck all smashed up and suspect that something was going on. Maybe they'd come looking, see Althea's truck too. Just maybe.

I headed on. Twigs cracking below me. The mist grew heavier again, tendrils reaching through the trees. When I looked down, I couldn't even see my feet, it was so thick. I could fall into a pit without knowing it.

But I had to carry on.

The trail was growing harder to follow. There was too much fog. Too much darkness.

A few steps later the flashlight went black.

I stopped, slapped the light against my hand. It wouldn't work. I took out the batteries and put them back in again. No luck.

I gave up and kept moving ahead, slower now, squinting and dodging trees. I gripped the flashlight tight in my hand. It was heavy enough to be a good weapon.

But against what? Kar had bested my grandfather who had a shotgun. Had crushed Hugin. What could I do against him?

Sarah, a voice said inside my head, *stop thinking that way. Just keep going.* I was sure it was my own voice—but why did it sound like Grandma Asmundson? She couldn't be talking to me. Not from heaven.

But a lot of strange things had already happened tonight.

My imagination was getting to me. All I knew was that I had to charge on, no matter what.

A sudden dark flash in my head made me stumble and fall to my knees. I felt claustrophobic suddenly, had an image of darkness, boards being moved, and could hear my brother whispering: *no no no no no.*

I knew what it was. I was feeling the same thing as Michael. He was being shoved in a shallow hole and covered with earth. I could sense him choking, clawing, fighting to keep the dirt from blocking his mouth.

My brother was being buried alive.

Then the image flew away from me and I was left crouching, feeling sick.

I got up again. Michael needed me. Grandpa. Angie. Althea. They all needed me to keep going.

But how would I find them? I'd lost the trail in the darkness and mist.

I looked up at the moon, a silver face peering through the trees. It wasn't bright enough to light my way.

I couldn't just stand here.

I gathered my courage and started walking in the direction that seemed correct. Looking for any sign that I was going the right way.

After about five minutes I began to panic. I was lost. I wasn't even sure where the road was . . . ahead of me or behind me. I might have made a circle. I could wander out here for days with no hope of finding anything.

I leaned against a tree. It was hopeless.

Then I looked up.

In the distance a light was glowing.

26

I ran towards it blindly, not caring if I fell or smacked my head against a tree.

It retreated. So I sped up.

I couldn't tell what kind of light it was . . . a flashlight? A torch? Maybe I should yell.

Just as I opened my mouth to holler, the light disappeared.

I picked up my pace, heading for the last place where I had seen it. Moonlight glinted through the tops of the trees, lighting some of my way. Painting everything white and silver.

I stopped when I heard a noise.

"Help! Help!" It was a small voice. Very far away and familiar.

I took a few steps. Listened.

Nothing.

I moved my left foot ahead.

"Help! Help!"

The cry came from directly in front of me. But there was nothing there. Just a bit of a clearing. A few bushes. Grass.

"Who is it?" I whispered.

No answer.

I moved my right foot.

Even in the moonlight I could see a dark round O in the ground. And I could hear splashing water.

"Hello?" I said.

"Hello! Sarah is that you?" It was Brand's voice. Yelling up from far below me.

"Brand! What happened?" I got down on my hands and knees, careful not to move too far ahead.

"I—I don't know. I was looking for Grandma. My flashlight stopped working and next thing I knew I fell down here—in a well." He paused. "I think someone pushed me though."

"Are you alright?"

"Yes. But—something looked down a few minutes ago, Sarah. It was big. Its head filled the hole. It was an animal I think."

I knew it was worse than an animal. "Can you get out?" I asked.

"I can't climb up. The walls are too slick. I'm treading water right now. Is there a rope or something up there you can toss to me?"

I looked around. "Nothing. How far down are you?" I couldn't see anything but darkness. I heard another splash.

"About thirty feet, I think. It's deep. I can just kind of see you."

"So a tree branch wouldn't work, then?"

"No."

We were quiet a second. "It—" I started, then cleared my throat, "—that thing that looked in at you has Angie and Michael. And Althea too." I paused. "We wrecked the truck."

"The '57 doesn't matter." I heard him breathe in. "Listen

Sarah, I'll be okay here. There's a ledge I can hang on to. You . . . you try and help Angie and Michael and everyone. Come back and get me."

"Are you sure?"

"Yes. Go. I can last for hours down here."

I paused. "Okay. I will. Take care of yourself."

"Just get there!"

Then I was off again. Running. Careful not to fall in the well.

A few hundred feet farther and the light appeared again.

A glowing light. With a tiny figure inside.

I realized what it was.

The boy. The ghost. Showing me the way.

A moment later I saw the cabin.

27

It was the cabin from my nightmare.

The door was half open, the house lopsided. Wind and rain had hammered on it for years, twisting it into an almost living shape. I knew the boards and logs had soaked up enough evil to stain them black.

Somewhere inside I would find everyone.

Or their bodies.

I had to stop thinking that way. But it had been so long since Grandpa was taken.

What hope was there?

The boy had disappeared. If he had ever even been there.

I swallowed. Somewhere behind me, Brand was treading water, thirty feet below the ground. I needed to hurry if I was going to do anything.

I snuck around the side of the cabin, using the trees as cover. I inched up to the wall and tried to look in the window. The glass was thick and round. It seemed to be made from the bottoms of old, dark, wine bottles. I couldn't see a thing through it.

I crept to the back of the house, looking left and right. I could make out an entrance to a cellar. I went up to it, bent down and listened, but heard nothing. I put my hand to the rope handle. Maybe there was some clue inside.

I couldn't pull. I didn't want to see what was under a cabin as horrendous as this one.

They can't be there, I decided. I released the handle. They can't be.

I went around the other side, found another window. It was even darker than the first one. I crept to the front of the cabin. There was a small porch and a half-open door.

I had to go inside. There was no other choice. I stole along the wall, up to the wooden floorboards. Fresh dirt was scattered in front of the door.

I stepped on the porch and the whole house moaned in protest, as if it knew I was there. I took another step and the board creaked. The wood was so brittle it could hardly carry my weight.

I set my hand on the door, staying to one side, and pushed slowly.

It creaked open.

I peeked around the corner. I couldn't see anything inside but shadows. I listened.

No movement.

I came around the corner, took my first step into the cabin.
Nothing.

I went farther, boards cracking beneath my feet. Was the cellar under me? Would I fall right through?

I took another step and another, till I was past the door.

My eyes slowly adjusted to this black, black darkness.

I could see a broken table in one corner, a chair. An old bed. All dimly visible.

This would be an awful place to live.

And to die.

I edged ahead. There was dirt piled here and there on the floor. The cabin smelled musty and rotten. Then I stepped again.

My foot caught on something and I fell, headlong, letting go of the flashlight, sucking in air, trying not to scream.

Down, down, down.

But not onto the floor.

I hit a body.

I pushed myself up. Something big and cold and once alive was below me.

I rolled away from it.

Right into another body. Two big, pale, glassy eyes stared into mine.

I bit my tongue to keep from screaming. I sat up, backed away again.

Then I saw the horns. Just above the eyes. The four legs and hooves.

They were deer.

And cows.

Dead and strewn across the floor. Even in the dark I could see that some of them were half eaten. I heard flies buzzing quietly, back and forth.

There must have been at least six bodies. It was hard to tell because some of them only had the heads left.

Torn apart as if by some wild animal.

I stood in the center of the cabin now. Looking around.

Had the same thing happened to Grandpa? To Michael? Angie?

Nothing seemed to be alive in the room. Maybe that was good.

I stepped over the body of a deer. I squinted my eyes and looked around.

But I couldn't see anything.

Then a glittering caught my attention, a movement in the corner of my eye.

The ghost boy was standing at the other end of the cabin.

28

He looked sad, lost, afraid.

I knew exactly how he felt.

"Bad," he whispered. His mouth kept moving but no words came out.

He stopped, seemed to be crying. His big eyes looking at me.

"I know," I whispered. "It's a bad place. I know, Eric."

His eyes widened when he heard his name. It really was him.

"Are you . . . trapped here?" I suddenly had an image of Eric still searching for his family in the trees after all this time. He didn't seem to understand my question. He kept blinking his eyes.

"Bad man," he moaned, *"bad man put dirt on me."*

It must have been Kormak, Kar's father. Fifty years ago he had buried this child. Then, how many years later, his son had come to take away my grandfather. What kind of a family were they? Evil ran in their blood.

I imagined Eric spending the last fifty years warning people away from this place. Not wanting the same thing to happen to anyone else. Maybe there was some way I could help him. To release him.

"You will be free," I promised. "Your mother will hold you again . . . soon."

He was crying now, big watery tears that fell from his face and disappeared before they hit the floor. I wished I could somehow hug him. I didn't dare move closer; he might vanish.

He wiped at his eyes. *"Under boards. Buried. Good. Buried old man."*

My heartbeat skipped. "Do you mean Grandpa?"

This question made Eric point down below him, stomping little feet that made no noise. *"Hurry . . . fast . . . buried . . . bad man coming."*

I stepped towards him.

"Bad man coming," he repeated.

Another step and he vanished.

I went to where he had been standing. Stood there. What did he mean?

A cry came from beneath my feet.

29

It was human sounding. Soft. A moan of pain. It was so familiar.

"Grandpa?" I asked, getting down on my knees. "Grandpa?"

Another whispering groan.

I felt around, found an edge on one of the boards. I pulled up with all my strength. Slivers bit into my hands, but still I kept working.

Finally, with a creaking protest, the board came up.

I looked down, couldn't see anything but blackness. I yanked up another board.

A sliver of moonlight came through a crack in the roof, lighting up the space in front of me. There was a thin oval, a nose, mouth, closed eyes. An old and wrinkled face. Half buried in the dirt.

"Grandpa!" I exclaimed. "Grandpa!"

I touched his cheek. It was cold, so cold that I feared he was dead.

His eyes opened, slowly. "Sarah," he whispered, his voice gravelly. I realized he probably hadn't had any water for over a day. "Sarah, you're here."

"Yes," I said, "Everything's going to be alright. You're alive.

I knew you would be. I'm going to get you out."

He blinked. "I can't move. I feel like I've been in a freezer for ten years. Now I know what a sirloin steak feels like." He tried to smile, but couldn't.

"Grandpa," I asked, "is it . . . the man . . . thing . . . is it what I think it is?"

He blinked. "Yes. Too much hate inside him to stay dead."

I swallowed. "He—" I said urgently, "Kar has Michael and Sarah and Althea too."

This seemed to wake Grandpa up. "Help me out of here. First close the door."

I went over and pushed the door shut.

"Now what?" I asked when I was standing over him again.

Grandpa blinked. "Listen very carefully. You must—Oh no!"

"What? What?"

"I'm getting . . . colder." A frightened tone had come into his voice, his words were slurred.

"Colder? What do you mean?"

"C-c-c-older . . . colder . . . whenever he gets . . . close . . ."

"I'll dig you out. Now."

"No." It seemed to take all of Grandpa's strength to get these words out. "No . . . time. You must save . . . the others. Leave . . . me."

"But . . ."

There was a rumbling sound outside, like thunder.

"Go," he whispered. "Speak *sofa um nótt*." He seemed to be rambling, not making any sense. "*Sofa . . . um . . . nótt*. Go . . . trust . . . your blood."

He closed his eyes.

A weight hit the door and it rattled on its hinges.

30

I jumped back against the wall. There was a soft *sst* sound as something sharp and thin poked into my back.

Then I felt a wet, warm liquid running down my back.

Blood! I was bleeding.

I felt behind me, discovered that the wineskin I was carrying had been punctured and was leaking water down my back. I had hit an old nail.

The consecrated water! I knew I needed it and here it was pouring out onto the floor.

I pulled the wineskin around to my front, desperately trying to find the hole.

It had been punctured on both sides, was nearly empty.

A second blow hit the door and the top hinge came flying off and tumbled across the floor.

I couldn't just stand there. I leapt over the dead animals and threw all my weight against the door. I picked up a piece of wood and braced it across the frame.

There was breathing outside, an angry, tortured sound. Human and animal.

"Blood. Hunnggr. Smell your blood." A harsh, raspy whisper.

With a roar, Kar crashed into the door again and the planks snapped inwards.

But the door held.

There was a moment of silence.

I couldn't hear any movement outside. Just the blood pounding in my ears, my heart beating loud as a drum.

But he seemed to be gone.

He couldn't have given up.

I leaned against the door, pressing my ear closer, straining to listen.

A fist came through an inch away from my nose. A hand as big as a shovel, with thick, hairy fingers, reached for me.

I ducked but he caught my hair, started to reel me in.

I pulled back. He had too much hair and was too strong—I couldn't escape.

With a desperate movement I grabbed the wineskin and poured what was left of the water onto his hand, yelling at the same time.

His skin hissed, smoke rose up. He screamed on the other side of the door, let go of my hair, and I fell to the ground.

I could hear him snarling outside the door, stamping and smashing into things. The cabin felt like it would cave in.

Then he ran crazily around, throwing his body against the thick log walls. The windows shattered, dust and wood and shingles fell in on me.

Again he piled himself into the walls like a battering ram.

He howled. But this time it was a retreating cry. Like he was running into the forest, away from the cabin.

31

I listened for what must have been a full minute.

Only silence. A whisper of wind in the trees. Nothing more.

I went back to Grandpa.

"Grandpa!" I whispered, urgently. "Wake up!"

He didn't move. I touched his face. He was even colder. But he stirred slightly, seemed to be breathing.

"I'm going to find the others," I said. "Then I'll be back. I promise."

I turned, went for the door.

But where would they be? Where would he hide them?

I remembered the cellar out behind the house. Of course, the only place.

I lifted the wood from the door, pulled it slowly open, peered out with one eye. The overgrown yard looked empty. The light from the moon had brightened, painting it all with white.

I stepped out, a piece of wood gripped in my hand for a weapon.

I went around the house, slowly.

Nothing. Kar was gone.

I came to the cellar door. It took most of my strength to lift it. Creaking, cracking, moaning in protest it came up. The hinges squealing like they hadn't been used in years. I let it drop.

The light of the moon shone over the first three earthen steps.

I started down, my wood in front of me like a sword. It felt flimsy and small. I knew it wouldn't help me in the slightest.

But just holding it made me feel better.

After a few steps I was covered with ebony darkness. I pushed on, the stairs seemed to go quite deep. It was cold in here. The cold of December still seeping out of the earth.

I could make out a small, cramped room stuffed with old, rotten potato sacks. Two support poles held the floor up. This seemed to cover only half the bottom of the house.

A step later I heard a small noise. A whisper of breath.

I tightened my grip.

But there was more than one person breathing. There were two, then three. I looked down.

Only inches from where I was walking were the faces of Michael and Angie, buried in the dirt, a newly made mound over top of them. A foot or two away was Althea.

All with their eyes closed.

I bent down.

Michael's cheek was igloo cold and covered with small cuts. Had he been dragged on the ground all the way here?

Angie was freezing too and one eye seemed bruised.

Althea had lost her patch. Her blind eye stared whitely at me, her good eye closed.

None of them were awake. When I spoke, no one moved.

I started digging Michael out. The dirt was soft and I found it easy. Within a minute he was free. It took a huge effort to pull him out of the hole.

Through it all he stayed sleeping.

I worked on Angie next, quickly unearthing her body. When I was finished I pulled her over beside Michael.

I started on Althea. About halfway through I heard a creaking noise above me. A heavy inhalation of air.

I turned to see the moonlight blocked by a huge shape coming down the stairs one slow step at a time. He brushed against the walls with his shoulders, hands out.

Then finally I saw his eyes. Cold, yellow, pitiless—they had changed. There was nothing human in them anymore, no emotions but anger and hunger. He stared right at me through the darkness. His elongated face was twisted into a grimace.

He slouched ahead, unblinking. He stopped to sniff at Michael and Angie.

I backed up, farther, farther.

Then I hit the earth wall.

Kar trudged towards me, his breath rattling in his throat. His hands out. His mouth moved in a chewing motion and I knew he could no longer speak. All he had was a lust for my blood.

Saliva dripped from the edge of his thick lips to the floor below.

I threw the piece of wood at him. It bounced off, harmlessly. He didn't even blink.

His form filled the cellar. He stepped over Althea. Lumbered closer and closer to me. Both his hands were out like huge claws, opening and closing.

I could see strangely shaped muscles bulging and flexing. He could tear me apart in an instant. Turn me to jelly.

He reached out. I put up my arms to ward him off. But still he pressed in on me, his hands touching me. They were cold and covered with earth, slime, and blood.

He forced me harder against the wall, squeezing now, his grip inescapable. His face was closer to mine. I could feel his breath—a cold, harsh wind. His deformed body smelled of rotting flesh.

My ribs felt like they would give. He was going to crush me against the wall.

His face leaned closer in. I saw his eyes, the color of a harvest moon, glowing with huge, pitiless pupils. *"Blood . . ."* he whispered, his words slurred through his thick, gray lips. Spit spattered my face. *"Blood of . . . Asmundson . . . must bleed."*

I could see yellow, thick, grainy teeth in his mouth. Sharp.

I closed my eyes. Felt myself curl into a ball, suffocating under his weight.

I would be dead in a moment.

This was the end.

One of these breaths, now so hard to breathe, would be my last.

I surrendered. Waiting. There was nothing I could do.

Then I felt a stirring. Deep inside me. A swirling. Of hope. Of the past. A place I had only visited in my dreams.

An old, ancient space inside my fourteen-year-old body. Echoing with voices.

Sarah. Sarah. Sarah.

For a second I felt all of my ancestors, back for a thousand years, in my blood, my heart, my spirit—urging me on. My grandmother, my great-grandfather, even Grettir the Strong were all there. I felt their power added to mine. They were telling me to breathe, reminding me who I was, lending me their strength, their knowledge. I inhaled and they seemed to cheer.

Sarah Asmundson. Sarah.

I set my legs. Then I pushed. Hard.

It was like lifting the weight of a truck, a boulder, a mountain. And still I used this new strength, lifting higher and higher.

Kar made a confused, almost startled, noise. He tried to squeeze me tighter, to fight back. He succeeded in pushing me down a little.

I felt a rush of strength and gave one final heave. Kar suddenly flew backwards, crashed onto the floor, and rolled into one of the support poles. It cracked. A small clump of dirt and pieces of wood fell from the roof, covering him.

He lay there on his back, waving his arms and twisting his neck, looking for me. He was like a beetle that couldn't right itself.

He screamed.

The voices, my ancestors, were gone.

Just me. Alone.

I knew I had to act quickly.

I stood up, rising to my full height, and came towards Kar. My feet were steady.

Kar turned to me. His yellow eyes blinked. His face seemed confused and angry. He tried to move his arms, to reach towards me, but his hands fell uselessly at his side. He opened and closed his fingers like claws.

He tried to scream again, but all that emerged was a hissing of air.

He seemed broken. Whatever gave him power was dying bit by bit.

But would it come back? I didn't know how long I had.

I stood right above Kar, looking down. He bared his teeth, yellow, sharp spikes. I knew he would tear open my throat if he could reach me.

I remembered what Grandpa had said. The words. Icelandic words. They came to me as natural as English. *"Sofa um nótt."* I spoke slowly, soothingly. He glared at me.

I knelt next to Kar. This time I almost sang the words—a lullaby. His eyelids slid closed. Then they opened and stared at me, anger making them glow red.

Was he waking up?

Didn't Grandpa say something about them cursing people? With their last bit of strength. A curse that lasted a lifetime.

"Sofa um nótt," I whispered. "Sleep. *Sofa um nótt."* His eyes held mine and I felt a dark emotion entering my thoughts, my spirit.

His curse.

He moved his lips, trying to mouth something.

"Sofa um nótt," I repeated, desperately.

There was a final flare of anger in his eyes. I felt a stabbing pain in the back of my head. My heart stopped.

Then nothing.

His eyelids slid together.

32

He stayed still.

Satisfied, I turned to the others. Althea was getting up, so were Michael and Angie, rubbing their heads.

"What happened?" Michael whispered. "I feel like I've been hit by a bulldozer. Where are we?" He turned to me. "Oh . . . Sarah, I had the weirdest dream . . . we crashed the truck and then I was dragged upside down through—"

"Quickly!" I hissed. "Get out of here!"

Michael blinked. Angie stared at me.

Only Althea seemed to understand. "She's right, get up, get out, now!"

With her voice added to mine, they listened. We stumbled up the stairs. Out into the open air.

"Where are—" Angie started.

"C'mon, you've got to help me!" Then I ran around the front of the cabin. "In here!"

They followed me inside. I started tearing at the boards in the floor, madly throwing them behind me.

"Hey, watch it!" Michael said. Then he paused. "Grandpa!

That's Grandpa!" He pitched in and Angie helped too.

Grandpa opened his eyes a moment later, stared up at me. He couldn't speak but he smiled.

It took all of us working together to drag him out of the cabin. We stopped when we were about a hundred feet away.

Then we sat there catching our breath.

Suddenly the cabin started to moan, to pitch and twist like a gale of wind had hit it. And with a final crash it collapsed in on itself, imploding, falling and falling down so that not a board was standing.

We stared at the dust, the wreckage.

"Someone's going to have to explain a few things to me," Angie said.

Grandpa looked right at me. "I have a feeling that a lot of this won't be easily explained."

I felt tired, all my strength was leaving me. Something brushed my shoulder and my heart leapt.

I turned to catch a glimpse of glowing light with a figure inside. A little boy smiled at me, then flew upwards. He seemed to be going towards the stars.

"Good-bye, Eric," I whispered.

With my last bit of strength I limped to the house. It took me a moment to find two good-sized planks.

I placed them across each other in the form of a cross.

33

We didn't forget about Brand. We tied our belts and clothes together and lowered our makeshift rope down and pulled him out. Then we walked through the trees silently.

The police found us on the road and after wrapping us with blankets and asking us a hundred and one questions, they took us back to Althea's.

My father and mother arrived the following day. Over the next few days the police returned and asked more questions. I explained to them what I could, left out what I knew they wouldn't understand. They looked through the wreckage of the cabin.

They never found Kar's body. Only old, partly disintegrated bones. They didn't know what kind of animal they were from. They were too big to be a bear or a human.

I wanted to get home. It would take me a lifetime to understand all this.

When we left, Grandpa gave me a big, long hug. "You're made of good stuff," he said. I squeezed him hard, then we were in the rented car on our way to the airport at Winnipeg. I felt older already. Maybe it had changed me.

We went into Gimli and I told my parents to stop at the *Ye Ol' Ice Cream Shoppe*. Brand was at the front counter. He came out and stood in front of me.

"Going?" he asked.

"Yes," I said. I glanced up at him and he smiled. He was so handsome that I almost forgot what I wanted to say. "I—I can't stay long. I just wanted to tell you . . . well . . . I had fun. Except for Grandpa getting kidnapped and all that stuff." I paused. The next part would be the hardest to get out. "I'm kind of hoping you'll write to me."

"Of course!" His smile got even bigger. "Will you come back next summer? We could go tubing!"

"I wouldn't miss it for the world." I hugged him and gave him a piece of paper with my address on it.

When I got to the door, I turned back. "Brand, do me a favor till next time we see each other . . . don't fall down any holes, okay? You might meet a rabbit you don't like."

He still smiled, though he looked at me like I was crazy.

I winked. "I'll tell you what it means next summer."

THE HAUNTING OF DRANG ISLAND

This one's for Brenda, with love.

And to all those unheralded English teachers out there.

This book also has a redhead in it, so I want to thank Lucy Maud Montgomery for inventing that spirited Canadian redhead from Green Gables. Oddly enough, L.M.M. was the third cousin of my great-grandmother Anna Jean Frost of P.E.I., so I can actually lay claim to some of the same genes.

I also want to thank Brenda Baker, Barbara Sapergia, and Anne Slade, three women who helped in the shaping of this book. And my Grandma Jean for always being such a great support.

And finally, thanks to Bob Tyrrell for some timely suggestions that opened up a whole new world of possibilities on Drang.

If you're looking for Drang Island, it's a ways past the north end of Vancouver Island. Keep your eyes peeled for thick fog, mist, tall cliff walls, and lightning. It can sometimes be very hard to find. Don't believe anyone who tells you it doesn't exist.

1

If you're gonna die, die with your boots on.

That's what my Grandpa Thursten used to say. It was the Viking code. "Remember, Michael," he'd whisper in his harsh, gravelly voice, "face whatever life has to throw at you with gritted teeth and grim determination. Never surrender."

I wished he'd given me a few more details. Like what to do if you and your father were stuffed into life jackets and trapped on the wild ocean in a tiny ferry piloted by a man who was three times as old as God. And let's say all the forces of nature were trying their best to send you to the bottom of that ocean, while lightning tore holes in the sky. Wind ripped the breath from your lungs. Waves pummeled you. *What would you suggest we do then, Gramps?*

I gripped the side of the boat. Dad was right next to me, one hand clamped on the bench.

A little more than thirty hours ago I was tapping my pen against my desk, waiting for the school bell to ring and finally announce the end of grade nine and the start of summer. At the time I was looking forward to getting away from a year of bad marks and failed friendships. If someone said I could beam myself back to that same desk right now and live my last year over again, I'd almost do it. Almost.

Harbard, the ferryman, faced Dad and me. "One of you will not return," he announced.

"What?" Dad yelled, struggling to be heard above the noise of the engine and the crashing waves. He had his baseball hat on backwards to prevent the gale from ripping it off. His round-rimmed glasses dripped with water. "What did you say?"

Harbard turned his head and glared, his deep-set eyes burning with anger, almost like he was mad that he'd allowed us on his ferry, that the storm was our fault. He looked as if he hadn't slept, shaved, or had a haircut since the sixties. Who would give this guy a license to run a boat?

He stared right at me. Could he read my mind? I leaned even harder against the back of the ferry, squirming away from his gaze.

"One of you will not return. I will take you both to Drang Island tonight, but only one will come back with me. It is *örlög:* fate."

A wave hurled itself against the bow, spraying us with water. Dad shielded his face. "You can stop kidding around, now," he said, half joking.

Harbard was staring forward again, fighting to keep the boat steady. He shook his head, making his yellow seaman's cap move back and forth. "No jest, not tonight. The Norns decree the shape of our lives, regardless of our wishes."

"You're scaring the heck out of me and Michael," Dad shouted into the gale. He sounded serious. I don't think Harbard heard him this time, at least he didn't make any reply to show he had.

"I'm not frightened," I said, quietly, "really, I'm not."

Dad glanced down at me. People always commented on how similar we were; we both had blue eyes and the same long, thin-boned features passed down to us by our Icelandic ancestors. The only difference was my father had sandy-blonde hair and mine was almost black. But I hoped I wasn't looking at all like Dad right now. There was an expression on his face I'd never seen before. Not fear, but something close to fear. He clenched his teeth; his jaw muscles bulged. He seemed like he was about to speak, then he turned away and stared across the ocean.

I followed Dad's gaze. By squinting my eyes I could pick out glowing spheres in the distance, zigzagging all around like restless fireflies and occasionally blinking out. They were the lights of the park, our destination. At least there was electricity on the island. We already had a spot reserved in the campground. But would we ever get there? I was sure we'd been lurching through the water for more than an hour since leaving Port Hardy. And every second seemed to be bringing us closer to the ends of the earth.

Another huge wave struck like a battering ram, forcing the boat to lean. It knocked Dad and me to the edge of the bench. The ferry kept tipping in the same direction. It felt like a huge hand was pushing one side upwards. The motor sputtered and several moments passed where I couldn't hear anything. Just silence. The boat leaned farther, so far that water began lapping over the side.

And I had the sudden feeling this was more than a wave: something bigger, underneath, lifting us higher.

And higher.

Then, just when I thought we were about to be tossed overboard, a clap of thunder crackled through the sky. The boat fell back the other way, crashed down into the water, and leveled out again. Harbard gunned the engine.

"Jormungand just turned over," Harbard said. The first word sounded like *yourmungond*. He rubbed at something hanging on his neck. A good-luck charm? "The god of the deeps spared us. This time. Many a ship has gone down in this very spot. Last year twelve sailors drowned. They found part of the hull. Nothing more."

"What's he talking about?" I whispered to Dad, trying my best to be tactful. "Is he nuts?"

My father put his finger to his lips, motioning me to be silent. "They told me back at port that this can be a bad stretch of water. But there was no sign of a storm when we left." He paused, glanced at Harbard. "And despite his looks, our ferryman came highly recommended. He's even part Icelandic."

Well, I should have seen that from the beginning. The crazy eyes, the need to talk about doom and gloom. Being Icelandic myself, I knew we were a race of people stuffed full of long stories and weird ideas. And it got worse as we got older. My Grandpa Thursten is the perfect example of that. He's eighty or so and all he talks about now is people coming back from the dead, or trolls chewing on the bones of sheep, or Norsemen yelling insults at each other from their boats.

Don't get me wrong. Grandpa's a fun guy. You just have to get used to his dark sense of humor.

Of course, after everything that happened while I was staying with him last summer, I took anything any Icelandic person said a lot more seriously. "Which . . . which one's Jormungand, Dad? Is he the giant wolf the Viking gods have to bind?"

Dad shook his head. "I don't want to get into all that stuff now."

"Well . . . just give me the short version."

Dad smiled. Maybe he wasn't as nervous as I thought. "Jormungand is the big snake who lives under the ocean and wraps himself around the whole world. He spends his time biting his own tail and swallowing whales that are unlucky enough to pass near him."

"Is he friendly?"

"No. Loki, the most evil and trickiest of the gods, and the giantess Angrboda had three monstrous children, each with enough power to destroy the gods. Jormungand was one of them. He started out as a little snake, but Odin knew how dangerous this monster would become. He threw him in the ocean and Jormungand grew gigantic. He waits down there until the end of the world—Ragnarok. The final, vicious battle between the gods and the giants. Jormungand is killed by Thor, the god with the hammer. Then Thor stumbles back nine steps and falls down dead, poisoned by Jormungand's venom."

"Oh. I see." Well, that was enough about that. Why weren't there any happy Norse stories? Ones where the good guys win in the end and everyone lives to a ripe old age. Or how about one where three travelers on a ferry don't sink in the ocean and become fish food?

Dad was staring into the distance again, lost in thought. We carried on without speaking, the boat's engine alternating between roaring and gasping as it struggled through the watery turmoil. The lights gradually came closer, turning into a sparse set of streetlamps set far inside a cove. A few small buildings were visible, huddled close together.

They looked tiny compared to what surrounded them—tall spires and walls of jagged rock standing high in the air. We passed so close to a finger of stone that I could have reached out and run my hand along its chipped surface. How many boats had it claimed? For a split second a bolt of lightning illuminated the cliffs. Every corner seemed sharp and unassailable, every crag dangerous.

So this was Drang Island. Who would want to call this place home? It looked about as friendly as Harbard's face.

We came out of the open water and into the bay. The waves were calmer here and for the first time I relaxed my grip on the side of the ferry. I got a good look at the buildings on the beach. They were cabins, old and unkempt, facing the water. Only one had light coming from the window. Behind them was a thick collection of trees, their branches reaching down towards the rooftops. A path had been cut through the trees, lit by two dim streetlamps. I assumed that would be the way to the campground.

We pulled up to a deserted wooden wharf and Harbard tossed a rope around a post and secured the boat. Dad and I gathered our gear and bikes and stepped onto solid wood. My legs felt all wobbly. My balance was off center. It was as if some part of me was still on the water, rocking back and forth. I planted my feet firmly and sucked in some air, then let out a long sigh. It was hard to believe that most of my ancestors had spent their lives on the wide open ocean. Tonight, I just wanted to be a landlubber.

We handed back our life jackets, then Dad started digging in his wallet for our fare. When we'd first boarded the ferry, Harbard had explained that he only accepted payment for his services after he reached the other side, just in case something happened on the way there. He'd said this with a slight smile at the time.

But now there was no smile. Harbard shook his head and motioned for Dad to put his money away. He stared silently, his gaze going back and forth between us. I had no idea what he was searching for. Behind all that hair and sunken face, he looked sad. A small version of Thor's hammer hung from a metal chain around his neck—it *was* a good-luck charm. "Your futures are not entirely clear," he whispered, hoarsely, "but I know one thing; it would be ill luck to take money from the doomed." Then he undid the mooring and limped to the front of the boat. Did he have a peg leg? I wondered. Harbard backed the ferry out of the dock, gunned the motor and steered towards the open water, leaving us staring at his retreating figure.

I looked at Dad. "What did all that mean?"

"I have no idea." He patted my shoulder. "It's probably nothing. We all get a little stranger as we get older." He scrunched up his shoulders, did his best Hunchback of Notre Dame impression. "See, it's happening to me already." I laughed and clapped politely.

Dad bowed, then lifted his backpack and used his right hand to guide his bike. "Pick up your stuff and don't forget anything, okay?"

"I won't." You'd think I had Alzheimer's the way Dad was talking. I grabbed my own backpack and bike.

Dad pulled up the collar on his coat and motioned me ahead with a nod. "I'd guess we're not too far from the campground. On the way we can stop at the Park Office, call home, and tell your mom and your sister we made it safe and sound. Your mom will be up late waiting for the call, I bet. But we better hurry. It feels like it might rain."

2

It did rain.

Hard. The forty days and forty nights kind that threatens to wash away everything on earth.

Luckily we'd found our little camping spot and had just finished putting up our three-person tent when the first drop made its splashy appearance right on the top of my head. We ducked inside. Dad flicked on the battery-powered plastic lamp and we unrolled our sleeping bags, unpacked the rest of our gear, and rewarded ourselves with a granola bar snack.

The tent felt safe, which calmed me down, because our walk through the campground had been unnerving. The place was as empty and about as welcoming as a ghost town, site after empty site lit by the occasional outdoor lamp set high on a post. The one good thing was the Park Office, a deserted log cabin where the phone actually worked and we were able to call home. When we were done, I pointed at a big sign on the wall that read WARNING: THE GENERATOR SHUTS DOWN AT 11:00 PM. Realizing we only had a few minutes, Dad and I ran to our site. We made it about halfway there before the lights blinked out, so we had to set up the tent with the help of a flashlight.

Safely inside, I listened to the rain. A million watery drummers drummed on the sides of our new home; it was beginning to feel like we might be in for two weeks of this. Even still, chances were good that I'd have more fun here than back in Missouri. On Drang I wouldn't have to try and make a whole new set of friends, like I'd had to last winter. Tried and failed, that is. I'd just started high school and unfortunately my two closest pals, the only people I really knew well in Chillicothe, had moved halfway through the school year and I wasn't able to find anyone else to hang around with. My twin sister, Sarah, had managed to fit in just like that. But she always seemed to be better than me at most things that involved making friends. And using her head.

For instance, she probably wouldn't have taken Dad's car out for a test-drive in the middle of winter. Especially not a year and a half before getting her license.

Anyway, that's something I'd rather forget.

There was another good thing about our trip; I was getting to spend time with Dad. You see, between looking after the farm, training bird dogs and doing his writing, Dad's a busy guy. To be entirely honest, I was surprised when he asked me to come to Drang. If he was only going to choose one of his children, I would've placed all bets on my sister. They just seemed to get along better.

I crawled into my sleeping bag. Dad had already wrapped himself up in his own downy cocoon, looking like a human caterpillar with glasses. He was jotting notes in his journal. Nearly every night for the last three years he'd been working on a book filled with modern-day Viking tales. It was called

How Odin Lost His Eye or something equally appetizing. He was extremely secretive about the book; he hadn't let me, Mom, or Sarah read a word of it. He said he wanted it to be a surprise when it was published. Part of the reason we'd come here was for him to do research.

"Do you know why they call this place Drang?" Dad asked.

"I haven't got a clue," I answered.

"Some Icelanders made a settlement at the north end. No one's sure when, but probably in the late 1800s. They hoped it would be a safe haven. Close to the salmon. But the island was so inhospitable their village failed and only one hardy soul stayed on. The place reminded them of the original Drang Isle, off the north coast of Iceland. You know, where Grettir died."

This was starting to ring a dim bell. "You mean Grettir Asmundson? Our ancestor?"

Dad rolled his eyes. "Your grandfather's been filling you full of tales, hasn't he? There's no easy way to prove we're descended from Grettir the Strong, but Drang *was* where he spent the last years of his life. You could only get up on the isle by using ladders. It was the perfect place for him to hide from his enemy, Thorir. But ever since Grettir had fought an undead monster, he couldn't stand facing darkness alone. The *draugr* had cursed him, saying he would always see his eyes in the night. So Grettir kept other outlaws as company. One of them was lazy and didn't pull up the ladders. Grettir's enemies braved a storm, made it to the island, and climbed up. Grettir was sick and they were able to kill him, but he still wouldn't release his sword. They had to cut off his hand. One man even chopped at Grettir's head and ended up chipping his blade."

"Now I *know* he's related to us. With a head that thick, he has to be."

"Oh, ha, ha." Dad set down his journal. "You know, this island has interested me for years. All sorts of rumors about it have rippled through the Icelandic communities."

"What kind of rumors?"

"Well, they say ghost ships are sometimes spotted in the mist. Viking longboats with dark sails and figureheads in the form of a long-necked monster. But no one's ever been able to board one. And you heard Harbard talk about the snake Jormungand. He actually believes in all the old myths that we call stories. He was born and raised on this island—that's what the folks said back at Port Hardy. That means he might be a descendant of the original settlers, so I hope I get a chance to ask him about their beliefs."

"We came all this way to talk to that psycho?"

Dad shook his head. "I didn't have a clue that Harbard existed until a few hours ago. But my guess is he knows more about Drang than anyone else. Even his name suggests that: Harbard means Graybeard in the old tongue. It was one of the names Odin used when he disguised himself." Dad rubbed the top of his head, checking to see if his bald spot had grown in. For the thousandth time today. "The real reason I came is because there are supposedly ruins from the original village somewhere on the north end, along with a series of caves that might have served as shelter for the pioneers. I want to see these places. And talk to any locals I can find. Some swear that the fetches of a great Norse sorcerer still flit around the island."

Dad got a kick out of saying strange words and leaving me to guess what they meant. "Fetches?" I asked impatiently.

"*Fylgja* they were called in Old Icelandic. Dark spirits created by a mage well-versed in the unearthly arts. He'd take his soul and make mirror images of it, then send them out to do his bidding. These fetches were used to spy on the enemy, to cause a disturbance, or to bring bad luck. They were invisible, unless you had second sight. Sometimes they could even be sent into people's dreams to deliver a message. They apparently helped drive the Icelandic settlers away from Drang."

"I see. This *is* going to be a fun vacation."

"I suppose now would be a bad time to tell you the snake population on Drang is extremely high; for some reason they breed quite rapidly out here, even though it's such a cold climate. There have been a number of studies done, but the scientists can't explain why there are so many snakes."

"Oh great." I slammed my head into my pillow in fake anger.

"I thought you weren't frightened of snakes."

"I'm not. But there's a difference between not being frightened of snakes and wanting to go to an island full of them."

"Would it help if I told you only three people in Canada have died from snake bites since 1956?"

"My luck, I'd be the fourth."

"Actually, the fourth one might have been a well-known scientist called Doc Siroiska. He came here last year and disappeared on the north part of the island. He was an expert on snakes. Some figure one finally got him."

I shivered. "That's great, Dad! Is this just some clever way to get rid of me?"

"Well, I always did like your sister better," he said lightly. I knew he intended this as a joke, but it still made me do a slow burn. I couldn't help but think it was partly true. Dad fluffed up his pillow, then set it behind his head and laughed. "You look a little scared, Michael. Cheer up! Tomorrow's going to be a grand day." He took off his glasses and placed them carefully in their case. "Good night."

I just nodded. Dad clicked off the light. About three seconds later he began to snore lightly. Was this a side effect of growing old?

I lay there, staring up into the darkness. I didn't feel quite ready to sleep.

A *schlick* sound came from outside the tent. Followed by a harsh, almost growling, noise.

Bears? I strained my brain, trying to recall if Dad had at any time mentioned creatures larger than snakes. I couldn't come up with a thing. It was probably just a stray dog.

The rain stopped. Dad's snoring didn't.

A can rattled.

I sat up. Dad was dead to the world. I thought briefly of waking him, then decided against it. I could check this out on my own. Grandpa had always said, "Fearlessness is better than a faint heart for any man who pokes his nose out of doors."

I found my jeans, threw on shoes and a shirt, grabbed the flashlight, and poked my nose out of doors.

A short distance away a branch snapped.

3

It took a while for my eyes to adjust. I crouched next to the tent, head cocked to one side, listening. A pale moon sent a few slivers of silver light through the pine trees, illuminating the abundance of plants and tall grass at the edge of the campground. Tendrils of mist floated a couple of inches above the ground. The air was muggy and smelled of damp, rotting vegetation.

A dull, repetitive, thudding noise started, then stopped. I swallowed and took a few steps towards the echoes, clutching the flashlight tightly. I didn't turn it on for fear of attracting attention to myself. The small road at the edge of our campsite was clear and straight. I could follow it and still be within sight of our tent.

I crept up to the road. Now metal was ringing against metal. I carried on, step by step, my shoes sinking in mud. Water soaked through the sides and into my socks. Before I knew it, I had turned a corner and couldn't see our campsite anymore. The sounds grew louder.

Rain still dripped down from the trees. I padded ahead, careful to avoid any large puddles, moving as silently as I could.

A dark shape flitted across the track about five feet from me, eyes glowing with pale yellow light. I jumped back. Leaves rattled as the creature disappeared into the brush.

Cat, I thought. It had to be a big black cat. It was the same shape. And just as fast.

I forced myself to go forward. This was stupid. If my sister were here, she'd have told me exactly the same thing. Or said something wise like, "Fearlessness is better than a faint heart, unless it's dark and you're alone."

I was too curious to go back now. Not before I caught a glimpse of who—or what—was making the noise. I rounded another bend.

A strange gray form shifted in the wind, going up and down. At first it looked like the back of a giant, ghostly bear, shaking itself. It grew larger, filled with air, then deflated and fell. I couldn't make sense of what I was seeing.

Someone cursed.

I took another hesitant step and things began to come together. It was a tent. A camper was trying to set it up in the middle of the night. So we *weren't* the only residents of the park.

I squinted. A black figure was bent over, hammering another spike into the ground and grunting, but it was a tricky job without any light.

I cleared my throat.

The banging continued.

I cleared it again. Louder.

The person stood straight up, held the tool like a weapon. "Who's there?" a gruff, muffled voice asked. "This is an axe. I'm not afraid to use it! Who's there?"

"Uh . . . I am."

The camper wore a waterproof sports jacket and stood a few inches shorter than me. The hood was up, hiding any features. The hatchet glinted in the moonlight. Small and sharp. "Be more specific! Do you have a name?"

"Yeah, it's Michael. Do you need some help?"

"No. Bug off!"

I took a step back. "Gee. Okay. Just askin'. But I do have a flashlight, you know."

"A flashlight? Why aren't you using it?" the man growled.

"I . . . uh . . ."

"Look. Turn it on. Shine it at yourself so I can see who I'm talking to."

So I did. The light blinded me, lit my face from below so I'm sure I looked ghoulish. My nostrils were probably glowing orange. "Oh," the raspy voice said, "you're just a kid."

This ticked me off. "Your turn." I pointed the light at the dark shape, but I couldn't see much. Just a nose and glaring eyes. Then he lowered the hatchet and pulled back his hood, revealing red hair cut short around the ears and two stern, angry eyes.

And soft lips.

My jaw dropped. "You're . . . a girl!"

"You're quite the detective," she snarled.

"I couldn't tell," I stammered, "it being dark and you talking so raspy." She looked about my age. I stared at her, my eyes wide. She was pretty, with a thin nose and ivory-colored skin dotted with freckles. "Uh . . . or is that your normal voice?"

"Will you point that light away?" she said, her voice sounding much lighter. She gestured towards the ground. "Better yet, shine it on the tent. That'd be helpful. At least I could pound in these pegs while you stand around in shock."

I lowered the flashlight.

"Thanks," she said. She began wielding the camp axe quickly, hitting the pegs squarely with the blunt end. She'd done this before. "Now point it over there!" she commanded. I moved the beam. She swung again. "And there." I adjusted the angle. A second later another peg was in the ground. She barked a few commands and tightened a rope.

I was still amazed that she was even here. Who was she? What was she doing alone in the middle of nowhere?

"Hold this." She gave me a pole. She looped a yellow rope through a hook on the top of the tent, then pulled up on the other side. With a click, her new home was suddenly high in the air and standing firm.

She came around to the front. "Your work is done. You can go now."

"But . . . but what's your name? How'd you get to the island?"

She laughed. "Don't worry. We seem to be the only people dumb enough to camp here, so I'm sure we'll run into each other again. I'll tell you then. Good night."

She slipped into her tent.

I stood there, my mind buzzing. Then, feeling suddenly awkward, like I'd just been dismissed by a teacher, I started for home.

4

I didn't sleep well. At first I couldn't stop thinking about the girl. Then finally I fell into a fitful slumber. I had a dream that I was at the far end of the island, surrounded by darkness. A thin specter, formed of malice and swirling dark-blue light, rose out of the ground and started walking south, singing softly to himself. I followed, drawn towards him like a magnet. I had the feeling he was searching for something. He made his way over a tree that had fallen across a long, deep crevasse, then he drifted for a distance and finally entered the campground and stole into our tent.

Once there he just glared down at me and Dad, radiating anger and bad luck. I stared up at him, finding it impossible to move. Then the vision ended and started over. I kept waking up and looking for the visitor, but the shape skulked into the shadows. I'd convince myself I was dreaming, fall asleep again, and end up right back in the same nightmare. Finally, after about half the night had passed, I drifted into sleep. I was exhausted.

Morning brought the sound of Dad humming to himself. I moved my arm and discovered my entire body ached.

"You gonna sleep all day, Michael?" Dad asked. "The early bird gets the worm, you know."

I opened my eyes and shook my head slowly, too tired to groan at Dad's cliché. He was clad in his blue jogging suit, sitting down, tying his shoes.

The sunlight was doing its best to turn the tent into a solarium. Birds chirped in the distance. Drang seemed like a completely different place than it had been eight hours ago.

I attempted to get out of bed, but all the muscles in my back tightened into knots. I forced myself to sit up. It seemed a year had passed since the last time I opened my eyes. Dim, dark shapes flitted in my mind, then vanished.

Dad was bent over, trying to open the tent door. "Some campers we are," he commented, running the zipper to the top. "We didn't even zip the flaps all the way down." He stepped outside.

Then I remembered what had happened last night before I went to sleep. About the girl. I searched around for my cutoffs. Maybe she was awake already. Or did I just imagine her?

Dad huffed and puffed, doing his warm-up exercises to get ready for his daily run. His outline was cast across the tent, a stretched-out cartoon version of him pumping his knees. Then he suddenly stopped. "Oh my God," he whispered. This was pretty alarming because he never uses the Lord's name in vain. Well, except if the car gets a flat tire.

I did up my shorts and headed outside.

Dad was standing beside the tent, his arms crossed. His face had that slightly red tinge that meant he was getting mad. "I can't believe someone would do this," he said.

There, scrawled across our brand new tent, was some kind

of graffiti. The words were bright red and partly blurred by the rain. They said: YU AR MARKED DED.

"It's some kind of tar," Dad said. "It's gonna be near to impossible to get it off."

I stared at the letters. It looked more like thick blood to me, but I didn't mention that to Dad.

There was a footprint in the mud. It was astounding; so large that whoever made it must have been at least seven feet tall. Alongside it were something like dog's tracks. A gigantic dog.

I felt a chill. It looked like giants had been hanging around our campground.

A gray, partially buried object caught my eye. Three or four feathers lay next to an odd, mud-covered lump. I leaned a little closer.

One of the feathers was stained red. And the lump wasn't a lump at all, but the body of a bird.

A headless pigeon.

Its head rested a few feet away. One dull black eye stared at me. "Dad, take a look," I said.

He came over. "What is—*ohhh*. What kind of vandals would kill a bird?"

"Kids," a voice said from behind us.

5

We turned. There, blocking out part of the sunlight, stood a heavyset man. He had a bulging stomach, thick arms, and wore a uniform with a gray shirt and brown pants. A Park Ranger patch was stitched to his right shoulder. "I'm Dermot Morrison," he said, looking at us over the top of his sunglasses. His voice was deep and he spoke like he was used to having people pay attention to him. "And like I said, it was kids."

"Kids did this?" Dad crossed his arms again.

I wanted to blurt out something about the size of the footprint, but my tongue was tied in a knot.

Ranger Morrison nodded. "Yeah, kids. They hit a few of the tents last night. Out for a fun time. They're bored, spoiled, rich punks who spend the summer here with their parents on the east side of the island. They sneak over to the campground to raise havoc." He smiled and turned away, like he'd just explained everything we needed to know.

"Well, have you caught them yet?" Dad asked.

"No," Ranger Morrison said over his shoulder. "I've got a few things to do before that." He stopped and faced us. "You can't just pick 'em up for nothing. You have to have your case together." He scratched the side of his nose. "But I'll get 'em. Don't worry."

"What's this graffiti supposed to mean?" Dad asked. The last part of his sentence sounded like *s'pose ta mean*.

"You a Yank?" the Ranger asked.

"I'm not sure," Dad answered. Morrison crinkled up his face with a look of utter confusion. "What I mean to say is, we're from Missouri. If you're a Yank, you're from the northern U.S. And Southerners come from the south. Missouri's right on the border between South and North, so I don't know which one I am. Probably a Yank, though."

"I see." The ranger gave us the once-over, as if he was sizing us for jail cells. Or an asylum. "Anyway, the graffiti, as you call it, don't mean nuthin'. They just want to scare people. I wouldn't pay it any attention."

"Should we be worried about them coming back?" Dad asked.

"No. I have a good idea who did this. I'll drop by their cabin today, invite myself in for coffee. That'll scare the crap out of those juvees. Don't you worry, I've got it under control." He eyed us up again, seemed to dare us to contradict him.

"You will tell us when you get them." The way Dad said this, it didn't sound like a question.

Ranger Morrison sniffed. "You'll find out, one way or another." He looked down, seemed to smile. "You should probably put that bird in the garbage. It's gonna be a steamer of a day today and it doesn't take too long for them to start to stinking." He paused, pushed up his sunglasses, and nodded to us. "Enjoy your stay on Drang."

He strode away, heading down the road.

Dad watched him go. "Michael, remember when I told you how friendly Canadians are?"

"Yes." He'd said this two or three times. Dad was born and raised in Canada, so he was pretty proud of the people up here.

"Well, Ranger Morrison is one Canuck who makes me go *yuck*." He winked. "I guess we shouldn't get too upset. It's all just a practical joke." Dad glanced at the pigeon, then back at me. "So should I flip a coin?"

"Flip a coin? Why?"

Dad's lips twisted into a wicked grin. "To see which one of us has to clean up the bird."

"You're older. You should do it."

"No, no, no, Michael—we're on holidays together and the key word is *together*. That means we split everything fifty-fifty. Besides, I brought you out here so you could learn something about responsibility."

Responsibility? Is that what this whole trip was about? Was Dad hoping he'd have a brand new kid who behaved properly by the time the vacation was over? I crossed my arms.

Dad had no idea he'd just offended me. He magically made a coin appear in his hand and was twirling it with his fingers. It was one of those gold-colored Canadian dollars. "Heads or . . ." He looked at the other side. ". . . loon."

"Do I at least get to keep the loonie if I lose?" I asked.

Dad nodded and flipped the coin skyward.

"Heads," I mumbled as it arced through the air. Dad caught the coin, slapped it on his arm, then turned to display it. A floating loon stared at me. I'd lost. Just another sign of my bad luck. He tossed me the dollar and I stuffed it in my pocket.

"Well, I'm going for my jog," Dad announced. "See you in a few minutes."

"What should I use to pick it up?"

"I'm sure you'll find something," he shouted. He was already at the edge of our campsite, pumping his knees up and down in a slow jog. "You've got a knack for being clever."

"I got it from Mom," I yelled, but he was gone, his feet a blur beneath him.

It took me a while to choose the right instrument for the job. I finally settled on the small silver shovel in our tool bag. I went around to the side of the tent and picked up the pigeon's head.

Its eye stared at me.

Then I carefully scooped up the body. A swarm of flies took off, buzzed around, then returned to their prize. I felt my stomach tighten and wished I could somehow do all this with my eyes closed. A few flies abandoned the bird and landed on my cheek. Their tiny legs tickled me, but I couldn't take my hands off the shovel to brush them off.

I crept over to the garbage, walking as carefully as possible. Finally I got to the can and gently dropped the pigeon inside. The flies followed.

I picked up the lid and placed it on top, whispering a small prayer. It seemed like the right thing to do.

"Bye-bye, Tweety Bird," a raspy voice said behind me.

6

I turned around, expecting to see the creeps who killed the bird.

Instead, who should be standing there but the girl from last night. Wraparound, mirrored sunglasses hid her eyes, making her look like a Star Trek crew member. She wore ankle-high hiking boots, blue jean shorts, and a black shirt scrawled with the words: *Reality stinks and so do you.* She was smaller than I remembered and she appeared fit. Energy seemed to crackle out from somewhere deep inside her. She smirked, then asked, "Poor little bird fall down dead?"

"Uh . . . yeah." Flustered, I opened my mouth again and out came: "It wasn't your bird, was it?"

I could've whacked myself on the head. What a stupid thing to say.

She stared at me, or I think she was staring because I couldn't see her eyes behind the reflective lenses. Her grin changed into a grimace.

Oh, good job, I thought. You've gone and made her mad.

"You've never been here before, have you," she said.

"No, I haven't."

She removed her shades. Her eyes glittered with humor and I sighed in relief. "Hey, welcome to Drang Island," she said, spreading her arms like a tour guide, "the weirdest island in the whole wide world." She stepped up and offered her hand. "By the way, thanks for the help last night. Sorry I was so defensive. I get that way when people sneak up on me in the dark. My name's Fiona Gavin."

"I'm Michael Asmundson." We shook. It felt a little awkward; I didn't quite get my hand all the way into hers. A sissy handshake. "So I . . . uh . . . see that your hair's red. Are you a Norj or a Swede or something?"

"A Norj? What's that? Some kinda nerd?"

"No, it's short for Norwegian."

She shook her head. "I'm Canadian. Born and raised in beautiful B.C. And I get the red hair from my mom. She's part Irish. Not that it's really your business."

"Sorry . . . I didn't mean to be snoopy."

"No harm done," Fiona said, rather matter-of-factly. She glanced past me at our campsite. "Looks like someone tried to redecorate your tent, too."

"Was yours hit?"

She nodded. "Yep, some kind of messy circular mark. If someone's going to be a graffiti bandit, they should try and pick up some artistic skills first. At least you can make out words on yours. It seems to say, 'You are marked dead.' It's like a threat or something."

"Yeah, but what does it mean? Who would write that?"

Fiona shrugged. "Who knows. Most people who do this stuff are just pimply-faced geeks, out to get a thrill. I don't imagine it'll get solved. There's only one ranger on the island."

"We met him," I told her.

"Great guy, isn't he?" She made a face like she'd just bit into a lemon. "There's not much he can do about the vandals but stamp his feet and huff and puff. There *are* a few wild ones who hang out on Drang. Me included." She winked. I almost blushed. "Of course, maybe it's some of the sheep-stealin' hermits in the bush, claiming their territory."

"Sheep stealers? What do you mean?"

"Last year a rich sheep herder tried to raise about thirty sheep here. Thought this'd be the perfect place to graze. Cost him a lot to ship them over. They all disappeared. People think it might have been the hermits, stocking up on their mutton."

"You seem to know a lot about Drang."

"Drang's my getaway place."

"Are you here alone?"

Fiona narrowed her eyes. "What's it to you?"

"I'm a secret agent," I answered flippantly, "It's my job to ask questions." I remembered how the weather had been the night before. "You arrived after us. How did you get here?"

"Kayak."

"You came in a kayak? Through all that wind and lightning?"

"The sky was clear when I left; the storm hit me about half-way across. Kayaks are pretty dependable. And the trip wasn't that tough 'cause I was angry and I paddle better when I'm angry." I must have looked confused by her whole story, so she added, "I didn't have that far to go. My parents have a cabin on an island south of Drang."

"Do they know you're here?"

"You don't know when to stop asking questions, do you?"
She looked like she was about to get real mad.

"Sorry," I whispered, and shut my mouth.

An uncomfortable silence passed between us. Then Fiona
pointed and asked, "Are those your bikes?"

"Yeah," I told her as we walked over to them. "They're rentals."

"They look pretty rugged." She lifted one up and let the front
wheel drop down, catching it on the second bounce. "Good
shocks on this baby."

"That's mine. I named it Sleipnir, after Odin's eight-legged
horse. He was the fastest in all the worlds."

"You named your bike after a horse?" She frowned.

"Uh. Well, yeah. In our family we name everything we
travel on or in; it's kind of a Viking tradition. Our boat is
called Verdandi, after one of the fates; our car is Hugi and it's
named for a giant who ran really fast. Well, fast as the speed
of thought. Our car isn't that speedy though, so it's kind of a
sarcastic joke to call it Hugi . . ." I trailed off.

Fiona had her hands on her hips, staring at me like I was a
lunatic. "How . . . uh . . . interesting," she said. "Is the rest of
your family as . . . uh . . . interesting as you?"

I opened my mouth to answer, but was distracted by the
sound of someone running down the road behind us. I turned
to see Dad huffing and puffing, taking his last few steps into the
campsite. His T-shirt was soaked and a thin sheen of sweat glistened on his face. He was losing some of his hair and it made
his forehead shine like a polished pink bowling ball. I'd learned
a long time ago not to tease him about his receding hairline.

Why'd he have to go for such a short run today of all days?

He stopped in front of us. The lenses on his glasses were

slightly fogged up and he was grinning mischievously. Fiona introduced herself. Dad said *hi* and raised one finger, as if he was about to start an important speech.

I knew he'd spit out something that would embarrass me. He always did whenever he found me with girls my age. He usually said things like "Michael has a birthmark on his behind" or "I hear my son's a good kisser."

Instead, he asked, "You two thinking of going biking?"

"Can we?" I blurted. "I mean—you don't mind if we borrow yours?"

"Go ahead." He took off his specs and started wiping them clean. He squinted at me. "You and I can go out tomorrow. Or the next day. We've got two weeks here."

"Do you want to go for a ride?" I asked Fiona.

"Yeah, sure," she answered, coolly. "But how about tomorrow? I was planning on taking my kayak out this morning."

"Oh . . . okay." I tried to hide my disappointment.

"I was hoping you'd come with me," she added, much to my surprise. "I know you can rent kayaks down at the dock. You ever been on one?"

"Yeah, a couple of times back home. Never out in the ocean, though. I'd be glad to tag along."

"Good!" Dad slipped his glasses back on. "I'll be rid of Michael for the morning at least." He winked at me, then said, "We still haven't had breakfast. You want something to eat, Fiona? Or are you gonna eat with your parents?"

Fiona glanced furtively from me to Dad. "Uh . . . no thanks. About breakfast, that is. I'll get some food at the tent and be back in about twenty minutes."

As I watched her leave, I thought about telling Dad that she was alone on the island, but bit my tongue. It really wasn't my business. And I sure didn't want Fiona upset with me.

"She seems nice," Dad said. "She from around here?"

"From one of the islands to the south, I think."

Dad nodded, rubbed his hands together. "How about scrambled eggs, Michael? And an orange or two?"

It sounded fine. He lit our one-pot camping stove and within a few minutes we were munching away on partly burnt eggs and bread toasted almost black.

"I can't imagine living here in the old days," Dad said. "It's fine today, in the middle of summer. But winter must have frozen the hearts of the settlers. Rain and snow and rain and snow. There are abandoned settlements on islands all around this part of B.C. Swedes, Finns, Icelanders, Danes; tough people, from a tough climate. And still they were beaten by this land—their bones buried in the earth or at the bottom of the ocean. And Drang is supposed to be the harshest of all the islands."

"Fiona said a few people actually do live here year round."

"Not many, I bet. A lone woodsman with a wood stove, a winterized cabin, and plenty of survival skills could make it, but you won't find any families out here. Even the ranger packs up in October and takes a ferry to Port Hardy."

"Does Harbard live on Drang?"

Dad shrugged. "I wouldn't be surprised. He seems the type. Sometime today or tomorrow I'll see if I can track him down. Trade him a drink for a few stories. I can always just wait by the docks until he shows up."

Dad stuffed his backpack with pens, paper, and notebooks. "Don't go too far out in the water. And don't be trying to show off, okay?"

"What's that supposed to mean?" I muttered.

"I'm just asking you to be safe. You have been known to do stupid things to impress your friends, right?"

He was talking about the car incident again. He'll still be talking about it on his hundredth birthday.

"I'll be as careful as I can," I promised. Apparently this was enough for Dad. He hiked his pack up over his shoulder and in a few moments he'd disappeared down the road.

7

I cleaned up our garbage, then plopped myself down on the bench next to the tent, sipping away at my water bottle. I felt tired, like I'd run a marathon or stayed up late cramming for an exam. I reminded myself I really hadn't had the best sleep the night before. And my short conversation with Dad was echoing around my skull. It seemed he was always expecting the worst from me.

A breeze rustled the branches of a nearby tree. I looked at the thick trunk and down at the roots, which were partly uncovered. In the old Norse stories there was a tree called Yggdrasill that went from the underworld to heaven. Its branches held up the sky and a mighty eagle sat on its topmost bough, with a hawk resting on his brow. At the tree's roots was the dragon Nidhogg: corpse eater. Yggdrasill would survive Ragnarok; even outlast the gods. Whenever I looked at any big tree, I couldn't help but think it was somehow related to the world tree.

I thought about Harbard still believing that all the gods and giants were alive. That the great wolf Skoll chased the sun down every night, and Hati, another wolf, pursued the moon. That Jormungand was sleeping in the water, waiting for the end of the world when he would rise and spew venom across the skies and earth. And what about all the ghosts and trolls that my grandpa was always harping about? Did Harbard also think they existed? How could anyone believe that? And yet last night, in the middle of the storm, I would have believed anything. If I'd been told that Thor was battling with the giants, causing all the waves and lightning, I would've said, "Of course he is. It's the only thing that makes sense."

I thought of my sister. If there's any other fourteen-year-old kid who knows her Icelandic heritage as well as I do, it's her. She would love this place. In some ways it was too bad that we both couldn't come along on this trip.

"Wake up, sleepyhead!" Fiona exclaimed from behind me. I almost jumped out of my skin. I tried to pretend she hadn't surprised me. "You must be the dreamy type," she added.

"You must be the type to sneak up on people."

"It's my specialty. Quiet as a cat and twice as fast. You ready for an ocean adventure?"

I nodded and got up. We made our way through the campground, past the Park Office, and down to the docks. We saw only two other campers. "It's getting busy down here," Fiona said, sarcastically. "Can hardly get through the crowds." I laughed.

I rented a kayak, a life jacket, and a double-bladed paddle from a grumpy old man who had a little shack next to the pier. He gave me back fifty cents and both quarters were dated before World War Two. Maybe it'd been a while since he'd had a customer.

Fiona's kayak was sleek and red, shining with new paint and sitting lightly on the water. It must have been worth quite a bit of money, so I couldn't help but wonder how rich her parents were. She got in. I found my kayak a little farther along the dock. The blue paint had been scratched and it looked like it had been torpedoed and put back together again, minus a few pieces. And yet when I climbed inside, pulled the spraydeck tight, and headed out into the bay, I knew I was in a good kayak.

"I think I'll call it Mjollnir, after Thor's hammer," I said, "'cause it cuts through the waves so cleanly."

Fiona rolled her eyes. She was only a few feet across from me, expertly dipping her paddle in and out of the water. "You know, your family needs help. There's more to life than Norse stories."

"Don't tell my grandpa that," I said. "He'd keel over. Or swear at you in Icelandic. My dad might even do the same."

"Did you tell him I was here by myself?" Fiona asked quietly. I thought about how I'd been tempted. "Did you?" she asked, a little louder.

I shook my head. "I didn't think it was any of my business. I figured you'd tell him if you wanted to. I'm assuming you're not in any trouble . . . are you?"

She paddled a few strokes before she answered. "No, I just need a break from everything. That's all. End of story."

I wanted to ask more, to find out what she needed a break from, but I didn't have the guts to open my mouth. Besides, I hoped maybe she'd tell me on her own.

Just as we were nearing the end of the bay, Harbard passed us in his ferry. There were two people standing at the back, holding the side and gaping at the rugged cliffs of Drang. They looked a little frightened. I wondered if he'd told them that only one passenger would return. Maybe it was some sort of traditional ferryman's joke.

He stared at Fiona and me as he went past.

"He's giving us the evil eye," Fiona whispered. Then she added with a raspy laugh, "We're doomed to crash into the rocks or get blown out to sea."

"Don't say that! He probably has the power to make it happen."

"I bet he does. Everyone in this area knows ol' Harbard. They say he's got second sight. He can even talk to spirits—you know—that channeling stuff."

"Really?"

"That's what they say. I don't believe in it myself."

"I do," I admitted.

"What?" Fiona set her paddle across the keel of her kayak. "You do?"

"Well . . . I've seen a ghost before."

"Oh, please."

"No . . . I mean it. One night about five years ago, my Grandma Gunnora appeared in my room. She told me she was going on a journey, but that she'd see me again someday. I thought it was really her, that she'd driven all the way down to Missouri to talk to me. But an hour later the whole family was awakened by the phone. It was Grandpa telling us that she had passed away in her sleep. Back in Canada."

"That's a little spooky. Did you tell anyone about her visit?"

"My sister, Sarah. No one else . . . except you that is."

I expected her to make fun of me, but instead Fiona just nodded and began paddling again. "Thanks for trusting me," she said a short time later. We were just outside the bay and the water was growing rougher. I had to work harder to move forward.

We went along the south side of the island, dwarfed by the tall cliffs. Gliding along silently, we kept our distance from the shore, where the waves smashed against solid rock. Occasionally Fiona would point something out, an interesting rock formation or an osprey cutting through the air. We didn't see any other bays or places to land.

I watched Fiona out of the corner of my eye. Her skill was impressive; every movement was smooth and perfect, like she'd spent her whole life in a kayak. Now that I'd seen her on the water, I wasn't surprised at all that she'd made it through the storm the previous night.

After an hour or so, I found myself getting dog-tired. I pulled up my paddle and Fiona did the same. The waves rocked us back and forth. "Where is it you live again?" I asked.

She pointed towards open water. "That way."

"I don't see land."

"It's there, I guarantee it. Straight south, paddle till your arms feel like they're gonna fall off, then go a little farther." She rubbed her biceps. "Speaking of arms falling off, I'm about ready to head back. How about you?"

"You took the words right out of my mouth," I said.

I slipped my paddle into the water and hit something solid. Which surprised me, because we were about a hundred yards from land. I poked my paddle down again. About a foot into the water, it stopped. "The water's really shallow," I said. "There are rocks right here."

Fiona looked over the side. "There can't be. They'd be marked by buoys to warn boats." She stuck her paddle in and it would go no farther than a few inches. "Gee, you're right."

The water was too murky to really see anything. I leaned closer, almost far enough to tip the kayak. It seemed something was moving below our boats. An enormous, dark green shape. Suddenly a long, smooth back, ridged with pointy vertebrae, broke the water between our kayaks, then disappeared.

"Did you see that?" I asked quickly, trying not to panic. "There's something right under us! What is it?"

"I don't know," Fiona whispered, as if she was afraid of waking it up. "Just stop poking it. We've got to get back to the bay."

She didn't have to tell me twice. I turned my kayak around, bumping the creature again with my paddle. How big was this thing? Then I pushed off and paddled madly away. I looked back after a few minutes and the water was still.

"It must have been a whale," Fiona said, sounding excited. "Can you believe it? We were that close to a whale!"

I was still gasping uncontrollably. "I thought it might be game over for us if it came to the surface."

"A whale wouldn't sink us on purpose. I wonder what kind it was?" She dug her paddle in and expertly spun her kayak so she was facing back the other way. I stopped paddling and struggled to turn my kayak. "It should surface again. They have to surface to breathe."

We watched the area for a full five minutes, but didn't see any more signs of giant mammal life. "I don't think it's around anymore," I said.

We started back to the bay. By the time we arrived I was pretty tired. Fiona was huffing a bit, too. I wouldn't admit it to her, but I was happy to have the dock beneath my feet.

When I returned the paddle and my life jacket, Fiona told the man we'd seen a whale. He looked at us like we were lunatics. "Whales don't come to this island anymore," he said. He had a smoker's raspy voice. "Not since something started eating them."

"What would do that?" I asked.

"Don't know, exactly. But I bet it wasn't a whale you saw, it was something else. Probably Drang's very own sea monster. People round here have been spotting it for ages."

8

"What a nut!" Fiona spun her finger in a circle next to her temple, the international sign for craziness. We were already a good hundred yards from the dock, well out of the old man's hearing. "There's gotta be something in the air out here that makes everyone zany."

"Yeah, he must be Harbard's cousin or something." I held my stomach. "I thought I was going to bust a gut right in front of him."

"We shouldn't laugh too hard," Fiona warned.

"Why?"

"Maybe he was right about the monster. Maybe it was the Son of Sisutl," she whispered, a wry smile on her face.

"What? Who?"

"Just a joke. The Natives in this area tell a story about Sisutl, a mighty snake with two heads, one on each end of its body. It could bring either great power or sudden death to any who encountered it. There's an old story that the Son of Sisutl, a gigantic sea serpent, still patrols this area, gobbling up lost sailors. My mom illustrated a children's book about it. The author cut out the gory parts and made the snake into a nice guy. But every island out here says they have a sea monster. They get more tourists that way."

We walked back to my campsite. "Um . . . we're still gonna bike tomorrow, right?" Fiona asked. She seemed kind of hesitant, like she expected I might say no.

"Sure," I said. "I'm all for it."

"I'll see you then." She headed off to her tent. I watched her go, her red head bobbing up and down. This was turning out to be a great day. I opened the flap to our tent and went inside.

Dad was snoozing, his journal lying open on his chest. He popped one eye open. "Okay, you caught me. I just needed a nap. The walking wore me out, I guess. How'd the kayaking go?"

"We had fun. Saw what the island looked like in the daylight. And we . . ." I paused. I didn't want to tell him about the whale. Knowing him, he'd overreact and say I couldn't go out again.

"And you what?"

"And then we came back. And here I am." I dropped down on my sleeping bag next to him.

"Well, I'm glad you had fun. I talked to a few locals and asked them whether they'd been bothered by vandals. They said it was the first time they'd ever heard of anyone writing on tents."

"Did they think it was kids?"

"Seemed the most likely culprits. I yacked at Harbard, too. He's busy today, but tomorrow he said he'd meet with me and tell me the whole history of the island. It took a lot of convincing, though. He's not really the social type." Dad sat up, gave me a serious look. "Did you sleep okay?"

I wondered if he'd seen me go outside during the night, if he was waiting for me to confess to it. "Yeah, I slept fine." "I didn't. I had quite a few nightmares. I remember one where I was still on the ferry, trying to bring it to shore myself, but I never seemed to even get close." So he'd had bad dreams, too. I was just going to tell him about my own when Dad dropped a bombshell. "Maybe they were caused by guilt."

"Guilt?" I said. This had really come out of left field. "What do you mean?"

"Well, I know you've had a tough time this last year. Your marks kinda prove that. I've been wondering if maybe it has something to do with me being gone so much. April to September is, well, half the year; so I feel like I've missed half your life. I just haven't been there for you."

I was floored, unsure of what to say or of what I was feeling. "Uh . . . it's okay, Dad. You made it to most of my basketball games . . . before I quit the team, that is."

Dad looked dejected. "I just don't do enough and I'm sorry. That's part of the reason I wanted to have this holiday with you. I'd hoped we could reconnect. I'm glad you found this new friend, but save some time for your old man, too."

So that's why he'd brought me on the trip, to get back in touch. "I will," I promised.

"Good." It looked like Dad was about to hug me, but I wasn't quite ready for that. I stopped giving out hugs when I was a kid. A moment of slightly uncomfortable silence passed. I couldn't think of anything to say.

"Let's make some lunch," Dad suggested. We did. Hot dogs and beans. Later we went for a walk, following the trails east of the campground. We didn't talk much, but there was something nice about just spending time with Dad. Although, I have to admit, I did find myself thinking about Fiona often.

That night I slept soundly. I didn't have any nightmares.

It was almost like a normal vacation.

9

Fiona showed up just after we were done breakfast. Dad had already left to find Harbard, though not before he made me promise not to bike too far into the woods. He'd heard from one of the locals that it would probably rain today. As far as I understood it, that was just normal weather in B.C.

"Aren't you ready yet?" were the first words out of Fiona's mouth. "I don't like to be kept waiting. I'm a type A personality."

"What does the A stand for? Abnormal? Or abrasive?"

"Oh, aren't you the funny one. It stands for 'About to go biking by myself.'"

"Kinda touchy, aren't you?" I filled my bottle at the tap and fastened it in the holder on my bike. "Don't worry, maybe later I can teach you a few *good* comebacks." Fiona stood there with her arms crossed, looking steamed. I chuckled and ducked into the tent. I came out with my biking gloves, my fanny pack, and my pride and joy: a black Nutech helmet with flames down the sides. I zipped up the tent.

"You gonna wear a sissy brain bucket?" Fiona asked. It didn't sound like a joke.

I glanced down at my helmet. I felt like dropping it on the ground and saying *naw, I was just kidding, ha ha*. But I remembered a rather gory film we were shown at school once about head injuries. I won't go into details; I'll just say that I never wanted my head to look like a squashed watermelon.

"I wanna keep the few wits I still have inside my skull," I told Fiona.

"Where's it you come from again?"

"Missouri."

"Do they make you wear those things down there?"

"Nope." I paused. "I just want to."

She raised both her hands, palms up, and shrugged. "Hey, whatever, it's a free country." She quickly lowered the seat on Dad's bike. Then she pulled her sunglasses from her back pocket, slipped them over her eyes, jumped on the bike, and jammed down on the pedal. Dirt shot from under the wheel and she launched onto the road. "Catch me if you can!"

I followed as fast as I could. A few hundred yards later, Fiona cut up a path. She didn't slow down for at least twenty minutes, heading over jumps, up and down sharp trails, most of them riddled with stones and roots that rattled my brain as I went pounding over them. It took all my energy to keep up with her. Thankfully, I'd done quite a bit of biking back in Chillicothe.

And my bike, Sleipnir, was perfect, even better than the expensive one I had at home. It responded to every bump like it had a mind of its own and knew exactly where it wanted to go. At one point I took a jump and thought I'd lost control, but when I landed the bike stayed balanced.

We were getting to be a long ways away from the campground. I thought about my promise to Dad to stay nearby, but there was no way I was going to ask Fiona to turn around. No way.

The path took us through a dense clump of gnarled trees that blocked out the sunlight. The farther along we went, the thicker the trunks became. Many of them had been around for hundreds and hundreds of years. They were so high I couldn't see the top. Not that I really tried; I didn't dare take my eyes off the track.

The shade was cool and the only thing that kept me warm was pedaling. Fiona showed no sign of slowing down. She dipped in and out of holes, weaving off the path and back on again. Once she came so close to a tree that her handlebars grazed it, chipping the bark. Then she zipped away, laughing. Wasn't she afraid of anything?

She was still wearing her sunglasses, even in this darkened area. It was a wonder she hadn't planted herself face first in the ground yet.

A short time later we broke through the bush onto an abandoned, mostly overgrown road. "They must have logged here," Fiona yelled, then she followed it. I was a few yards behind. The trail had two separate tracks and was wide enough that it felt safe to look around. The trees were getting so large I imagined their roots digging down into underground lakes. Their branches formed a tunnel above us.

I sensed something moving to my left. Keeping pace with me. I blinked, wondering if it was a trick of the shadows. Or a deer? Or coyote?

I slowed, stared. There it was again. A dark shape, bounding through the underbrush, rustling the leaves and branches. I stopped and squinted, trying to spot it once more. A pine cone rolled out into the open. I padded up to where it had come out.

Fiona had pulled up about fifty yards away. "What are you doing?"

"I thought I saw something."

She spun quickly around and wheeled back to where I stood. "What?"

"There's an animal in the trees." I pointed. The leaves were shaking.

"I don't see anything."

I leaned down and peered into the bush. I remembered the thing that had crossed my path the night of the storm. "I could swear I caught a glimpse of eyes. Are there any animals on this island about the size of a cat?" I asked.

"Not that I know of. Are you sure it's not your imagination?"

"I saw something!" I crept forward until I had a clear view of the area where I had last seen signs of movement. There was nothing but a patch of empty ground. "At least I think I did." I shivered. Now that we had stopped moving, I was cooling down. Fast.

"It was probably a rabbit," Fiona offered. "Let's get going. Maybe there's some open space ahead where the sun'll warm us up. I'm freezing."

Fiona sped down the trail again and I struggled to keep pace. She turned a minute later and headed up another thin path lined with trees. I stopped and glanced back the way we'd come.

Sunlight barely penetrated the branches, making the leaves glow yellow and green. A black shape, about the size of a small dog, shot across the road and disappeared. It moved so fast I couldn't tell what it was.

I shook my head. It was probably twice as scared of us as we were of it. At least that's what I hoped. I waited for another couple of moments, but I didn't see anything else.

10

Fiona chose a path that was uphill, steep and winding, so I really had to get up off the seat to push the pedals down. My legs started to burn, and still we climbed higher and higher. When we finally reached the top, she stopped.

I pulled up behind her. We were in a clearing, high on a hill. Below us was the wide open ocean. No other islands could be seen, only the shimmering blue water, endless and looking like it would be impossible to cross. The sun was behind us, so I knew I must be looking west onto the Pacific.

One section of the island jutted out into the water, giving us a clear view of its edges. There were sheer cliff walls that dropped forty or fifty feet down to the water. Drang was really a natural fortress, like Alcatraz on steroids.

Large birds circled around the rocks, occasionally diving down into the ocean to catch unsuspecting fish. Waves smashed up against Drang's side.

I undid my water bottle and took a sip. Fiona did the same.

Peering down the hill, I spotted a small log cabin. It had a sod roof and was surrounded by about twelve obelisks placed in a semicircle, each about half as high as the cabin. They were like a partially completed wall, meant to protect the home. How on earth had they been carried there?

A vegetable garden was growing near the edge of the cliffs. It looked to be healthy and full of green plants, but we weren't close enough to see what kind. Three thin scarecrows stood guard, shirts flapping in the wind.

"Who do you suppose lives there?" I asked, pointing out the cabin to Fiona.

"You want to sneak down and take a look?"

"Not on your life."

Fiona laughed. "They don't make 'em too brave in Missouri, do they?"

"They don't make us stupid either," I retorted.

Fiona's laugh grew louder and I could feel myself getting really angry. Who did this girl think she was? I thought of how my ancestors, like Grettir the Strong, would never let anyone make fun of them. I got off Sleipnir, kicked the kickstand down, let the bike go, and started stomping towards the cabin.

Fiona stopped laughing. "Where are you going?" she shouted after me.

"Where do you think?" I undid my helmet and latched it to my belt.

"Hey . . . I was just kidding . . ." Suddenly her tone became urgent. "Get down! Hide!"

"What?" I stopped.

She was pointing frantically at the cabin. "Someone's there!" She had taken off her sunglasses to get a better look.

I knelt. A man was limping out into the open, next to the garden. His hair was gray and wild.

I snuck back up the hill to Fiona. "It's Harbard," I said.

"I can see that. I didn't know this was where he lived. He's one of the few who actually stay on Drang year round. He's half Viking and half Native, you know."

"Half what?"

"Indian. His tribe used to live here. A long time ago, before the rest of us came. His dad was some Scandinavian or Icelander, but his mom was from the Kwakiutl tribe."

"Where's his tribe now?"

"Dunno. Guess they got smart and left."

Harbard began hoeing his garden. He seemed pretty harmless. "Is this his land? Is he going to be mad that we're here?"

"What he doesn't know won't hurt him," Fiona said, bravely. "Though we should probably be careful. There's a rumor he catches stray kids and boils them up for stew."

"What? Get real!"

Fiona laughed. "Just kidding. I actually haven't heard anyone say anything bad about ol' Harbard."

"You almost had me going for a second there. You're not bad at pulling someone's leg. Not as good as me, of course."

This made her eyes glitter with mischief. "I bet you a dollar I can get you again. Right now."

I didn't like the sounds of this, but I wasn't going to back down. I pulled out the coin my father had given me. "You're on."

Fiona grabbed the loonie and shoved it in her pocket, saying, "I might as well have it, because I'm gonna show you who's the better trickster." She put a hand to her mouth and howled like a wolf. Loud.

"Hey!" I tried to stop her. Her cry echoed around us.

Harbard jerked his head our way. He shielded his eyes from the sun, squinted.

"What are you doing?" I barked. This was one guy I didn't want to annoy.

"He's not the fastest runner in the world. We can be gone before he gets anywhere near us."

"You're crazy!"

"Oh, don't be such a . . . uh-oh."

Harbard had made his way to the woodpile. He was now holding a large axe. *"Draugr!"* he yelled. *"Fardur burt!"* He grabbed the chain around his neck with his free hand. Was he trying to ward us away? Did he think we were evil spirits? Fetches? *"Galdrakarl! Flya!"*

Then he whistled, sharply. A long, black hound slipped out of the cabin, ears pricked up. It was the biggest dog I'd ever seen. It could probably bring down a deer on its own. Harbard snarled a command.

"We better get outta here," Fiona whispered. She didn't sound as brave as she had just a minute ago. "Fast."

The dog stared in our direction. Then began loping towards us.

In a heartbeat I was on my bike and pedaling like a maniac. I glanced back to see Fiona right behind me. We went up a few feet then down into a gully, trees blurring past. I didn't care which direction we traveled. I just wanted to put as much space as possible between Harbard's dog and us.

We took a long loop on a thin, winding path, then twisted back and forth. By this time I was wondering if I'd ever find my way home to the campground.

I glanced back. There didn't seem to be anything following us.

We headed up another hill. The way was getting even rougher and some of the stones looked sharp enough to puncture my tires. We climbed higher and then sped down into a valley that was crammed with long, green grass that hid a lot of oversized, jagged rocks. The sun beat down; sweat dripped into my eyes, blurring my vision.

The path dipped steeply. My stomach lurched and I grabbed tight onto the bike, praying it would bounce across the stones beneath us, hoping I could somehow manage to stay on. I wasn't even wearing my helmet. It was still strapped to my belt. If I fell here I'd be torn to shreds, all the bones in my body broken.

We were now rattling our way across flat, stony ground. The whole area had been smoothed out like a riverbed.

Suddenly there was nothing but empty space in front of us. I slammed on my brakes. Fiona ground to a halt a yard or two behind.

We were on the edge of a deep ravine that stretched in either direction as far as the eye could see. It was as if the whole earth had cracked open, dividing the island in two. The chasm was fifty feet wide in some places and only about ten in others. Below us was a drop of a hundred feet or more. Sunlight didn't penetrate far enough to illuminate the bottom. All we could see was a swirl of mist and gloom.

It took me a second to catch my breath. I was glad to see Fiona was winded, too.

"I had no idea this was here," she spat out between gulps of air. "I wonder how far it goes?"

I shrugged. I scanned the open area behind us. There was no trace of the dog.

"I'm sorry," Fiona said.

"What for?"

"For . . . for playing that trick on Harbard. Getting us in trouble. I sometimes do things without really thinking first. It was dumb."

I opened my mouth to say *yeah, it was really dumb*, but the look of genuine sadness on her face stopped me. "Well . . . it's alright. We seem to be okay."

"Yeah, except I dropped my sunglasses. That dog's probably chewing on them as we speak." She glanced up. "At least there are a few clouds in the sky now. I won't be squinting all the time."

"Well, we can't go back that way. I hope we can find another path home."

"That shouldn't be much of a problem. There are lots of trails out here." She pointed in a direction I believed was east. "Maybe if we push our bikes towards those trees we'll find another way, though I'm not quite up to the long ride back yet. Mind if we find some place to sit for a while?"

"Good idea," I said. We headed across a flat space, carpeted with grass and stones. We were only a few feet from the chasm. I kept looking down, enthralled by the depth of the hole.

After a few minutes of walking, Fiona motioned in front of us. "See that?"

I nodded. A hulking, ancient pine had fallen across a place where the crevice wasn't that wide, forming a bridge. We neared. Ashes surrounded the splintered remains of the trunk. It still smelled of fire.

"I bet this got hit when that storm came through," I said. "There was some pretty wicked lightning."

The whole area looked familiar to me, almost like I'd been here before, or at least seen it. It was the weirdest feeling, since this was my first visit to Drang.

Fiona kicked her kickstand open and left her bike standing next to the stump. She grabbed onto a branch and climbed up the fallen tree. She held out her arms for balance, padded back and forth, then did a graceful pirouette and bowed. She stood with her hands on her hips, looking like a female Indiana Jones. "You know, I wonder if anyone else has even walked on that side of the island. We could be the first. You up for it?"

I remembered my promise to Dad. I knew we were a long way from camp right now, that if anything happened Dad would have a tough time finding us.

Fiona was staring at me. "I can't stand around all day," she said.

As long as I was careful, nothing would go wrong. And besides, sooner or later I had to take charge of my own life. I gave the tree the once-over. It was long and thick and seemed to be sitting pretty solid. It didn't look that dangerous.

"Okay," I said, finally, "let's go."

With some difficulty I climbed up. I gulped some air and led the way across, picking my way past branches, being careful to step right in the middle of the tree, not on the sides where the bark was loose. When we were about halfway across, I decided to look down. Dark, pointed cliff walls and sharp rocks beckoned to me. They spun in my vision. A thin, silver line of water glistened in the depths.

I stepped too far to one side and slipped.

11

"Here! Grab on!" Fiona was lying on her stomach, reaching down.

I clung to a thick branch, my feet dangling in empty air below me. "I can't reach!"

She moved a little closer. The branch started to creak. I couldn't pull myself any higher, so I kicked out with my foot, found the edge of the tree, and pushed up.

We linked hands and with her help I climbed to the center of the fallen tree. I sucked in enough air to fill a zeppelin.

"You gonna live?" Fiona asked.

"Yeah," I said, once I'd calmed down and stopped feeling like throwing up. It took everything I had just to stand. My legs were wobbly and I didn't trust them anymore.

Fiona was right behind me. "Don't look down until you get to the other side. It makes it easier."

Now she tells me, I thought. I concentrated on my footing. We slowly moved along the trunk, using the tree branches for balance. It took a lifetime and then some to get to the other side. I was sure my hair had gone gray.

We jumped down. Fiona rubbed her hands together. "We better get back before nightfall. I'd hate to cross that in the dark."

I didn't want to cross it again at all. "What time is it now?" I asked after noticing that my watch was missing from my wrist. It was likely still sitting in the tent, next to my sleeping bag.

Fiona shrugged. "I don't wear a watch in the summer. But it's sometime around twelve or so, I'd guess. Enough time to take a gander around this place and get back for hot dogs. Which reminds me, did you happen to bring anything to eat?"

I dug in my fanny pack, came up with two pieces of beef jerky, a granola bar, and a caramel candy. We split everything, except the candy. I bowed deeply and offered it to her, saying, "Sweets for the sour."

"I hope you enjoy your joke, 'cause I'm gonna enjoy the candy." Grinning, Fiona snatched the candy out of my hand.

It felt kind of nice to make her smile. We sat in the open on two bench-sized stones and ate. Didn't say too much. I watched birds arcing through the sky.

Fiona stretched out her legs and sighed. "So what's Missouri like?"

"Hot most of the time. We live out on a ranch near Chillicothe."

"Is your dad a rancher?"

"Kind of. Dad trains bird dogs."

"Bird dogs? Do they have wings?"

"No." For a second I wondered if she was serious; then I saw the smirk on her face. "They're dogs that hunters use. Dad comes up to Saskatchewan every year in the late spring for a few months to train them. It's just too hot and muggy in

Missouri. Our hired man is doing it right now, while Dad takes a break."

"You must get sick of the barking."

"You don't even hear it after a while." I found myself wanting to tell her about my father. "Dad's a writer. Or a collector, I guess. He likes to collect modern versions of all the Norse myths and folk tales. He has a book contract with one of the big publishers in New York. He just has to finish the last chapter. He's been working on the whole thing for three years."

"Man, that's a long time," Fiona said. She picked up a small stone and tossed it about twenty feet. It rolled into the chasm. She then looked me right in the eye and asked, "So, do you have lots of friends down there in the States?" Her eyes were a light shade of green and I gotta say I was spellbound by them. They were the kind of eyes you'd expect on a Valkyrie. Fierce, proud, perfect, glowing with—

"Hello! Earth to Michael." Fiona waved her hand in my face.

"What? What did you ask me?" I asked.

"Do you have lots of friends or do you bore them to death with long pauses in your conversations?"

"Uh . . . no, not too many friends. We came to Missouri two years ago and I found a couple good pals. But their fathers were laid off by a manufacturing company and forced to find work out of state. So about halfway through the year they moved, and I was kind of on my own."

"I know what you're saying. I just started going to a private school in Victoria. Mom and Dad thought it would be better for me. 'Course, I didn't know a soul there."

"Well, I must admit, I'm not completely alone. I actually hang out with my sister quite a bit. We're twins."

"Really? So, tell me: If she studies for an exam, do the answers appear in your head, too?"

I laughed. "No. If they did, I'd be a straight-A student. She always gets higher marks than me. Specially this year."

"It must be great to have a sister. I'm an only child."

"Really? That must be tough."

"What do you mean?" She narrowed her eyes slightly.

"Well, who do you blame your mistakes on? That's what siblings are for."

She laughed. "I just blame everything on my parents."

"I guess that works," I said. "So what do your parents do?"

"Dad's a prof at the University of Victoria. Mr. Engineer of the Year—whoopty-do." Fiona twirled her finger in the air. "And dear ol' *Mom* is a graphic artist."

"Don't you like them?"

She shook her head. "I don't have to like them, do I? Just lump them. They're kind of hard to get along with sometimes. Well, most of the time. Always telling me what to do. And I don't know if you noticed, but I'm a little headstrong. At least that's what they keep telling me." She grinned.

"Is that why you came to Drang? To get away?"

Fiona nodded. "An unplanned vacation. I had a fight with Mom over this summer school she wants me to go to. It's for musically gifted children."

"What instrument do you play?"

"Ukulele."

"Really?"

"No." Fiona gave me this look like I was about as smart as a toad. "Piano, when I'm forced to. It's what all the hoity-toities make their teen prodigies play. Or violin. Registration is this weekend, so I slipped out the back of the cabin. Mom and Dad probably won't notice I'm gone until they call for me to get in the car. I'll go back tomorrow and get yelled at in stern, authoritative tones."

"Won't they be looking for you?"

She shook her head. "I've done it before. Their new approach is to ignore anything bad that I do. They figure I just want attention."

"If you really want their attention, just crash your dad's car."

"What do you mean?"

"Last winter, I told some guys on our basketball team that I drove Dad's Mustang all the time. It's a '67. I was just bragging, trying to impress them. So they dared me to bring it to practice. I did and gave a few of them a ride. But it was a wet, snowy day and the wipers weren't really working. Plus, the windshield fogged up. Next thing I knew I hit a post in the parking lot and the car got hung up on it. The guys piled out and I was left there."

"Did you wreck the car?"

"Not really, just dented the fender. And gave it a flat tire, too. It was more a trust thing. Mom and Dad didn't have much faith in me after that. Not that I was all that high on their 'People To Depend On' list before."

"I take it you don't have your license yet. How old are you, anyway?"

The question surprised me. My heartbeat quickened. "Fifteen . . . that is, I turn fifteen in a few days."

Fiona nodded wisely. "I remember when I turned fifteen."

"When?" How old was she?

"Two weeks ago. Mom and Dad bought me the kayak. They didn't guess I'd be using it so soon."

Just fifteen. It wouldn't be long before we'd be the same age. There was something kind of nice about that.

Without any warning, Fiona elbowed me. I almost shot straight in the air. She was squinting into the distance. "You know that animal you saw in the woods?"

"Y-yes."

"What if I told you I just spotted it?"

I scrambled to my feet. "What? Where?"

Fiona pointed at the tree we'd just crossed. "I saw it about halfway down the trunk. It wasn't very big."

Walking as quietly as we could, we moved towards the tree, eyes peeled. We were only a few feet from the edge of the chasm. "Can you see it?"

She motioned. "There, it's in the branches, coming towards us."

Then I saw it, about thirty feet away. Or I saw something. It was there but indistinct, an ebony shape, rustling from shadow to shadow, hidden by pine needles, hardly making them wiggle. It hadn't seen us yet. As it came closer, I still couldn't tell what the creature was. It was dark and blended in with its surroundings.

We crouched near the edge of the chasm, behind the topmost branches of the fallen tree. Staring. Now our little visitor was completely hidden by green. A branch moved. A second later, a pine cone fell into the depths. Then the animal darted across an open space into more shade. It stopped about two yards away from us, didn't make a sound for a few minutes. I wondered if it had heard something. Or had it picked up our scent?

I put my finger to my lips and Fiona nodded as I grabbed a broken stick the size of a baseball bat. It had been burned on one end.

I used it to slowly part the branches.

We peered in. Nothing. I lifted another section of needles. Something there?

I leaned closer, pushing the stick farther into the branches.

And finally, there it was, the strangest creature I'd ever seen. Its hairless body seemed to shimmer, though it was dark as tar.

Two eyes narrowed. It hissed. It wasn't a cat-like sound at all.

"Michael, I think—"

The animal burst from the tree and into the air, straight at me. It grew larger, stretching taller and wider, looking almost human. I thought I could see claws and a gaping mouth riddled with teeth. I threw out my hands. The thing hit my chest, but it had no weight. Instead it seemed to pass right through me.

Its touch froze the blood in my veins. My muscles stiffened. I wobbled, then caught a stone with my heel and collapsed backwards onto the ground. Rocks jabbed my spine and my ribs. The last bit of air in my lungs whooshed out of me.

I turned my head to see the thing bounding across the plateau. It was small again and seemed to be scampering on two legs, heading at odd angles, back and forth, like it was lost. It wasn't shaped like any animal I'd ever seen. It hopped over an outcropping of stone and disappeared.

"What on earth was that?" Fiona asked.

I waited for my breath to return. Then I slowly, carefully, sat up. "I have no idea, but I don't ever want to see it again."

Fiona was standing next to me now, looking concerned. "It didn't hurt you, did it?"

"Not that I can tell." I poked at myself. To my amazement there weren't any scrapes or sore spots on my chest and arms.

She extended her hand, helped me to my feet. Her grip was warm and sure.

"It didn't even hit me," I said. "It's like it passed right through. Did you see what it looked like?"

"No, only a blur."

"Did it . . . did it seem to get larger, then shrink down again?"

"What?"

I rubbed the back of my head. "It changed size as it came at me."

"That's just your imagination. The thing wasn't any bigger than a cat." I wasn't sure if she was right, but I didn't want to argue anymore. Fiona looked towards where it had last disappeared. "Do you think it was following our trail?"

I shrugged. "Who knows."

Then I remembered why this place looked so familiar. It had appeared in the nightmare I'd had our first night on Drang. I'd followed a specter over a fallen tree.

How could I dream something and then actually see it, days later?

I glanced at the real tree and at our bikes, waiting on the other side. Things seemed safer over there.

Fiona caught my eye. "You're not thinking of going back, are you? Not so soon. We've only been here a few minutes."

"Yeah, and look what's happened." I resisted telling her about my nightmare. After all the Norse stuff I'd babbled about, she probably already thought I was a bit crazy.

Fiona punched my shoulder, softly. "Don't be a party pooper. Why don't we explore this direction, away from that . . . that . . . whatever it was?"

"What if there are more of them?"

"Well . . . we won't poke them with a stick. They'll probably just run away like that one did. C'mon, let's take a look around."

My body was still feeling stiff. It'd be good to walk some of it out, I decided. I wouldn't want to get back up on that tree bridge with aching muscles.

We headed westward across an open plain littered with smashed rocks. It looked like Thor himself could have been here, testing out his hammer. Or maybe giants had played a vicious game of Murder Ball. We picked our way around the debris. Green grass and small trees still found a way to grow, working their way in between cracks and into small patches of soil. I was glad I had good hiking boots on and equally happy when a cloud drifted between us and the sun. I'd been sweating like a pig; I hoped I didn't smell like one.

Soon the rocks grew in size and the ground sloped upwards. We squeezed by two stones that could have been brought over from Stonehenge. This part of the island was much rougher.

"I've never seen anything so desolate," Fiona said. We came to a small rise, but all that lay in front of us was more of the same.

Fiona led me down a narrow path that gradually descended a long way. It became a pass, with rocks on either side of us. We went from shade to light to shade and finally stumbled into a small ravine. Fiona turned a corner and immediately stepped back, almost into me.

"What is it?" I stopped.

She pointed at a steel pole sticking out of the ground.

Next to it was a body.

13

Actually it was half a body.

Of a goat.

And it looked like someone had torn it in two and left just the top part. The animal was chained to a thick steel pole that jutted straight up into the air. It would have taken a pretty big guy to hammer that rod right into the rock.

A few feet behind the goat was an obelisk, similar to the ones at Harbard's except this stone was as black as a starless night. It was set flush against the rock wall. Runes were printed in red across its surface. The grass, which had managed to sprout in corners and cracks all across the ravine, was dead all around the stone.

Flies buzzed. I caught a whiff of the carcass and felt the urge to barf.

"That's pretty gross," Fiona said, "about the grossest thing I've ever seen."

We moved upwind from the goat's body. I ran a hand through my sweat-slicked hair. The sun turned this spot into a frying pan—the day wasn't getting any cooler.

I stepped to the other side of the animal, where I found a piece of stained, woolly hide and a pile of broken bones, some small and brittle, others thick and heavy. Vines had grown around part of a rib cage, but most of the bones looked like they'd only been there for a short while. None of the remains appeared human.

"Some psycho must have tied it up and killed it," I said. "Who would do that? And why?"

Fiona shrugged. "I don't know." She bent over and poked at the piece of hide with a twig. "Doesn't this look like sheep skin? Remember those sheep that went missing? Maybe they all ended up tied to this stake."

"Kind of a *baaad* way to go," I quipped.

Fiona rolled her eyes and grimaced. "That's not even funny."

"Sorry," I said. "It's an old habit, passed down from my ancestors. Dad says the Vikings used to make jokes all the time when they were in a tight spot."

"I'm sure they were funnier."

"Probably. How about this one? This Viking guy snuck up on another guy named Thorgeir and tried to kill him with an axe, but he missed, ran away, and left his weapon behind. The next time Thorgeir saw him, he planted the axe in his skull, saying, 'You forgot your axe.'"

Fiona smiled slightly. "Now that is funny."

"At least he didn't say, 'You axed for it.'"

She groaned and took a few steps away from the goat. Or me. I wasn't sure which she wanted to avoid most.

A green blur caught my eye. I focused on it, just in time to see a four-foot-long serpent slide into a hole near my feet.

"Snakes!" I exclaimed. "I just saw one."

"Yeah, that's normal." Fiona was kicking the metal pole. It didn't budge. "There are always tons of snakes on Drang. They're not dangerous. Well, except for the rattlers. If you get bit by one you just can't move around too much or you'll make the venom spread faster. My father explained the whole process to me: first you'll feel pain, then nausea, chills, and dizziness. You know, all the same things you experience on a first date."

I forced a laugh. If only she knew how close she was to the truth. It was time to stick to a more comfortable topic. "Dad said this island is known for its snakes."

Fiona nodded. "Some guy named Doc Siroiska came to study them and some other odd stuff on Drang. Last year. It was a big deal 'cause he was one of them superstar scientists like David Suzuki."

"Oh yeah," I said, pretending I knew who David Suzuki was. "What was this doctor's name again?"

"Siroiska."

"Hey, I think my dad mentioned him, too. Didn't Siroiska disappear?"

"Yeah. They figure he fell into a chasm or the water. Or got lost in a cave. They searched the whole island and the surrounding ocean. Never found a trace. Reporters said he probably wanted to vanish. Apparently he was bankrupt." She paused. "But some of the fishermen who pass by this end of the island say they hear his ghost calling out, warning people away from here. Spooky, eh?"

I looked down the snake hole. It reminded me of a ground squirrel burrow. Moist air and a smell of wet dung drifted upwards. There were probably hundreds of serpents nesting down there. I edged cautiously away, even though I knew most snakes wouldn't bite unless they were provoked.

I heard something splashing. I followed the sound, heading towards the edge of the ravine.

There was about a ten-foot drop into the water. It would have been straight down, except someone had carved out a slide from the solid rock. It looked like a stone age version of a water slide, but it was about twenty feet in width. Waves splashed against the bottom, making the swishing sound.

I called Fiona over and asked, "What do you think this is for?"

"Beats me." She knelt down and ran her hands across the top edge. "What's all this stuff?" Her fingers were covered with greenish flakes, each the size of a quarter. "It's like fish scales or something."

"The snakes probably suntan there."

"Oh yuck!" She wiped her hands together, trying desperately to clean them. "Look, these things just cling to your fingers."

The slide was worn smooth, as if something had traveled against the rocks a thousand times over. It was a fairly steep slope; one false step and we'd slip straight down.

About a hundred yards away, an immense shape broke the surface of the water, then vanished into the blue depths.

"Did you see that?" I asked.

"Yeah, maybe it was the same whale we saw yesterday. I didn't spot a fin, though."

Neither had I. I stared, waiting for it to appear again, but the ocean was calm now.

My eyes were drawn to a black mark on the side of the ravine. It was a twisting serpentine symbol that looked like a snake biting its own tail. The paint reminded me of the stuff that had been used for the graffiti on our tent.

"Jormungand," I said.

"What?"

I walked over to the image. "He's a giant snake from Norse mythology. The Vikings believed he would one day rise out of the ocean and spew venom across the earth and sky."

"Sounds pleasant. Did he ever do it?"

"Yes, but Thor was there to stop him. They'd been enemies ever since Jormungand was born. Thor fought against him three times. Once, as a trick, the giants turned Jormungand into a tiny cat and dared Thor to lift him. He did and was able to get the cat to raise one paw, which amazed the giants because he was really lifting the giant snake. Another time, when Thor was fishing with a giant called Hymir, the giant caught two whales. Thor didn't want to be outdone, so he rowed into deeper water, cast out his hook with a bull's head for bait, and snagged Jormungand. Thor actually pulled him up and tried to pound his skull in with his hammer. But before he could kill the monster, Hymir, who was scared of Jormungand, cut Thor's line. Thor and Jormungand met for the last time during Ragnarok: the final battle of the gods. Thor slew the serpent, then died from the poison."

"Kind of a tough way to go."

"Yeah, but when you're a Viking god, you gotta expect that you won't die in your sleep. Most of the gods were killed during Ragnarok, but a new world rose up from the old one, with many new courts and buildings fairer than the sun."

Fiona was giving me an odd look. If I wasn't mistaken, it was something like admiration. "You seem to know a lot about this stuff. You're smarter than I first thought."

I let her insult slip by. "I've been told these tales over and over since I was a kid. My parents are myth junkies."

"So who do you suppose painted this snake thing?"

"Dad said some Icelanders built a settlement on Drang. Maybe they did it, marking this as some kind of sacred place."

"What would they use it for?"

"Well, I'm tempted to say sacrifices, but that just doesn't make sense. Most Icelanders have been Christians for almost a thousand years."

She traced the outline of the snake with her fingers. "When was the settlement here?"

"Dad didn't know exactly. The late 1800s or so. Or maybe that's when they left. I don't remember."

Fiona pointed at the dead goat. "I've got news for you. *That* has only been here for a week at the most. It could have been killed just last night. I'd guess someone else besides the settlers has a thing for this snake. Or for chopping up livestock."

"I don't know about you," I said, not wanting to sound too frightened, "but I think it's time we headed back."

Fiona nodded. "You're right. I've had enough weirdness for one day."

Behind me, something whispered. I whipped around in time to catch a glimpse of the creature that had attacked me earlier. It disappeared into a hole atop the cliff walls.

Fiona saw it too. "Was it that thing again?"

"Yeah, but it's gone. I wish I knew why it's following us."

For the first time, Fiona looked worried. "Let's just get out, okay? I don't want to be here anymore."

I stepped over the goat and started up the path. Fiona followed close behind. After about five minutes of walking she stopped and looked back, her hands on her hips. "I don't think this is the trail we were on before."

"What makes you say that?" I asked. "I'm sure we took the right one."

"We may have started on the right one, but somewhere we took a wrong turn. I think."

"Are we going south?" I asked.

"It's hard to tell. This path is always twisting one way or the other."

"Do you think we should go back and make sure?"

She shook her head. "I don't want to see that mangled goat again. Besides, we've come this far. And maybe we are on the right track; it could just look different going this way."

We trudged on. Once or twice the sun shone down on us, but mostly it was blocked by the rocks and trees. A few clouds drifted through the sky, casting cool shadows. My body and head were still sore and I thought again about when that thing had touched me. Had it given me some disease?

Soon I grew parched and I couldn't stop myself from picturing the water bottle I'd left on my bike. What I wouldn't do to have one sip from it right now.

A noise snapped me out of my little dream. Footsteps. Loud footsteps. Just behind us. I stopped, turned, and listened for a second.

Fiona stopped too. "What is it?"

I heard a bird or two and the rustle of leaves in the breeze. "Nothing," I told her. "Just dreaming, I guess."

We climbed up another small hill and onto a plateau. There, laid out before us, were several domes made of piled rocks. The mounds were each about ten feet high. Vegetation had crept across everything, adding a green tinge to the desolate area. A few crooked trees poked their trunks up out of the dirt, looking forlorn and wasted.

"What are these?" Fiona asked, moving to the largest of the mounds, then going around the far side. I followed. There was something familiar about its shape. I'd seen one before or a picture of one. The dome was broken open, huge stones had been cracked to pieces and rolled aside, leaving a gaping hole. The inside of the mound was hollow, dark, and uninviting.

And yet on some level it beckoned to me. I edged slightly forward, not really aware that I was moving. Was there whispering coming from inside that darkness? I felt an urge to get out of the light and go inside.

I slowly stepped ahead, came right to the edge of the opening. It was colder here, but still I moved forward. Did I hear shallow, raspy breathing now? Or was it the breeze whistling through the stones?

I caught a sudden whiff of something long dead and terribly rotten.

14

The stench was thick and overwhelming. I reeled back and coughed, covering my mouth. My stomach tightened. I felt like I was about to be sick.

"What's wrong?" Fiona asked. She rested her hand on my shoulder.

I shook my head. "It stinks inside," I said, hoarsely. I stumbled a few feet away and examined the dome warily. Rain and wind had worn the rocks down.

Now I knew exactly what these were, had seen a hundred pictures of them in books on Scandinavian history. "These are cairns: burial mounds." I cleared my throat. "And I think they're pretty old. It looks like thieves got into this one."

"Is this how the settlers would've buried their dead?" Fiona asked. Her voice was a little shaky.

"Maybe." I glanced around. I edged nearer to the opening of the cairn, wanting a better look at the stones. "But there aren't any crosses or markings. Most people would want you to know who was buried here. My ancestor, Grettir the Strong, used to go into cairns like this and fight the ghouls who lived inside."

"Yeah, right," she said. The way she rolled her eyes made me smile.

"Okay, so the stories are mostly made up, but you've got to give the Icelanders credit for their superior imaginations. According to the sagas, Grettir would go inside the cairn, kill the monster, and come out with all the treasure. And there was lots of treasure. The greatest chieftains were often buried with their wealth, even with their horses sometimes."

I shuffled a little to one side. The sun was coming from the wrong direction to allow light into the mound, so I couldn't see the interior clearly. Despite that, an object glinted in the darkness. "Looks like the thieves missed something," I said. I moved in closer, holding my breath, wondering if I had spotted an axe or a medallion.

"Don't go in there!"

Fiona's voice startled me. "Why?"

She looked pale. "Someone dead once slept there . . . or still is. Just let them rest. It's giving me the creeps."

The glittering blinked out, then reappeared. It was a circular light, almost like an eye. It vanished again. I edged away. "You're right. Besides, it would probably bring me bad luck."

Fiona's face was tight with worry. "Let's find our way home," I said.

We hurried to the end of the plateau and followed another path that led upwards. We climbed higher; patches of grass appeared.

We walked briskly for another ten minutes. Finally, the landscape opened up. We stopped at the top of a rise. The sun was about three-quarters of the way through the sky. The heat took some of the chill from my bones. Fiona leaned against a ledge. "Let's have a rest. I'm exhausted."

I inhaled, filling my lungs. Fresh air helped drive away the fear I was feeling only minutes before. I hadn't realized how much I'd needed a good gulp of oxygen.

I took a few steps to the edge of a small cliff and looked down. We were now quite high up. Birds arced through the air below us. Beyond them was a green valley with a small stream meandering through it. But the area looked damaged, like a war had been fought there. Clumps of trees had been knocked down in a haphazard pattern.

"Hey, are those houses down there?" Fiona pointed to a group of tall pines.

I squinted. Camouflaged by the trees were three long log houses with grass roofs. One was almost completely fallen in. Another was missing its door. Only the house in the middle looked like it would last the whole day. The land in front of the homes was overgrown with brush and weeds.

"They're definitely houses," I said.

Something small dropped to the ground behind us. I turned, but there was nothing there, only a pebble rolling across the path. And yet I had the feeling something, or someone, had just been standing a few feet away.

Fiona was still eyeballing the buildings, shaking her head. "Who built those lovely condos?"

"These could be the ruins from the old settlement. The place doesn't look like it's been lived in for quite a while."

"Uh-oh, I've got some bad news," Fiona said.

"What?"

She pointed to the west. "There's rain coming."

A gray and heavy barrier was moving along the ocean quite a distance away, but I knew it wouldn't be long before it swept across us.

"We better hurry and find a way back," I said. "I don't want to be caught in a downpour. Especially not out here."

We started looking for a path home. The only one we could find led us north, down towards the ruins.

Soon we were out of the rocks and onto grassy soil, thick with nettles and oversized weeds. I was relieved that it was no longer a struggle to find safe footing, but I didn't like the direction we were forced to travel. Thorny brush made an impenetrable wall on either side of us.

"We have to keep going," Fiona said. "I still can't see any easy way to head south. We may have to follow the shore as far as we can."

The vegetation grew heavier and the land boggier as we descended into the valley. My nostrils filled with the stink of fungus. The smell drifted right out of the ground, growing stronger with every footstep. It was too wet here for normal plants to thrive. Only the ones that grew in shade and on the undersides of things took hold. Large green pads of moss had choked out some of the grass. We stepped over the occasional rotted log.

Fiona pointed at an old pine that had been split in two. A small column of smoke still rose from it. A number of other trees nearby had received similar blows. "This place looks like it was shelled by lightning."

I nodded. The hair on my scalp and arms was tingling as if the electric blast had left a residue of energy in the air. "I'd have hated to be standing in the middle of the storm," I said. "Just one bolt would've cut my whole body in two."

"I guess that'd give you a split personality," she joked.

"Oh, ha, ha! With quips like that, you're working your way up to being an honorary Icelander."

My words were lighthearted, but I was starting to feel nervous. A vicious storm was on its way, so death by lightning seemed a very real possibility. This got my feet into motion. The valley widened. We crossed a small, sluggish stream using algae-covered rocks as stepping stones. I slipped near the far side and soaked my left shoe.

Fiona grabbed my hand, saying, "I think you need a bit of help with your balance."

I stepped, squished, stepped, squished, next to Fiona, enjoying the feeling of holding her hand. The day seemed a lot brighter. I could march on for a thousand miles or so, no problem.

Unfortunately, there was trouble almost right away. We were nearing the ruins. They looked even worse than they had from a distance. Beams broken, doors rotted, mold growing along the windowsills. Vines had crept up the walls and clung onto every corner. Two of the roofs were caved in as if they'd received a blow from a massive fist. I couldn't see any easy way to go around them.

"We'll probably find a path or two on the other side of this place," I said. "When these people were here, whoever they were, they must have made some sort of trails. Maybe they're not completely grown in."

"I hope you're right."

We walked slowly up to the three houses. It'd been at least a hundred years since anyone had lived here. Maybe longer.

Along one of the houses was a shallow pit. In the pit was

a large, flat stone with runes written across it, like the ones I'd seen in books on Norse mythology. The stone was cracked in the center and stained with a splotch of red. It looked like someone had only recently dug it up, because fresh dirt was piled over to one side.

I was about to point this out to Fiona when a quick movement at the edge of my vision startled me. Before I could scream, a long arm had reached out and grabbed me by the elbow.

"What are you doing here?" a man grunted.

15

Fiona gasped. I turned to face my attacker, fists up and ready to fight.

It was my father. His jaw muscles were clenched, his eyes narrowed, and he looked about ready to kill me. "What the hell are you doing on this end of the island?"

"I—we—got lost," I stammered, moving a few steps away.

Dad shook his finger. "Do you know how far you've come? I told you to stick close to home."

"We were but we just . . . uh . . ."

"We found some pretty cool paths," Fiona finished.

Dad ignored her. He crossed his arms. "Do you know how long I had to argue with your mom to get her to let you come on this trip?"

I clammed up, not sure what to say. I couldn't believe he was flipping out on me in front of Fiona.

"Don't you have anything to say?" Dad asked.

"I'm sorry," I mumbled. "We didn't mean to go this far. We did get lost, honest."

Dad let out his breath. "Where are your bikes?"

"Back there." I motioned over my shoulder. "On the other side of those rocks." I deliberately left out the fact that we'd crawled across the ravine on a tree. And traveled down a bunch of mountain paths.

"Well," Dad said finally, "you're here. There's not much I can do about that now." Was he cooling down? He stared at me, his face unreadable. Then he uncrossed his arms and his look softened. "I was going to show you this place tomorrow anyway."

"Why?" I asked, pretending I hadn't already figured out where we were.

"It's the remains of the settlement I was talking about."

"Really?" I said. "That's cool." I wondered if he could tell I was trying to get on his good side. "How'd you get here, anyway?"

"I rented a boat." He gestured towards a tall, finger-shaped cliff. "It's tied up in a bay over there. This morning I met Harbard and he told me about this place but wasn't interested in ferrying me here. He said I'd already given him enough bad luck to sink seven ships. Then he warned me to be good and gone from this end of the island before dark, because that's when all the spirits from the underworld are loosed and Hel herself walks this valley." Dad shook his head. "I can't tell if he has a really strange sense of humor, or if he's just the most superstitious man in the world."

"Maybe it's a little of both," Fiona offered.

"I hope so. Harbard did mention he might come by this way to make sure I didn't drown. Then he went off, saying he had to work in his garden." Fiona and I exchanged a glance. We'd seen Harbard in his garden, alright. "Anyway, Drang is exactly the place I needed to see. It should really help me figure out the last story in my book. Harbard was kind enough to tell me a little of the island's history. All about the Icelanders who settled here and the hardships they encountered." He paused, then added, "And all the murders that took place."

"Murders? What the heck are you talking about?" Fiona asked. "Uh . . . I mean, what murders?"

I waved my hands. "No! Don't get Dad talking about anything gory. He won't stop."

"You want to know what happened, just as much as she does," Dad said. I actually didn't, but I figured I was in enough trouble, so I paid attention. "It's an interesting but strange story. Harbard said fifteen men, nine women, and a few children, led by a man named Olavr Tryggvason, came by way of Victoria and landed here in the summer of 1896. They were all Icelanders and they had dreams of forming a new community on Drang. They had no idea how inhospitable this island could be."

"Did the weather drive them away?" Fiona asked.

"No," Dad said, "it was the Mórar ghosts. At least that's what the settlers said. When they first arrived this was a peaceful, warm valley. They knew they didn't have too many months of good weather left, so they quickly built these three longhouses to winter in." Dad led us over to one of the buildings, knocked at the wood wall. "Solid structures, with open hearths in the center to keep everything warm. The fall was rainy and miserable—nothing that would discourage an Icelander. But when the first major winter storm struck them, two of the women froze to death in a matter of hours. It was an unnaturally cold night. The settlers' woodpile was buried under ten inches of ice and their food supply dwindled along with their hope. The ocean was too rough to cross, so they were stuck here. Then the Mórar appeared.

"Apparently the Mórar would first just follow people around after dark, cracking branches and thrusting their ghostly faces in front of travelers. Then they became more aggressive, straddling the rooftops and slamming doors. They were led by an absolutely malevolent specter whom the settlers called Bolverk. They believed he was able to make the dead walk. That's dead animals *and* dead humans. One of the men was apparently attacked by his own dog who had died and been buried the day before. The dog still had dirt caked in his fur. It took three big men with clubs to kill the hound for the second time."

Dad motioned at one of the openings beside us. "Later that night the two women who had frozen to death appeared and probably stood right here, scratching at the doors and windows, begging to be let into the warmth. No one dared open the door. The next morning they found their corpses outside. The settlers said prayers over the women's bodies, then took them out in a boat and dropped them into the wild, rolling ocean.

"But that was just the beginning. Bolverk sent a fetch into one of the settler's dreams. It drove the man so insane, he awoke, grabbed an axe, and chopped several of his sleeping fellow settlers to death, then fled. Olavr called together all the men to go into the night and find the murderer, but no one would, so he journeyed out on his own and brought him down."

"Killed him?" I asked.

Dad was rubbing the top of his head, checking out his bald spot. "Probably. At least he was never seen again. When Olavr returned, the others held a vote and decided to leave, even though the ocean was nearly impassable. Olavr stayed on saying his work wasn't finished."

"What work?" Fiona had her arms crossed. I'd never seen her look so serious. She seemed older somehow.

"I don't know. Harbard didn't explain any more than that."

"Well, what about the ghosts?" I asked. "Where did the Icelanders think they were from? Were they Indian ghosts?"

"Exactly! What about the ghosts!" Dad pointed one finger in the air and waved it around to add emphasis to his words. "I had the same question. I found a couple things here that shed a lot of light on the story of the settlement. And maybe why it went so wrong. If you believe in bad luck, that is. Come here." He led us around the corner of the ruin. A part of the wall had collapsed and the earth had sunk down, almost like an underground chamber had fallen in. "I was snooping around here, just soaking up the atmosphere. And I found this." Dad knelt and pushed some of the dirt away from the side and revealed a line of disintegrated timbers below the longhouse. "This building was constructed on top of an older one. The settlers probably didn't even know it was there. Now, it's pretty strange that there was another house here. I know the Natives didn't make homes like this. But there's more."

Dad led us back to the stone we'd been looking at a few minutes before. He adjusted his glasses, squinted down. "That rock has probably been here longer than the settlers' longhouses."

"Why does it have red marks on it?" I asked.

"Uh . . . I'm not sure," Dad said. "The runes are the most interesting thing about it. I'm a little rusty at reading them, and many aren't familiar to me, but it looks like they're part of a prophecy. Or some kind of chant about the end of the world. It says: *An axe age, a sword age, shields will be bashed, then a wolf age, a fang age, and brothers will be drenched in the blood of brothers. Take this sacrifice, Father of wolves, Sire of snakes. Unleash your son, Jormungand. A new world will rise from the venom and fire.*"

Dad's last words echoed around us. "But people haven't written with runes for hundreds and hundreds of years," I said. "Did the Icelandic settlers make this stone?"

"No," Dad answered. "It wasn't them, If my guess is right, Vikings built the older structure and carved the runes almost a thousand years ago. And those Vikings were called the Mórar."

"The ghosts settled this place?" Fiona was looking about as confused as I felt. "What do you mean?"

Dad gave her an almost wicked grin. He got a big charge out of reeling people into his stories. It was probably a genetic thing, passed down through generations of storytelling Icelanders. "They called them the Mórar, which means ghost. There were always lots of names for spirits depending on which part of Iceland you were from: fetches, *afturganga*, *skottur*, *draugr*. The more names you knew, the better. There was power in naming things. Sometimes that would be enough to dispel them.

"So Mórar was just another name for ghosts. But it's *also* the name of a group of Icelanders who, about a thousand years ago, were banished from northern Iceland near Reykir. In fact they were from the same area our family came from. It might even have been our ancestors who drove them out of Iceland. Kind of neat, eh? We drive them away, then a thousand years later we find their resting place."

Actually it didn't sound neat to me. I found it a little unnerving.

Dad leaned against the longhouse. "The Mórar were the

worst of the worst, accused of sorcery and unholy sacrifice and said to be closer kin to wolves than men. They worshipped Loki and his two giant sons, Jormungand and Fenrir. The Mórar's leader was a sorcerer named Bolverk." Dad paused. "Bolverk is another one of those names from the old days. Odin used it whenever he was going to do something bad."

"You mean Odin was a bad guy?" Fiona asked.

"He was both good and evil, full of pride and greed just like many people are. The Vikings believed Odin was the highest of the gods, but most Norsemen worshipped Thor. They liked him because he was a tough, strong, honest god. Simple and straightforward. This meant a lot of tricks got played on him, but he was still the one all the gods turned to when they needed some extra muscle. But as much as the Icelanders identified with Thor, they never forgot to pay their respects to Odin, the one-eyed Allfather.

"Anyway, the name Bolverk means 'worker of evil.' And if the legends are even partly true, this sorcerer lived up to his name a hundred times over. Drinking the blood of snakes to prolong his life, sacrificing horses that had been run until they were slick with sweat, and other macabre stuff like that. The people of northern Iceland chased the Mórar away before they grew too strong.

"They fled across the North Sea and eventually made their way into what's now Russia. They plundered for a time, until their ships were sunk by Byzantine soldiers and they were forced onto the land. No one heard of them again, though there are legends that a few of them survived and were able to make it to the east coast of Russia and build a longship. From there they might have struck out to find a new home. And landed here."

"They came all the way from Russia?" I asked. "Isn't that a little far?"

"It's not entirely impossible. The Vikings expanded as far west as Newfoundland, as far south as Sicily and Greece, and as far east as the Ural Mountains of Russia. They were amazing navigators and loved the ocean unlike any other race. The Mórar were among the hardiest of them all. But if they landed here they were likely only a few in number, with no resources. One bad winter would have meant the end of their food supply and of them. Or they may have died of sickness."

Dad fell silent. The clouds had shifted across half the sky, blotting out the sun. A cool breeze was snaking its way through the valley. I shivered.

16

"Come this way." Dad led us into the one longhouse that still had its roof intact. We stopped a few feet inside the door. Gray light filtered through cracks in the wall, revealing a cobwebbed interior and a dirt floor. Another door, half disintegrated, was open at the far end. Two walls, which used to separate different parts of the building, were now collapsed.

"There . . . it's a bit warmer in here," Dad said, then carried on like a teacher who'd been interrupted halfway through a lesson. "Whether the Mórar were here or not is a moot point. It'd take a team of archeologists to prove that. But the Icelandic settlers believed the Mórar ghosts were here. And that was enough to make them leave. I have no idea why Olavr chose to stay." Dad paused. "He was quite the man though. He lived on Drang until his death in 1947." Then Dad turned to me and said, "You've already met his son."

"I have?"

"Yeah. Harbard. Olavr married at an old age. Longevity was one of his family's traits."

I found it hard to imagine Harbard having a father. Had he

been just as grumpy as Harbard? Thinking of his dead father reminded me of the cairns. "Did Harbard mention the burial mounds?"

"Mounds? Where?" Dad asked.

I told him. Then decided I should tell him about the dead goat, too. He listened intently. "The cairns must be quite old," he said when I was finished. "The settlers wouldn't have built them; they buried their dead in the sea because they feared their bodies would fall under the control of the Mórar. And I don't think the Natives would've built mounds like that. I have no idea what the goat thing is all about. No idea at all. It does make me wonder about the runes on that stone out there and why it's been stained red, almost like it was part of some ceremony. Sure am curious about who dug up the stone in the first place." He paused and I saw the worry on his face. He glanced at his watch. "It's almost supper time. We should head for home." Then he looked at Fiona. "Were your parents expecting you to be away this long?"

"Well . . ." Fiona started. She cleared her throat. "To tell you the truth, they actually don't know I'm even here."

It took a moment for the words to register with Dad. "What do you mean?"

"We had a misunderstanding. I kinda slipped away from home and came to Drang on my own."

"You've been here for almost two whole days? Won't they be sick with worry?"

Fiona couldn't meet his eyes. She looked at the ground, her jaw muscles clenched. "Yeah, probably by now. I guess I was too mad to really care." She fell silent.

No one said anything for a few uncomfortable moments. But

I heard something. A familiar sound was beginning to register in my brain.

Footsteps. Outside. Soft, determined footsteps.

"Close the doors," I whispered.

"What?" said Fiona.

"Close the doors!" I yelled. I ran to the front of the house. A light, misty rain had just begun turning everything outside to silver. I yanked on the door, but it wouldn't budge.

"Michael! Have you gone off your rocker?" Dad was a step behind me. "What are you doing?"

Then a wolf's howl cut through the air. Just a few feet away.

It was a long, mournful wail, drawing some secret hidden panic and fear from deep inside me.

"A wolf?" Fiona whispered, her voice shaky. "But there aren't any wolves on Drang Island."

17

We stood, paralyzed by the sound.

A second wolf answered the howl, their voices overlapping.

"They're right outside!" Dad stepped past me, grabbed hold of the door, and yanked it shut. Part of it came away in his hands. "Quick, close the other door!"

Fiona was the first there, tugging at the door. I dashed across the room, joined her, pulling until the door was shut as tight as possible. The wood was flimsy. I found a long piece of half-rotted timber and lodged it across as a brace.

We gathered in the center of the room. I picked up a stone that had fallen from the hearth. Fiona dug in her pocket and pulled out a jackknife. She opened the blade. It was about three inches long.

"If we just stay still," Dad whispered, "they might go away."

None of us moved. We breathed in and out as one.

There was growling. Then a gruff word was spoken by a man and the wolves fell silent. I strained my ears, but all I heard was the wind whistling through cracks in the house. A pitter patter of soft raindrops on the roof. Water dripped down onto the floor.

There was a two-inch-wide hole a few feet away from me that looked out to the front of the longhouse. I crept up to it and put my eye to the opening. Outside it was dull, misty. Lightning flashed in the distance, backlighting the trees.

Then something moved, covering the hole. I was looking into a large human eye sunk into a pale, mottled face, the color leached from the iris, the pupils black. An eye that blazed with anger and power.

The stone I'd been carrying slipped out of my fingers. I couldn't back away or cry out: the eye held me in place, silenced me. Strength drained from my body straight into that glowing orb. Never to return. Even my heartbeat slowed, the blood in my veins seemed sluggish.

Something huge exhaled on the other side of the wall, its breath a thick, ice-cold vapor wafting in through the cracks, chilling my skin. A scent of sweet decay followed, as if it had been eating flowers. The shape leaned closer against the wall. A low creaking sound came from inside the wood; the timber was bending slowly. The eye neared. Grew larger.

"Chose you," an eerie voice rasped, *"I chose all three of you."*

I tried to open my mouth, but it was frozen shut. A new break appeared in the wall, directly across from my throat. White, thin fingers wiggled, slowly reaching in, quietly pushing aside the rotted wood.

"What do you see?" Dad asked. His voice came from a great distance, almost another world. "Is there anything out there?"

I sucked the slightest bit of air into my lungs, tried to force it back out in the form of a word. Failed.

"Michael?" Fiona asked. "What's wrong?" Her questions echoed around me.

The hand was getting closer. Grasping at the open air, fingers brushing my Adam's apple.

"Michael," Fiona's voice floated nearby. "Are—"

The hand grabbed hold of my neck, yanked me against the wall, trying to pull me through the wood. I found some last bit of strength and pushed back, struggling against it as the fingers tightened around my windpipe, cutting off my air. Fiona yelled something, clutched my shoulder, and heaved. Dad did, too. Still, we weren't strong enough.

The man on the other side began to laugh, a deep, rumbling guffaw that shook the longhouse.

Then metal flashed, the laughter was cut short, and I was free. I fell back, gasping for air. I glimpsed a white, long-fingered hand with the jackknife embedded in its wrist. There was no blood. The hand was yanked back through the hole.

Dad drew us away from the wall.

"Who's out there?" Fiona gasped. Her eyes were wide and wild.

"Stay calm," Dad commanded, his voice cracking. "We've got to stay calm. What'd you see, Michael?"

I rubbed my throat. "J-just an eye. And then a hand. I couldn't tell who or what it was."

"Well, I guess we've got more than wolves to worry about," Dad said, sounding desperate. He barked orders like a general. "Grab a piece of wood or a rock. Keep your eyes open, tell me if you spot anything. We can only hope we've scared him off."

I didn't think so. Not after looking into that pool of anger. And why didn't he cry out when he was stabbed? Didn't it hurt? And if that didn't hurt, then what would?

I found a long stick, thick enough to deliver a substantial

blow. Fiona had picked up a similar weapon. We gathered in the center of the house again, keeping as far away from the walls as possible.

"We might have to make a run for it," Dad said. "If it's just a man, maybe we have a chance. I haven't heard the wolves for a while; whoever it was must have scared them away."

"Where do we go?" I asked.

"Towards the boat," he answered. "I'll lead the way."

"But—" Fiona started.

A booming crash cut off her question. Something had landed on the roof and was stomping around up there, pounding on the wood. The timbers shook, splinters and sod rained down. The noises ended suddenly.

Then came a thud as if a heavy weight had hit the ground. The door at the front rattled so hard it nearly fell off. Then the shaking stopped.

"He's playing with us," Dad said, softly. "It's just a game for him."

Our attacker started pounding on the walls, chunks of wood flew across the open area, one of the boards snapped in two, and I glimpsed a shifting figure. Then silence.

But not complete silence. Now there was the sniffling of an animal and a low growl reverberated through the interior of the longhouse. Finally, a word, whispered so deep it was really little more than a rumble: *"Ormr."*

Dad sucked in his breath. The word had some meaning to him, but he didn't share it. "We have to get out," he whispered.

Something began moving along the floor at the front of the house. A long, thin apparition. It appeared in the light, then disappeared. Followed by another and another, coming out of holes in the ground. Ebony-skinned shapes that slithered across the floor towards us.

I heard a rattle, like a baby's toy. Shaking back and forth.

"Snakes," I whispered.

A second rattle shook. A third. Serpents were advancing in waves.

"Get out!" Dad yelled. "Out the back!"

We ran. I was first to the door, pulling off the piece of wood that I'd put there to block it. A dark shape shot from a nearby ledge, latched onto my right wrist. Pain burst in my flesh, burned all the way up my arm. I looked down to see the green, glowing eyes of a serpent staring into mine.

18

Its fangs were sunk deep into my wrist and it was trying to wrap its ink-black body around my arm.

I screamed. Shook my arm until the snake flew off and landed on the far side of the hut.

Then Dad pushed me into the open.

We ran blindly, out behind the longhouse and up a small embankment made treacherous by the soft rain. Dad led us higher, through bushes, our feet pounding madly in the earth. I grabbed at branches, using them to pull myself up. I looked back. No one seemed to be following us.

We didn't dare slow down. My arm ached with a numb pain that was spreading from joint to joint. Hadn't Fiona said something about staying still if you got a snake bite? How movement would hurry the poison through your veins?

We charged on. Dad was only a few steps ahead, breaking the path, but I had to struggle to keep up. His legs were so long I started to lose ground. We cut through a series of low-hanging trees. I covered my face with my arms and crashed through them into the open.

A dark figure was right in my path, arms stretched out and its mouth wide. It was one of those creatures we'd seen before, but this one was even larger than the last. It hissed, loudly. I fell to one side, trying to avoid touching the beast, rolled over, and looked up to see that it had vanished yet again. I was alone. Dad had run ahead without me.

Fiona cried out from a long distance away. I'd lost track of her and somehow she'd lagged behind. She yelled again, her voice echoing, making it hard to tell where it was coming from. She sounded like she was in pain.

I spotted a flash of her red hair in the mist. "Dad!" I shouted, hoping he would somehow hear me. "We've lost Fiona. She's still back there!"

I ran towards her, over rough land, past dead pine trees. I found her on the ground, pulling at her foot. It had been jammed between a rock and a twisted, thick tree root. "Help me!" she yelled.

I bent down, started yanking on her leg until she let out a cry of pain. "You're gonna break my ankle!"

"Can we undo your boot?" I asked, quickly looking around for signs of danger.

"I tried. The laces are double-knotted. They're too slippery to get a grip on."

"Then hold on. We have to do this the hard way." I grabbed onto her shoulders and tugged, digging in with my feet. She grunted, pushing with her other leg. Finally, her foot broke free and we landed in a heap. I scrambled to my feet and helped her up. "Can you walk?"

She nodded and looked around. "I nearly tripped over one of those stupid little creatures. Then I was caught in this root.

The thing laughed at me, then went running back towards the cabin."

"I saw one, too," I said. "They seem to be all over the place."

Rain was now tapping heavily against the leaves. The drops were getting bigger. Branches snapped in the distance.

"Where's your father?" Fiona asked.

"He mustn't have heard me call to him. He's probably up ahead, looking for us."

We hurried back across fallen trees and up to the top of the valley to where I'd last seen Dad. There was no sign of him.

"I think this is the way to the boat. He must have gone there," I whispered. "I hope that's where he went."

"Should we keep going?"

I looked back. There were rows upon rows of trees, fog twisting through them. He could be anywhere. "I don't know," I admitted.

Then I heard a shifting sound, a shuffling in the mist that rolled towards us, growing thicker. A shadow lumbered forward through the haze: a man-like shape. Dead trees fell and live ones shook as each step sent a shock wave through the ground.

A voice reached us, a strange, eerie singing.

Hullabulla lullabulla
bones and red blood
in a dark flood.

Each step he took made the pain in my arm double. Every note in his song mesmerized me. I felt drawn towards his presence. An ever-widening circle of power, getting nearer and nearer.

Hullabulla lullabulla
heart in red blood
in a dark flood.

Fiona was standing as still as a deer caught in a car's headlights.

Then from another direction came a different man, dressed in rags, shambling out of the mist, waving his arms. His skin white and dead looking. His mouth moving wildly, guttural words pouring out. *"Go wan get out ov ere! Un! Un!"*

"Run!" Fiona yelled.

The urgency in her voice broke the spell. I ran with her along the path, scrambling through the trees. We dashed wildly down a low hill. All the while a ghostly voice called from behind, laughing, whooping, and mocking us as we fled, making me feel that every motion was futile. We'd never get away.

We burst out of the trees into a large bay, sliding the final few feet down an escarpment. We skidded to a halt among sharp piles of scree. "There's the boat," Fiona yelled. It was a small one sitting lopsided and lying partly out of the water. It had an outboard motor.

We dashed along the thin line of sand for about fifty yards, forced to splash through a few inches of water. My father wasn't anywhere to be seen. "Start it!" Fiona yelled as we climbed into the boat. "Start it!"

"But we can't leave Dad!"

"Just get out into the water!" She pointed behind me. Two wolves, one gray and one black, were loping across the beach towards us.

The boat was too far onto the sand to go anywhere. I jumped

down and pushed it into the bay until I was up to my hips; then I climbed aboard. The second I was in, Fiona yanked back on the pull start. The motor sputtered. She tried it again. The wolves were nearing, splashing through the water in their mad dash towards us, tongues hanging out between their jaws. Their eyes glowed red.

The waves drove us back towards the shore.

"Again! Try again!" I yelled.

Fiona flicked a switch, pressed a button. Then gave it another desperate pull.

The motor fired and she hit the gas. I fell back and we plowed a few feet into the water.

But it wasn't far enough. The black wolf leapt and landed halfway inside the boat. It dug in with its back legs, threatening to capsize us. It snapped its jaws. Some of the fur was missing from its head, revealing white skull beneath. One of its front paws had no flesh at all, just claws and bones.

I grabbed an oar and whacked the beast, but this only seemed to enrage it. The wolf now had its hind leg hooked on the edge, was about to climb in. I smacked it again. At the same moment Fiona cranked on the tiller, launching the wolf into the sea. It disappeared under the waves.

Then we were away. Farther and farther, out into the deep part of the bay. We circled around. The waves were growing higher. Wind pasted my hair to the side of my head. "Stay close, Fiona. Dad may show up." We looked back. The wolf had crawled out of the water and joined its companion on the shore, waiting for us.

I found two life jackets under the seat and we quickly pulled them on.

"We can't stay out here forever. We'll run out of gas," Fiona said.

"We've got to get help. We'll have to go back to the campground. Let's head this way," I said and pointed west.

Fiona gunned the motor and we started out of the bay. I looked back. The wolves were still there, eyes glowing, teeth bared, but I saw no sign of the ghoulish men. Or of Dad.

We roared out of the bay, the cliffs sloped up before us. On the edge of a precipice stood a tall man, wind stirring his garments and small black shadows dancing around him. He was holding onto another man by the scruff of the neck. I recognized Dad's shirt. His head was hanging down. Was the man going to throw Dad from the cliff?

I yelled at Fiona to look up.

The man gestured with a staff, out at the ocean.

In the distance the sky looked clearer. There was another boat coming our way. Maybe they had a radio or could help us. Just as I stretched out my arms to wave them down, a giant shape rose up in the open water.

We struck it with the force of a battering ram.

The boat disintegrated under us.

19

By all rights I should've been slammed to pieces against the shore. Or drowned and dragged down to the depths.

Instead, I bobbed to the surface and drifted. Salt water stung my eyes and the scrapes on my body. I don't remember even trying to swim. All I recall is staring at the darkening sky and listening to the water swishing all around me. But I was moving. Not back and forth with the waves, but ahead. Like I was being pushed by a single, determined wave. Carried onwards and away.

At times I thought I could hear Fiona moaning.

Then a dark hull appeared; a motor revved down. Two hands clamped onto my shirt and I was dragged from the water, lifted by strong arms, and dropped down onto a wooden deck like a landed fish. A harsh voice spit out words that exploded around me. There was a pause in this barrage as another catch was hauled in and dropped next to me.

I opened my eyes to a grizzly beard and sky blue eyes glowering down at me.

Harbard.

"You're alive," he said, sounding disappointed. "You looked like you'd become a shade. What were you doing in the water with a storm about to start?"

I couldn't answer. My tongue was trapped in my mouth, feeling swollen by salt.

From beside me came a moan, then coughing. Fiona was lying there, stirring as if in a fitful sleep. A cut on her forehead bled freely.

Harbard leaned closer. His teeth were stained yellow. "I saw you on the hill above my home. You and your friend. Taunting me. Bad luck comes from bad doings."

He was getting too close. I tried to push him away, but all I could do was lift my right arm a little and drop it to my side again. At least this attracted his attention to the snake bite. His eyes opened wide in surprise. "You've been bitten!" He grabbed my wrist, pulled it towards him like he'd forgotten I was attached to it. He prodded at the wound, sending a bolt of pain down my arm. "*Draumur snákur,*" he mumbled. The words gave me a chill. "Where did you get this bite?" Harbard was squeezing my arm now. "Tell me!"

I opened my mouth, but only a hiss of air came out. My vocal chords seemed to have dissolved. Harbard pulled a flask from his jacket, twisted off the cap. Before I could move he latched onto the back of my head, yanked me up, and dumped a burning liquid into my mouth. The concoction blazed a trail down my throat and into my stomach. I sat up, leaned over, and coughed for a painful minute. Finally, I spat over the side of the boat.

"Answer me," he commanded. "Where did you get this bite?" Then a sudden look of genuine fear came over him and he said with more urgency, "Where is your father?"

"Back there," I pointed. I'd finally found my tongue. "He's back there. Not safe." Harbard kept asking me more questions, but I found it hard to put everything that happened into words. I did my best. When I mentioned the burial mounds, his look of concern turned to horror.

"One was broken open? Then my father's work is undone. And the *afturganga* is loose."

"Who?" I coughed.

He handed the metal flask to me. "Drink this. Be still, or you'll make the venom spread."

"What! Am I poisoned?"

"No. Only your mind will be poisoned. Sit there and don't move." He pointed at the far end of the ferry. I pulled myself backwards and could barely find the strength to lean against the side of the boat. Only my mind would be poisoned? What could that mean?

Fiona lifted her head, looked at me. "I have a splitting head-ache," she announced. Then she closed her eyes. The cut on her forehead had stopped bleeding. I reached out to touch her shoulder and try to wake her up.

Harbard gunned the motor, knocking me back, cracking my skull against the bench. Now I was really awake.

"Where are we going?" I shouted.

"To the dock. I'm taking you back."

"But what about Dad? He needs help right now!" I struggled to get up. My legs folded under me like a newborn colt's and I slammed into the deck.

"Stay still!" Harbard scolded. "I'll try to find your father. You two are of no use to anyone now."

I didn't have the energy to argue with him. Harbard urged

every last ounce of speed out of the ferry, sending us crashing over waves, charging towards our destination.

I pulled myself closer to Fiona, leaned against her, but decided to let her sleep. I softly pushed an old fishnet beneath her head, hoping that would give her some comfort. Then I examined my arm. There were two holes just past my wrist, oozing blood. The wound tingled and that part of my arm felt deadened. The tingling seemed to be spreading through my body.

I couldn't stop thinking about my father and the man on the cliff holding him by the neck. The image sickened me and at the same time angered me. What did that bushman—or whatever he was—want with him? With any of us?

He'd said, *"I chose you. I chose all three of you."* Which made me think he had something to do with the graffiti on our tent, that he could have been following us from the moment we set foot on this island.

After what seemed hours, Harbard turned into the bay that led to the campground. I pulled myself up enough to see out of the boat. We charged at the dock so fast I thought we'd collide with it. Then Harbard reversed the motor and we banged into place next to a post. I fell over. He limped up to me, grabbed my good arm.

"You'll get out here," he explained. He lifted me and dropped me onto the dock. Air whooshed out of my lungs. A moment later I heard Fiona shout, "Hey, what are you doing?"

Harbard groaned from exertion. Fiona landed beside me. "Ow!" she cried.

Harbard tossed the flask onto my chest. "Drink the rest of this. When they come for you, tell them to wrap you in blankets. And to feed both of you garlic."

Then before I could move, he was gone, the ferry plowing out into the bay. I stood slowly.

"What was that old turd doing with us?" Fiona asked. She was sitting up now, holding the side of her head. "And why are you so pale?"

20

I showed her my snake bite. She studied it carefully. "It's a clean wound, no swelling. Did you see what kind of snake it was?"

"It was black, that's all I know."

"Good." She sounded relieved. "It wasn't a Pacific rattler then. They aren't black. And they're the only poisonous thing in these parts."

"Harbard knew what it was. He called it by a weird name. 'Dramer snaker' or something like that."

Fiona frowned. "That could mean anything."

I nodded. "It's probably an Icelandic name. Though it does sound a little like 'dream snake,' doesn't it?"

"Whatever it is, you should probably put some antiseptic on it."

I held my arm up against my chest. "What about you? That's a nasty cut on your head."

"Yeah. It feels like someone was playing hockey inside my skull." She gently touched the wound. "I think the boat must have hit one big rock. But it seemed like it rose right out of the water on its own."

I swallowed. "What if it wasn't a rock?"

"What do you mean?"

"Well, you said it looked like it rose out of the water on its own. What if something did?"

"Like a whale?"

"No, some kind of sea serpent. I know it sounds nuts, but we've seen it twice now, just the back of it. There's even a place where people sacrifice goats to it. Maybe it really exists. Maybe Harbard's not as crazy as we think he is."

"You can't be right," she said softly. "You can't be."

We were silent for a while. This was almost too big to comprehend. I offered Harbard's flask to Fiona, but she took one whiff and handed it back. I drained it. The substance returned life to my limbs. "We need to get help. We're gonna have to find the ranger," I said.

"He's probably already looking for me. My parents would have called him by now."

"Does that mean you want to stay here?"

She shook her head. "No. I guess it's time to talk to Mom and Dad. This isn't exactly a normal trip away from home anymore. Besides, it'll take both of us to convince the ranger that there's something really bizarre going on here."

A few minutes later we were in the center of the campground, looking at the front of an old, square, tin-roofed building. The words PARK RANGER were stenciled on the door. The wind and rain had faded the words and cracks were creeping through the wood.

Fiona went in first, saying, "Whatever you do, don't mention sea serpents." The floors were hardwood and there was a long counter that ran from one wall to the other. It looked like a bar, except there were no bottles or glasses hanging from the roof. Maps were pinned to the wall beside a bulletin board with a big sign that said, "DON'T FORGET THE LONG WEEKEND RUSH!"

There was no one around.

I stepped up to the counter, found a bell, and rang it.

The *ding* sound echoed around us. We waited.

Ding.

A door opened behind the counter and out came Ranger Morrison. He was smiling until he saw us. Then his face became grumpy. He bellied up to the counter. "What do you two want?"

"We have to report a missing person," I said.

The surprise showed on the ranger's face. "A missing person?"

"Yes, my dad has been captured."

Morrison looked from me to Fiona. "Is this some kind of stupid joke?"

I shook my head. I felt numb.

"Who did it?" he asked. "And where?"

I repeated the story, speaking slowly, awkwardly at first, explaining our bike trip, meeting up with Dad, and about the one man who hounded us at the longhouse and the other who later came out of the woods, waving his arms. Ranger Morrison eyed me with contempt and seemed to be biting his tongue, but his face turned pale when I mentioned Harbard.

"Harbard's looking for him?" Morrison asked. I was glad there was at least one person on this island he respected. "This sounds too much like that Siroiska thing all over again, mystery upon mystery. And almost a year to the day since he disappeared. You two sit down." He gestured at some chairs set by the wall. Fiona and I sat. Morrison grabbed a medical package from behind the counter, trudged over, and handed it to Fiona. Then he disappeared into the back, came out a minute later with two cups of tea. The bags were still floating in the steaming water.

He looked down. "What's your name again?"

"Michael Asmundson."

He gestured at Fiona. "And you?"

She straightened. "Fiona."

"Fiona who?"

"Fiona Gavin." She sounded almost proud when she said this.

"Where are your parents?"

This was it, I thought. She was going to be in trouble.

"Gone," she answered after a short pause. "To Seattle. On business. I'm on holidays with Michael and his dad."

The lie came pretty easily to Fiona. Like she'd been practicing it all day. I wasn't sure if this was a good time to lie or not.

Morrison stared at her, then at me. "I think you two made half this stuff up," he said heavily. "But my instincts tell me to believe the other half. Now I just gotta figure out what to do." He took a couple of steps away, then said to me, "The funny thing is, I was looking for you and your dad at about eleven this morning."

"Why?"

"Because your sister called here. It sounded kind of urgent, though she wouldn't tell me what it was." He pointed at a pay phone on the wall. "You can use that if you want. I'll be busy for a few minutes." He went into his office.

Fiona grabbed a plastic spoon from the table, removed her

tea bag, and had a sip. Then she dug in the medic kit, found an antiseptic, and poured some on my bite.

"Ouch!" I cried. "Aren't you supposed to warn me first?"

"It wouldn't be half as much fun." She patted it gently with a cotton ball. It seemed like the wound was shrinking already. She stuck a bandage to my skin. "I had to lie to him," she whispered.

"Why?"

"Because if he knew I'd run away, he wouldn't have believed our story. He obviously doesn't know anything about me; maybe he hasn't checked his messages or something. I'll phone my parents when we're done here." Fiona felt her forehead. "How's my cut look?"

"The blood's all dry. It's really not much more than a scratch," I answered.

"Too bad. I was hoping to get a cool scar." She smiled at me, then poked through the medic kit, examining its contents.

"Is there garlic in there?" I asked.

"Garlic?"

"Yeah, Harbard said we should eat garlic."

Fiona shrugged. "I doubt there's garlic anywhere on this island. He's probably being superstitious. Maybe he eats it all the time." She paused. "That would explain why he doesn't have too many friends."

I grinned. Then I shivered. My body still seemed out of whack. I sipped the tea. It did warm me up, if only for a few minutes.

I knew I should phone home to at least tell them what was going on. And to find out why Sarah was calling.

"Your dad's gonna be alright," Fiona whispered. And then

she started saying something else, but her words faded out. My arm grew numb. A part of me receded from everything. I closed my eyes, then opened them again.

All the color had drained from the room. Everything was painted in gray tones. Something moved in the corner of my vision and I tried to look directly at it, but it stayed just out of sight. For a second I thought I'd seen a black, human shape. Watching us. A leering smile on its ebony face.

"Michael," it hissed.

21

The thing started to move closer, coming fully into my vision, reaching towards me with long, spidery fingers.

"*Michael. Michael.*"

I blinked. The room swirled back into full color.

"Michael." Fiona tapped gently on my head. "Michael, are you there? Hello!"

It took me a moment to register what she'd just said. I looked around, but the dark form had vanished.

"Sorry, I just kinda spaced out there," I explained. "I'm gonna walk a bit." I stood, then meandered slowly around the room, trying to get my bearings while Fiona watched me. I spotted a small clock and was surprised to see it was seven fifteen at night. I went to the phone and dialed home collect.

"Are you alright?" Sarah asked before I could even say hello.

"Y-yes, of course."

"Are you sure?" She sounded like she didn't believe me. "I had this awful feeling just moments ago that you were in danger. Like something bad was—I don't know—glaring at you. Waiting for the right time to strike. Is everything okay?"

I looked around the room. Blinked. I still couldn't see any more strange shapes. "Yes, I think we're safe. We're in a police—that is—a ranger's office. Uh . . . is Mom home?"

"No, she went to town. What's going on, Michael?"

I told her about Dad—about everything—as quickly as I could.

"I see," she said, slowly. She didn't sound surprised at all or else she was really good at hiding it. "Now some things are making sense."

"What things?"

"I had a dream last night. About the island you guys are on. It was . . . it was a saga dream, Michael. Like Grandpa talked about, a dream that is more than a dream. I saw you with a stone in your hand. You said something about using it to shake the roots of the world tree. And there was this storm full of Valkyries and warriors, all charging across the sky to battle."

If there was anything I'd learned in my life, it was to trust Sarah when she said she'd had a dream. She once told me to stay home from a school trip, so I did, pretending I was sick. One of my classmates accidentally had his arm broken in several places at a metal factory. I always wondered if it was supposed to have been me.

"Do you have any idea what the dream meant?" I asked.

Sarah was silent for a moment. "It had Yggdrasill in it. The world tree."

"Yes, I know what Yggdrasill is." We were always competing with each other to see who knew more about the old Norse myths.

"Something more is going to happen there at Drang. Something big. And it has to do with life and death, because

Yggdrasill is the tree that goes from life to death." She paused. "Look, just get off the island. It isn't safe there."

"You're overreacting, Sarah," I said. "Everything's going to be okay." But part of me agreed with her. We should leave and let the ranger and the police handle everything. But what about Dad?

"Just don't do anything . . . I don't know . . . brave or stupid. Swear on Grandma Gunnora's grave," she whispered. In our family this was the strongest oath we could make.

"I swear."

Ranger Morrison came out of the back room. He started talking to Fiona.

"I should go," I said.

"Take care of yourself, Michael. Okay?"

"I will." I hung up.

"Are you ready?" Ranger Morrison asked me.

"Ready for what?"

"To show me where to look for your father."

"What he's saying," Fiona explained, "is he doesn't trust us."

22

"Listen kid!" Ranger Morrison snarled. "I'll make up my own mind about this so-called sacrificial place. I need to see it with my own two eyes, then, if necessary, I'll radio for help from there. The Mounties don't appreciate being called in for nothing."

"You're risking my father's life by delaying," I said.

He glared down at me, then spoke slowly and clearly. "I do things by the book. Now let's get going while we still have a few hours of light." He headed toward the door. I exchanged a glance with Fiona, who still looked boiling mad. I knew we only had one choice.

"We have to go," I whispered. "What about your parents?"

"I'll phone them when we get back."

We followed Ranger Morrison down to the dock and climbed into his boat, which was slightly larger than Harbard's. After putting on our life jackets, we headed out to sea. A line of clouds cloaked the top of the sky, gathering like unraveling spools of dark wool that shrouded the north end of the island.

The next few minutes drifted by. I stared at the rock walls of

Drang as they blurred past, waves crashing relentlessly against the gray stone. I saw a small bay with a dock and a series of stairs that climbed up a low cliff. I assumed that was where Harbard lived.

The boat roared on, battling the water. The clouds above us were growing heavier.

"Do you know who would kidnap his dad?" Fiona asked the ranger.

Morrison furrowed his brow. His jaw was set and I wasn't sure if he was going to speak. "I don't," he finally admitted. "Maybe someone who lives in the bush. I often get reports from fishermen who see smoke on the north end of the island. What did Harbard tell you?"

"He spoke about his dad," I said, "when I told him the burial cairns were broken open. He said something like 'my father's work is undone' and that 'something was let loose.'"

Morrison cocked his head to one side. "I haven't a clue what that means. I came here long after his father was dead. People say he was just as strange as Harbard."

The ocean was growing harsher and my stomach answered with a familiar queasiness. I looked back towards the land as we rounded a corner. I spotted the slide made of stone. "We're here," I shouted. "This is it."

Morrison pulled down on the throttle and cut the engine to quarter speed. We floated to the base of the slide. It took him a few moments to moor the boat to an outcropping. "I'll go up first. You two follow when I pass the rope." For someone who was overweight, he climbed the slide with surprising ease.

He stood at the top. "It smells like a slaughterhouse," he yelled. Then he attached the rope to a small tree and lowered it down.

I headed up the slide, digging in with my feet. Fiona was one step behind. When I got to the top, Ranger Morrison was staring at the ravine. His face was ashen. "Maybe there really is something going on."

The bones were still there. So was the stake and a freshly killed goat.

A thin trail of blood led from the goat to the slide.

23

"You did say there were two men, right?" Morrison asked.

"Yes," Fiona answered. "One came out of the woods at us. Shouting."

Morrison pointed at the steel pole. "Do you have any idea what these guys hoped to accomplish with this . . . this sacrifice?"

I looked at the symbol of Jormungand. "I can't believe I'm saying this, but I think they were going to summon something."

"Like a séance?" the ranger asked.

"No, a special ceremony to bring something up that slide. A sea monster."

Morrison shook his head. "That doesn't make any sense. Who'd be dumb enough to believe in sea monsters?"

Me, I thought. "Someone does," I said. "That's why they built this place."

Morrison stepped closer to the stake. We followed, carefully finding our footing on the steep slope. The closer we got to the goat, the harder it became to inhale. It was like the air was thicker here, the gravity stronger. A few pellets of rain landed, stirring up the smell of the dead animal.

The moment I got near the steel pole, the bite on my arm flared up with a burning pain and my heart stopped beating. I wobbled for a second.

"Michael, what's wrong?" Fiona asked. She grabbed my shoulder.

"*Harrrrrt,*" I moaned. The blood was frozen in my veins. What was wrong with my heart?

I opened my eyes. The world had drained of all colors but two—I was seeing everything in black and white. Shadowy shapes were flitting around us, darting here and there, pointing and laughing. Two of them pulled on Morrison's pant legs, but he didn't notice. A dark silhouette slipped right in front of my face, its mouth a huge smile. It stuck its hand in the middle of my chest and I felt a sharp pain.

THUD-THUD-THUD-THUD.

I pulled back. Blinked again.

My heart was beating. Air filled my lungs. The real world returned.

Both Morrison and Fiona were staring at me. "Sorry," I whispered, "I felt queasy for a s-second. I just need to sit down." Fiona took me to a large, flat-topped stone. I sat. I was still wheezing, so I took off my life jacket and let it fall behind me. Fiona settled in next to me, put one arm around my shoulder.

"I had some kind of hallucination," I admitted. "And I had one back at the office, too. I think it's the snake bite. Harbard said it would affect my mind."

"What did you see?"

"Black shapes. Dancing around us."

"I did too, just a moment ago," Fiona whispered. "They looked like the creature that followed us today. Then they vanished."

We were silent for a moment. "What if they're real?" I asked. "What?"

"I just . . . I wonder why we both saw them? It's like we're looking into an invisible world. And they seem to be following us everywhere on this island. Just like fetches."

"Like what?"

"They're these kinda ghost things. Dad told me about them. I think that's what we're seeing." I looked at her; she seemed dazed. "What do you think they are?"

"I don't know," Fiona answered slowly. "I just don't know what's real anymore."

Ranger Morrison was now a few feet away, staring at the dead goat. "I'm gonna radio the Mounties," he announced. The wind had picked up and was making the short, wide sleeves on his shirt flap.

"It's about time," Fiona whispered, low enough that he couldn't hear her.

Morrison walked to the edge of the slide, then stopped. "Oh my God," he said. He quickly made his way down the rope, disappearing from sight. A second later the boat started up.

"What's he doing?" Fiona asked. She stood and took a few steps towards the slide. "He's leaving us!"

I got to my feet, each bone creaking, and shuffled closer to the water, forcing myself to move. I pushed my cold hands deep into the pockets of my shorts.

Morrison was pulling away, yelling into his microphone. Far above him giant storm clouds gathered.

"Maybe he has to get out in the open to radio for help," I said.

Morrison put the microphone away. He circled over towards

the cliff walls, where rocks pointed to the sky like teeth. The surf crashed against them. He stopped the boat as close to the jutting stone as he could, then plucked a long pole from the deck. It had a hook on one end.

I felt suddenly sick, staring out at the churning water and somehow knowing what I was about to see would be bad. Very bad. Is this what my sister experienced when she got one of those *good guesses*?

Then something else grabbed my attention. In the murky distance, out beyond the island, a form broke the surface. It was like a whale, but larger and too distant to discern. Waves washed up against it. I squinted. It slipped under the water.

A moment later it appeared again, farther away, then just as quickly disappeared. Had it been here feeding? Had we interrupted it?

I looked back down at Morrison. He'd just dipped the pole into the waves. He moved it around in a circular motion; then it caught on something heavy. With much effort he slowly hauled his catch into the boat.

It looked like a human body. With white, lifeless limbs.

It was about the size of Dad.

24

"Oh no," Fiona whispered.

The boat revved up and Morrison turned it towards us. He cut through the water, slowing to a quick stop right next to the slide. He then bent over and urgently pushed down for a few moments. He was doing CPR. Finally he lifted the figure up.

I saw scraggly hair, a slightly balding forehead. Loose, swinging arms.

Dad, I thought. *Oh no. Not this . . . this can't happen to my father.*

He looked pale. He'd lost his glasses. What would I do if he was dead?

Then Morrison squeezed my father's stomach. Water sluiced out of Dad's mouth. He coughed for a few wretched moments, but didn't awaken. He was alive, at least.

My mind was a blur of questions, emotions. Had they tried to sacrifice him? Had he been thrown in the water and left to die? Would he survive this?

The ranger lowered him, gently resting his head on a pile of fishnets in the end of the boat. He yelled up to us, "Your dad was floating facedown when I saw him. I thought he was dead, but he's still breathing. He's badly cut up though."

A wave slammed the boat against the slide. Morrison fell over, then cautiously pulled himself back to his feet, keeping a tight grip on the edge.

"Can we come down?" I hollered, gesturing to Fiona to get ready to climb down.

"In a moment. Somehow I'll have to get this boat steady."

The ocean was much rougher now. A thick, swirling breaker of clouds unfurled from the sky above us like a wave, lightning sparking its dark underbelly.

Within a minute it hit us full force. Ice-cold rain sliced down, biting into my skin. Wind struck my body. I stumbled back a few feet, struggled to keep my footing. Fiona and I leaned against each other. I grabbed her hand.

"We have to get down to the boat now!" she yelled. I nodded, shielding my eyes from the downpour. We had stumbled a yard or two away from the edge. I couldn't even see the water anymore. Or the boat.

But I thought I could hear the ranger yelling at us, his voice angry and urgent.

A clap of thunder shook the whole ravine, rattling my vertebrae. Lightning flashed directly above us, making the hair on the back of my neck shoot straight up. It was way too close for comfort.

Then a whispered song like a lullaby drifted into my ears.
Hullabulla lullabulla
bones and red blood
in a dark flood.
I turned to see where the song was coming from. Lightning

shot down again, revealing a deep-blue, pencil-thin apparition standing in the ravine, one arm raised, like he was pulling strings on a puppet. A second later the figure was gone, swallowed by darkness.

"Fiona!" I screamed. "Let's go!"

I struggled to pull her right up to the edge of the slide. Her hand slipped out of mine, then immediately she shoved it back into my grip. She seemed to weigh a ton.

Then I heard her cry like she was a mile away from me, which didn't make any sense because I was still holding her hand. Her ice-cold fingers clung to mine.

I turned back to look at her. A specter scattered behind me, the feeling of someone's hand in mine disappeared. I heard ghostly laughter, then nothing. What was going on? A trick?

A fetch. It had to be. Doing its master's bidding.

Fiona yelled again. Her voice was muffled.

"Get down here!" Morrison shouted. He was struggling with the pole, prying at the rocks in an attempt to keep his boat from slamming against them. "This boat's gonna break apart any second!"

"Fiona's gone! Someone took her!"

"What? Get down here! Now! We'll bring the Mounties back and find her."

I took one look at the waves, him fighting against them. I saw the prone figure of my father laid out across the deck.

What was the sensible thing to do, I wondered. Climb down, get in the boat, retreat to the campground and wait for the police to unravel this mess? That was the sensible thing to do. But nothing about any of this was sensible. I couldn't do anything for Dad now. And I couldn't leave Fiona to these madmen.

"Come here!" Morrison commanded.

"No," I said, not sure if he could hear me. "No! Take my father back. I'll find Fiona."

The ranger yelled something at me as I started running wildly towards the end of the ravine.

25

The ground had grown slippery. Light had drained from the sky, soaked up by the clouds. Soon total darkness would fall. I scrambled around, hoping to discover a clue to where Fiona had gone.

In misty darkness I tripped over the body of the goat and fell, accidentally hugging its wet hide. Dank, dead air slipped out of its lungs. Its eyes were open and dull. I recoiled, falling back against the metal post.

So many sacrifices had happened right here. So much violence. And I was lying right in the center of it all. I felt paralyzed by claustrophobia. How many animals had died in this spot?

I wasn't going to be next. I pulled myself together, sat up. A glowing light caught my eye. I saw that the black obelisk at the edge of the ravine had been moved, revealing the mouth of a cave. The light had come from the inside.

I padded slowly up to the opening. It seemed to exhale an unearthly stench of carcasses and filth piled up and left to rot. I took my last deep gulp of air, pulled my collar up to cover my mouth, and crept inside. The interior was tall; glowing stalactites hung from the roof like the teeth of an enormous dragon. I took a few more steps, hesitant to go too far. I stopped, listened. My own breathing echoed in the corners.

I thought I could hear the sound of footsteps and voices somewhere deep in the rock.

A shuffling noise came from just behind me.

I spun around in time to see a bulky figure step out from a hidden alcove. He filled the doorway, blocking the dim light.

I slowly backed away into the cave.

"Done be fraid," a thick voice slurred quietly. *"Im Sirska. Juz want talk."*

I stepped back, panicked, and hit a wall, bumping a stone. It rattled across the floor.

"Done be fraid." He shuffled a few feet in my direction, then stopped. He was a heavyset man, certainly not the one I'd seen pointing at us in the rain just moments ago. *"Im Sirska. Siroska. Frend."*

There was something familiar about what he was saying. I could almost make out the words. *Sirska. Siroska.*

And then it suddenly made sense. "You're Siroiska," I whispered. "Doctor Siroiska."

"Yessss," he rasped. His voice was so hoarse I could barely make out the words. *"Siroska, ma name. Once."*

"Then you're alive."

He slowly shook his head. A sad motion. *"No. Dead. Im dead. He killed me."*

"What?" I asked in disbelief.

"Bolverk. Sorcerer. He came to me in dreams. I was alone, doing my research. Hullabulla, he sang. He led me to his grave and I opened it. Then he killed me. On the rune stone."

"But, you're here, talking . . ."

"*Dead. Heart stopped beating many, many months ago. He kept me like this to do his work. Never resting. So cold. Always another sheep. Another goat. Until everything was set.*"

Siroiska had gone crazy. That was the only thing that made sense. He'd spent a whole year trapped at this end of the island. And what was that about sheep and goats? He'd killed them?

"*Dead,*" he repeated. "*All dead inside me. No more dreams.*" He staggered into a shaft of dim light that came from some opening in the ceiling. I could make out his face now, checkered with gray and white patches, the skin hanging loose. His eyes were lifeless marbles that searched the room blindly for me. Was he out of his mind?

Or was he telling the truth?

He shook, struggled to take another step, then fell to his knees. "*He made me this way. He did this. I tried to warn you. To get you to go away.*"

I remembered now. I'd seen Siroiska before, when we were running from the longhouse. He'd come out of the forest, waving his arms. "Who were you warning us about?"

"*Bolverk. Evil spirit, now flesh.*" Bolverk, the name burned in my skull. Somehow I knew it had to be him. "*Bolverk chose you and your father, said he knows your bloodline, knows your family came from the same land as him. Many years ago. He tried to feed your father to the worm. It refused. Bolverk believes he will have better luck with a smaller gift.*"

"Fiona? Is that what you mean? Where did he take her?"

Siroiska struggled to lift his finger. He pointed past me. "*There . . . there. Find her. If you can. She's there.*" He was falling down farther, crumpling into himself. "*I'm fading. He no longer needs me. He has what he wants."* Siroiska was now collapsed in a heap on the floor. *"Leave me. I should have been gone long ago."*

"I'll send someone to get you. The Mounties are coming. You'll be safe again," I promised, knowing that somehow this was impossible.

He didn't answer.

I felt along the wall until I found an opening that went the same direction he'd pointed and started down the tunnel.

26

I traveled as quickly as I could, navigating over the rough ground. The walls around me glowed dimly.

I passed openings that led into other caves, all honeycombed beneath the earth. Some echoed with the sound of splashing waterfalls. Others smelled of decaying flesh. I tried to stick to the passage in the center, holding my arms out to stop from banging into a wall. I could only hope there weren't any hidden chasms.

Then I heard Fiona's voice. I turned a corner and pressed myself flush against the wall.

A dimly lit figure stood in the center of a chamber, one hand clasped on Fiona's arm. He was clad in dirty rags that hung in strips wrapped loosely around his body. He was tall, thin, his shoulders disproportionately wide. His face was hidden by a hood and he held a long, intricately carved staff in his hand. Circling around him were the two wolves; their claws clicked against the stone. Light emanated from somewhere. I looked for candles. Even a flashlight. Then it became apparent: the man himself was glowing softly.

"Let go of me!" Fiona moaned. "Please, let go!"

"Do you know me?" the raspy voice drifted out from somewhere inside his hood. Waves of dread filled the tunnel, filled me. *"Do they still try to protect the children from me, the crib breaker? Do they still whisper the lullabies of fear?"*

Lullaballa bulla

the blood runs down

Lullaballa bulla

Bolverk wears darkness on his crown.

His singing was surprisingly soft and musical. It had a powerful effect, drawing me towards him. The bite on my arm flared with pain, began to burn, then turned cold. At some level I responded, moving forward, pulled by an irresistible force. First one step, then another. I was powerless to stop myself.

One of the wolves looked towards me, two red slits for eyes. I shuffled ahead, turning the corner. Then the echoes of his song died and I was able to hold myself still. The wolf slowly turned away. I edged back into my hiding place.

"Do they still sing of me?" Bolverk asked, a harsher edge to his voice. Fiona didn't answer. *"Do they fear my return?"*

"I—" Fiona sounded hoarse. He was squeezing her arm, forcing her to speak. "I—I don't know."

He met this with a long silence.

"So many years," he whispered, finally, *"the wolf chasing the sun. So many days spent sleeping, all the languages of men drifting into my skull. All the ancient dreams waiting for life. And then, to waken in my cairn wearing this filthy flesh. I will wear new flesh soon."*

He looked down at Fiona. *"You are small. Warm. The perfect morsel for a god."*

I remembered the goat that had been torn in half. I shuddered at the thought of the same thing happening to her.

"Tonight you shall rest in *Niflheim*. When you tell Modgud your name and lineage, let her know it was Bolverk who sent you. And that I will never dwell in her halls."

Niflheim. The land of the dead. Fiona was doomed.

My arm was burning again. I looked down at it, squeezing with my other hand, trying to stifle the pain. The snake bite had begun swelling up and oozing dark blood. It was as if just being near Bolverk had caused the reaction.

Bolverk's voice faded—they were gone. I stepped into the chamber where they'd been, only to discover several openings, each wide enough to travel down. Fiona and Bolverk were in one of the tunnels now, but which one? In a fit of panic I chose one, ran through it, blood pounding in my ears. Everything was closing in on me, stalactites scraping my head, until finally I came to a dead end. Bones were scattered around as if something had been trapped there long ago.

I ran back to where I thought I'd started and picked another tunnel, running madly down it. Finally, at the edge of exhaustion, I stopped and leaned against a wall. All this aimless wandering wasn't getting me anywhere. But what could I do? I'd starve to death down here if I couldn't find a way out. No one would know what had happened to me. I thought of my father lying unconscious in the boat. Had Morrison been able to get him safely back to the campground?

What would my dad do in this situation? My sister? I tried to stay calm. Maybe that was the best thing, to just slow down.

I closed my eyes. Pictured Fiona. I couldn't even imagine what must be going through her mind. For the first time in all the madness, the thought of my father's pain, of Fiona's plight, was too much. Tears welled up in my eyes. What could I do for either of them? For myself?

My arm throbbed again. My vision shifted; suddenly I could see that other world again. Several fetches were gathered in front of me, pointing and laughing at my suffering.

I couldn't stand it. I bellowed, kicking out at them, my legs going right through their bodies. This only made them cackle harder. I chased them until my lungs felt like they would burst. The fetches vanished with a hissing noise. Bad luck. That's all they were. Bad luck on four legs. Another sign that I was doomed.

Something reflected from the floor a few feet in front of me. I walked ahead to where I'd seen the flash. I found the object: it was small, round, and metallic.

It was the dollar coin. Whether on purpose or by accident, Fiona had dropped it. Maybe my luck was changing.

I pocketed the coin. At least I knew I was going the right way.

A slight breeze brushed my face, carrying the scent of fresher air. I was closer to freedom than I'd thought.

I staggered ahead. A hundred yards. Two hundred. The cave ended abruptly and I found myself on the edge of a cliff that dropped eighty feet to the churning ocean. Night had fallen while I was under the earth; a full moon peered between clouds, casting pale light. To one side of the cave was a narrow path leading up through some trees. I followed it. Branches rattled above me. The trees didn't look like any I'd ever seen. They were twisted in on themselves and grown together like each branch was trying to strangle another.

How far away were Fiona and Bolverk? And what would I do if I caught up with them?

The gale was colder now, like some forgotten winter wind had been waiting to be unleashed from the sky. My skin had turned to gooseflesh. My right forearm had swelled up and become deadened. I could barely move my fingers.

CRACK!

The noise came from behind me. Bolverk was here! Or his wolves.

I was about to run when a familiar voice snapped, "I told you to eat garlic."

27

It was Harbard, limping towards me out of the trees. A blue, glowing light surrounded him; my vision had switched to that other world.

"You don't listen very well, do you?" he said. His brow was furrowed. He was soaking wet and dirty, as if he'd been crouching out here for hours. He gripped a small axe in his hands. "If you'd eaten garlic there wouldn't be any swelling and you wouldn't be seeing what you see now. The second sight isn't meant for one so young." He ran his hands in front of my eyes and the glowing light vanished. He pushed something into my right hand. "Squeeze this."

I slowly opened my deadened fingers and saw a smooth, palm-sized stone. Runes were scratched across its middle. "What . . . what is it?"

"A piece of rune stone. Like the ones that protect my house. It is etched with *helgan*, the word that will ease all wounds. And take away second sight."

A sharp pain pierced my arm. I squeezed the rock and the ache ebbed away.

"It works!"

"Of course. Why wouldn't it?"

I felt my wrist. The bleeding had stopped.

From somewhere far ahead of us in the woods came a low thudding sound. "Where is . . ."

"The *afturganga*: the one who walks after death," Harbard said, simply. "Bolverk has gone on to complete his task." Harbard's teeth glinted in the moonlight; he looked almost savage. "My father buried him and his companions. Under stone. I should have seen the signs, that he was awake again." He grabbed my shoulder and pushed me down the path. "You will help me. We must move now, there is little time. Your friend is alive, but not for long."

I followed Harbard. He led me past tree after twisted tree; nothing seemed to have grown straight on this side of the island. A mist seeped out of cracks in the ground as if the earth was trying to cover up what was about to happen. Or was it old, malevolent spirits, forcing their way to the surface to watch? To add their evil to the night?

I shivered. Harbard stopped briefly to give me his jacket, then gruffly commanded me to keep moving.

The way grew even steeper. I used my left hand to grab at roots and small bushes and pull myself higher. Harbard moved quickly and with ease; his limp was hardly noticeable. I wasn't going to let any old man outdistance me.

We climbed, not stopping for anything. The wind had picked up again, swirling the fog around us. Pellets of rain stung my skin. We journeyed higher, step after step into the thickening gloom.

Soon a booming noise filled my ears. Deep, echoing drums laden with doom.

"He's begun!" Harbard quickened his pace, flicking mud and water all over me.

We reached the top, a small plateau covered with stones and outcroppings of rock. We crawled to the far side and peered over the edge. Below us was the small bay Fiona and I had fled in the boat.

"This is where the Mórar landed, so many lifetimes ago," Harbard said. "They climbed up onto the island and died, their bodies wasted from being at sea so long. Washed by rain, shrouded by snow. Their evil sank into the very depths of Drang."

The light of the moon penetrated the clouds, outlining everything. Tendrils of swirling mist floated above the water. There was a long rectangular rock near the edge of the bay, surrounded by waves. Torches had been fastened to each corner and were burning brightly, the flames flickering back and forth in the wind. The booming grew louder.

"Where is the sound coming from?" I asked.

"The Mórar. Bolverk's companions are in the underworld, standing on the shore of corpses, pounding the summoning drums. They are close to returning to life. That is why we can hear them so clearly."

I was silent. I couldn't comprehend what he was saying.

"Jormungand comes," Harbard said. "From the deep, they call him." The drums beat faster, heavier. "Once, many ages ago, Jormungand was a friend of my mother's people; the guardian of the island. A son of Sisutl." Harbard pointed at the rectangular rock. "The shaman would stand on that stone and speak with him. But now Bolverk has twisted the guardian, turned him into something vile. He taught the great serpent to eat the flesh of animals, not the green plants of the mother. Jormungand has refused to feed on your father. Bolverk hopes to lure him here and offer him smaller human flesh."

A motion attracted my eye: gray robes flapping in the wind. Bolverk was crossing the bay, dragging Fiona towards the rock. At the very sight of him Harbard sucked in his breath. So did I.

Both Fiona's wrists were bound together by ropes. Bolverk yanked her ahead, wading easily through the water. He pushed her down on the stone, but she twisted out of his arms, landing with a splash. She was going to get away!

Fiona kicked desperately through the waves, but she couldn't use her arms. She sank below the surface. Bolverk waited, unconcerned. I opened my mouth to yell at him, to get him to save her. Harbard gripped my arm, silencing me. A few moments later Bolverk reached into the water and pulled her into the air. She gasped, gulping in air.

Before she could get her bearings, he roped Fiona to two posts, tying her tightly so her arms were stretched out and she was forced to stand. Bolverk backed away.

Fiona struggled but the bonds were too tight. The waves crashed up against the stone below her.

Harbard got to his knees. "I must go down there."

"I'll go, too."

"No. You'd be little help. I must do this; my father taught me how to deal with him. But up here . . ." Harbard seemed to smile slightly, ". . . yes, up here you will give me a big hand."

He reached into a holster on his belt, pulled out a pistol with a thick barrel.

"A gun? Do you expect me to shoot someone?"

"No. Bullets would mean little to Bolverk. This is a flare

gun." I should have guessed by the size of the barrel. "Only one flare remains. I will signal and you'll fire it above Bolverk's head."

He handed the gun to me. It felt heavy and old like a swash-buckler's pistol. I searched for a safety.

"Careful," Harbard whispered, "it has a hair trigger."

Then he started looking for a way down. A second later he was gone.

28

I settled into place, holding the flare gun with my left hand. Despite the healing stone my right arm was still useless, so I was worried about my aim.

Bolverk stood on the beach, his arms spread wide. The wind blew his garments into long, flowing ribbons that trailed behind him. He banged his staff in time with the drums. Waves washed in, splashing him.

Lightning sliced jaggedly through the sky, hitting a stone about thirty feet from me and pulverizing it. The heat seared my skin, left me momentarily blinded. Acrid smoke filled my nostrils.

I blinked. My sight returned and I could see Bolverk in the same place, chanting. The drums grew louder, more hypnotic; a beat as ancient as the earth. I found myself wanting to hit the drums, to stand and let the rhythms move through me. The sounds spoke of a past that lay half forgotten inside my heart, as if I had once believed in all the old gods and spirits, believed the world had been formed in burning ice and biting flame.

For a split second my vision slipped back into that other

place. Four hulking, glimmering figures were at the edge of the beach, pounding on transparent drums. Fetches danced around them, darting in and out.

The stone in my hand pulsed and the vision ended. At the same moment a massive form broke through the water, then disappeared. I stared at the shifting waves, now growing even higher.

Hurry, I thought, urging Harbard on, hurry!

I glimpsed a movement on the beach. Harbard had made his way to the bottom and was creeping around huge stones. A light rain drizzled down.

Another flash of lightning created two shadows above him on one of the rocks. Four-legged shapes with huge jaws. The wolves!

Harbard moved into the open, unaware he was being followed.

I yelled, but the drums and the crashing of waves were too loud. The wolves loped along, closing in for the kill.

"Harbard!" I screamed again. The wind ripped the words from my mouth.

I pointed the gun at the wolves. My hand was shaking and slick with sweat. I used my right hand to steady my aim. Pulled the trigger.

Click.

I pulled again. *Click. Click.* It wouldn't fire. The flare gun had become too wet or maybe it was too old. I tried to see how to open it, but in the dark it was impossible. I held the gun out once more and pulled the trigger all the way back.

SSST-POOM. A red flare fell like a comet, making Harbard turn. The light revealed the wolves leaping through the air. Harbard threw up his arms. Then darkness.

I dropped the gun, pushed myself up, and ran as quickly as I could across the slippery rocks, searching for a path that would lead down along the rock walls. I searched desperately, squinting my eyes in the dark, and finally I discovered the narrowest of trails. I shoved the healing stone in my pocket and moved as quickly as I could along the path. The occasional bolt of lightning lit my way.

I only looked down once and that was enough. I was at least forty feet up from the ground. If I fell I'd be nothing but a pile of broken bones, to be feasted on by crows and flies.

I worked my way over rocks, bumping my side against the cliff. I slipped and grabbed at an outcropping to save my skin. The path grew narrower still. I clung to the wall, but my wounded arm was nearly useless. The rocks were sharp and slick. It was taking too long. Somewhere below me I heard the growl of a wolf. Harbard would be torn to pieces by now.

I quickened my pace.

A few feet ahead I could see the path widen. But first I had to cross a section just inches wide. I took a step. Then another. The ledge crumpled underneath my feet.

I plummeted down, arms flailing, looking for something to grab. Lightning flashed, revealing twisted, snake-like roots. I latched onto one, stopping my fall.

A second bolt of lightning revealed a single tree that had somehow clung to the side of the cliff for years, defying the rock, the lack of soil, defying the wind and rain that had pounded on it. The tree had worked its roots into the cliff wall and somehow found nourishment.

I held onto it tightly with my left hand, wrapping myself in the roots. Warmth returned to my limbs. The wind wasn't as harsh here. I had the odd feeling that the tree was lending me its strength. And then I remembered the dream my sister had told me about, the one with the Yggdrasill tree.

I felt her presence near me. I closed my eyes and thought I could hear my ancestors—my Grandma Gunnora, Grettir, Great-Grandfather—all urging me on, whispering that I had work to do, my family's work passed down from generation to generation. I started to lower myself using the tree roots as ropes. Finally I reached the ground and could look across the bay.

The drums had stopped. One of the torches was out, the other flickered madly in the gale. Bolverk was gone. All I could see was Fiona on the rock, struggling against her bonds.

A few steps later I was splashing through six inches of water. The ocean was making its way, wave by wave, into the bay.

Closer, I heard the snarl of wolves. I spotted the outcropping where I thought Harbard was and hurried towards it.

I rounded the rock and there was Harbard, still very much alive, but cornered by two wolves.

29

The gray wolf was limping. It looked like Harbard had injured it with the small axe he gripped in his hand. But the wolves had done their own share of damage. Harbard's right arm was hanging down, blood dripping from a wound that had been torn above his elbow. He had a crazed look on his face as if the gash had turned him into a berserker.

The limping wolf moved to one side of Harbard, the black one to the other. Their hides had been stripped here and there, were flapping loose, revealing white ribs. The gray wolf had no fur on its legs at all, only white bones, clicking and clacking with each movement. Harbard moved back and forth, facing one wolf, then the other, but he couldn't change position fast enough.

The black wolf leapt, its mouth wide. Harbard spun and sank the axe into its skull. It fell dead, seemed to clatter into pieces. I was already running to Harbard when the gray wolf plowed into his back. Its jaws clamped down on his shoulder. He screamed and tried to roll away but the wolf had him. I jumped the final yard and tackled it, my head smashing into its ribs. I grabbed the wolf's fur, tried to pull it off Harbard, but bits of flesh and bone came loose in my hands. The pieces of flesh were cold as ice.

My ploy succeeded too well. The beast turned on me, fangs bared. Its tongue was black and dry. It dived for my throat and I fell back, pushing at it. Trying to keep it away.

Steel flashed. Harbard's axe was buried in the wolf's skull. It staggered, let out a low moan, then the red light of its eyes faded. It collapsed on top of me. I shoved the thing off me and rolled away from the revolting stench of the carcass.

Harbard was lying on his back, bleeding from the shoulder. "A bad throw," he said, his voice grave. "I was aiming to chop his head right off. But I *was* using the wrong arm."

A loud, grinding noise came from the water, like one of the cliffs had shifted closer. An unearthly moaning shook me to the core.

Water had splashed in and now reached up to Harbard's chest. He looked half awake. I got up and dragged him to higher ground. His eyes were rolling around in their sockets and he was moving in and out of consciousness. Without warning, he grabbed me, saying, "Ragnarok comes. The earth will be consumed by venom and fire," then closed his eyes.

I left him, pulled the axe out of the wolf's skull. Its body had mostly dissolved and was being bumped towards shore by waves. I was surprised how calm I was, as if I was seeing the most natural sight in the world.

The moaning was louder now. A sound that seemed to signal the end of the world.

I heard a cry for help. I dashed towards Fiona.

30

The water grew deeper, making it harder and harder to run. Bolverk was somewhere out of sight. I charged towards the stone, waded to the front of it, and Fiona finally saw me. "Michael," she said, her voice hoarse, "I've had a very bad day."

"Hold still. I'll cut you loose."

I chopped at the rope, but it was thick and made of tightly bound hair. And I was handicapped, having to use my left hand. "Hit it again!" Fiona shouted. I struck twice more and the binding snapped. Fiona slipped to one side, then steadied herself.

"Take the axe," I yelled.

That familiar blaze entered her eyes. She grabbed the axe from me and whacked the rope again and again. The blade refused to bite. I climbed onto the stone, trying to find a way to help. A blast of wind nearly knocked us into the water.

Then, just as Fiona began to make headway, she stopped in mid-swing. "It's here," she whispered.

I glanced up as a glistening, vast shape crashed down into the waves. Part of the stone suddenly gave way. I slipped. The only thing that stopped me from rolling into the water was my grip on Fiona.

I pulled myself back and we scrambled to our feet. "I dropped the axe!" Fiona struggled against the remaining rope. "Help me untie this!"

I reached towards the rope, yanking at the knots. They were too tight and wet. We struggled together, trying to loosen them. Finally, success, and we both pulled. Fiona's arm was freed.

A hard object whacked my shoulder and I froze. Something blurred past my eye, struck Fiona and she, too, stood stiff.

Bolverk had arrived, his staff crackling with blue energy.

31

"*Infidel!*" Bolverk whispered. "*Ragnarok is here! You cannot stop the unstoppable.*"

I still couldn't move. The wind hit me full force, but my feet were glued to the stone.

Bolverk stood beside us. "*Ormr,*" he bellowed. Words as ancient as all my ancestors, words that described nightmares. "*Midgardsormer.*"

A roaring sound from the darkness answered him. The water began to bubble.

"*Ormr,*" he spoke again.

Lightning slashed the sky, its light revealing a dark green form, moving towards us like a giant wave. A long snout floated in the air, the head rising higher and higher. Serpentine eyes the size of shields glared down, two glowing pools of rage. This was a face even Thor would fear.

"*Jormungand,*" Bolverk whispered, "*son of Loki, accept these gifts.*"

He bowed and stepped back a few yards, leaving Fiona and me frozen there.

The serpent's eyes flickered at us. This was the god of the island. Once a guardian of men, now an eater of flesh. It hovered like it was about to strike.

Sarah's voice drifted into my head. *I dreamed you will use a stone to shake the roots of the world tree.* I didn't know if it was her or a memory of her, but the words were clear.

What could it mean? What stone?

The feeling that my twin sister was somewhere nearby calmed me, loosened my arms. The stone, I thought, the healing stone. I slowly pushed my right hand into my pocket and pulled out the stone.

Jormungand watched me, breath hissing between his fangs.

But what was I to do? Throw it? Would that drive him away? I thought of Thor, how he had slain the serpent with his hammer, then had fallen down dead from the venom. Pitting anger against anger. Steel against tooth and coil. Was that the way to victory? How do you fight something so enormous it could swallow the sky?

I lifted the stone above my head, showing it to the snake. He glared and hissed again.

Anger couldn't be at the root of the world. Something always rose up again, always came back. Even in the Norse myths, when all the battles were fought and most of the gods dead, a new world rose from the old. A world of light and warmth. Of life. Grandpa had told me all about it.

"Friend," I spoke, my voice cutting through the wind. "You were once our friend."

I lowered my arm.

Jormungand blinked. He dropped his head slightly.

"*No!*" Bolverk cried. The serpent looked his way.

Bolverk was silent now. He lifted his staff, waved it slowly back and forth. Jormungand mirrored the movement, his head drifting from side to side. Finally, Bolverk held the staff still.

"Midgardsormer," he whispered.

Jormungand snapped open his cavernous month, displaying two fangs, dripping venom.

He lunged at us.

32

The stone platform disintegrated beneath our feet. Fiona and I were thrown into the water, the weight of the beast knocking us farther down. Panicking, I kicked up with all my strength until I broke the surface. I could hear Fiona floundering through the waves beside me.

Just as I found my footing a hand grabbed me from behind and forced me back under. I slipped to one side and struggled up again. Bolverk clamped onto my shoulder. I hammered at him and his hood fell away, revealing his raging face, all white and skull-like, one socket empty, the other holding a large, glowering eye. His mouth was uncannily big and thick-lipped.

I pushed at Bolverk, then punched my fist into his eye and broke free, making him drop his staff.

"Meddling infidel!" Bolverk latched onto me again, digging his thin fingers into my neck. He lifted his free arm.

Jormungand rose up behind him, silently. Higher and higher, water dripping from his scales.

Bolverk seemed to sense the serpent's presence; he lowered

his arm, released me, and faced Jormungand. He began backing slowly away.

Jormungand dived, his mouth gaping, and Bolverk screamed. Then was suddenly silent.

A massive wave knocked me to one side. The last thing I heard was Fiona yelling, "Michael!" Then I was under the water again, kicking against the pull of an undertow. Deeper. Deeper. Down to the bottom.

But something bumped me, forcing me through the water with one big whoosh. Lifting me up above the waves, leaving me near the shore. Fiona found me and we swam back together. I led us to the end of the bay, splashing through shallow water, finally climbing onto the rocks.

An immense and majestic serpentine shape rose in the distance, glinting with silver moonlight. I could just make out its shining eyes and a snake's snout before it dived gracefully into the ocean and was gone.

33

Together, Fiona and I had the strength to help Harbard to the top of the cliffs. He was in much better shape than when I'd left him, though his arm seemed broken. "It's just a scratch," he said. He guided us to where he'd left his ferry.

He wouldn't let us drive. He planted his feet, grabbed the wheel tightly, and piloted us through the water. The sun was just beginning to rise, bringing color back to the world.

When we reached Harbard's cabin, his dog greeted us at the door.

"You don't have to fear him," Harbard said. "Surt knows the difference between good and bad. Unlike many people."

The dog stepped aside and we went in. I was surprised to find Harbard had a TV and a police radio.

Soon we had the Mounties on the line and were told to wait right where we were. They informed me my father had been taken on a fisherman's boat to a hospital in Nanaimo before the storm had completely enveloped the island. He was in intensive care, but he had come to and asked about me.

Dad was going to be alright. It took a moment for this to sink in.

Harbard kept talking about axe ages and sword ages and wind ages and wolf ages. He seemed lost in some strange world. At one point he looked me in the eyes and smiled. "Snake slayer," he said.

We had to wait for a long time. Fiona told me what it was like to be in the caves with Bolverk. We didn't talk about Jormungand or anything else after that. It seemed too soon. She eventually fell asleep, but I found that even a snooze was an impossible prospect. There was too much to think about. I couldn't slow my brain down. I kept hearing Bolverk's final scream and seeing the serpent disappear beneath the waters.

The bite on my arm had nearly disappeared, though it still ached.

Hours later several RCMP officers showed up, along with Ranger Morrison. "You're a brave kid," was all he said to me. Then a gray-haired Mountie named Sergeant Olson introduced himself. He and another officer asked me questions and I answered as best as I could, telling them what I thought they would believe. When they were finished, the sergeant shook my hand, which still hurt. He said a ride to the hospital was waiting for me in Port Hardy. Then he left to search for any sign of Bolverk.

I found out later that the Mounties discovered the bones of a man in the caves. They used dental records to prove it was Siroiska. The coroner said he'd been dead for over a year. Days later a huge human skull with one extraordinarily large eye socket washed up on shore. It dissolved in a Mountie's hands.

About twenty minutes after the police left, Harbard got up and convinced us that only he could get us home across the water. "I won't even charge you," he said.

Soon we were in his ferry, cutting through the waves. I sat beside Fiona at the back. I looked out nervously at the ocean.

"Jormungand sleeps now," Harbard whispered. He must have caught my glance. "We'll make it to the other side."

He was right. The water was calm and easy, the ferry cutting a smooth path through it. Harbard's prediction about my father and me had turned out to be right. Only one of us did return with him. I was just thankful it hadn't been any worse for Dad.

We landed at a small dock on an island. Cabins were set on a hill, looking down on us. It seemed too real, too perfect, after being on Drang. Fiona got off and I climbed onto the pier with her.

"Well, I guess this is it," she said. "Good-bye, so long, and all that. I hope you'll drop me a note sometime, let me know whether you've made it home."

"You know, I learned something these past few days," I said.

"What?"

"That if I can make friends with you, I can probably make friends with anyone."

She grinned, showing her dimples.

Then I did something that completely surprised me. I kissed her. Quickly. On the lips. I stepped back.

Fiona stood there, stunned. For the first time since I'd met her, she was speechless.

"Good-bye," I said. "You'll have to try a holiday in Missouri sometime. It's nowhere near as weird."

She nodded but didn't answer.

I got back in the ferry and Harbard started to slowly pull away. Fiona was still staring at me. Finally she pointed and her shout drifted across the water. "I'll write you!" she promised, "as long as you don't tell me any more Norse stories!"

I must have smiled for the rest of the trip. Before I knew it we'd landed at Port Hardy and I stepped onto the dock with a great sigh of relief.

Harbard grinned. For him there were no long farewells. "Good-bye, Thor," he said. Then he was heading away, as if it had been just another day's work.

A tall, middle-aged Mountie was waiting at the end of the pier. He led me to his car and we headed to the hospital to see my father.

Dad would finally have the perfect chapter to end his book.

THE LOKI WOLF

THE LONG WOLF

This novel is dedicated to my brothers David, Ken, and Brett, who have all supported me in their own ways. And no, none of the characters are based on any of them.

And I'd also like to dedicate this novel to all the Icelanders out there. Thanks for letting me borrow bits and pieces of your wonderful stories and heritage. I may have inadvertently changed the schedule for the Nordurleid *bus to Hvammstangi and the Icelandair flight from New York to Keflavík. They will be running at the proper time from this moment forward.*

I would like to thank my wife, Brenda Baker, for her editing skills and my publisher, Bob Tyrrell, for the same. I also want to give a special tip o' the Viking helmet to Jón Jónson for reading a rough draft of this novel and to Brynjólfur Gíslason, who was kind enough to tell me a little about his hometown of Hvammstangi. And I perhaps owe the most to Snorri Sturluson (1179–1241), who was an Icelandic historian, poet, and chieftain best known for his Prose Edda, *a prose account of the Norse myths. Without his version of the myths, these books wouldn't have been possible.*

1

One week before my trip to Iceland, I died in my sleep.

Not a real death, of course. Very few healthy, fifteen-year-old girls pass away in their beds. No, I died inside one of my own nightmares. In the dream I fell from a great height—a cliff or a tower—and every bone in my body shattered when I landed on a pile of pointed stones. I awoke immediately, lying in a chilling pool of my own sweat. I didn't sleep again for hours.

The next night I drowned in a wild ocean, the undertow pulling me down until water filled my lungs. Or was it the undertow? Did something—a giant sea serpent perhaps—have a grip on me? The last thing I saw before waking was the surface getting farther and farther away.

On the third night the worst nightmare—the very worst—invaded my mind. I was running barefoot through a deserted town in a strange country, the Northern Lights drifting through the sky. Soon the town disappeared and I sprinted across a rocky plateau, gasping for breath, my long red hair flowing in the air. Loping behind me was a gigantic wolf, its jaws snapping together and tearing off pieces of my flesh. There was no blood. No pain. But bit by bit he swallowed chunks of my body until nothing of Angela Laxness remained.

I awakened, sweating and cold. I had somehow knocked over my night table, breaking my lamp. The noise was enough to bring my mother to my bedside. I couldn't explain to her what had frightened me. In fact I could barely speak; I was too busy trying to catch my breath. She held me like she used to when I was a kid, whispering, "It's going to be alright, Angie. It's just a nightmare. You're safe. You're safe."

I dreamed of the giant wolf the next three nights in a row. My parents believed these nightmares were happening because I was worried about my upcoming trip to Iceland. Though I've traveled to Canada and to a few of the states near our acreage in North Dakota, I've never been across the ocean. "It's just your subconscious working through the new experience," my father said. "It's nothing to be ashamed of. You'll be safe. You'll be with your grandfather and your cousins. You'll get to see the farm our family came from."

I nodded and said, "Yes, you're right, I'll be safe."

My parents weren't going along because this trip was Grandpa's Christmas gift to the grandchildren and he wanted to show us the sights on his own. I'm sure Mom and Dad had considered calling the whole thing off in the last few days. I didn't know if I'd be that upset about missing it.

You see, I'd had nightmares like this a few weeks after my younger brother, Andrew, died in a car accident. He was traveling with our neighbors to a hockey game and they were rear-ended by a large truck. It was a miracle anyone survived. Our neighbors did. My brother didn't.

It all happened five years ago, when I was ten. I had a recurring nightmare where the sides of a car were closing in on me until I couldn't breathe. Nothing anyone said or did could make the nightmares go away. Then one night Andrew appeared in my room, looking the same as he had in life, medium-length blonde hair, a warm smile. Except he was . . . ethereal. I think that's the right word. He touched my shoulder and whispered, *"Just let it go, Angie. There was nothing you could do. Let it all go."* Then he was gone. I haven't had a nightmare since.

Until the wolf came loping into my dreams.

My parents told my grandfather all about this phantom wolf. Grandpa Thursten is my mother's father and he's Icelandic to the core. He lives in Canada just outside Gimli, Manitoba, the site of the largest Icelandic settlement in North America. He knows every story about ghosts, dreams, Norse gods, and wolves.

The night before we were supposed to leave on our trip, Grandpa phoned and quietly grilled me with questions: *Do you remember the very start of the dream? Describe the wolf. Was it gray? Why were you barefoot? Were there stars or a moon in the sky?* I answered everything with as much detail as I could. Then he was quiet.

"What are they about, Afi?" I said into the receiver. *Afi* is Icelandic for grandfather. We grandchildren rarely use it—only when we want to let him know that we're serious.

"You'll be alright," he said, "I promise. You will be alright."

2

I am telling this in the wrong order.

I should have started out by saying who my ancestors were and who I am. That's how all the Icelandic sagas begin—I know this because I've read most of the ones in my mom's collection. And all the Norse myths too. They always start with "so and so" was related to "so and so" and then "so and so" got in a boat and killed "so and so." And they end by telling you who "so and so's" offspring was. In Iceland it's important to know who you're related to.

That must be why Mom spends her spare time researching our family tree. She and Dad are constantly trying to find out more about who we're descended from, what deeds defined their lives, what land they lived on, and how all of this made us into who we are today.

They even know which bones belong to which side of the family. "Our past is written all across your face, Angie," Mom has often explained. "Your green eyes come from your father's side, your thin cheekbones are just like your grandma's, you can thank your Grandpa Thursten for making you so thin—"

"—and your red hair is a freak of nature," Dad would always interject. They never did explain why I ended up being left-handed, even though they were both righties.

Then they would tell me stories about the "so and so's" we're descended from. Inevitably the lecture would end up with a story about Grettir Asmundson, a hero who lived in Iceland many years ago. He was known for being big and mean and for beating up on a few ghosts and undead monsters. He was also an outlaw, but Mom and Dad usually glossed over that part.

Whenever my parents were done their lesson in genetics, Mom would sum it all up with: "If you don't know your own past, you can't know who you are."

So I will begin by saying, I am Angela Laxness, the daughter of Deidre and Jón Laxness of North Dakota. Through my mother's side of the family, the Asmundsons, I can trace our ancestry back to Grettir the Strong, a famous hero.

It's a big deal in Iceland.

3

The worst place to put someone with a fear of heights is a window seat in a jet that's about to climb 30,000 feet above the Atlantic Ocean. Yet that's the seat Grandpa Thursten gave me. "It's better to face your fears," he whispered, his lips curling into a knowing smile.

Easy for him to say. He fell asleep before we'd even left the tarmac at New York. He missed me digging my fingers into the armrests until I broke one of my nails. It would take a couple weeks to grow it back to the right length. I held my breath as the weight of the Boeing's momentum crushed against my chest and we took to the air.

A hand gently touched my shoulder and I tensed up.

"Take a deep breath," my cousin Sarah whispered from behind me. Grandpa's seat was back and Sarah was able to squeeze her hand through the open space. I'd admitted to her earlier that I wasn't looking forward to hurtling through the sky at hundreds of miles an hour. "Breathe in, then out. Everything will feel a lot better once you've got some air in your lungs."

I heard Michael, Sarah's twin brother, chuckle, and I felt a sudden anger. He was always being the smart aleck. I turned to tell him to shut up, but the jet engines kicked into overdrive, forcing me against the seat.

I eventually did take a breath. And another. And another. Until I thought I'd hyperventilate. I'd braided my hair because my mom said it would be easier to travel without it flapping all over the place—I was sure the braids had loosened and individual hairs were sticking up like porcupine quills. So much for looking sharp on my first trip to Iceland.

After several hours of flying I actually began to get comfortable, staring out the jet's window into the early morning darkness, trying to spot land. We'd been served a meager breakfast of bagels and slightly warm scrambled eggs. I was surprised my stomach wasn't upset. I had control of my breathing, my heartbeat had slowed, and I'd unclamped my hands. Maybe Grandpa was right; it *was* better to face your fears. At least I could look out at the wing and see that it was still attached.

"Have you had any more skull guests?" Grandfather asked.

Two seconds ago he was asleep in his seat, snoring softly. Now he was wide awake, his deep blue eyes staring into mine. He had a rather big, slightly crooked nose and he looked like each lesson he'd learned in his lifetime had given him a wrinkle—and there were lots of wrinkles. His thick white hair was styled like Einstein's.

"Skull guests?"

"Dreams, I mean. They used to be called skull guests in the sagas, because they came and stayed—like bad guests. Did any more of them drop by?"

"No. Not since we talked on the phone. I don't remember

having any dreams at all last night." And it was true. The big, bad wolf had left me alone, off loping through someone else's nightmare, I'd supposed, looking for another Little Red-headed Riding Hood.

"Good. Perhaps they meant nothing, then."

Perhaps? What did that mean?

"They did get me thinking, though," Grandpa continued, "about Thorgeir Tree-Foot."

"Who?" Michael asked. Grandpa's seat was leaning far enough back that Michael and Sarah were able to peek at us, their blue eyes glittering, white-toothed grins splitting their thin faces. We were the same age, they were my best friends, and we had a lot in common, but I have to admit there was something a little odd about them. First, it kind of freaked me out how similar they were—dark hair, pale skin, with their heads absolutely crammed full of old Norse myths and legends. They weren't identical twins, but every time I saw them they appeared more and more alike.

Despite that, I was happy to spend some quality time with them. They lived in Missouri and we hadn't had much of a chance to talk in the last year or so.

Grandpa narrowed his bushy eyebrows. "So none of your parents has ever mentioned my dad, Thorgeir Tree-Foot?"

"Our great-grandfather was called Tree-Foot?" Michael asked, that typical smart-aleck tone in his voice. "So that's why I'm always tripping over my own feet."

"That's from not being able to chew gum and walk at the same time," Grandpa Thursten quipped. He waited for a come-back, received none, so he carried on. "Do you know how he got that name?"

This was starting to sound familiar to me. Mom had told me this story when I was younger, but I couldn't remember any of the details. "No," I admitted.

"Your great-granddad had dreams just like yours, Angie. Potent dreams. Every night for a fortnight he dreamed he was going to lose his leg. It would get caught in a trap. Or he'd be building a fence and his axe would slip and sever his leg below the knee. Or, and he always said this was the most terrifying dream, a great serpent came from beneath the water and bit it off, leaving him in the middle of the ocean, trying to swim home with only one leg. The outcome of the nightmares was always the same: he would awake covered with sweat and reach down to be sure his leg was still there."

I shuddered. The passengers across the aisle—an old guy in a brown beret and his middle-aged wife—were glancing our way now, which inspired Grandpa to raise his voice even louder. He'd use the intercom if the stewardess would let him.

"One day my father had to take a trip from Bjarg to Hof, twenty miles or so across some of the most treacherous ravines in north-central Iceland. It's not far from Thordy's farm, where we'll be staying." Thordy was one of Grandpa's nephews. I recalled Mom and Dad telling me some sad story about his wife dying, but I'd have to ask Grandpa about it later. He was too deep into this story already. "Make no mistake, the homeland is a place of beauty and death. One moment you'll be admiring a breathtaking waterfall; the next you'll be at the bottom of a cliff, watching the ravens descend to pick your bones. Your great-granddad was only nineteen at the time, unmarried, and searching for summer work. He'd heard that a sheep farmer was looking for help, so he hiked through the mountains, whispering the ancient rhymes his father had taught him, lines to ward away the specters and the mischievous little Huldu Folk. He had three shiny pebbles in his pocket to leave as an offering at any cairns he passed, because he believed every ghost in Iceland desires some kind of tribute."

Grandpa was starting to really wind himself up now. He even glanced over at the couple across from us to be sure they were still listening. My heart started going a little faster in anticipation.

"But the journey was longer than my father thought it would be and it was getting close to nightfall. Soon he was alone on one of the passes, far from any crofts. All he heard was the *tick tack* of his walking stick on the path. A storm gathered overhead.

"Soft footsteps echoed off the rock walls. Then came a sound of sniffing and a low, unearthly moan that made the hairs on the back of my father's neck stand up. He quickened his pace, knowing some evil thing was behind him. He muttered all the names of the undead in hopes of dispelling his pursuer. He wasn't afraid of anyone who was alive, but he knew the ghosts of this pass and the *Uppvakningur*—those who walk after death—were to be feared."

I was holding my breath. I let it out between clenched teeth. Ever since I was a child, Grandpa had been telling us these stories about men who walk after death and monsters thirsting for blood. Every year I thought I'd outgrown them and every year I discovered I was wrong.

"A rock fell over behind him, the breathing became louder, and he began to run across the plateau, believing he was fleeing for his very life. The paths were hard to see in the darkness and he lost his way. His pursuer growled to one side of him, so Father went the opposite direction. A few minutes later he could hear someone scrambling over stones behind him. Father knew he was being herded like an animal to the slaughter. Finally the plateau narrowed and he was trapped, with a thin ledge as his only escape. He hugged close to the cliff, shuffling as quickly as he could along the path—his eyes set on freedom and safety ahead. Something was thrashing about on the plateau behind him, but he didn't dare look back.

"When he was halfway across, there was a sudden rumble above. A small boulder hit him, then another, and finally a hail of rocks and debris knocked him off the path. He rolled and tumbled down, end over end, coming to a stop at the bottom of a ravine. A large boulder had crushed his right leg to the earth, pinning him below the knee.

"He looked around. Bleached skeletons of animals surrounded him, their bones broken in two as if a carnivore had been sucking on the marrow. Beside them were three human skulls, their brainpans cracked open.

"He heard a rustling sound followed by a heavy-throated roar. The noise came from the far end of the ravine. To his horror a black bear slouched towards him, slaver dripping from its huge jaws. He had never seen a bear before and he knew none had ever roamed Iceland. And yet here was one of the beasts. He tried to fend it off by throwing rocks but it descended without hesitation, clamping its teeth into his shoulder. Father beat at it with his hands, yelled with all his might But it snarled and shook him back and forth, playing with him as if he were nothing more than a doll.

"It wasn't until the bear had dragged him partway out from under the rock that he was able to grab the nearest half of his walking stick. It was thick, and the broken end was as sharp as a stake. He used all of his strength to jab it into the side of his attacker, through the thick hide and between the ribs, aiming for the heart.

"The bear screamed, a noise that sounded almost human. For the rest of his life my father heard that cry echoing in his nightmares. The bear halted and glared down at him with raging eyes. It opened its massive jaws, took a step forward, then fell over to one side and lay still. It moaned, sucked in its last breath, then slowly turned into a man, a stick embedded in his chest.

"Your great-grandfather dragged himself out from under the rock and crawled to the end of the ravine and upwards. His right leg was useless. It took all of his will to climb higher, repeating an old saying over and over in his head to keep himself going: *Cattle die, kinsmen die, I myself shall die, but there is one thing I know never dies: the reputation we leave behind at our death.* He made it to a wider trail and was discovered a few hours later by a group of traders heading for a spring market in Reykir. When they brought him back home the doctor had to remove his leg. They replaced it with a wooden stump. And that was how your great-grandfather got the name Thorgeir Tree-Foot and how his nightmares about losing his leg came true."

Grandpa settled back in his seat, a satisfied look on his face. Was this supposed to make me feel better about my own nightmares? I leaned back against my seat and tried to relax. The old man across the aisle was still gripping the armrest. I hoped Grandpa hadn't given him a heart attack.

"What did that saying mean?" I asked. "It sounded kind of morbid."

"My father had no desire to be known as the man who died alone in a chasm. He wanted people to remember him as someone who never gave up."

"What did he think attacked him?" Sarah asked. I was surprised at the serious tone of her voice.

The jet hit some turbulence, rattled for a moment. Were we in trouble? Where was the life preserver? Under the seat? I tried to remember the stewardess's emergency instructions.

Grandpa waited patiently until the shaking stopped and the plane was once again steady in the air.

"Your great-grandfather came from a different time than you or I. He believed the bear was really a shape-shifter, a son of Loki. My father had more superstitions than priests have prayers."

"What's a son of Loki?" Michael asked. "I haven't heard about them."

"Well, they were these—uh—mythical creatures who could make themselves look like you or me, or shift into an animal like a bear or a—" The pilot announced that we were about to land. "It's a long story, it has to do with Loki and a giant's curse and how Iceland was created. I'll have to tell you later."

The engine slowed and the Icelandair Boeing 767 began to descend. My stomach lurched. I hoped the pilot was still in control. I looked out at a hazy, silvery-misted darkness.

Below us, glittering white and black like an uncut diamond, was Iceland. The country of my ancestors.

4

The landing was anything but smooth: the plane shuddered and hopped down the runway, tires squealing like banshees. The high-pitched metallic sound reminded me of my brother's accident—of what he would have heard in those final moments. I closed my eyes, which just made things worse. Time stretched out so it felt like an hour before we ground to a halt. My ears were ringing, my breath shallow. I unclenched one hand from the armrest and the other from Grandpa's leg.

"Thanks for letting go," he said. "I couldn't feel my toes anymore."

I was slipping into a strange state of jittery confusion. Grandpa's words echoed around me and I couldn't hear anything else. The other passengers moved in slow motion, pulling their luggage from the upper compartments, putting on their winter jackets.

I slowly sucked in some air, then let it out through my nostrils. That seemed to help. I did it again, swallowed, and my ears popped, releasing a flood of muttering and rustling sounds. People were moving at a normal speed. I stared out the window.

It was still dark. We had pulled up beside a rather odd-looking building that could have been mistaken for a large, modern church. It was called the Leifur Eiríksson Airport.

"Are you coming?" Grandpa asked. "Or you gonna take the plane home again?"

"I—I'm coming." I gathered enough of my wits to grab my handbag and get my jacket from the upper compartment. The jacket was still folded carefully and I was glad to see there weren't any wrinkles in it. I made my wobbly way towards the front of the plane, tagging along behind Michael and Sarah.

The stewardess said good-bye to us and Grandpa told her some joke in Icelandic that made her laugh and blush. He was still a charmer, even though he was older than the hills. I glanced in the cockpit and saw the co-pilot wiping sweat off his forehead. Maybe I wasn't the only one who thought it had been a rough landing.

Grandpa, done with his flirting, led us down the ramp and along the entrance tunnel. We were among the last people off the plane, so it seemed like the place was deserted.

"Did you go through a growth spurt, Michael?" I asked. He was about half a head taller than Sarah and me. "I thought we were all the same height."

Michael puffed out his chest, proud as a peacock. "It's the tall tales Grandpa's been telling—they finally had an effect on me."

"Tall tales? Is that what you think they are?" Grandpa, who was a full head taller than Michael, reached down and messed up Michael's hair, grinning like crazy. "Why you ungrateful little ingrate. If you weren't my own flesh and blood, I'd give you—"

We stepped into the terminal. Grandpa stopped, grimaced

and turned pale, dropping his shoulder bag to the floor. "Uh
. . . uhhnn . . ." he moaned. He rubbed at his chest and began
tottering like he was about to fall.

"What's wrong?" I asked. We gathered around, trying to keep
him steady. I grabbed his hand. It was cold as a chunk of ice.
Sarah and Michael held either arm. The remaining few passengers jostled by us, heading for an escalator. A young woman
stopped momentarily to see if she could help, but Grandpa just
waved her away. She walked on, glancing over her shoulder at us.

Grandpa's lips were set in a tight line, his face ashen. He was
trying to speak. He blinked slowly.

"Afi," Sarah whispered. "Afi."

His eyes momentarily closed and I thought he would pass
out, then blood came back into his cheeks and he shook his
head. He knocked three times on the wood wall. "No . . . nothing's wrong," he whispered, hoarsely, "just . . . just the land
spirits saying hello." He inhaled. "Iceland knows when one of
its own comes home. It's been too many years. That last trip
was with your grandmother, on her birthday."

"What was all the knocking for?" Michael asked.

"To get on the good side of the spirits and the Huldu Folk."

I shared a glance with Michael and Sarah. A *do-you-think-he's-
going-crazy* glance.

"Don't look so worried," Grandpa said. He laughed as he
regained his color. "It's an old habit, nothing more." He sucked
in a few more deep breaths. A minute later he gently pushed us
away. "I don't want to stand too close to you kids, your silliness
might infect me." He was definitely back to his old self.

He picked up his shoulder bag, led us through customs and
over to our luggage. Despite our protests he carried his own

suitcase, marching straight out the front doors of the airport. I slung my backpack over one shoulder, Angie and Michael grabbed their own bags, and we struggled to keep up.

Outside, the only light came from streetlamps scattered throughout the nearly empty parking lot. Oversized snowflakes drifted like moths down to the ground, covering the waiting taxis and buses. I zipped up my jacket. Sarah did the same with her parka, which was so thick and puffy she looked like a gray marshmallow. I was glad I had Thinsulate in mine. I still appeared slim but I'd stay warm. At least I hoped I would.

"What time is it?" Michael asked.

Grandpa made a big production of checking his watch. "It's about eleven in the morning. The sun should be out at noon."

"Noon!" I exclaimed. "How long does it stick around?"

"Till two in the afternoon." Grandpa held out his hand. He caught a snowflake, watched it melt in his palm. "Enjoy the sun while it's here because it won't be out at all in Hvammstangi."

"It'll be dark all the time?" Sarah asked. She and Michael had the same surprised look on their faces. They could have been mistaken for identical twins.

"Near enough to dark." Grandpa grinned, his eyes glittering. He'd obviously been waiting for this moment for a long time. "I guess I should have told you a bit more about Iceland before bringing you here. I'm getting forgetful in my old age."

What kind of crazy holiday had I signed up for?

At least it looked like the right season. Snow glistened from the surrounding pavement and buildings. A Christmas tree, lit by multicolored lights, stood near the front of the airport.

It would be kind of weird not to have my parents around on Christmas day. And to be celebrating hours before them. Mom had given me some gift money, which I planned to spend on an Icelandic sweater. For the first time it dawned on me that they would be on their own Christmas morning. I wouldn't be waking up and walking down the stairs to see what was under the tree. Mom and Dad would be alone, with both of their children gone.

I felt my eyes water.

"The snow will melt in a day or two," Grandpa predicted. "Then it'll start to rain."

"Rain?" Michael asked. "Is this gonna be a wet Christmas?"

"It's the warm water currents that keep ol' Iceland heated up. Did I mention the wind'll probably blow most of the time too?"

More good news, I thought. Was there no end to the surprises?

Grandpa waved his hand and a taxi pulled up. Soon we were heading to Reykjavík, the capital. The sky had grown brighter, though I had yet to see the familiar sun. We sped down the road, Sarah and Michael pointing when we spotted the ocean. The rocky land was a bleak and almost sinister picture, with mountains looming in the distance. "It's so barren," I whispered. "It's like winter on the moon."

"NASA used to practice moon landings in Iceland," Sarah explained. She was sitting in the middle seat, squished between Michael and me. "It was formed by volcanoes and continental drift. Even the ice ages couldn't put a stop to the volcanoes."

"When did you get so smart?" Michael poked her in the ribs. "You weren't smart a few days ago. Even a few seconds ago."

Sarah held up a travel booklet, then used it as a shield against further attacks. "It's all in here."

"If we have time," Grandpa said from the front seat, "I'll take you to the largest volcano, Mount Hekla. In the Middle Ages they believed it was one of the vents of hell itself."

"Sounds like a hot place to go," I quipped.

"Please, Angie, I can only handle one smart mouth at a time," Grandpa said, pointing towards Michael. The twins laughed in unison.

We passed a few cottages and larger homes, then crossed a bridge, turned a corner, and there was Reykjavík neatly laid out before us. The city looked small and tidy, like we'd stumbled on a fairy-tale town.

We drove through the outskirts, gawking at the tall houses. Some were light blue, others gray, even red. We bumped down various narrow streets and passed a number of giant churches with tall, bell-shaped spires.

"Exactly where are we going, Gramps?" Michael asked.

"To the bus depot. Thordy will be waiting for us in Hvammstangi. I'm sure he'll be glad to have some company. He's probably been pretty lonely since his wife died."

"What did she die from?" I asked. "Mom just told me she'd passed away, but didn't say what from."

Grandpa turned to face the three of us. We leaned closer. "It's really quite sad. Two summers ago Kristjanna didn't come back from an evening walk. The home croft has some really rough land up on the plateau. When I was a kid we'd lose at least one sheep a year to the cliffs. Thordy went out looking for her and was gone for days. The family and the local constable organized a search party and scoured the area. The hired man finally discovered Thordy in a cave, far back in the mountains, with his wife cradled in his arms. She was dead and he was completely distraught, moaning and rocking her as if she was just sleeping. No one knows what killed Kristjanna. There was no sign of an aneurysm or anything like that, just one tiny wound behind her left ear."

"The poor woman," Sarah said. "And poor Thordy, too."

"Yeah," I said. "Is he doing alright now?"

"He sounded okay on the phone. But that's part of the reason why we're staying there," Grandpa explained. "To keep him company."

The cab pulled to a stop in front of a rectangular, two-story building: the bus depot. People in long coats walked around. Other younger people were wearing backpacks. No one seemed to be in much of a hurry. The sky was still dark.

Grandpa paid the driver and we began lugging our luggage to the depot. I was happy I'd managed to jam all my belongings into my leather backpack. Both Sarah and Michael had their gear stuffed into two large canvas travel bags. They looked like something the military would use. Or a hockey team.

"Just wait here," Grandpa said. "I'll pick up the tickets. You can stare at the pond across the way."

5

The pond, as Grandpa had called it, was really a small lake of water across the street, guarded by a few trees. A pint-sized tower sat on one bank. Buildings were reflected in the waves in the dim light. I wondered how this land would have looked when our ancestors first arrived on their Viking boats. Somehow they had built a city from nothing, making a place of safety and warmth.

A four-passenger plane buzzed above the water and over us, so near we ducked. "The airport's right there," Michael said, pointing at a landing strip behind the bus depot. "Man, they sure pack everything close together."

A minute later Grandpa came out with a handful of tickets and led us to a red bus with white lines across its side. The name *Nordurleid* was on the front. It was about half the size of a normal bus. I set my backpack on top of the other luggage and lined up behind Michael and Sarah.

The driver was a long-armed man with a beard as thick as unraveled wool. He greeted us with two gruff words: *"Gódan dag."* We all said *hello* back to him. He took our tickets, motioned to the bus, and began throwing our luggage in the storage compartment.

Inside, there were only about five other riders, though at least fifty seats. "Better settle in," Grandpa said, "it's a long way to Hvammstangi." He paused, gave us a sly smile. "Hey, that could be a song." He began to sing to the tune of "It's a Long Way to Tipperary." *"It's a long, long way to Hvammstangi, but my heart's right there."* Grandpa bowed, then sat next to a window.

We started on our way. The wind whistled through the spaces between the sliding windows; cold drafts of air ran across my bare neck like ghostly fingers. I pulled on the window, but it was shut as far as it could go. I huddled in my jacket, hugging myself.

About ten minutes later it dawned on me how quiet we all were—which wasn't that strange for Sarah, but Michael's mouth usually ran at 200 rpm. I glanced over at him. He was staring ahead, his eyes glazed over. "You on another planet, Michael?" I asked.

"No, I'm—"

"Dreaming of Fiona," Sarah interjected.

"Shut your—" Michael began.

"What?" I cut him off. "You're still writing to her? This must be serious. Is she your true love? Your one and only? Your reason for—"

"Please, stop this soap opera!" Grandpa shook his head. "This trip will be long enough without hearing about the heart-wrenching agony of teen romance. We're about ten hours away from Hvammstangi."

"What!" Michael exclaimed.

"I'm kidding. Couple more hours should do it." Grandpa

pointed out the window. "The coast is that way. In fact we're not far from an outcropping that's sometimes called Skrymir's nose."

"Is Angie's side of the family descended from Skrymir?" Michael asked. "Is that why her nose is so big?"

"My nose isn't big!" I shouted. And it wasn't. It was petite. Maybe even too small, the Laxness nose I'd inherited from my father. "It's nowhere near the size of the Asmundson nose."

"Please, you two, stop squabbling!" Grandpa shook his head, feigning shame. "Just use those big ears you all inherited from me for listening. I'll tell you who the sons of Loki are. It has to do with how Iceland was created, not by these so-called continental drifts, but by one of the gods." He cleared his throat, a universal sign that he was about to start one of his stories. "You see, one day Loki, the trickster god, dared Thor to battle with the largest of the giants, Skrymir. He was a hundred times taller than Thor; his very shoulders held up the sky. Thor tracked him down, which wasn't hard considering the size of his tracks. He challenged Skrymir to a fight, then began swinging his mighty hammer, Mjollnir, again and again at the giant. The battle raged across all nine worlds, over mountains and lakes and valleys. Villages were crushed by the giant's feet, fissures torn in the ground by Thor's hammer. Through it all Skrymir laughed, saying, '*Shoo shoo pesky red-haired fly.*'

"Loki hatched a plan to help Thor defeat the giant. The trickster god slyly asked Skrymir to prove his strength by catching a hundred whales. Skrymir waded into the ocean. Thor jumped aboard a boat and paddled after him. While Skrymir was under the water searching for whales, only his head was exposed above the waves. Thor leapt atop him, hammering at his skull.

Wherever he struck, rocks and flame spewed forth. Then ice and snow. Rocks and flame, ice and snow. Finally Thor gave the giant such a powerful blow in the center of his skull that Skrymir's entire body turned to stone.

"Skrymir's final words before his lips froze in place forever were a curse on Loki, telling him that his children would be forced to live on this new island as outcasts. Many ages later Loki betrayed the gods and brought about the death of Baldur, the most loved and beautiful of all the gods. The gods hunted Loki and his shape-shifting children down and turned Vali, Loki's favorite son, into a wolf. He killed his brother Narvi, whose entrails were used to bind Loki in a cave. Vali then fled, bounding away across the water to the land where the sun shines at midnight. To Iceland."

Wow. Someone getting his guts torn out. Grandpa was reaching a new height in storytelling gore. I hated to think what he'd come up with next.

Grandpa opened his mouth to say something, then closed it and rubbed his chin. "And that was that," he finished, quietly. "At least that's all I can remember."

The lights went out. I turned, looked through the window. We were in a tunnel.

"We're just going under the fjord," Grandpa explained. "No need to get all antsy."

We eventually came out the other side, but the sky appeared much darker. Almost black.

"So is that how the myth ends?" Sarah asked. "With Vali coming to Iceland."

"Oh no," Grandpa said slowly, ". . . well . . . myths and folktales never really end. You should know that by now. They become part of other stories. The Irish monks were the first to land on Iceland. A few of their journals survived and they mention that they sometimes saw feral people in the shadows of the mountains. They called them *lupinus* and believed they were the spawn of the Devil and that they could shift their shape into wolves or bears or whatever creature they wanted, as long as it was about the same size as they were—though most seemed to like being wolves for reasons I can't imagine. The creatures would even take the form of a familiar monk, just to lure other monks to their lair. The monks wore bells on their belts, which they rang to keep the evil ones away."

"The Vikings who came and chased off the monks spoke of the *úlfr-madr*, the wolf men. Icelanders in the 1500s wrote about these shape-shifters building their own farms and taking human shapes to blend in."

"Where did all these stories come from?" I asked. "What are they based on?"

"Human imagination. But your great-grandfather believed they were the sons of Loki. He saw one once. In fact that's how he got his name, Thorgeir Tree-Foot. You see, it all started when he was taking a trip from Bjarg—"

"Repeat! Repeat! You told us this story on the plane," Michael said, then seeing the confused look on Grandpa's face, he softened his tone. "This morning, remember?"

Grandpa glanced back and forth between us. "I did, didn't I? Right. It seems so long ago." He drew in a breath. "Sorry about that. I usually only tell my stories once a day." He crossed his arms and sat back. "I'll try to think up some new ones," he promised. Then, as if wanting to retreat from us, he closed his eyes.

Sarah gave me a worried look as if to say: *What's up with Grandpa?* I shrugged my shoulders.

We traveled for some time in silence, the bus somehow managing to stay on the thin, snow-covered highway. Grandpa looked like he was asleep now. I studied his face, the wrinkles, and the white hair. He did appear older than last year. A lot older.

I shook my head. I didn't want to think about him aging. He was in his late seventies, wasn't he? That's still young for an Icelander. But when he'd had that little dizzy spell in the airport, I'd thought, briefly, that something was seriously wrong.

I glanced at my watch. It was one thirty in the afternoon, Icelandic time, and the sky was already dark. It had been a lifetime since I'd rolled out of a New York hotel bed early in the morning to catch the flight. I needed a serious rest. I closed my eyes and slept fitfully. We stopped twice in small towns, but since Grandpa didn't move I just closed my eyes again.

The sound of the engine slowing down woke me. We had turned into a gas station. Before I was even fully awake, we were standing outside, our luggage in our hands, watching the bus pull away.

"That's strange," Grandpa said, after surveying the area. "Thordy's supposed to be here to meet us." From where we stood, the whole town appeared empty. "I sent him a letter telling him exactly when we would arrive. Even called him a couple of days ago. We'll head downtown. It isn't far. Travels aren't over until you're safely indoors."

Which apparently meant *Let's Start Marching*.

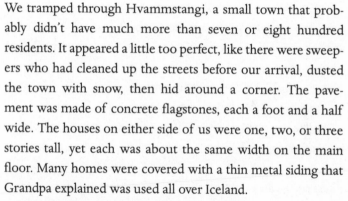

6

We tramped through Hvammstangi, a small town that probably didn't have much more than seven or eight hundred
residents. It appeared a little too perfect, like there were sweep-
ers who had cleaned up the streets before our arrival, dusted
the town with snow, then hid around a corner. The pavement was made of concrete flagstones, each a foot and a half
wide. The houses on either side of us were one, two, or three
stories tall, yet each was about the same width on the main
floor. Many homes were covered with a thin metal siding that
Grandpa explained was used all over Iceland.

"It looks like protection from meteorites," I said.

"Yeah," Michael agreed. He took a black headband out of his
jacket pocket and slipped it over his ears. "Is it closer to space
up here? We're not gonna suddenly be sucked into the atmosphere, are we?"

Grandpa made a *harrumph!* sound and tramped even faster
through the snow. We marched down what appeared to be
Hvammstangi's main street. A huge Christmas tree with glittering lights stood on one side of the block. Across from it was

cal tavern, a place called the *Hôtel Selid*. Grandpa went

gh the front doors leaving us shivering outside.

o this is northern Iceland," Michael said between clattering

. "It's even colder than I thought it would be."

This is nothing," I said, shivering. "You two have been in Missouri far too long. You need a taste of a good North Dakota blizzard to remind you what cold really feels like."

"Everything seems so old here," Sarah whispered, a tone of awe in her voice. "Not just the buildings, though some of those are quite ancient, but the land. Just so much older than anything around Chillicothe."

The town was beginning to look familiar to me, like I had seen it in a photograph. But the memory was so strong it felt as though I had maybe even stood right here, exactly where I was standing.

"Are you alright, Angie?" Sarah asked.

"Yeah, your brain freeze or something?" Michael added.

I shook my head, ignoring him. I couldn't remember where I'd seen this place before. "I'm just getting my bearings, that's all."

Grandpa came out of the tavern a moment later accompanied by a middle-aged man who was wearing a sweater and walking like he didn't feel the chill. He grumbled a few words in Icelandic when he saw us. Grandpa answered, then laughed. The man remained sour.

"I can't get a hold of Thordy, so we're gonna catch a ride with my new friend, Brynjólfur," Grandpa explained. "He just wanted to make sure you didn't bite. I assured him you've all had your shots."

"Funny, Gramps," Michael said, "you're a real riot."

Brynjólfur led us to his vehicle, which was some sort of large, four-doored jeep with oversized, knobby tires. Judging by the dents and chipped paint, it had been through a couple of near-death experiences. We climbed in and started bumping down the road before I could even find my seat belt. I quickly dug around in the seat, coming up with a few pieces of garbage, and finally uncovered both ends of the belt. I didn't feel safe until I'd clicked them together and tightened it around me. The heater barely puffed out enough hot air to defrost a patch of the window directly in front of Brynjólfur. He turned out to be a worse driver than the jet pilot. Maybe they were cousins.

Minutes later we were on an icy highway, heading inland. After a few miles of jouncing around we turned and bumped down a country road into a valley. There were the occasional signs of civilization, lights of farms here and there, all made eerie through the frost-covered windows. The lights grew fewer and farther between until we were in a land of darkness lit only by our headlights. The road roughened and a dim bobbing glow came into view, grew brighter. The jeep rattled to a stop in front of a house. It was one story high, plain looking, and painted white with a beat-up, four-door, four-wheel-drive truck parked out front. No lights were on inside. Across the yard stood a smaller, older looking home that appeared to be built right into the hillside. Behind them both was the shadow of another building.

Brynjólfur didn't get out of his jeep. He waited until we had all our bags piled beside us, then mumbled a parting word to Grandpa and jammed down on the gas. The jeep's tires spun on the ice, spitting a few pieces of gravel our way. Seconds later his taillights disappeared into the night.

"Wow!" Michael said. He stared at the sky above him.

There was no moon. The air was alive with shifting, glowing lights, brighter than the stars and so close they appeared to be skimming the top of the house. It awakened the oddest familiar feeling in me. I felt like I'd been here before, too. *Deja vu all over again.* The hairs on my arms and the back of my neck began to stand up. A cold chill crawled down my spine, a chill that didn't feel like it would go away anytime soon.

"The Northern Lights," Sarah whispered. "I've never seen them so bright. And so close."

"They're a sight for sore eyes." Grandpa craned his neck, trying to see as much of the sky as possible. "I grew up under these lights. We're definitely home." He cleared his throat. "Well, no sense getting hypnotized by the *Aurora Borealis*, not when we could be hypnotized by a blazing fire instead. Now remember, Thordy is my brother's son. So he's your . . . well . . . uncle, I guess. I hope. Or is he a cousin? Well, just call him Uncle Thordy, either way. He'll like it." Grandpa picked up his suitcase. "I don't know about you, but I'm ready for some old-time hospitality."

He strode ahead and rapped loudly on the thick door. There was a long silence. Grandpa let out a frosty, exasperated breath and pulled back his arm to give the door another good pounding, but the muffled sound of footsteps coming down a hall stopped him. They grew louder, the floor creaking like there was a huge weight moving across it. Uncle Thordy sounded like he was a giant.

The door squeaked open half an inch and a shadow stared down at us. All I could see was a glowering eye.

A gruff male voice barked something in Icelandic.

"Four weary travelers, looking for some room at the inn," Grandpa answered in English. "And some coffee!"

"Who are you?" the man asked. "Tourists? You trying to find the guest farm? Are you lost?"

"No," Grandpa laughed, "not lost. I'd recognize the croft I grew up on. It's me—Thursten Asmundson, home for the holidays."

The eye swiveled back and forth, back again. "Thursten?" the man snapped. "But he's in Canada. Not due until tomorrow."

A porch light flicked on, the high-watt bulb momentarily blinding. Grandpa bowed, a wide smile on his face.

"You're Thursten?" the man asked gruffly. "I thought you'd look different."

"I look the same as I did when I saw you ten years ago, Thordy, might have gained a wrinkle here or there."

"It—it is you. Uncle Thursten!"

The door suddenly slammed shut. I expected a warm greeting; instead we stood staring, waiting for it to open again. "I'll be right there!" Uncle Thordy exclaimed loudly, then opened and closed another door inside the house. Finally he yanked the front door open again and came out.

He was a tall, barrel-chested Icelander, his thick beard and hair speckled with gray. I'd guess he was somewhere in his late forties. His face had the familiar big-boned Asmundson look, with a long jaw and a rugged nose. He had three serious-looking scars that stretched from his right eyebrow into his hairline. He was wearing a pair of slippers, but didn't seem to mind tramping through the snow. He gave Grandpa a rib-crushing bear hug. "You've arrived early! What a surprise!"

"Surprise?" Grandpa wheezed. He coughed and Uncle

Thordy stepped back. "But we're here when we said we'd be, Thordy."

"You are?" Uncle Thordy scratched his head. "What day is it?"

"Thursday, all day," Grandpa said.

"Oh no! Oh, I'm so sorry." Uncle Thordy put one hand to his forehead like he was stricken with a sudden migraine. "I'm a day behind, I haven't been getting much sleep. I've been so confused. I was supposed to pick you up today. I'm sorry."

"It's alright. Everything worked out. It just added to the adventure of it all. The kids had fun in Thorstein's jeep."

"You survived a ride with Thorstein?" Uncle Thordy regarded the three of us. "You are tough. Look how big you three are. I've only seen pictures of you when you were tots, though I've heard quite a bit about you. The twins and Angie, our North American roots. You're all grown up!"

"Uh . . . hi," Sarah said. We all introduced ourselves and shook his hand. It was warm and strong. He was also wearing a layer or two of aftershave lotion. Very strong stuff.

Uncle Thordy grabbed two of the nearest bags and lugged them towards the house. "Let's talk inside." We followed him.

I was the last one through the door. I bumped it closed with my hip, set down my backpack, and was hit by a blast of heat. At least Uncle Thordy believed in using his furnace. Maybe I'd finally get the chill out of my bones. The second thing that hit me was a slightly rotten scent in the air. A smell like the garbage had been left out too long.

7

"Just toss your coats in the closet and throw your boots on the mat," Uncle Thordy said, opening up the closet door. "Then get your bodies into the living room."

I found a hanger and gingerly hung up my jacket. It had been expensive and I didn't want it to get creased. As I went to close the door I noticed a big axe hanging on the closet wall, large enough to take out a good-sized tree with a few whacks. Why did Uncle Thordy need such a gigantic axe? Iceland wasn't exactly the most wooded area in the world. I closed the door.

Uncle Thordy led us down the hall and past the kitchen. The smell I'd detected at the front door lingered more heavily in the air here, but the kitchen was tidy. Maybe that's why Uncle Thordy hadn't opened the door right away—he was too busy hiding the garbage. It crossed my mind that he might not be into bathing too much. Which I knew wasn't the norm here—Icelanders spent every spare moment jumping into hot springs.

Uncle Thordy guided us into the cozy warmth of his living room. Actually, it was more like a library than a living room. Two large shelves sat on either wall, stuffed with books of all sizes. I was happy to see Uncle Thordy was a reader, just like the rest of the family. I'd have to sneak a peek at his collection; maybe there were some sagas I'd never seen before. Of course, it wouldn't do me much good if they were all in Icelandic.

Next to one of the shelves was a scrawny Christmas tree, dotted with tiny versions of the Icelandic flag, a few scattered ornaments, two lines of lights, and a lopsided star that pointed at a corner of the ceiling. It looked frumpy, but it was good to see something similar to what we'd have at home. I guessed Uncle Thordy had given us his best shot at decorating.

I dropped my backpack and collapsed on a forest green couch, sitting as near to the brick fireplace as possible. A fire danced across two logs. I held out my hands, let the heat warm my fingertips.

"I'll show you where you'll be sleeping later," Uncle Thordy said, "but for now, tell me about your trip."

"It was bumpy," Michael said.

"And rough," I added. "Did we mention it was bumpy?"

"A character-building experience," Grandpa said. "Unfortunately these three weren't starting with much character." He winked at Uncle Thordy.

"We inherited all we got from you," Michael quipped.

"Well . . . I—I don't have a comeback. You got me that time, Michael. Guess I'm training you a little too well."

Uncle Thordy grinned at the bantering, then furrowed his brows. "I am sorry I wasn't at the petrol station to meet you. I lost track of time. It always happens in the midwinter. There are so many hours of darkness you start to wonder when to sleep and when you should be awake. Soon your waking life becomes a long, slow dream. I am so sorry."

"You're forgiven," Grandpa said. "There's only one thing that would make up for it: a big, hot cup of . . ."

"Coffee! It's on its way." Uncle Thordy leapt up and went to the kitchen. The living room only had a view of the kitchen table, but not the rest of the kitchen, so I couldn't see what Uncle Thordy was up to, but with all the banging it sounded like he was conducting a symphony of pots and pans.

"Don't be too hard on ol' Thordy," Grandpa whispered. "He hasn't been the same since Kristjanna died. He even looks different, more tired, I guess. I hardly even recognized him."

A few minutes later Uncle Thordy returned with a tray full of cups and a huge metal pot of coffee. He smiled and triumphantly lifted the blue pot. It looked like something straight out of the pioneer days, covered with dents. He poured us each a cup without asking whether we wanted one. "This'll get your heart going," he promised, handing me a cup. I saw the dark bags under his eyes, the lines on his face. The scars above his right eyebrow added to the impression that he'd had a hard time lately. I knew what a heavy weight grief could be; it must have taken years off his life.

The coffee was thick as oil and steaming hot. I glanced at Sarah and Michael, who were both staring at their own cups like they'd been given poison. I'd had coffee a few times before, but this was way different. Like the long lost ancestor of coffee. I took a sip and it tasted about half as good as it looked. It was hot enough to heat my innards, though, and I was thankful for that.

"This is what Icelanders drink?" Sarah whispered. "No wonder so many of them look grumpy."

Uncle Thordy had slipped out and was back again with a plate heaped with flat, blackened pieces of bread along with strips of meat. He set it on the coffee table in front of us. *"Hangikjöt* and *flatkökur,"* he announced.

"That's smoked lamb and hard bread to you," Grandpa explained.

We dug in. The bread *was* hard as cement, but I was able to bite off a big enough chunk to discover that it was fairly tasty. And the lamb melted in my mouth. I was so famished I could've eaten a ton of it. We hadn't had a bit of food since breakfast on the airplane. Uncle Thordy returned a third time with a plate of stuff called *gravlax*, which was made of salmon. It tasted salty.

"If I'd been more organized I'd have had a real meal prepared for you. Maybe even some *svid."*

"Oh, you should save that for special occasions," Grandpa said. "Plus it'd probably freak Michael out."

"Freak me out, why?"

Grandfather brushed crumbs off his shirt. "It's singed sheep's head, sawn in two, boiled, and eaten fresh."

Michael turned pale, along with me and Sarah. I was the first to voice our opinion. "Ewwww!"

"We never waste anything in Iceland," Uncle Thordy began, "it's part of—"

A knock on the door cut his sentence short. He shot out of his seat, spilling coffee on his hand. "I'm not expecting company," he said, wiping the coffee on his pants. "Just wait here." He walked down the short hall and out of sight. The front door creaked open, letting a gust of wind come into the living room. It settled at our feet and chilled my legs. I slid closer to the fire.

Uncle Thordy spoke in hushed tones and another voice answered. There was a soft clunk, then the door closed.

A moment later a man followed Uncle Thordy into the room. The stranger pulled back the hood of his jacket and a few flakes of snow fell to the floor. I was surprised to see a young guy about my age, his black hair slicked back. He had a thin, fine-boned face, dark skin, and his lips were curled into a friendly smile.

"This is Mordur, my hired helper. He saw my lights were on so he came by," Uncle Thordy explained. Grandpa stood and reached out his hand. Mordur gave him an exuberant shake, saying, *"Gott kvöld."* Grandpa winced slightly, like Mordur had squeezed too tight. Mordur shook everyone else's hand, saying "Good evening" in English each time.

When he came to me, he held my hand for a few seconds longer than the others and stared at it like it was an interesting butterfly that had just landed on his palm. I was surprised how warm his hand was—burning hot. He looked me in the eyes, his were a swirling gray.

"Sugar," he said.

"Wh-what?" I muttered. I started to blush.

"Sugar. I come by for sugar." His English had a bit of an accent to it. He let go of my hand. He seemed—well—almost like he was struck with a sudden bout of shyness. "For my coffee. It makes it much . . . uh . . . more good tasting." He turned to everyone. "Welcome to Iceland! Christmas is best time to be here. The best time, I mean. It is when you get all the good food."

"Please, join us," Uncle Thordy said. "The coffee's hot."

Mordur shook his head. "No thank you. I still have to finish dishes. Your family is here to celebrate the holiday. That is good. Have you warned them about the thirteen Santa Clauses?"

"Thirteen Santa Clauses!" I said, a little too loudly. Mordur looked my way, giving me a warm grin. His eyes strayed to the top of my head, then back. Was my hair a mess? "B-but there's just one Santa Claus, isn't there?"

"Not in Iceland. We do different things here. The thirteen Santa Clauses are the *Jólasveinar*. It means 'Christmas lads.' They are very small. Imps! I think that is the word you use. There is *Stúfur*, the itty bitty one, and *Pottasleikir*—he licks pots people leave out—*Bjúgnakrækir*, the sausage snatcher, and ten others. One comes every night for thirteen nights before Christmas and puts a gift in your shoe. Unless you are bad, of course. Then they do a bad thing. Like steal your sausages or hide your lipstick."

"Only in Iceland would they have *bad* Santa Clauses," Michael said, between bites of bread. "We're a morbid people, we are. Thirteen brats handing out presents."

"Careful," Mordur warned, shaking his finger, "the *Jólasveinar* know when you talk bad about them. You will end up with a rotten potato in your shoe."

"It's all he deserves," Sarah joked. Mordur smiled at her and I felt a sudden twinge of jealousy. She already had a boyfriend in Manitoba, why was she flirting with him?

"Tonight is the twenty-one of December, *Gluggagægir's* night. He is the window peeper. And if you are really bad, Gryla, the old hag mother of the *Jólasveinar*, will go and eat you."

"This is starting to sound more like Halloween," I said. Mordur turned towards me again. "Tricks, treats, and monsters."

Uncle Thordy set down his cup of coffee on the side table. "Don't you three listen to Mordur. He's inherited his father's long-winded, storytelling genes. And don't worry about being devoured by Gryla. The only old hag near this croft is Gunnvor and all she eats is regular food. As far as I know."

Genuine surprise showed on Grandfather's face. "You mean she's still alive? She was ancient when I was a child. I thought she would've died years ago."

Uncle Thordy rubbed his beard. "Oh, she's alive alright. Alive and kicking. I can feel her beady eyes on my back every time I head out to the pasture. She puts the spook in the horses, too."

"Then she hasn't changed." Grandpa Thursten shook his head in disbelief. "She used to come down to where we played by the marsh and threaten to break our bones and throw us in a cairn if we kept making a racket."

"She may be Gryla in disguise," Mordur said, laughing. "Anyway, I do need sugar, then I will depart with all your wonderful guests." He slapped his forehead. "I mean leave you with all your guests. Sorry, my English is rusted. It has been months since I used it." He shrugged.

"It's okay," I said, "your English is a thousand times better than my Icelandic." I smiled, then wondered if I had salmon stuck in my teeth. My cheeks flashed with heat. For the millionth time I cursed my pale white complexion. I was probably as red as the nose on Rudolph the Red-Nosed Reindeer. Mordur glanced at the top of my head again and I resisted the urge to pat down my hair. Sarah caught my eye and winked.

Mordur followed Uncle Thordy into the kitchen and came out with a small paper bag of sugar.

"It was good meeting you all," Mordur said, then left. A moment later the door down the hall opened and banged shut.

"He's young for a hired man," Grandpa remarked.

Uncle Thordy nodded. "He is. Just sixteen. He's the son of my previous hired man, Einar. Einar drowned last summer while fishing at sea. A terrible, tragic accident. He left Mordur with nothing but a few months' savings and the clothes on his back. His mother lives in France and didn't want anything to do with him."

"How'd he learn English?" Sarah asked.

"Mordur isn't much for school, but he's smart as a whip. He picked up his English from tourists and other Icelanders. We all know pieces and bits of two or three different languages. He's good at most everything he wants to be good at and the animals do what he says, so I decided to keep him around. Plus I felt a debt to his father. Einar was a dependable man."

"It's always a comfort to work with someone you trust." Grandpa rubbed at his chest as if he had some sort of sharp pain. When he saw us all watching him, he grinned. "What are you staring at? Haven't you seen an old man try to keep down a burp before?" He looked at Uncle Thordy. "Do you have any plans for us tomorrow?" he asked.

"To let you sleep as long as you want. None of the relatives arrive until tomorrow night."

Grandpa nodded. "Sleeping in sounds like a great idea. Maybe in the afternoon I can drive you kids to Bjarg. It's where Grettir the Strong grew up. We might even be able to take a trip to Drang Island, where Grettir died. Though I don't think we'd want to climb around there this time of year."

Grandpa always spoke as though it was just a couple of years ago that Grettir the Strong was alive, but in fact he lived sometime back in the 1100s, long before I set foot on this earth. According to my parents, Grettir spent most of his time fighting other Icelanders and the undead. I've always been glad our family let go of that tradition.

Grandpa reminded us we all had orders to phone home once we got to Uncle Thordy's, no matter what time it was in the States. Michael and Sarah went first and talked to their parents for a few minutes. When it was my turn my mom picked up the phone on the third ring. It was so odd to hear her voice sounding crystal clear, even though she was thousands of miles away. She and Dad were just sitting down for a late supper of hamburgers and homemade French fries. She asked me questions about the trip and I answered them all in a daze. When it came time to say good-bye, all I could say was, "I miss you."

"We miss you too, dear," Mom said.

I joined everyone in the living room and we talked for another half hour. My eyes started to burn, my lids grew heavy. It had been a long, trying trip and jet lag seemed to have caught up with me. Uncle Thordy saw one of my yawns. "It doesn't matter what country you're in," he said, "a yawn means the same thing. I'll show you to your rooms."

We grabbed our luggage and Uncle Thordy led us down a short hall, the walls white and bare. Sarah and I would share a room. Michael had to settle for a cot in Uncle Thordy's tiny office. Grandpa took a room down the hall from us. We said good night to Uncle Thordy and Michael.

"I'm glad to have you girls along," Grandpa said quietly to us. "I do feel lucky to have grandchildren like you two. And Michael, of course."

"Have a good sleep, Afi," Sarah said.

As he turned away I noticed a dark spot on the back of his shirt. "Grandpa, what's that?"

He turned to me, then looked over his shoulder at where I was pointing. It was a red stain.

"Did you cut yourself?" Sarah asked.

"Not that I know of," Grandpa answered. "I'll check it out in the mirror. Guess I must have leaned on something sharp. Good night." He closed the door.

Once we were in our room I dropped my backpack next to a cot. I went to the washroom and decided to have a quick bath. The water here got hot real fast. Maybe it came directly from a hot spring. My hair actually looked okay. I'm not sure why Mordur kept staring at it. A few minutes later I was clean and perfectly toasty.

8

"How are you feeling now, Angie?" Sarah was sitting up in her bed, reading a thick paperback novel. "I know you're not much into airplanes." Her brown hair was undone so it fell across one shoulder. She'd let it grow since the last time I'd seen her and it made her look more sophisticated.

"I'm better," I admitted, towel drying my hair. It was down to my shoulders. It'd be a while before it would catch up to Sarah's. "Once we landed I calmed down. Of course the bus ride didn't help much. Or the car ride."

"It hasn't exactly been an uneventful trip so far, has it?"

"It was a little weird how Uncle Thordy forgot to pick us up." I grabbed my brush and began working on the tangles in my hair. "And then he wasn't all that friendly until he found out who we were."

"Maybe they're more paranoid here than we are at home. Or more superstitious. But I got the same vibes. He was relieved to see it was us."

"Do you find the house a little stinky?" I asked.

Sarah nodded. "I don't think Uncle Thordy's all that careful about keeping everything clean. Plus I think he's a little
depressed. I get the feeling if we lifted the rugs we'd find a lot
of dust bunnies."

Done with my hair, I dropped my brush on the night table
and tucked myself under the biggest, thickest comforter I'd
ever seen. We were quiet for a few moments. There were tons
of things I wanted to ask Sarah, about her boyfriend, how her
mom and dad were, what was new in her life, but I just couldn't
find the energy.

But somewhere beneath all my tiredness, my heart was beating double-time. The coffee had kicked it into high gear. The
last thing I needed was to be tossing and turning all night.

"Don't take this the wrong way," Sarah said, measuring each
word, "but you don't seem as, well—up—as you usually are.
I always think of you as being Suzy Sunshine, but you're not
quite like that right now. Is everything alright? Or is it just the
long trip?"

Sarah had a gift for being able to sense my deeper moods
better than anyone, even my parents. "I—I've been thinking
about my brother a lot lately. The closer I got to this holiday,
the more I thought about him."

"It's been five years, hasn't it?"

"Yes. A long time. But the older I get, the more I miss him. Or
the more I understand what it means to not have him around
anymore."

"I miss him too, Angie. Andrew was a great kid. As much as
Michael gets on my nerves, I can't imagine what it would be
like if he was gone."

We fell silent. What else was there to say? He was gone and we missed him.

But there *was* something else. I opened my mouth to tell Sarah about the nightmares I'd had back at home, but then couldn't spit out a word. I had an overwhelming feeling that if I spoke about them, they would return. Better to leave them be.

There was one other thing bothering me, though.

"Do you think Grandpa's okay? He seems tired. More tired than I've ever seen him."

She frowned. "He is looking older. And he tried to tell us the same story twice in the same day. He never used to do that."

"I hope he's okay," I said.

"He probably needs rest, that's all. It was a heck of a long trip. I still can't believe we're here. Actually in Iceland. Where our family comes from." She yawned and blinked sleepily several times. "You know, I think I'll be a lot more excited about it tomorrow. How about some shut-eye?" She waited for me to nod, then clicked off the lamp. "Nighty-night."

"Good night," I whispered, my eyelids slowly shutting down. Sleep. Exactly what I needed. A chance for my brain to rest.

I hoped I was too exhausted to dream.

9

Probably the worst nightmare in all of the old Norse myths is the one that haunted Baldur. Baldur was the purest of the gods. He was beautiful, wise, and gentle, and the son of Odin. No one wished him harm. Yet one night he had awful nightmares that made him twist and squirm in an attempt to escape the dark phantoms. He woke up, his body gleaming with sweat. He tried to remember each shape he'd seen and dispel them from his mind. But he failed. The skulking dream creatures crept away only to return again whenever he closed his eyes.

None of the gods could figure out the meaning of the dreams. Finally Odin went down to the underworld to ask a dead seer what the dreams meant. She told him Baldur would die soon, and his death was a sign that Ragnarok—the end of the world—was coming. There was nothing any of the gods could do to stop either event.

When I closed my eyes and slipped towards sleep, I had a nightmare that equaled the evil of Baldur's bad dream. Once or twice I thought I heard rustling outside the window, but I couldn't pull myself out of the dream world. When I finally fell into a deep sleep, my head was full of constantly changing images; skull guests, and floating specters that terrorized me. Snow swirled around, fire burst from the ground. Viking armies battled each other, falling down dead, only to rise up again and continue the fight.

Then the wolf from my other dream returned, loping across the battlefield. But this time, instead of eating me bite by bite, he leapt through the sky and seized the sun, spattering blood across the world. A second smaller wolf swallowed the moon.

Through it all was the sound of scratching, like someone was scraping at a piece of glass with a knife. Or pulling their nails across a chalkboard. And somewhere in the background was my brother's voice, sounding out like a distant bell.

I woke up halfway through the night, sweating like I had run a marathon. I didn't want to fall asleep again because I knew the shapes were still there, somewhere beyond the shadows in my brain, waiting for me. I lay awake, staring at the ceiling, pulling the comforter tight. My arms soon grew tired, my body ached, and, despite my fears, my weary eyelids slid closed. I slept.

10

"Breakfast!" A loud knock on the door jarred me awake. The lights in the room were on, burning into my eyes. "Breakfast!" Uncle Thordy repeated. "Get up and grab it while it's hot!"

I blinked and sat up. "I thought the plan was to sleep in today."

Sarah was already dressed in jeans and a red lumberjack-type shirt: heavy, warm, but not exactly the height of fashion. She was sitting on the bed pulling her hair into a ponytail.

"Guess the plan changed."

"Well, I need about ten more hours of being zonked out. It's always weird sleeping in a new bed."

"You certainly rolled around a lot last night. I heard you kick the wall a few times." I tried to remember the nightmare again, but couldn't put together enough of the dream to explain any-thing to Sarah. It was like a big puzzle missing half its pieces. "It's not surprising," Sarah continued. "I don't think our bodies were meant to travel across the Atlantic in less than a day."

I pulled myself out of bed and started digging through my backpack. All my neat packing had been jumbled together during the trip. I tugged out a pair of black jeans that were loose fitting, but didn't make my hips look too big. I slipped them on and wriggled into a dark blue sweater. For some reason my red hair always looked better when I was wearing that color. There was a small mirror on the dresser, so I grabbed my make-up bag and examined myself.

Bags under my eyes. Hair pointing every which way but straight. I looked like I'd spent most of the trip with my head out the airplane window. I did the best I could with my brush.

Sarah's face appeared in the top corner of the mirror, a wicked smile on her lips. "Mordur won't be at the breakfast table," she whispered.

"Oh, please." I stopped teasing my hair long enough to make a face at her.

"I saw the way he looked at you. He kept staring at your hair. Maybe he has a thing for redheads."

"Yeah, right, and maybe I'll get struck by lightning in the next five seconds."

"Hope you brought a lightning rod." She went back to her bed, pulling on some socks.

"What do you suppose is for breakfast?" I asked, changing the topic.

"I don't know for sure, but I can smell it. Eggs and maybe bacon. Hurry up before Michael wolfs it all down."

I gave up on my hair. It would pass for being combed. I took a moment to pull the curtain aside and glance out the window. Even though my watch read *10:15* AM, it was still dark out. What kind of holiday was this going to be if we couldn't see anything?

The window was double paned and I noticed the outside one

was etched with three scratch marks. A tuft of gray hair flut-
tered in the wind, caught in a crack in the wooden sill.

"Sarah, take a look at this."

She came to my side, put her hand on my shoulder. "What's
that?"

"It looks like dog hair. How did it get there?"

"I don't know. It's kind of high up for a dog." She stared at
it for a moment, pressing her nose up to the glass. "Maybe it
was one of those Santa Claus imps—*Gluggagægir*, the window
peeper—who came last night."

"And left some hair?"

"I'm kidding," she said, laughing. "I don't know what it's
from."

My rumbling stomach stopped me from brooding about it
much longer. We went down the hall to the kitchen.

Michael was too busy chewing to say hello, so he just gave us
a little wave. Uncle Thordy stood by the oven, a greasy spatula
in his hand. Eggs and bacon were frying in a big iron pan, spitting grease across the stovetop.

"Sit. Eat." Uncle Thordy pointed at two empty chairs at one
side of a heavy wooden table. The moment we sat down he
plunked two plates in front of us and gestured towards a bowl
of white stuff. "That's *skyr*," he explained, "made from cow's
milk." I'd seen it before. It was like butter but white. Mom and
Dad would slather it all over their toast or crackers whenever
they could get their hands on some. It tasted much better than
it looked. "Dish up!"

Toast was piled on a plate beside a hill of fried eggs and
bacon. There were sliced bananas, a box of Kellogg's Corn
Flakes, and a selection of cheeses. The cheese was a little old

and musty. Maybe that's the way they liked it in Iceland. I dished up and started eating. The eggs had been fried so long that the yolks were solid and the whites partly burnt. The bacon was crisp. Michael was eating a bowl of some steaming porridge-like substance.

"Where's Grandpa?" I asked between mouthfuls.

"He's a little under the weather," Uncle Thordy said, bringing over a pitcher of water. "In fact I'm concerned about him. He's coughing and sweating a lot and has a bit of a fever, but won't let me take him to the doctor. He said he's been tired for the last few weeks, but something really hit him hard last night. He's going to stay in bed today and try to recuperate."

Sarah, Michael, and I exchanged worried glances. "We'll have to check on him after breakfast," Michael said. "Cheer him up with our youthful exuberance."

"I'm sure he'd like that," Uncle Thordy said, "but don't turn on the light. He says his eyes are sore."

We ate quietly for a minute or so. I grabbed a piece of toast and spread some *skyr* across it. "This is a great breakfast."

"I'm glad you like it. It's just so . . . so nice . . . to have company out here. Makes me feel safer. I mean, makes the house seem not so empty."

I glanced over at Sarah. She raised one eyebrow.

"I've heard so much about you kids, too," Uncle Thordy continued. "Thursten's very proud of you three. Doesn't stop talking about you. And I know there's something special about you twins."

"Special?" Sarah asked.

Yeah, I wondered. Why were they special?

Uncle Thordy stared straight at Sarah. "You twins have a certain skill for solving problems."

"I don't know what you mean," Sarah said.

"I just . . . I guess, I'm just trying to say that I know you're good kids, that's all. That we're leaving the family name in good hands."

"Uh, thanks," Michael said.

I wasn't sure if I should be offended. My last name was Laxness, not Asmundson—so I wasn't carrying on their family name. I decided Uncle Thordy wasn't intentionally trying to leave me out. Maybe he'd forgotten my last name.

We ate silently. Uncle Thordy offered us more coffee, but we politely said no. "Aren't you going to eat?" Sarah asked him.

"I had some toast before you got up. I never did much like breakfast. Why don't we say good morning to your grandpa now?"

Grandpa Thursten's room was down a low-ceilinged hallway. The door was made of wooden planks and had a rounded top. It looked ancient.

"It's all that remains of the original house," Uncle Thordy explained. "I had the rest added on about fifteen years ago."

I knocked gently. We waited, but there was no answer. I knocked again, slightly harder, and listened. "Come in," a faint whisper drifted through the wood.

I pushed on the door and it creaked open on a cramped, musty-smelling room. The light in the hall lit enough of the room for us to see a chair and a desk, but Grandpa's bed was still hidden by shadows. It took a moment for my eyes to adjust. "Don't just stand around, get in here," a hoarse voice commanded.

I took a few steps with Sarah and Michael right behind me. Grandpa was lying on his side, his head sunk into a pillow, his face pale and pasty looking, and his eyes dull. The rest of him was hidden under the blankets. He coughed. "I seem to have caught a little bug. I'll be up and at 'em by tomorrow morning. Guaranteed."

I doubted it. I guessed he had a couple days in bed by the way he was looking. Maybe even a week.

"Don't worry," Uncle Thordy said from the doorway. "Mordur promised to show them the croft house and the rest of the farm this morning."

"Good, I wanted them to see the old croft. I spent countless hours out there with my dad. It's where I learned most of the stories I know. It's an important part of our family history."

"I'd take them," Uncle Thordy said, "but unfortunately I have some business to attend to in town. I'll pick up something for supper at the supermarket. A few of the relatives want to drop by tonight. Will you be up for visiting?"

Grandpa answered in Icelandic. Uncle Thordy nodded solemnly, then he forced a smile.

"I'll be ready to give the whole world a good kick in the dustbins," Grandpa whispered and began coughing. I didn't know what to do. We just stood there listening to his painful gasping. Finally I found a glass of water by his bed and handed it to him. "Thanks," he whispered.

"We should let him rest," Uncle Thordy suggested.

I patted Grandpa's open hand. It was clammy. "Angie, stick around for a moment," he rasped. "I want to talk to you about what I got Michael and Sarah for Christmas."

"Sure," I said.

Uncle Thordy put his hands on Sarah and Michael's shoulders and guided them out of the room, saying, "Guess we better go. It's bad luck to hear what your Christmas present is going to be." He closed the door softly.

"Actually, Angie, I have to ask you something," Grandpa whispered. "It's about the nightmares you had before we left."

11

"What do you want to know?" My throat felt suddenly dry.

"I'll explain. Just help your ol' grandpa sit up, okay?"

I bent over him, pulling awkwardly on his upper arm until he was in a sitting position. He coughed once more. "Shouldn't you be going to a doctor?"

"This is a minor ailment."

His pillow was out of place, so I tugged on one edge, revealing a small stain of blood. "You're bleeding again."

"It's that pinprick in my back. It itches like crazy. I don't know how I got it." He rubbed the top of his left shoulder and shook his head. "My father would be laughing now. He lost his leg to that bear and not once did he utter a word of complaint. And here I am whining over a mosquito bite." He leaned back. "Could you pass me the water, please?"

I handed him the glass and he slowly sipped a mouthful. "That's better." He gave the glass back and I set it on the bedside table.

I pulled the chair away from the desk and sat next to him. He stared, measuring me with his eyes. "Last night I had the same nightmare as you had when you were back home. A wolf chased me across an open stretch of land. And he devoured me piece by piece."

The wolf wasn't just in *my* head anymore. "How could you have the same dream?" I asked.

"If I follow what I know of psychology, it's just my sub-conscious acting out the same story you told me. I somehow dreamed a similar dream because you had described yours to me."

"And do you believe that? That you're just . . . just mimicking me."

He smiled and his face wrinkled up so it looked like old paper. "I've been around a lot longer than most psychologists. I've seen more strange things than the average person. And I've learned to trust my instincts."

"What are they saying?" Each word he spoke was adding to my fear. I didn't want to know any more about that dream; I didn't want to think about it at all.

"The dream is more than just my brain exorcising its demons. It's a sign. A signal. I think it means we should be careful."

"Careful of what? We're safe here, aren't we?" I asked. I couldn't help but think of the fear I had sensed in Uncle Thordy.

"As far as I know, but I . . . well, years ago, if I was worried, I'd never say anything to you kids. I'd just try and handle it all myself. But now you're older. I have to trust you and let you know what's going on in my brain, even if it sounds crazy. So tell me, do you remember anything else about your night-mare?"

I shook my head, then paused and raised one finger. "Wait, yes, when we were in Hvammstangi I felt like I had been there before. The town was in my dream. I ran through it. And so were the Northern Lights."

"It's almost like you saw the future."

"I don't like to think that. Isn't deja vu just a trick your brain plays on you? It could be my imagination. It *has* to be."

"Maybe," he said, sounding doubtful, "but you wouldn't be the first of our clan who's seen something before it happened. Or the last."

I didn't want to know things before they happened. I didn't want *those* kinds of dreams. They always seemed to be about bad things.

"You probably think it's strange to dream of this place," he continued. "I know you were born in North Dakota and raised there, Angie, but this is where you come from. Where all of us Icelanders come from. This is your family's farm."

"I had another dream last night," I admitted, and then explained it to him as best I could.

"Armies that battle each other. A wolf who bites the sun." He counted on his fingers as he spoke. "Another wolf who swallows the moon. That's Skoll and Hati, they've chased the sun and moon for all of time and finally caught them during the final battle between the gods and the giants."

"I dreamed of Ragnarok, Grandpa. Why would I dream of the end of the world?"

He gave a half-hearted shrug. "Don't worry, the world's not coming to an end. It's just about a personal battle, I think. Inside your head. The worst thing about dreams is they aren't meant to be understood by the logical part of our minds. So I don't know if I can make sense of this latest dream. And one thing we should remember is to never completely trust dreams."

I crossed my arms and leaned back in my chair. "What's that mean?"

"Well, for example, I once had a terrible nightmare where I went to a restaurant with your grandma. I ordered a chicken dish, you know that one with Swiss cheese and ham inside. And I choked to death on it. Well, I woke up before I actually died in the dream."

"And have you ever choked on chicken?"

"Not yet. But I refused to eat it. The dream felt so real it had spooked me away from chicken. Your grandma just laughed and after a few months she made me eat a whole plate of fried drumsticks." He chuckled. "It sure was good. But I shouldn't joke. I do think there is something important about your dreams. I just wish I could think straight; my sinuses are aching too much. There is something else bothering me in the real world."

"What?"

Grandpa leaned ahead slightly, speaking more quietly. "Your uncle. He's—I don't know if you can sense it—but he's not right in the head yet. He's still so full of grief over his wife. He forgot to pick us up because he's depressed. Many Icelanders get depressed in the winter, it's so dark for so long. It's only natural. But his sadness is deeper somehow. And he's frightened, too."

"I know. I could tell."

"It's probably just his imagination, that's all. He has a right to feel scared, I guess. His wife died a strange, unexplainable death. Who knows what really happened in that cave." He paused. "You know, I'm starting to sound a little too paranoid. Your grandma always used to say I had more superstition than brains." Grandpa closed his eyes. He had the longest white eye-lashes I'd ever seen. "God, I miss her," he said quietly, "I really, really miss her. Sometimes it's so hard to go on without her."

I'd never seen him look so weak, so sad. He'd always been a tower of strength to me. I put my hand on his shoulder and he opened his eyes and smiled. "You've got some of her traits," he whispered. "It's funny, really, we're all like beads on a string following one after another, going on forever. Asmundson after Asmundson."

"And Laxness after Laxness," I added.

"Yes, you're lucky enough to have two strong bloodlines run-ning through your veins." He shook his head. "I do wish I'd paid more attention to your nightmare back home. Maybe I would have called the trip off. I just want you to tell your cous-ins to be careful. I didn't feel comfortable talking in front of Thordy about this stuff. That's all."

"I'll tell them," I promised. I leaned down and kissed him lightly on the cheek.

"Now I can sleep a little better," he said, closing his eyes.

12

I found Sarah, Michael, and Uncle Thordy in the living room. Uncle Thordy was standing next to the fire. "I hope you don't mind spending the morning with Mordur," he said. I couldn't think of anything better. "He'll show you around the place. I have a meeting with the banker, otherwise I'd be your guide. I do apologize. I thought you were arriving later today, so I set up appointments in town. That way I'd murder two birds with one rock. I'm so stupid sometimes."

"Uncle Thordy," I said, "you're not stupid. Not at all. You just made a mistake. Back home we call that *pulling a Michael*."

"Don't even start with me, Angie," Michael warned.

"*Pulling a Michael*," Uncle Thordy repeated. He furrowed his brow, showing confusion. "I'm not sure what you mean."

"It's a joke," I explained, "like Michael makes mistakes and so we . . . uh . . . name mistakes after him."

"Oh, I think I see." Uncle Thordy stroked his beard, pretending to be thinking heavily. "I kind of like that."

"I don't." Michael crossed his arms and feigned anger. "It's deflammatory."

"I think you mean defamatory," Sarah corrected.

"Sorry about that, cuz," I said to Michael, only half meaning it. "I was just trying to . . . uh . . ."

"You were just trying to cheer me up," Uncle Thordy finished. "I catch on now." He put his hand on my shoulder, gave it a squeeze. "You're good kids. I wish I could spend the day with you instead of in some stuffy office asking for better interest rates. But that's what being a modern man is all about. Is there anything you need to know before I go? Like where I keep the coffee? Or the cookies?"

"Actually," Sarah said, "I do have a question. What did Grandpa say to you?"

Uncle Thordy frowned, which made the bags under his eyes darken. "When?"

"A few minutes ago," Michael said, "when he spoke to you in Icelandic while we were visiting him. What didn't he want us to know?"

"It wasn't a secret. He was just thanking me for . . . for taking care of you. And saying it was good to be home. And he reminded me that he was born in that room."

"Born in that room?" I said. "Couldn't they get to the hospital in time?"

"They probably didn't even try. People were pretty independent in those days. Home births were common."

It sounded kind of scary to me. No doctors. No nurses. Just hot water and towels. Grandpa definitely did come from a different time than me. A whole different world. I couldn't imagine sleeping in the same room I was born in.

"I have to get ready to go to town." Uncle Thordy went down the hallway and a moment later we could hear him opening drawers. "Mordur should be here soon," he yelled from his room. "I packed some lunch for your trip. It's in the fridge. Just throw it in the backpack hanging in the closet. It'll be easier to carry."

Someone knocked on the front door.

"Will you get that?" Uncle Thordy shouted.

I suddenly thought of the state of my hair. I wasn't going to answer the door. Not with Mordur on the other side. "Uh, excuse me," I said, making a beeline for the bathroom.

Sarah's voice followed me. "Don't forget to wet down the rooster tail on the back of your head!"

I closed the door to the bathroom, shutting out her and Michael's laughter. I took a good look at myself in the mirror. It wasn't as frightening as I thought it would be. I used a damp facecloth to rub water on my hair, an old trick my mom had taught me. It wets all parts of your hair evenly without soaking it. I found a brush in the cabinet and a few seconds later my red mop looked passable. Even a few curls had shown up. I washed my face and cursed the fact that I'd left my make-up bag in my room.

Michael and Sarah let out a huge guffaw. I hoped they weren't laughing about me. I wiped the facecloth across my face once more. I decided not to worry about my make-up, it was still pretty dark out. I checked my hair for about the fifth time, breathed in, and opened the door.

In the hallway a framed picture caught my eye. It was a large photograph of Uncle Thordy and his wife, Kristjanna, with mountains in the background. It was hung so that the light in the ceiling lit the image perfectly. Kristjanna was beautiful, a sturdy woman with strong cheekbones and long blonde hair, like she'd walked out of the pages of a saga. And Uncle Thordy, with his arm around her and a smile on his face, looked like a different man. About twenty pounds thinner. No bags below his eyes. His beard trimmed. And no scars above his eyebrow. It nearly brought tears to my eyes, just to see them together. The picture couldn't have been much more than three years old. Uncle Thordy probably stopped and stared at it every day.

Michael, Sarah, and Mordur were standing in the front doorway. I joined them. Mordur was dressed in a thin, gray winter coat. He was an inch or two taller than Michael, with slightly wider shoulders. He smiled at me, showing white, straight teeth. "Ah, Angie, right? Welcome to my group tour. You had good sleep?"

"I did. I had a perfect sleep. One of the best I've had in ages. It sure was a good one."

Sarah gave me a discreet kick, her way of telling me not to babble.

"So no thirteen Santa Clauses visited last night?" Mordur asked. "I am disappointed. I guess you were all good. Any gifts in your shoes?"

"I did find some lint in mine," Michael said. "What does that mean?"

Mordur feigned sadness, wiping away an imaginary tear. "It is going to be a skinny Christmas."

"Lean Christmas," I corrected, softly. "I think that's what you mean."

"Yes." He patted my shoulder. "Thanks. A lean, skinny Christmas for you, Michael. Sorry."

Uncle Thordy came out in fresh clothes, his hair combed

back. He smelled like he'd dived into a tub of Brut. Maybe depressed people didn't bathe much.

He winked at us and did up the buttons on his collar. "I've got to make the banker think I'm a dependable businessman."

Mordur spoke to him in Icelandic. It sounded like a question. Uncle Thordy narrowed his eyes slightly, looking a little angry. He snapped three words, glanced at us, regained his composure, and said, *"Bless."* Which meant good-bye, in Icelandic. And with that he grabbed his coat from the closet, gave us one more wave, and was gone out the door. A moment later his truck started up and he roared away.

"What was—" Sarah began to ask.

"No time for talk! Not now!" Mordur said quickly. He seemed to be forcing his lips into a smile, pretending nothing was wrong. "Let's get going. Not much light." He clapped his hands together. "Chop! Chop! Chop it! Dress hot, with big layers. You can peel them off if you get toasted."

Sarah narrowed her eyes, then went to the closet, came out with her thick coat. I grabbed my own and slipped it on, along with my black mittens.

"You'll need something for your head," Sarah reminded Michael.

"Yes, Mom," he said, stuffing his headband into a pocket. A few moments later we were all dressed in our warmest winter clothes, standing at the door.

13

Mordur escorted us into the yard. It wasn't dark out anymore, but it wasn't day either, just some kind of state between the two. There was enough light to turn the snow yellowish. One edge of the sky was brighter than the other, so I assumed that was east. I now saw that Uncle Thordy's farm was in a valley, surrounded by big hills and two rows of cliffs.

"Our lunch!" Michael suddenly exclaimed and rushed back into the house.

"That's Michael, always thinking with his stomach," Sarah said. We laughed.

Remembering the tuft of hair I'd seen earlier in the morning, I walked around the side of the house to our bedroom window. There were tracks in the snow below the sill, but it was hard to tell what had made them. The gray hair I'd seen stuck to the window was more like wool. I picked it up, let it float from my fingers.

It landed beside a small cloth sack that had been bound at the top with a string. The side was ripped open and the contents were gone. There had been something red inside.

"Ready for big tour, Angie?" Mordur shouted. They were already walking across the front yard, away from me.

"Uh . . . yes!" I looked down at the bag again, then rushed to join them.

Uncle Thordy's house was the newest part of the farm. The whole yard was an odd mixture of new and old, like there were three different time zones here: kind of old, really old, and ancient. We passed a small, crumbling home, which was about fifty yards from Uncle Thordy's and built into a hill. It was made of wood and sod.

"Do you like my house?" Mordur asked.

"You live in there?" Sarah asked. "Do you have hairy feet?"

"Hairy feet? No." He looked confused. "Why?"

"It's just like a hobbit hole," she explained. "You know, from *The Lord of the Rings*. They were these—uh—little people who had hairy feet. Imps, sort of."

This information didn't end his confusion. "I have simple needs," he said, finally. "I do not own phone. No television, only radio. I like my home. It has history. And my feet are not hairy, I swear."

He flashed a smile and led us through the yard. We stopped in front of a rectangular building with a pitched roof that sagged towards the ground. It had seen more than its share of winters.

"Is this the barn?" I asked. "It's kind of old, isn't it?"

"Why build a new barn?" Mordur said quickly, sounding almost insulted. "This one still stands." It was like I had just asked the stupidest question in all of history. Or perhaps whatever he and Uncle Thordy had quarreled over was still bothering him. "This is more than a barn," he explained, his voice softer, "it is the old home, too. No one is sure when it was built. Uncle Thordy said his grandfather arrived in 1912 and this was here, made by first crofters. It may be two hundred years old and is still strong as the first day it stood." He opened a wide door at one end. "It is our sheep shed now."

He flicked on a switch and four dim bulbs glowed from the ceiling. Inside, huddled against each other, were about fifty sheep, their coats a dirty gray. An overpowering stink of manure hung in the air, accompanied by a feeling of moistness, like all the sheep's exhalations were filling up the barn.

"I assume that's the sweet smell of sheep dip," Michael said, one eyebrow raised. The expression made him look like a really young version of Grandpa. I couldn't help but remember Grandpa's words: *We're all like beads on a string, going on forever, Asmundson after Asmundson.*

"Yes, stinky sheep dip," Mordur answered. "Watch your feet 'cause it will stick like glue to your boots. This is where our flock winters. The goats and the sheep. They do not get out until after the lambing season at the start of May."

"Not even for a breath of fresh air?" I asked.

"No. Snow comes down hard here. And no warning either. Letting them out during winter is a good way to kill them. Just ask the crofters who were slow with bringing in their flock this fall. They had big problems."

Sarah leaned over to pet one of the sheep. Its coat was so thick it looked like a frizzy ball with matchsticks for legs. "They seem friendly enough."

"They think you will feed them." Mordur led us farther into the barn. The sheep parted and formed into groups, watching us like curious children. There were a few bearded animals, nowhere near as fluffy—goats. It was warm inside the barn, so I unzipped my jacket.

"Hot, right?" Mordur unbuttoned his coat, revealing a thick, gray sweater. "This was home to people back in the old days. Before we got heat from the geothermal pools at Laugarbakki."

"They'd live with their sheep?" Sarah asked.

"And cows. The bunks were right above the cows' stalls. It made smart sense. You keep a good eye on the animals. And they gave off warmth. And you didn't have to walk far to get milk."

I couldn't imagine having to fight my way through a crowd of livestock every time I needed to go outside to the bathroom. It'd be even worse getting ready for a date with all those sheep staring at you.

Mordur opened a gate into another pen. "Wait until you see the old croft house in the far pasture. Compared to it, this barn is heavenly."

"It sounds really *baaaaaaahhhd*," Michael said, doing his best impression of a sheep.

Sarah looked supremely annoyed. "Even you shouldn't sink so low, Michael."

"Never underestimate how low I will go, sweet sister." Michael bowed.

Mordur took us into the far corner of the barn where two ponies stood, staring at us. "This will be our transport."

Grandpa often spoke glowingly about the Icelandic pony. He called it the most dependable four-legged vehicle in the world. They looked like normal horses compressed into about only two-thirds of the size. One was brown and the other gray, their manes dark and wild, their long tails flowing down to the straw-covered floor.

We helped Mordur bridle the ponies, then led them out into the fresh, open air. They followed without the slightest bit of fuss. "Don't we need saddles?" I asked.

"Bareback riding is not hard. Right, Sleipnir?" Mordur patted the gray pony's forehead. "We will trade turns. It is a long way and there is just four hours of good light, so we had better be quick. I will give you hand up."

He stood beside the pony and cupped his fingers into a stirrup. I'd ridden horses a couple of times before at Michael and Sarah's place, so I knew what to do. I put my left foot in his hand and grabbed the reins. He lifted me carefully and I was surprised at his strength. Then suddenly he lost his footing and slipped to one knee. I fell against him but he was able to hold me up. I had to put my hand on his shoulder to balance myself. "I have got you," he said, gently raising me up again.

The horse stayed perfectly still. I slid my right leg over it, holding the reins in my left hand.

Mordur backed half a step away, keeping one hand on the horse. "Sorry," he said quietly, grinning, "your hair made me— how you say—blinded?"

Was it a compliment? "It does that sometimes," I said and returned his smile.

"You get better grip if you hold the reins in the other hand," he suggested.

"I'm a southpaw. This *is* my best hand."

Mordur gave me a cute but bewildered look. "Southpaw?"

"It means I'm left-handed," I explained, pretending to write with my left hand. "Southpaw is just an expression from back home."

He stared at me blankly. "Well, use either your north or south paw. Just hold tight."

I grinned. Sarah was already on the second horse. She sat up straight and her legs came down past its belly, about two feet from the ground.

"They have seven speeds," Mordur explained, "none very fast. This way." He motioned and started walking towards the hills, with Michael plodding along beside him.

"Giddyup." I shook the reins and the horse paced behind them. I stroked its neck and it raised its head in a sort of salute.

"What are their names again?" I asked.

"That is Sleipnir and the brown is Nonni." Mordur was powering his way through the snow, which was getting deeper the farther we got from the buildings.

"Sleipnir?" I said to Sarah, who was riding right beside me. "Isn't that the name of Odin's horse?"

"Yeah, Sleipnir had eight legs and could travel through all the worlds, even down to the underworld." Her ponytail barely bobbed as she rode. It *was* a smooth ride. "Remember the story of how Baldur died from a poisoned dart? And Baldur's brother, Hermod, borrowed Sleipnir and rode all the way to *Niflheim*, the land of the dead. And he begged Hel, the female keeper of the underworld, to let Baldur live again."

"I remember," I said, "that's when Hel said Baldur will only be brought back to life if all the creatures in the world weep for him. But Loki wouldn't shed a tear, so Baldur had to remain in the underworld." I ran my hand across Sleipnir's mane. "There were a couple of other stories about Sleipnir, too, weren't there?"

"Odin races Sleipnir against a giant with a horse named Gold Mane," Michael added, "and he wins hands down."

Mordur was looking at us with open wonderment. "I'm impressive!"

"You're impressed, you mean," I corrected.

He immediately covered his face with one hand, as if to hide his shame. "Yes, I am impressed. You three know a great much about the old myths. And Uncle Thordy said you all are somehow related to Grettir. He is a big hero around here."

"We're Asmundsons through and through," Michael said.

"Except me. I'm a Laxness," I added. "I get my Asmundson blood through my mom. And with a grandfather like ours you have to be able to quote from the myths or the sagas till the cows come home." I paused. "Or should I say till the sheep come home?"

Mordur chuckled, Sarah and Michael groaned. You can't please everyone, I thought. Mordur gave me another of his perfect smiles. There was something about him being out in the open with the landscape all around that made him appear even better looking. He belonged in a painting. "Laxness?" he asked. "That is not a common name."

"It was easier to say than Svéinurdarson, our family's original last name. When my great-grandfather landed in Canada, they asked him what his last name was, and he thought they asked him what farm he was from in Iceland. So he said 'Laxness.' And the name has stuck ever since."

We headed through the valley, most of it desolate and covered with a thick layer of snow. Soon the farm was far behind us. The mountains loomed on the horizon, never quite letting us see the sun. The light was so different here than back in North Dakota. It was like being in another world entirely.

"Hey, isn't that Uncle Thordy's truck?" Michael pointed

to the road, which was far below us now. A white truck was parked in a turnoff.

"It is. But I do not see him. Maybe he had a problem," Mordur said, squinting his eyes. "He is close to home. If it is a deflated tire, he will be able to fix it on his own."

We turned and continued on. Soon the hills blocked our view of the road. Mordur didn't ask to ride either of the ponies, and when I suggested he should take a turn, he said he was used to long walks.

Michael wiped his forehead. "Well, *I'm* ready to take a pony for a spin."

I surrendered Sleipnir to Michael, but not before patting the horse on the neck and thanking him for carrying me. Michael launched himself onto Sleipnir's back. He looked rather comical, his legs hanging so low his boots dragged through the snow. "Does this thing have power steering?"

We ignored him and plodded along. Soon we were at the end of the valley and climbing towards a plateau.

"The summer pasture is high up but not far," Mordur explained. After about forty minutes or so, we passed within a few hundred yards of a tiny church set into the side of a hill. A large stone cross stood near the front door like a guardian.

"Who would build a church out here?" Michael asked.

"The old crofters," Mordur said. "There are many churches in Iceland. It was a sign of your goodness to build a church on your land. And wealth."

"Can we go see it?" I asked.

He shook his head. "Not today. Too far long. It looks near, but there are hard paths. And it is high up. It is built so the back overhangs a cliff."

We slogged through the snow. My legs were aching slightly and my toes felt a little frosty, but it wasn't anything I hadn't experienced before. A little farther on I saw the glint of glass high on a plateau above us. An old, gray house stood on the edge of a large cliff overlooking the ravine. I stopped and pointed at it. "Who lives up there?"

"Gunnvor and her son. That house is made of huge stones. The only stone home in this area. Gunnvor is the one Thordy spoke of last night—very odd, very mean woman. They have no church on their land."

"What's that mean?" Sarah gently pulled back on the reins to get Nonni to stand still.

"There has not been a church built. Their family did not want one. They rarely come down from their place. Who knows what they eat. And when they do show up in town, it is at odd times. Funerals, weddings, town meetings. Always angry and never invited."

"They? How many are there?" Michael asked.

"Gunnvor and her son. Her husband died a long time ago. Gunnvor believes Thordy and his farm are too close to hers, that he is really a sitter—uh—a squatter on their land."

"But hasn't our family owned this place since before the twenties?" I said. "They must have if Grandpa was born here."

"Yes, but Gunnvor's kin were up there lots of years ago. They were first to arrive. They do not care about government-made maps or land titles." Mordur made an odd motion with his hand, like a sign to ward away evil. "I dislike to talk long about them. I get the feelings Gunnvor is staring at us right now." He stepped up his marching speed and led us higher, onto flat land. I kept glancing over my shoulder until the house had disappeared.

"These are the grazing flats." Mordur motioned like a tour guide. From this height the farmhouses were out of sight. The land here was smooth and rounded like the inside of a shallow bowl, made white with snow. "In the spring it is green with grass and marshes and a bright sun. I spend many hours out here watching our flock, daydreaming, reciting the sagas."

"I bet you'd kill for a TV," Michael said.

"There's no reception. It is too far from transmitters," Mordur replied.

"Actually, I was just kidding," Michael said. "A joke."

"Oh, I see . . . I see it." Mordur grinned. "A TV would be great fun. But I find books far easier to carry."

A chill wind hit us, whistling over the rock formations and knocking back my hood, making my hair fly all over the place. I tugged the hood back into position.

"We had better get inside," Mordur said. He led us around a large pile of boulders. About twenty yards away, leaning to one side and looking like it had been through several different wars, was the legendary croft house.

14

It was a lopsided, two-story dwelling that had been built against a hill. The bottom shell was made of wood, and slices of turf were piled against the walls. It looked barely big enough to fit five sheep comfortably. At the top was a rounded loft with a dormer window and a slanted roof thick with snow. Somehow this glorified bunkhouse had stood against all the snow, sleet, and wind nature could throw its way. Crags rose up behind it, dwarfing the place.

Mordur pointed at it. "Here lived one of the first crofters with his sheep, horse, and dogs. And his wife and four children."

"It must have been a tight fit," I said.

"Everyone stayed warm in winter."

"This is what Grandpa wanted us to see?" Michael asked. "A sheep shack?"

Mordur pulled back his hood. "This *sheep shack* has bigger history than some castles. It is what Iceland is about—people working hard to make a living. Fighting against snow, rain, bad prices. The real Iceland heroes are the old crofters. They deserve respect. Your family is part of this croft house's story. Your grandfather spent his childhood summers up here."

"I bet all he did was talk to himself and make up bad jokes," Sarah said.

The wind had doubled, whipping my hair against the side of my face. I pulled my neck scarf tighter. "Will this place keep us warm?" I asked.

"It will block the breeze." If Mordur thought this was a breeze, I'd hate to see his idea of a storm. He led us closer. "I stayed up here most of last fall watching the flock. It is a good shelter." The front door was big enough for a cow to go through. Mordur yanked the door open and it nearly fell off. It was hanging by one rusted hinge. Michael and Sarah had dismounted and were about to tie the horses to an old post. "No, bring them in," Mordur said, holding the door wide. "This is where they stay."

We led the horses into a cramped space that was half a foot taller than their heads. We had to stoop to enter. The air was stale; cobwebs hung down from the ceiling. Two stalls stood along one wall. Mordur gestured. "There were maybe twenty lambs and two horses here in the old days."

"They must have stacked them," Sarah said, pulling Nonni farther into the stable.

"Stack them?" Mordur gave her a quizzical look. "Oh, I see, no—they just squish them together. They were plenty happy when spring came."

"Where's the rest of the place?" Michael asked. "You don't sleep on this straw in the summer do you?"

Mordur motioned above us. "Follow me."

He took the reins of both horses and tied them in separate

stalls. The wind whistled between cracks, stirring the dust and the old straw. It was going to be a long, cold walk home. Of course, if it was gusting in the right direction it might push us all the way back to Uncle Thordy's house.

Mordur stopped at a seven-runged ladder that led to the ceiling. He climbed to the top, pushed on a corner, and a trapdoor opened. "Climb up," he said.

Michael went first. Sarah brushed a cobweb off her shoulder. "This is not what I expected from a European vacation."

"I was hoping for a dip in one of those famous Icelandic hot springs, myself," I said.

Sarah laughed, then turned and started up. By the time I got to the top, Mordur had already lit an oil lamp and had set it in the middle of the room on a metal stove. The place stunk of must and dry manure. There was a washbasin imbedded in one wall and three sleeping benches stuck out from another. There wouldn't have been much privacy. An old, lumpy-looking mattress rested on the middle bench. A table, slightly larger than a newspaper, was nailed below a windowsill. The shutters were latched closed, but the "breeze" was still trying to force its way in, rattling them.

Sarah sat on a bench. "A whole family would stay up here?"

"They must have been pretty short," Michael said.

"They were good benders." Mordur was hunched over, dragging a wood chair across the floor. "Icelanders are smarter than most people think. Let's lunch."

I headed towards one of the wood benches, avoiding the grungy mattress. My foot kicked a small object and I looked down. A dead mouse. "Gross," I said, jumping away. I knocked over something. It was a slim wooden box about ten inches long. It broke open on the floor and three rolled-up pieces of paper fell out.

"What're you doing, Angie?" Michael was sitting on a three-legged stool, one hand under his chin like he was thinking real hard. "Some kind of new dance?"

"I just about stepped on that dead mouse."

"There is a lot here." Mordur didn't sound too worried. "They like this place."

I was going to be extremely careful where I sat. But first, I picked up the paper scrolls and partly unrolled one, revealing lines of writing. The paper was quite thick and felt rough around the edges. "What are these made of?"

"Calfskins," Mordur answered.

"Yuck!" I dropped them right away. This place was a junkyard. I'd probably caught a hundred diseases in the last few seconds. "What on earth are they doing here?"

He grinned. "They belonged to my father. In the old days the Icelanders would not have much paper—not enough trees—so they wrote stories on dried and stretched calfskins. Dad liked to study history of crofters, so he made these on his own. This is how sagas were preserved."

I picked one up gingerly and looked at the words. "They're in French. Are they . . . uh . . . a diary?"

"I cannot read it. Dad spent some years working on a French fishing troller and lived in Paris. He met my mother there. These letters might be to her, but he and her were—uh—how do you say it? Not good company together."

"We know what you mean," Sarah said softly.

"If they're not for your mom," Michael asked, "then why are they in French?"

Mordur shrugged. "Maybe he wanted to keep them secret. Not many Icelanders know French."

"What are they doing in the croft house?" Sarah asked.

"They were a big hobby of my father while he watched the sheep. I found the skins last fall in the walls when I set mouse-traps."

"I don't think they're a diary," I said, scanning them. "They might be a story."

"Why?" Mordur asked.

"I recognize one word: *loup-garou*. It means werewolf. Was your dad a writer?"

"He did tell tales. Maybe he wrote some down." Mordur took the calfskins from me, looked at them for a moment, then rolled them back up. "There is another thing," he said and reached into a corner of the box and pulled out a long, slender metal object. It had four sharp edges that tapered down to a point and was about twice the length of my index finger.

Michael brought his chair closer. "Is that a spearhead?"

"Yes. There are tiny figures carving into it. I think Dad made it, too. There is a drawing of the spearhead on one of the calf-skins."

"He was a talented guy," I said.

"Yes," Mordur agreed, "he had lots of big projects. He wished to be known as the crofter who made the old days come to life."

"'Cattle die,'" I quoted, "'kinsmen die, I myself shall die, but there is one thing I know never dies: the reputation we leave behind at our death.'"

"Why did you say that?" Mordur asked.

"It's something our grandfather taught us, from a story about

421

our great-grandfather," I explained. "I guess I just wanted to say it looks like your dad succeeded. He's created some real beautiful things. I'm sure people around here remember him as a historian. This stuff should be in a museum."

Mordur nodded. "You are right. One thing we Icelanders worry about always—what people will think about us after we are gone."

"I bet Grandpa can read the calfskins," Michael said. "He's from Canada. I'm sure he knows a few words in French. I remember him translating the French on a cereal box for me once."

"I will show him then." Mordur carefully placed the calfskins and the spearhead inside the wooden box and clasped the lid shut.

The gusting wind picked up outside, rattling the sides of the croft house. Drafts of cold air crept across the floor, rose high enough to make the flame in the oil lamp flicker. The place wasn't exactly windproof.

Michael opened up our lunch and grabbed some *hardfiskur*. He passed the bag to us. I took an apple and a strip of the dried fish. Even in the dim light of the oil lamp, the fish didn't look all that yummy. I handed the remainder to Sarah. "I have a question," Sarah said to Mordur. "It's about Uncle Thordy. And if you don't want to answer it, I'll understand."

Mordur was silent for a few seconds, his face serious.

"I answer what I can. But remember, he is my boss *and* my friend. He has done much for me."

"I understand," Sarah said. She bit her lip, thought for a second. "When we first arrived, he seemed . . . I don't know . . . frightened. Like he expected something bad to happen. Do you know why?"

"He has not been good since Kristjanna died. It is over a year and a half. Before that Thordy made the jokes and would whistle while he worked. He is all nerves now. He—I don't know how much I should let spill."

"He's family," Sarah said softly. She briefly held Mordur's hand, which made me raise an eyebrow. "We want to help him if we can."

"Well, he sometimes goes into deep sadnesses. He stays in the house for lots of days, leaves the lights off. He told me I was never to go in, unless he lets me in. Other times he leaves for a week without telling me. It is like he is trying to go away from everything. And I do not complain, but I do most of the work now. I rounded up all the sheep on my own last year. And there are troubles with money."

"Is that why he's going to town today?" Michael asked.

"Yes. Thordy wants another loan to keep the farm going on. He is not good with the books. He used to be most good. But what is going on in his head is what really bothers me. Sometimes I see his shadow in the window, staring out at the yard for hours, waiting for something to appear."

"But maybe there's some other reason for it. Did someone rob the place?" I asked.

"No, nothing like that. Part of it is a little—uh—bad thing we have been having on the croft. It started after Kristjanna's death. We lost two kids."

"You mean kids have died?" I asked.

"He means baby *goats*, Einstein," Michael explained, rolling his eyes.

"Uh . . . I'll shut up now." I took a nervous bite of the *hardfiskur*. It was as hard as it sounded, but not bad once you chewed it for a while. I swallowed, and the lump scraped its way down my throat.

"These goats disappeared without trace. We knew they were gone, because their mothers made such a noise. It is a terrible sound when a mother goat loses her kid. It upsets the whole flock.

"Thordy and I split up and looked low and high for them. My dog, Tyr, and I stumbled across their remains. They had been dragged onto a rock shelter high above the plain, their bones spread across the ground and broken in half. All the marrow was sucked out. The flesh was eaten."

I felt cold. I slipped my hands inside my jacket pockets. Mordur was staring into the flame of the lamp, looking hypnotized. "Thordy was not happy. We called the local constable and tried to figure what did this. Not a fox. And men are the only other meat eaters on Iceland. There were rumors about a mountain man—a criminal who lives in hiding—but the tooth marks were too sharp.

"Nothing more happened for months, and we got the sheep safely home, but that winter was *fellivetur*, a slaughter winter. Deep snow. Very cold. In the old days they had to kill all livestock because they would have nothing to feed them.

"On one evening when the moon was high and bright, I was out shoveling off my roof. It had just snowed. I stopped to rest and heard Tyr bark a warning. I climbed down and real fast made my way out into the deep snow. But his barking got far and farther away. Then it became growling and yelping and finally he was silent. I ran quick through hip-deep snow, the moon showing me my way. I rounded a corner and saw a big, gray thing feeding on the body of Tyr. It looked up at me.

Its eyes glowed with orange light. They held me and I could not move, a cold chill going through my bones. The creature backed away, seemed to almost smile. Then it ran off into the night."

He stopped. The wind continued to buffet the croft house, shaking the shutters. It wasn't getting any warmer inside.

"Has anything else happened since?" Michael asked.

"Two more lambs died. We did not find their bones. But they were safe in the barn before they disappeared."

"What do you think it was?" I asked.

"Maybe just a wolf that rode an ice floe here. About every twenty years one shows up. I do not know how it got in our barn, though. There are no holes wide enough. Thordy and I spent the summer patching. And it could not open the latch; you would need hands for that."

"You didn't want to bring us out here, did you?" Sarah was using *the stare*, the one where she knows there's an answer, and if she stares long and hard enough you'll spit it out.

"What?" Mordur looked stunned by the question.

"That's what you and Uncle Thordy argued about before we left." She kept staring at him.

He pursed his lips. "Yes, we had a disagree. I . . . I wasn't sure if it was safe. He said it was daylight, there was no thing to fear . . ."

The window shutter banged open as if a fist had struck it. A blast of snow and biting wind swept over us. Mordur struggled towards the window. He grabbed the shutters and was able to close one, but not the other. Michael jumped up beside him, pushing on the second shutter until Mordur could latch them both shut. With Michael's help he jammed a post against them.

"It is really storming big. I could not see much past the window. This was not in any of the radio forecasts."

The sudden chill had knocked the last bit of warmth from my body. "Let's go home. I don't want to be stuck out here for Christmas."

Mordur peered through the cracks. "We had better wait. It is a whiteout. The paths would be very not good. It will blow by soon. Of course, if you do not like the weather now, just wait five minutes, it will get worse."

"What?" Michael said.

"It is a saying. A joke. We will be okay. And Thordy knows where we are. The world would not end if we stayed the night."

"It'd be pretty close," Sarah whispered. I wrapped my arms around myself.

"Why not start a fire?" Mordur opened the grate on the stove. He carried an armful of what looked like brown squares from a pile by the wall and threw them in the potbelly. Then he took a hand shovel full of gray-black chunks from another pile and tossed them inside.

"What's that?" Michael asked.

Mordur lit a match. "Peat. I dug it up from the marshes east of the house. And dried sheep's dung. It burns good." He tossed the match in and seconds later a fire appeared. "Logs are hard to find up here."

"Is it gonna stink?" I asked.

"You will get used to it,"

Yeah right, I thought. At first I stayed as far away as I could, but soon the stove began to cast off heat, so Sarah and I edged closer, holding our hands near the stove, letting our palms grow warm.

There was a grating sound from downstairs. Then a slam. The horses whinnied loudly and banged around inside their stalls.

Michael looked up from the fire, eyes wide. "What the heck was that?"

15

We listened for what seemed an eternity. The wind continued to hiss through the cracks, but I couldn't hear anything else. Michael took a step towards the trapdoor and the floorboards creaked below his feet. Mordur motioned him to be still.

The beams that held up the croft house began groaning. The sound became louder and harsher and I realized it wasn't the beams making the noise. It was something else. A growl reverberated somewhere below us.

"There's something down there," Sarah whispered.

The growl grew deeper. It was unlike anything I'd ever heard. It worked its way into my nerves, my bones, my spine so that I couldn't move.

The others were frozen in place too, all straining to hear the next noise. The flames in the stove died down and a coldness crept into the room. Even the oil lamp grew dimmer.

The horses had remained silent and I imagined them pressed up against the sides of their stalls, tied tightly, eyes wide with fear, not wanting to attract the attention of the intruder.

Mordur reached for the fire poker and gripped it tightly. "We should not have come here." He took a step towards the trap-door, then stopped as if he wasn't sure what to do next.

The growling grew louder. The support beam in the center of the croft house creaked like a weight had leaned up against it. A heavy hissing noise drifted through the floorboards.

I came slowly out of my shock. There were cracks in the floor, so I knelt and looked through one. It was dark down there, except for a frail band of light.

I could make out a thin shape next to the support beam. It wasn't that large, maybe four or five feet tall. It was standing on its hind feet and appeared to be covered with fur. Its head was hidden in shadows. It was definitely some kind of animal, but not one I recognized.

"I . . . I think I see it," I whispered.

It turned towards me, as if it had heard my voice, and revealed a long snout.

"What . . ." Michael began. I looked up, motioned him to be silent.

I peeked back down and the thing had moved out of the pale light.

One of the horses neighed sharply, then the other. A board snapped. A roar, this time so loud it drowned out the horses' cries, echoed through the floor. A second timber broke, then came the clomping of hooves, a crash.

A large, dark blur shot through the band of light—one of the horses. He smacked into the side of the croft house. The neighing of both horses became louder, higher-pitched, so that they weren't even the noises of horses anymore. They sounded almost human, like they were being tortured.

Then there was a thud. Now there was only one horse

neighing, its voice ragged. It wheezed out its fright, stomping and struggling against an unseen attacker. Roars and growls echoed through the trapdoor.

For a moment the horse stood in the light and I could see its gray hide. It was Sleipnir. Four gashes stretched along his side; one leg looked broken. He tried to neigh, but only blood bubbled out of his mouth.

A gray shape jumped onto his back and clung to him. Sleipnir let out a frightened, gurgling whinny, kicked up his front legs, and jumped out of the light. The whole croft house shook.

We looked at each other. Mordur was still holding tightly to the fire poker. Michael, who had been frozen in place, shifted his weight and the floor creaked, loudly. There was an answering rustle from below us. Then came an odd, childlike cry of discovery from a few feet below the trapdoor. Like a prize had been found.

Us.

16

The ladder creaked as rung by rung the intruder climbed up. Next came a sniffing, a great inhalation of air. This was a hunter who had tasted blood and now wanted more. There wasn't a nerve in my body that would function. Ice ran through every vein, weighing me down.

We stared at the trapdoor. It lifted slowly, hinges squeaking with rust. A snout tested the air for several seconds, then the thing pushed its head up into the chamber and turned towards us, its eyes glowing orange. The creature looked human, except for the protruding canine snout and a covering of dark gray fur. It opened a wolflike mouth and let out a low growl. Dangling from its teeth was a strip of hide, flesh still attached.

It brought up a hand, not a paw, but a hand—with four clawed fingers and a thumb.

Before it could climb another step, Mordur yelled, launched himself through the air, and landed on the trapdoor, knocking the beast to the ground with a great thump. It roared and a second later the trapdoor, which Mordur was still lying across, was struck from below, lifting it up a few inches and nearly throwing Mordur right off.

"Help me hold it down!" he cried.

Michael got there first, kneeled next to Mordur, adding his weight to the door. I forced each muscle into motion, stood up. The trapdoor was hit a second time and one of the hinges flew into the air, deflecting off the roof.

I found a long post and slid it across the door, between Michael and Mordur. There were two rings on either side that had been nailed into the floor. Sarah grabbed the other end of the post and helped me guide it towards the opposite ring, but it was too big to fit cleanly.

A third blow hammered into the wood. Michael was knocked off and Mordur fell away, clutching his ribs.

"Quick!" Sarah hissed. "Push it through."

I shoved the post. It caught the other ring and I forced it into the hole, blocking the door. Michael and Mordur had jumped back on the door, braced themselves for an impact.

None came.

There was a knothole in the center of the trapdoor, large enough to see through. I leaned over to peer through it and was hit by a scent of rotting flesh. Then a large, hypnotizing eye filled the hole, swirling with orange and gray colors. It mesmerized me. A voice began to speak in my head in a language I'd never heard before. But the message was clear: *Surrender. Don't struggle. Don't resist. There is no escape.* The eye stared right into me, seemed to know who I was. My body became weak.

"Annnngggie." Michael's voice sounded slow and thick. "Annngie whatttsss wwrrronngg?"

Someone leaned in beside me. Sarah. Close enough that she could see through the hole. She gasped, then backed away. "Geh-eh-ttt gonnnne!" she yelled. Her voice freed me slightly and I was able to inch away. She had stoked the fire, lighting the room, and was now holding a heated metal poker. "Get gone!" she commanded. *"Fardu burt! Draugr! Flydu!"*

She ran forward and shoved the poker down into the knot-hole. The thing below us screamed and pounded so hard against the trapdoor that the wood cracked. Another wail followed, like a child that had been denied a toy.

We could hear the creature running and the noise of the door to the outside crashing open.

Sarah lowered the poker.

"Is it gone?" Michael asked. "Is it gone?"

I slowly released my grip on the post. My body ached. I bent and peeked through the crack in the trapdoor, afraid I would see that eye again, hear that voice. But there was nothing. Snow was blowing in through the door; already a small bank had formed on the ground.

"What the hell was that?" Michael asked.

"It was . . . it was . . ." I was shaking, my hands cold. "I thought it only went after sheep, Mordur."

Mordur was still kneeling on the trapdoor, holding his ribs. He pushed himself to his feet. "That was not what attacked my dog. That was too small."

"You mean there's something larger out there?" I asked.

"I do not know. Perhaps," Mordur said.

"Well, that's great news," Michael said. He looked at Sarah. "And what were *you* yelling? Some kind of hocus pocus?"

Sarah shook her head. "It was from the sagas. I read it a long time ago. It just came back to me before I hit that thing in the eye."

"Well, it worked," Mordur said, "but for how long?"

17

We armed ourselves with whatever we could lay our hands on—Mordur found a large hunting knife, Michael a board, Sarah kept the metal poker. I picked up a walking stick. We waited, listened. When we finally thought it was safe, Michael slid the pole out of the rings and slowly lifted the trapdoor. Mordur leaned into the hole, craned his neck so he could see into all corners of the lower croft room. "It is gone," he said. He climbed down the ladder, holding the knife in one hand. Michael, then Sarah, followed.

I decided the walking stick was too thin to be a good weapon, so I searched around for something else.

"Angie, what're you doing up there?" Michael yelled through the trapdoor.

"I'll be down in a second." I found another fire poker leaning against a chair, and next to it the backpack that Michael had used to carry our lunch. A few inches away was the box of calfskins. It seemed to be my job to clean up after these guys. I gently put the box inside the backpack and pulled it over one shoulder. I grabbed the poker and went to the stove, twisting a key on the oil lamp. The wick sank out of sight, the light died. I stumbled across the floor to the trapdoor and climbed down the ladder.

The front door had been knocked off its hinges; snow blanketed the ground floor. Mordur was bent over one of the horses. "Poor Sleipnir. Look at his throat . . ."

Sarah turned away. "It's terrible." I was glad to be standing a few feet away, I couldn't see anything clearly.

Mordur stared at Sleipnir, his face grim. "Thordy and I will come back to bury them. They will be good here for now. With the snow and cold."

Mordur stood up and stared out the entrance, holding his knife out in front of himself. "I do not think that . . . that thing will be back soon. It will be holed up somewhere with a sore eye. The snow is cleared, maybe enough to make home. Are you ready to go?"

"We don't have much choice," Michael said. Sarah was already tightening a scarf around her face. I pulled my zipper up. I didn't want to spend another moment in this place.

We entered a world of whiteness. There was a splash of red next to the broken door. I stepped closer and found a small cloth sack on the ground, just like the one I'd seen back at Uncle Thordy's house. It had been torn open and a black liver-like thing sat on the snow.

"What's that?" I asked.

"Butcher bag," Mordur said. "Livers and hearts and organs. For fox traps."

"I saw a bag like that near the house," I said. "What's another one doing here?"

He shrugged. "I do not know. But we better go home."

We marched through the snow, which had now gathered into huge drifts. The occasional blast of wind tried to knock us off our feet and coated our eyebrows and scarves with wet snow. We struggled through high banks, frosty air rising from our mouths. I had no idea what time it was anymore. The light behind us was fading.

On the plateau, the snow made everything look even flatter. There was no horizon, just a blank world. Somehow Mordur found the way. We traveled in single file, one step behind him. He would turn to help when there was a long drop or a difficult area to cross.

We hardly spoke. Sarah stumbled and Michael let her lean on his shoulder. They walked this way for quite a while, helping each other. I thought of Andrew and what it would be like if he were still here. Tears welled up in my eyes.

I was growing colder and rubbed my cheeks to get the blood flowing, then tightened up my scarf.

Mordur halted every once in a while and searched around as if trying to see some invisible pursuer. I sped up so I was a step behind him. "I got your dad's letters," I yelled above the wind.

"Did you?" He looked surprised and relieved. "I forgot them from my mind."

"I knew you'd want them." I wanted to say something else. Something about his father perhaps. Maybe I'd tell him I knew what it was like to miss someone you cared about.

Mordur cast another glance backwards, but before I could open my mouth to tell him what I was thinking, he shouted, "Hurry! Soon there will not be any light left."

The sky was now gray. How long had we been out here? I picked up my pace, gave up on talking. Every ounce of energy was funneled towards putting one leg in front of the other. I couldn't help but think that there was something in the snow behind us, pursuing us.

The feeling of running away reminded me of my nightmares. Were they warnings about what attacked us in the croft house? Or was there something worse out there?

When I first spotted Uncle Thordy's house, I let out a small cheer. The porch light flickered and Uncle Thordy's truck was parked outside. We broke into a run, kicking snow ahead of us.

We burst into the house without knocking. Uncle Thordy met us in the hall, his fists clenched. "You're back!" he exclaimed, dropping his hands. "Are you alright?"

At first none of us spoke. Whatever he saw in our faces must have answered his question. "What happened?" He looked directly at Mordur. "What happened?"

"The *úlfslikid*, it attacked us."

18

Uncle Thordy's eyes widened. "During the day! Where?"

"In the croft . . ." Mordur began. He sucked in some air, held his side. "I . . . I think we must sit down."

"Come in, come in." Uncle Thordy motioned with his hands. "You all look like you've been dragged through *Niflheim* and back."

We kicked our boots off, dropped our weapons, and tumbled into the living room. Uncle Thordy locked the door and followed us. The lights of the Christmas tree reflected in the window and the fireplace was blazing. It looked like heaven. I collapsed on the easy chair and loosened my jacket. I set the backpack at my feet. Michael and Sarah plopped down on the couch, both still dressed for outside. Mordur leaned against the wall beside me, favoring his right side.

"You okay?" I asked.

"Yes," he wheezed, "just a little bump."

"Why don't you sit?" I said, patting the armrest of my chair.

He gave me a mocking salute that only made him wince more, then sat carefully. "Thanks," he whispered.

Uncle Thordy had gone into the kitchen. He returned with a tray full of coffee in huge gray mugs. I grabbed mine eagerly, the comforting smell filling my nostrils. I sipped. It almost burned my tongue.

"Where are the horses?" Uncle Thordy asked.

"Dead." Mordur leaned one arm on his knee, trying to take pressure off his chest. "Both dead."

There was the sound of a door opening and footsteps plodding down the hall. Grandpa stumbled like a sleepwalker into the room, his face as pale as the white bathrobe he was wearing.

"Uncle Thursten, careful." Uncle Thordy got up and tried to guide him to a seat, but Grandpa just waved him away. Step by slow, careful step he closed in on his target, then turned and lowered himself onto the couch beside Sarah. He looked like he'd aged ten years in the last ten hours. His eyes were bloodshot. His lips curled into a painful smile. "Don't stop on my account," he whispered hoarsely, "things were just getting interesting. Please, though, for an old man's sake, start at the beginning."

So we did. First Mordur spoke, then we found our voices. Sarah would explain something and Michael and I would add our bits. It was a jumbled story, like piecing together a nightmare. I drank the rest of my coffee; my body was finally starting to warm up. I took my jacket off.

When we finished, Grandpa cleared his throat. It was a gross, phlegmy sound. He looked at Mordur. "So you think this—we'll call it a wolf—is different than the one you saw before?"

"Yes. But it was dark both times. Maybe it grew large in my memory."

Grandpa thought this over for a second, then turned to Uncle Thordy. "How many attacks have there been?"

"Four," Uncle Thordy said. "Just on animals though. The only evidence we've found are tracks."

"Wolf tracks?"

"No, not exactly. They are larger. But signs of claws in the print. The tracks always disappear after a few hundred yards. And, up until now, it's only happened at night. Dogs won't follow the beast, they just spin in circles and yelp. The constable is baffled by them." Uncle Thordy wiped sweat from his forehead. The thick scars above his eyebrow glistened. "I thought the nephews would be safe. I'd never have allowed a trip to the old croft house if I thought this could happen."

"It wasn't like anything I'd seen before," I said, thinking of its glowing eyes. "It climbed the ladder. It had . . . hands."

"Hands?" Uncle Thordy repeated.

"Did it bite any of you?" Grandpa asked.

We all shook our heads.

"Any scratches?"

Again, we shook our heads. Grandpa let out his breath, like we'd answered an important question.

My thoughts were getting tangled. I wanted to yell *What's going on?* Grandpa seemed to know more than he was letting on. Maybe Uncle Thordy did, too.

Another part of me just wanted to curl up in some corner and hide. Too much was happening.

"I . . ." Mordur began. "I have a favor to ask from you, Mr. Asmundson."

"It's Thursten," Grandpa said. "And what's this favor?"

Mordur reached down for the backpack, opened it, and

pulled out the box. He lifted the lid and gently took out the calfskins. "These were hidden in the croft house. My father wrote French on them. Michael said you would read it."

"French?" Grandpa echoed. "I can't say I know much of it. My wife dragged me to a French class for a few months before we went on a holiday in Quebec. I watch hockey games on the French channel, but that's about it. At least I know when they say, 'he shoots, he scores.' I'll give it a try."

"There is also this." Mordur held the spearhead in the palm of his hand so everyone could see. It glinted in the light. "I think Dad made it."

"He kept himself busy," Uncle Thordy said. "That's one thing about Einar. If he wasn't reading some old book about Icelandic history, he was trying to recreate it. Some of the professors at the university would even phone him and ask him questions. He showed me a paper that one professor had written that quoted him. He was pretty proud of that."

"May I hold it?" Grandpa said, and Mordur handed the spearhead to him. "That's a fine piece of metalwork. Light, sharp as a razor. And all these symbols carved on the sides. This must have taken a long time." He gave the spearhead back. "I wish I could have met your father. He sounds like quite the man."

"He was," Mordur said.

Just then I saw the slightest movement in the kitchen window. There was a face staring in at us.

Then it was gone.

"There's someone outside," I said.

19

"What?" Uncle Thordy turned towards the kitchen, following my gaze. "Where?"

"In the window," I answered, my voice cracking. "Just for a second. Someone looked in."

Uncle Thordy got up, went into the kitchen. Michael and Mordur followed. They stood at the window peering through the glass.

"Th-there," Sarah whispered. She was still seated next to Grandpa, pointing at the window in the living room. "Someone's there."

I turned. Glaring through the pane was an old, female face, eyeballs the size of boiled eggs, glaring from me to Sarah to Grandpa. The reflection of the Christmas tree lights made it seem like the woman was looking in at us from another world.

The old woman's scratchy voice carried through the windowpane. She was shouting in Icelandic.

"It's Gunnvor," Uncle Thordy whispered, amazement in his voice. "I haven't seen her for years."

The name sounded familiar. Then I remembered Grandpa

had talked about the old woman who lived on the hill. Only hours ago we'd seen her stone house at a distance. So this was Gunnvor.

"She says she's lost her child," Grandpa said. "She says we stole him."

Uncle Thordy strode farther into the living room. "Gunnvor," he said loudly, as if he was speaking to someone who was hard of hearing. He shouted something in Icelandic and pointed to the front door.

Gunnvor grunted a reply.

Uncle Thordy raised his voice even louder, repeated the words.

She disappeared from the window.

We followed Uncle Thordy to the front door. He opened it and called Gunnvor's name a few times, then muttered under his breath like he was cursing. "Mordur, get the flashlights from the kitchen. I'll need help to find her."

Mordur went towards the kitchen, grimacing like he was trying to hold in the pain. Maybe his ribs were broken.

Sarah was already pulling on her coat and heading for the door. "I'll help."

"I'll hold down the fort," Grandpa said from his seat.

I wasn't sure if I wanted to go outside. The woman didn't look all that friendly. And who knew what else could be out there? Michael went out the door too, so I pulled on my jacket and, as I did, noticed a tear in the shoulder. Perhaps I'd caught it on something in the croft. It felt like a bad omen.

We filed out into the front yard. The snow had stopped and there wasn't a breath of wind. The Northern Lights were back, dancing like angels through the sky. We circled the house, but the only sign of Gunnvor was a sled she had left next to the fence.

"There," Mordur said, pointing his flashlight towards the barn.

I could just make out Gunnvor past Uncle Thordy's shoulder. She was wrapped in a large fur coat and crouched in the beam of the flashlight. She wore a cloth cap, but her long gray hair was loose and falling past her shoulders. She glared at us, then pushed open a gate and trudged towards the barn, moving pretty fast for someone who looked older than Iceland itself. Had she walked all the way here from her home?

Sarah must have come to the same conclusion. "I think that's one tough ol' woman," she whispered.

"Gunnvor!" Uncle Thordy yelled. "Wait!"

She grunted something over her shoulder.

"She's going into the barn," Uncle Thordy said, anger in his voice. "She's going to frighten all the sheep. The crazy old hag. Why won't she stay where she belongs?"

He stormed off to the barn, flicked on the lights. We followed him through the front door. The sheep were gathered in one corner, huddled against each other, looking at us, their legs shaking.

Michael closed the door and we walked to the far end of the barn, passing through a gate. There was a large pile of straw in the middle of a stall. Gunnvor was on her knees, throwing handfuls of it behind her. A soft whimpering sound came out of the pile.

We stood back as first a leg appeared, then another, then a chest and arms, and finally the face of a boy, maybe ten years old. His features were wild with terror, and both his eyes were

bruised and swelling. He was foaming at the mouth and holding up his hands to block the light. Strips of clothing covered
him and there were scratches on his chest, arms, and cheeks.
Dried blood stained his body.

"He's been mauled," I said. "He looks awful."

"*Scratches*," Gunnvor barked over her shoulder in a thick,
accented English. She turned back, whispered softly in an
almost singsong voice completely unlike her previous grunt-
ings. "*Onni. Onni. Onni.*"

How could such an old woman be his mother?

"What is wrong?" Mordur asked. "What happened?"

Gunnvor turned her head. "He wanders. He is feebleminded."
She stared daggers at Mordur. "I know you. Einar's brat.
Snoopy as your father. Look where it got him."

Mordur didn't flinch. "How did your son get those scratches?"

"Not your business, whelp," she hissed. She cast her eyes to
Michael, Sarah, and me. "And stop staring at me. You smell of
the New World. Thorgeir Tree-Foot's little brood comes back
to stink up the farm." She turned to her son.

A light of recognition came into Onni's eyes. He suddenly
reached out and with a sharp cry and sigh flung his arms
around Gunnvor's neck. She lifted him from the straw. I saw a
mean-looking gash below his right eye.

A cloth bag fell from his hands. It was torn open, and something that looked like liver slipped out onto the floor. Just like
the bags I'd seen earlier in the day.

Gunnvor kicked at the contents. "Who baited him?" Her
eyes were blazing with rage now. I edged back, afraid of what I
saw in her. "Which one of you?"

No one spoke. I looked at the ground to avoid her glare.

"One of you did," she said. "I would crush your bones if I knew which one." I didn't doubt her. There was steel in her words. Her skin was wrinkled and her gray hair wild about her shoulders, but her thick body looked strong. "If this is one of your tricks, Thordy, you will pay." She pointed a pudgy finger at him, still clutching Onni in her arms. Uncle Thordy straightened his back and narrowed his eyes like he was getting ready for a fight. "You try to cover up your scent with perfumes, but you cannot hide from me." She spat at him, then strode past us, through the gate and out of the barn.

"We can help you," Uncle Thordy said, running after her. We followed.

"No help, not from you," Gunnvor grunted. "Just home. Away from your kind." She carried Onni to the sleigh and wrapped him in blankets. He had calmed down. His eyes stared listlessly at the sky.

"You can't drag him all the way home," Uncle Thordy said, taking a step towards her, then stopping himself, as if he feared she would lash out at him. "Not through all this snow. Please, come inside, we can look after his wounds."

"This isn't enough snow to bother a *real* valley dweller." She pulled on a rope, tying her son to the sleigh.

"But . . ." Uncle Thordy began.

"*No*," Gunnvor said, sharply. She began dragging the sleigh, each stride long and solid. She headed into the east, the Northern Lights swirling above her.

20

A slight breeze was stirring. Clouds had filled in the edges of the sky. Large flakes of snow started falling, getting thicker by the moment. The worst part of the storm may have passed, but Old Man Winter wasn't done dumping snow on us.

We went back inside the house. Grandpa was still in his seat, coughing so hard his face had turned red. Sarah quickly brought him water and he thanked her before tipping back the glass. I sat in the same chair, with Mordur, happily, back on the armrest again.

Uncle Thordy looked down at Grandpa and shook his head. "You should be in bed, Uncle Thursten. You're in no condition to meet any of the relatives. They said they'd come as soon as the roads were cleared. Of course, I'd rather take you to the doctor."

"No doctors. Just bring me coffee," Grandpa whispered hoarsely, "thick and black as a witch's brew. Only two places to get the best coffee in the world: Gimli and right here at Thordy's. Coffee the way it was meant to be. It'd bring a statue to life."

"How can I argue with someone so wise?" Uncle Thordy went to the kitchen and returned a moment later with the coffee. Grandpa could barely hold it, but he managed to sip without spilling a drop. He glared over the steaming cup. "Stop gawking at me . . . you'd think you'd never seen a man drink coffee before."

We sat back. Maybe he *was* starting to feel a bit better.

"So what happened?" Grandpa asked.

Uncle Thordy told him, and the rest of us added our two cents.

Grandpa nodded. "So she's still as testy as ever."

"She claimed someone baited Onni," I said. "With a bag of . . . of animal innards. And I saw a similar bag this morning outside my window. And at the old croft house."

"It was a butcher bag," Mordur explained. "I do not know where he found it."

"We better get a head count on our sheep tomorrow, Mordur," Uncle Thordy said. "I have an idea where some of those organs may have come from."

"What do you mean?" I asked.

"They looked fresh," Thordy explained. "They might have been *gathered* tonight."

I didn't even want to think about what that meant. Sarah was kind enough to change the topic. "Did you see much of Gunnvor when you were a kid?" she asked Grandpa.

"A few times. And she looked exactly the same as she does now, the poor woman. It's like she doesn't age—or she was born old." He lowered the cup of coffee, resting it on his knee. "She once came down and gave my father what-for because his goats were bleating too loud."

"Isn't she a little too old for children?" I asked.

"I'm not sure whose son he is," Uncle Thordy said. "Or even where he came from. Maybe she adopted him. Mr. Gunnvor died years ago—before I was born. At least no one's seen him since around that time."

"So how old is she, then?" I asked.

Grandpa exchanged looks with Uncle Thordy, who shrugged. "I'd guess she's in her nineties," Grandpa finally answered, but he sounded uncertain.

"And she gets around like that?" Michael said in disbelief. "She cut through two feet of snow like it was nothing."

"I don't know how she does it," Grandpa said. "I should have asked her though. I need a little of her energy now."

I could have used some too, if only to keep track of my thoughts. One suddenly occurred to me: What did my hair look like? I bit my tongue to keep from laughing at myself.

Uncle Thordy cleared his throat as if he were about to speak. We all looked at him, but he just stared back, then shook his head. His face appeared even more tired and depressed, like someone had let all the air out of him. He stood, went into the kitchen, and returned with the same cheeses we had seen at breakfast and some dried, smoked cod.

I devoured everything I could get my hands on. Michael and Sarah dug in too. Even Mordur took a handful.

"I think I'm starting to like this food," I whispered to Sarah.

"It does grow on you. Maybe we're getting tougher."

"So what was wrong with that boy?" Michael asked.

"Your guess is as good as mine," Grandpa said. "I'd bet he suffers from some sort of intellectual disability."

"He was covered with blood, though." I helped myself to a chunk of cheese. "What was that from?"

"Maybe he was attacked by the same thing that attacked you," Grandpa suggested.

"No. He would be . . ." Mordur crossed his arms, shivered. "A child would be torn in two."

"There has to be a connection," Grandpa said. "Odd that he would show up here on the same night. And naked. How did he make it through all that snow?"

Uncle Thordy cleared his throat again. His face had become stony. "Actually, it would be easy. He . . . he was in a different form when he walked through the blizzard. His wolf form." Uncle Thordy's voice was solemn, each word said without emotion.

"He what?" Grandpa Thursten asked.

"He's an *úlfr-madr*. A shape-shifter who can become a wolf. Just like the one who killed Kristjanna. That's why he was naked. That's why he's covered with blood. He's the one who attacked you kids at the croft house."

I leaned back into my chair. I didn't like the certainty in Uncle Thordy's voice. I glanced at Grandpa, expecting him to refute this wild claim, but he was wearing his best poker face. He watched Uncle Thordy with curious eyes.

"You think I'm wrong, don't you?" Uncle Thordy accused, jabbing a figure towards Grandpa. "You think it's all in my messed-up head. But you weren't there in that cave. You didn't hold your dead wife in your arms. One of Loki's offspring poked a hole behind her ear and killed her, like it was a game. Maybe it was even little Onni." Uncle Thordy had clenched his hand into a fist and was squeezing so tight it shook. "And now he's got Gunnvor acting as his mother. How do you think she's lived so long? He's shared some of his blood with her. Taken over her mind so she looks after him while he sleeps between kills." Angry red splotches appeared on Uncle Thordy's face. "They don't age like we do. He's probably fifty years old and he looks ten. Who knows where his real parents are."

He lowered his fist, glanced back and forth between all of us. His eyes burned momentarily into mine, daring me to speak out against him. He blinked.

"We all know how much you miss Kristjanna," Grandpa said softly.

Tears began to trickle down Uncle Thordy's cheeks. He gritted his teeth, wiped at his eyes. "Excuse me," he said, quietly. "Forgive me. Forgive me. I am not a good host today." He lifted his bulky body from the chair and trudged down the hall to his room, the scent of his aftershave lingering for a minute. The door closed.

"Uncle Thordy is not feeling well," Grandpa Thursten said, "and I don't know if he'll be better any time soon. It's never easy to get over the death of a loved one."

I remembered standing on the basement stairs at home, watching my father cry so hard that he shook. This was years after Andrew's death. Dad clutched one of Andrew's hockey sweaters in his large hands and cried and cried. I backed slowly up the stairs and left him to his sorrow. Then I went to my own room, closed the door, and bawled into my pillow. Grandpa was right. It wasn't easy to get over the death of someone you loved.

"Grief has been bad to Thordy," Mordur whispered. "My father said when the search party found him they could see big change—he already had ugly bags under his eyes and his hair had turned more gray. Even our dog barked when he came near. Tyr did not know him anymore." Mordur hesitated for a moment, then added, "But I am believing Thordy is right."

21

"Why do you say that?" Grandpa raised his bushy eyebrows.

"Because . . ." Mordur rubbed at the side of his neck like he was trying to ease a kink ". . . because my dad once said a story to me. In 1950 a local crofter wounded a female shape-shifter feeding on a reindeer. He caught her in a net and dragged her to the town square at Hvammstangi."

"How did they know she was a shape-shifter?" I asked.

"She had the head and body of a wolf, but she was walking on two legs. She lived only for a few days. They took photographs. I looked it up. There are articles in the library about the strange woman-wolf, even a drawing. People came from every corner of Iceland just to stare at her."

"Did you see the photos?" Sarah asked.

Mordur shook his head. "None were good. Just a shadow lying against the stump of a tree. When she died, her body fell all to pieces. My father went to see her a few hours before that. He said it was the most very frightening thing he had ever laid his eyes on. But he felt sorrow. She was tied to a stake and left to rot while strangers stared. Dad said he had many nightmares after. His mother tried to say it was a circus trick, but he could not believe her. It had looked too real."

"Perhaps he was right," Grandfather said. He coughed another phlegmy cough, then said quietly, "It was my brother Jóhann, Thordy's father, who found that shape-shifter."

We did simultaneous double takes. "What?" I said. "You . . . you knew about this story?"

Grandfather nodded solemnly. "Yes. My brother phoned and told it to me. I was already living in Manitoba then. He was very excited . . . I thought he had dreamed up the whole thing. Jóhann had a real gift for exaggerations and he was a little scatterbrained at times. He insisted he had caught a shape-shifter; he even sent me the faded photographs of the lump against the tree. I told him he'd been hoodwinked. Up to his dying day he swore it was a true story. Maybe I shouldn't have doubted him so much." Grandpa coughed again. "There is one thing that bothers me. Jóhann said he could hear a high-pitched howling for weeks afterwards. It sounded like a younger wolf. He believed there was one more."

"Oh great," Michael said, "is it Onni, then?"

Grandfather fell silent, his lips a tight line. He drank from his coffee.

22

The fire crackled loudly, and I almost jumped out of my seat. I was definitely getting too wound up. No more coffee for me.

"You know, I'd like to see what your father wrote on the calf-skins," Grandpa said suddenly. Mordur pulled them out of the wooden box and handed them to Grandpa, who unrolled one and held it up to his face. He squinted, lifted his glasses out of his pocket, and fumbled to put them on. "*Je suis* . . . uh, I am . . . uh . . . It keeps mentioning this name, Skoll, over and over again. And it mentions Kristjanna, too."

"Uncle Thordy's wife?" Michael said. "Why would it mention her?"

Grandpa shrugged. He rubbed at his temple like he was trying to ward off a headache.

"It has the words *loup-garou*," I said. "We thought it might be a story."

"A weird one, if it is." Grandpa had opened the third scroll. "And there's a drawing of the spearhead. It says it's Jón Arason's spear. I wonder if that's Bishop Arason."

"Who?" Sarah asked.

Grandpa wiped some sweat from his forehead. "Bishop Jón Arason was from the sixteenth century. He was sometimes called the last real Icelander because he stuck to his beliefs. In fact he was beheaded by his enemies for those beliefs. He was an historical figure, but, of course, this *is* Iceland—there were folktales about him, too."

"And they had something to do with the spear?" Mordur asked.

"Yes. And an *úlfr-madr*. One of the stories is about a woman whose husband went missing and was later found torn to shreds. They called in the bishop and he told the local black-smith to forge a spearhead much like the one Einar drew on the calfskin. The bishop dipped the spearhead in holy water and marched into the hills. Hours later, a great howling and screaming was heard. In the morning, Bishop Arason returned with a broken spear. The woman asked him if he had killed the creature and he said, 'Speak of the Devil and you give him life.' In other words, the deed was done, don't give the Devil any more of your time."

"Why would Mordur's dad make the spearhead?" I asked.

"Either it was just a hobby or he believed an *úlfr-madr* was loose. And not just any shape-shifter, but a 'pact-breaker'."

"What do you mean?" Michael lifted up the last piece of cheese and bit into it.

Grandpa squeezed his temples. He was beginning to look even more pale. "Well, legend says that around the time Bishop Arason was alive, all of Loki's children made a secret pact with the Icelandic leaders. They promised not to harm another human as long as the shifters were left alone. They took human shapes and lived among us. My father used to tell us tales about the shape-shifters who broke the pact; every hundred years or so, one would give in to the temptation of feeding on human flesh. Like the shifter who attacked him."

Mordur was leaning in, an eager look on his face. "Does the calfskin say more?"

Grandpa stared a bit longer, his eyes scanning the lines, his brow furrowed. "I'm having trouble focusing. Would it . . . would it be okay if I borrowed these tonight? I—I'd like to take a look at them under better light. Maybe I can tell you something in the morning."

"Oh . . . yes," Mordur said, a little disappointed. "I will wait."

"I had better go to bed, then," Grandpa said and rubbed his eyes. "Either that or prop my peepers open with toothpicks."

"Uh . . ." Sarah began. "Are we going to be safe here?"

"Of course," Grandpa said. "If that boy really is a shape-shifter, he looked to be in no *shape* to return tonight." He paused. A flicker of light came to his eyes. "No shape, to be a shape-shifter. Ha! That's a good one." He wheezed out a laugh as he tried to get up. Sometimes Grandpa was such a goof. I glanced over at Mordur and rolled my eyes in feigned embarrassment. He smiled and nodded. My heart skipped a beat.

Michael gave Grandpa a hand up. "Who knows," Grandpa continued, "in the morning we may wake up and have a good chuckle at all our theories hatched in the middle of the night. *Góda nótt.*"

"Good night," we replied.

"See ya in the morning," Michael said to us as he guided Grandpa to his room.

Sarah looked across at me, then at Mordur. She yawned suddenly—a yawn that looked completely fake—and got up.

"Well, I think I'll hit the sack too. Nighty-night." A second later, Mordur and I were alone.

The fire was dying, making the lights on the Christmas tree glow all the brighter. Mordur knelt down, grabbed a poker, and pushed the logs around so the flames grew higher. "This will burn down in a minute. I will stay until then."

"Good," I said, a little too quickly.

Mordur gave me a look. "Good? Why?"

"Uh . . . well . . ." I couldn't get my words in any logical order. "I just don't feel sleepy yet."

Mordur hadn't stopped looking at me. "Red hair is good luck."

"What?" I nervously ran my hand through my hair.

"It was a saying my father said. He maybe made it up. He believed every time he met a woman with red hair it was a good-luck day."

"Did he have a thing for redheads?"

Mordur nodded. "Yes. He and I had a lot in common."

It took a while for this to sink in. "So am I good luck to you?"

"We will see," he said. "I have not met too much girls from outside Iceland who know the old myths as well as you."

"How many girls do you know from other countries?"

"Just you." Mordur poked at the logs. Sparks flew up, but the flames were dying. "I wish this all was not happening right now," he said, his voice turning serious. "I wish I knew what my father wrote on those calfskins." He stared grimly at the embers.

"I'm sure Grandpa will figure out your dad's letter," I said softly. "And if he can't, there must be someone in town who can read French."

"I hope so." Mordur didn't sound hopeful. "This day has made me wonder about how my father died. He drowned while fishing. Just another Icelander stolen by the ocean, out trying to earn a couple kroners while work on the farm was slow. But there was something—how do you say?—spooky?—about it. Heim, another fisherman, said he saw a figure rise out of the water and pull my father down into the waves."

"Really? What do you think it was?"

"He said it was like a man, but covered with hair. No one else spotted the thing. They just saw my father standing at the edge of the boat in a stormy sea. Then gone. I thought Heim was making up the story. Heim likes his bottle, he is a great big drunk kind of guy. But now I do not know. Maybe the story was true."

We watched the flames die down until they were just red embers. Mordur poked at the logs again. One broke in half, burned brightly for a moment, then faded. "You know that female shape-shifter? My father spoke me about her just before he went to work on the fishing boat. He said he wanted me to think about the story. When he got back I was to tell him whether I thought it was true."

"Why would he do that?"

"I did not know. I thought he was just having fun, he liked to make the jokes. Now I wonder if it was a test. If I said I believed the shape-shifter was real, he might have spoken me what he was writing about."

Even though I wanted to be wide awake for this time with Mordur, my eyelids wouldn't cooperate. I kept talking, hoping it would keep my energy up. "You know, it's weird, but Grandpa told us that our great-grandfather killed a shape-shifter. Now we find out that Uncle Thordy's dad killed one, too. It's like this valley is cursed."

"It is," Mordur said softly. He got up onto his haunches, felt his side.

"How are your ribs?" I asked.

"Better. Just bruises. Nothing worth complaint." The last ember grew dark. "I should go home." Mordur checked that the chain-link curtain on the fireplace was closed tightly.

I went with him to the porch, flicked on the outside light. His house was only about fifty yards away, visible through a small window. It was calm out now, though it hadn't stopped snowing.

"Will you be alright there? Your place looks so small."

He smirked. "Are you worried for me, Angie?"

"Well . . . yes, of course."

He scratched at his temple, like he was thinking real hard. "Does that mean you like me?"

"I . . . uh. Well . . ." My tongue was tied in triple knots. "I—I don't really know you. But I like you."

He grinned. "I know. And I hope all this bad time goes away, soon. Maybe even tomorrow. You are not here for long. It would be good to talk more. You could speak to me about what it is like to live in America."

"That would be nice." My heart had sped up and butterflies were fluttering inside my stomach. "Really nice."

"Well, I go. And do not be worried about me." He pulled the spearhead his father had made from his pocket. "This will protect me," he joked. "Good night, Angie."

He walked out into the fresh, thick snow. I watched until he disappeared into his house and the light came on.

23

I went to my room and threw myself down on top of my cot. "So let me get this straight," I said to Sarah, who was still up, reading. "Mordur's not related to us? He's the son of the hired man? So . . ."

"So you can kiss him," Sarah finished.

"Hey, wait a minute, that's not what I was figuring out," I said, though it was *exactly* what I was figuring out.

"Well, if you did think that, you wouldn't be alone." She fluffed her hair, acting like some kind of model. "Lucky for you, I'm already taken."

I huffed out a sigh. The coffee was still zigging around my system, and everything else that happened was zagging through my brain. "This has been the weirdest day of my life," I announced. My body was drained. I felt immensely tired and yet I couldn't do much but sit up in bed and stare at the wall, wrapping the comforter tightly around me. I wanted to collapse into sleep, but it was impossible.

Mordur seemed different than any other boy I'd met. Exotic, I guess. I wanted to find out more about him. It must have been hard growing up with his mother living somewhere else and not wanting to spend time with him. And to not have a dad anymore.

"So what do you think it is?" Sarah asked, startling me.

I was so busy daydreaming I'd forgotten she was in the room. It took me a moment to figure out what her question was about. "I don't know," I answered slowly. "Something that's very smart."

"What if I said I believe Uncle Thordy?"

Just a few hours ago I would have called her crazy. But now I simply asked her why.

"Did you see when it was coming up the ladder into the loft? Its head . . . it was animal-like, but there was something human about it. You said it seemed very smart—smart enough to climb a ladder and lift up a trapdoor. Smart enough to get into the barn and steal a sheep. And the way it moved was unlike anything I'd ever seen. But it wasn't much bigger than that boy. Just very, very strong."

"Onni had a mark near his eye. Almost like he'd been hit with a fire poker."

Sarah nodded. She didn't seem surprised by this information. "Do you remember the story Grandpa told us on the plane?"

"About Great-Grandpa and the bear?"

"Why do you think he told us that story?"

"I don't know. To scare us. To pass the time."

"All good reasons. But he really believed it. He told it with such conviction, like he was seeing it through his father's eyes. I have a theory, Angie. I think we're all connected to our ances- tors. We share the same genes, the same dreams, and often the same lives. Think of Grettir the Strong. I've actually had dreams about him. How many battles did he have against evil in his life?"

"He fought a lot of ghosts and things. And people too, don't forget. He was an outlaw."

"Yes, but he's remembered for being a hero. We have . . . the essence . . . of each of our ancestors somewhere in our muscles, in our minds, and perhaps most importantly in our spirit. And sometimes that stuff just comes out."

"Like when you yelled those Icelandic words back in the croft house?" I said.

"Yes, it was partly what I read, but partly what was passed down to me, like one of our ancestors had been in a situation like that and knew what to say. What do you think?"

I'm about two steps from freaking out, is what I wanted to say. That only two days ago I was safe at home in North Dakota.

Sort of safe. Back at home I'd had the nightmares.

"We *are* connected to our ancestors," I answered. The hair on the back of my neck slowly stood up. I described the dreams I'd had about the wolf.

She listened silently, nodded. "I've had dreams like that too; seeing things before they happened. I once dreamed Michael was going to break his arm on a school trip. I even felt it crack. I convinced him to pretend he was sick and stay home. One of his classmates ended up breaking his arm at a tour of a metal factory. Kind of weird, but so what? So you and I seem to be a little psychic. Does it mean this wolf-thing is real?"

"My gut tells me one thing," I said, "but my brain tells me this is all our imagination." I lay back against my pillow. "There's still something bothering me: the quarrel Mordur and Uncle

Thordy had about us going to the croft house. Why did Uncle Thordy let us go if he believed this creature was out there?"

Sarah sat completely still for a moment, almost like she was meditating. "Do you think we were bait? He's had a year and a half to really learn how to hate this wolf-thing. Maybe he thought he could get rid of it."

"But to risk our lives—"

My words were cut off by the smashing of glass and a fearful cry from Grandpa's room.

24

Sarah and I sat frozen. Something heavy bashed against the wall, shaking the house. Grandpa yelled again, more a cry of anger than fear this time. Deep, loud growling, all too familiar, floated under our door. Then came the sound of a struggle followed by a sharp yelp.

"Grandpa!" I yelled, running out of the bedroom and down the hall. I pushed my way inside his room, Sarah one step behind me.

The lights were out and it was freezing because the window had been smashed. Glass glittered on the floor, catching moonlight. I couldn't see Grandpa.

Michael charged in, blinking the sleep out of his eyes. "What happened?"

Sarah clicked the light switch. The shade on the ceiling was partially broken, but the bulb flickered with enough light to show that Grandpa was in the corner, crumpled against the wall. I rushed up to him. Something pierced my right heel, but I ignored it. "Grandpa," I whispered, leaning down, touching his cold face.

"Afi," Sarah said from beside me.

He was out cold. His left cheek had two crisscrossing lines of scratches that looked like claw marks. Thankfully they weren't deep. Lying beside him was a small letter opener, blackened by blood. I pointed it out to Sarah. We surveyed the room. The desk was broken, along with the lamp beside it. Shredded paper had been scattered across the floor.

Grandpa opened his eyes. It took a moment for him to recognize us. "I got him," he wheezed. "Loki's offspring is fast, but I got the big beast. Right in the chest." He was clutching one of the calfskin pages. It had been torn almost in half. A chunk had been bitten out of the top.

"Let's move him to the living room," Sarah said. I took one arm, Sarah another, and Michael grabbed his feet. We lifted Grandpa and he felt unnaturally light. We carried him down the hallway and Michael kicked at Uncle Thordy's door as we passed. We didn't pause to see if he was awake. We lay Grandpa on the couch.

He sighed. There were several tears in his pajamas revealing cuts in his skin, but none seemed life-threatening and he'd stopped bleeding. His breath was ragged. Michael pulled a blanket off the back of the couch and we covered him.

"I could only read some of Einar's warning," Grandpa said hoarsely.

It dawned on me that he meant the writing on the calfskin.

"Einar knew. He knew. He said there are two of Loki's children in this valley. One was called Skoll, the Scarred One. The wolf who ate the sun. He liked to kill his victims slowly, by poking one claw behind their ear."

Grandpa gasped and pressed a hand against his chest. He

looked at Sarah and me. "I know what Odin said to Baldur," he whispered. His eyes slid closed.

Sarah put her hand on Grandpa Thursten's arm and shook him gently, but he remained unconscious. "We've got to take him into Hvammstangi, to the hospital. Go get Uncle Thordy."

I went to his room and pounded on the door. "Uncle Thordy, wake up!"

I hit the door again. "Grandpa's been hurt. Wake—"

The door opened on its own. A chilly breeze ran across my skin. I reached around for the light switch, flicked it on. The room stunk like rotten meat, such a strong stench I had to cough. The bed was made. The window was open.

How could he live in such a gross-smelling room?

I ran back to the living room yelling, "He's gone, Uncle Thordy's gone!"

"I'm going to call the police," Michael said. "This is getting too damn weird." He went into the kitchen and scrambled around, looking for a phone book.

I knelt down. My foot was aching. I lifted it, found a dark stain on my sock. A shard of glass stuck out near the heel. I gritted my teeth, pulled out the glass, and tossed it in the garbage. I found tissue in the kitchen and stuck it down my sock to mop up the bleeding. I'd have to do a better job later. I sat beside Grandpa and squeezed his hand. It was cold.

"Who's this Skoll Grandpa was talking about?" I asked Sarah.

"He said Skoll was the wolf who ate the sun. Maybe it's the same wolf who appears in the myths during the final battle."

"I dreamed about a wolf eating the sun," I said. "What's that mean?"

"I don't know." Sarah shook her head. "I just don't know at all."

"Well, what did Grandpa mean about knowing what Odin said to Baldur?"

"It was the great secret of the Norse myths. At Baldur's funeral, just before they were going to light the ship on fire, Odin whispered a secret to Baldur, but no one knows what it was."

"Why would Grandpa say that?"

Sarah's eyes were wet. It took her a moment to finally say, "Because he believes he's going to die."

"No," I whispered, tightening my grip on Grandpa's hand, feeling him there, very much there but getting colder and somehow further away.

25

"They're going to try and send an ambulance," Michael said as he came into the room. "The *logga*—the police, or whatever they call them—are coming too. *If* they can plow through all that snow. I guess the storm was twice as bad around Hvammstangi. The main highway is blocked."

"What if no one makes it here?" I asked. Grandpa's hand was like ice now. "I don't know much about first aid."

"If Grandpa gets worse, we'll have to phone back and get advice." Michael knelt down next to the couch. "The woman on the phone said it's just important to keep him warm."

Sarah had her palm on Grandpa's forehead. Grandpa's eyes were closed, his face solemn. "He doesn't seem to be waking up. He has a heck of a fever, but at least he's breathing. That's a good sign."

"What if he's in a coma?" I asked. I tucked Grandpa's hand under the blanket, then went to the end of the couch and covered his feet. "What are we going to do?"

"What can we do?" Michael asked. "Should I look for Uncle Thordy?"

"Go outside?" Sarah shook her head. "We don't know what's out there. We're safest right where we are."

"What about Mordur?" I said. "We can't just leave him alone."

I went to the kitchen window, scraped at the ice, and peeped through the clear spot. "The light's still on, so I guess he's awake," I said on my way back to the living room.

"We could phone him," Sarah suggested.

"He doesn't have a phone, remember?" I said.

Michael stood, his hands balled up into fists like he was gearing up for a fight. "Someone will have to go over there. But one of us has to look after Grandpa."

"How do we decide who stays?" Sarah asked.

"Rock, paper, scissors," I said. It was a hand game we'd played since we were kids, often using it to decide who would ask our parents for extra ice-cream money. We held out our hands. Mine was shaking slightly, even though I tried to hold it still. "On the count of three, loser stays."

Sarah counted aloud. On three, both Michael and I put our hands out flat, meaning we chose paper. Sarah made a fist.

"Paper covers stone," Michael said. "I guess you'll have to stay, Sis."

"We don't have time for a best out of three, do we?" she asked. She hugged both of us quickly. "For good luck," she explained. "Now hurry back."

We threw on our winter clothes and jammed our feet into our boots. I went back to the kitchen and found a large flashlight in the cupboard, heavy enough that it could be used as a weapon.

Sarah had pulled a chair up beside Grandpa and was holding

one of his hands in both of hers, concentrating as if she were praying. She didn't look up as I passed her.

Michael grabbed the axe from inside the closet and hefted it in his hands. "Let's go," he said and we stepped out into the open. It was still snowing lightly, but the air was calm. Despite that, we had a tough time slogging through the snowbanks, sinking up to our knees and higher. The tires on Uncle Thordy's vehicle were completely buried, and they were big tires. I had a sick feeling that it would be ages before an ambulance or cops got here. We were too far from town, and if the roads were clogged up anything like Uncle Thordy's driveway, they'd be completely impassable.

The moonlight seemed to be growing dimmer and dimmer, as if somewhere in the heavens something was taking bites out of it. I thought of the wolf who chased the moon through the sky. Too many of my dreams were becoming reality.

Mordur's outside light served as our guiding beacon. When we got to the house we discovered the door partly open, a small bank of snow already building up against it. The light from inside the house revealed tracks that were quickly being filled in.

I yanked on the door and it got jammed in the snow, but there was just enough room to stumble inside. "Mordur!" I shouted. What I saw pulled me up short. A pitcher had been shattered on the floor, shards of glass scattered across the tile. The table was knocked over, along with a stack of books. One wall was a bookshelf, more books were lying beside it. "Mordur!" I cried, running into the bedroom. I flicked on a light switch but nothing happened. I pointed my flashlight around, saw an unmade bed. The tiny room was empty.

Michael stood in the doorway of the bathroom. "He's gone," he said, kneeling down next to what looked like a broomstick. "But he didn't go without a fight." The stick was actually a handle that could have come from a pitchfork. Clamped at one end was the four-edged spearhead. A book was open beside it, full of illustrations.

"It looks like Mordur was doing some research," Michael said, lifting up one of the books. I glanced back at the spear. Next to it was a pool of blood.

"He's been hurt!" I said. I looked closer. Streaks of blood led to the door.

"I'm not sure what to do." Michael's face was pale. "I don't think we can take that thing on."

"Maybe it's weaker now. Grandpa wounded it. And Mordur might have, too. Maybe this isn't his blood. It—"

A low moan came from just outside the open door. Someone was crawling in the snow, trying to get in the house.

"Do you see that?" Michael whispered. He gripped the axe with both hands.

I bent down slowly, slipped my hand around the shaft of the spear, and lifted it, feeling its weight, light and balanced like it would strike a straight blow. We stayed still.

There was another moan and a man lifted his head, trying to look into the house. "*Help*," a soft voice said. "*Help me*."

His hand grasped the bottom of the door, pulled it open farther.

It was Mordur, crawling through the snow, trying to squeeze himself inside. His face was bruised, a cut bled on his forehead. His eyes swiveled in their sockets like he was trying to focus. He looked right at me and pushed his hand out towards me.

I moved to help him, lowering the spear, but Michael grabbed my shoulder. "Wait! I see something else."

A tall shadow was visible just outside the door, a figure slightly hunched over. It had a grip on Mordur's leg.

"Help me . . . get inside," Mordur whispered. "The shifter is right here."

I raised the spear, Michael brought his axe up, and without any signal from the other, we charged ahead. The shape was becoming clearer. And larger.

Just as we got to the door, the creature jumped back. It kept a tight hold on Mordur, dragging him out into the deep snow, like it was playing a game with us. It crouched over Mordur. Its long, muscled back was covered with matted hair. Tattered clothing hung from its body. Its red eyes glared at us over a long snout. In a heartbeat I knew that our worst nightmare was true.

Another shape-shifter, larger than the last, stood just feet away.

Compared to the one that had attacked us at the croft house this one seemed full grown.

"Skoll," I whispered.

It seemed to nod when I said its name. We stepped towards the beast and it jumped up and thrust its arm into the air.

The light over the door burst, showering us with glass and electric sparks.

26

We lifted our hands to guard our eyes. In that moment the shape-shifter had begun running from us, dragging Mordur by the feet like he was a rag doll. "There!" I pointed. They were a good ten yards away already. Mordur called to us, lashing out with his arms, trying to get a grip on something and pull himself free. His head bounced through the snowbanks.

Michael and I ran after them, sinking into the snow. We passed the barn and headed towards the plateau. The farther we went, the deeper the snow got, but we were able to keep them in our sight for a little while at least. Mordur made one more cry for help, then they disappeared over a rise. All we were left with were tracks.

I flicked on my flashlight, carrying it in one hand, the spear still in the other. Here and there, splashes of blood stained the snow.

"That better not be Mordur's blood," I said.

"I just hope he's still alive when we find him," Michael said, gripping the axe with both hands, looking like some kind of insane tree cutter. "Did you see how huge that thing was?"

"It's Skoll. The one mentioned in the calfskins."

"I was beginning to figure that out," Michael said. "But I was hoping I was wrong."

We ran as fast as we could, following the beam of my flashlight. I wasn't exactly sure of our direction, but it seemed we were climbing a hill heading towards the grazing fields. I turned back and the lights of Uncle Thordy's house shone like distant stars.

A few steps later, we lost the footprints. They just stopped, like the shifter had vanished. I pointed the flashlight in a wide arc, but all the snow ahead of us was untouched.

"Where did they go?" Michael was huffing, sweat glistening on his face. Steam rose from his skin, looking ghostly in the moonlight. We headed blindly into the open snow.

The sound of Mordur screaming stopped us in our tracks. We listened, trying to pinpoint the direction.

"Up there." Michael pointed to a rock wall barely visible a short distance away. It was about six feet high. "It's coming from up there."

We cut through the snow, climbed the wall. At the top, the land was flat again. The flashlight revealed a gray patch of cloth hanging from the branch of a small bush. A sickening feeling came over me.

"It's part of Mordur's sweater," I said, pulling the tattered rag off. I held it in the same hand as the spear. "He's probably freezing to death. He . . ."

"He'll be alright," Michael said. "If that thing wanted to kill him, it would have done it right away. For some reason he's keeping Mordur alive."

Clouds had cleared away from the moon. Rocks and snow

were outlined in a cold, blue light. "The tracks start again up there," Michael said, pointing. Then he turned to look back. "I want to know how that thing got from there to here, while carrying Mordur. Did it jump?"

Another cry came from the distance. Like Mordur was in pain.

"Let's go," I said, aiming the flashlight ahead. We dashed on, following the tracks until they took a sharp turn.

"Wait!" I yelled, holding up my hand. "Don't take another step!"

Michael stopped. "What is it?" I pointed the flashlight down. There, just in front of us, was a huge chasm.

"I didn't realize we were getting up so high," Michael said.

I looked over the edge. One more step and we both would have ended up down there, our bones broken, the snow slowly smothering us. My knees felt suddenly weak.

I edged back. Sucked in a deep breath.

"You okay?" Michael had his hand on my back. "Can't you breathe?"

"I'm . . . fine. We've got to keep going. I just won't look down anymore."

I turned, continued on, following the tracks. We struggled through the snow, across an area littered with large stones. It was like a giant had been bashing at the side of the mountain and this was where the chunks had landed.

We crawled up an embankment. I had to go one-handed, my other hand clutching the spear, the flashlight stuffed in my coat pocket. It would have been near impossible for the shifter to drag Mordur up here. It was at least six feet straight up, but at the top we found the marks again. A piece of Mordur's sweater was torn and hanging from some rocks.

"The shifter is leaving this trail on purpose," I said. "He wants to be sure we don't get lost."

Michael's face looked pale and cold in the light of the flashlight. "You're right. But what can we do? We have to try and rescue Mordur."

We kept on going. It wasn't until we had climbed the next rise that we stopped and stared, frozen in our tracks.

A stone house stood across from us. It was built into the side of a mountain. The roof sloped down from high above, stopping near the ground. Just below the roofline, candles flickered in the windows. It was probably one of the oldest stone homes in Iceland, ten times older than anything I'd seen in North Dakota.

I knew it was Gunnvor's.

27

The footprints and drag marks led to a small barn that sat off to one side of the house, across a snow-covered pasture. I turned and looked down the way we'd come. Two tiny lights were all I could see of Uncle Thordy's farm.

"We better keep quiet," Michael said, looking around, the axe in his hand.

"And out of sight," I added, switching off the flashlight. The moon cast a silvery glint over everything. Michael led. I followed silently behind him, keeping a good, strong grip on the spear.

The barn seemed even older than Uncle Thordy's, a low, flat building with a door in the center, barely big enough to fit a horse through. One side of the building was partially collapsed. We passed through a broken wooden fence and stopped. The barn shifted, making it creak like it was on the edge of collapse.

"The tracks go in here," Michael said and slowly pulled the door open. We stood back for a moment, not wanting to enter the pitch blackness. I flicked on the flashlight, checked as far as I could see, and took the first step inside.

The place was empty. I took another cautious step and Michael followed me in.

The air smelled old, musty. The straw on the floor had turned gray with age. I swept the flashlight around, lighting up different corners of the barn. A large roof beam had collapsed, so the ceiling at the far side of the barn sagged nearly to the floor. The remains of a stall stuck out of one wall. At one time it might have held a cow, but there was no sign of any animals anymore.

Nothing had been kept in here for years. I swung the light around again. My cheeks tingled and I worried it might be frostbite.

"Where is he?" Michael whispered.

Then my light caught a gray cloth lying in the far corner. "Michael, what's that?"

We ran to it, ducking under the roof beam. It was another piece of Mordur's sweater. Beside it, opened like someone had been interrupted having lunch, were three cloth bags, each bursting with livers and hearts, laid out like a sacrifice.

"Do they ever stink," Michael said, holding his hand over his nose. "You could smell them from a mile away."

"Uhhhn," someone moaned. "Whazzhapp—"

Above us, the beams creaked. Slowly we raised our heads.

28

Before I could point my flashlight up, a black shape landed with a thud on Michael, forcing him to his knees, then face first to the floor. The axe flew from his hand. I screamed and dropped the flashlight.

"Get it off me!" Michael yelled, desperately struggling with his attacker. I grabbed the flashlight, pointed it, only to see it wasn't a wolf, but a man. A man in a tattered gray sweater. Michael thrust with all his limbs, flipping the man over. He landed on his back, where he lay, still silent. Michael scrambled away, climbed to his feet.

We crept towards the body and I shone my light in its face. Mordur.

His face was deathly pale, his cheeks scratched. His eyes flickered open for a moment. "Uhhhn," he moaned again, then shut his eyes.

"He just fell on me," Michael said. "Or he was pushed."

I quickly flashed the light around the barn again and up into the rafters. No one was waiting there for us. "Skoll's gone," I said. "He must have left before we got here."

Mordur had a gash on his forehead, but the blood was dry. I knelt and put my hand on his neck. It was warm, his pulse strong. I breathed a sigh of relief. At least he wasn't dead. Not yet, anyway.

"Mordur," I said and gently pulled up one of his eyelids with my thumb. I shone the light into his eye. It was rolled back in its socket. "Wake up, Mordur."

Mordur's clothes were ripped all over, right down to his skin. His sweater had huge chunks out of it, showing his white undershirt.

"Take a look behind his ear," Michael said urgently and knelt down next to me.

We tilted Mordur's head, pulled back an ear. I wiped away a patch of dried blood and found a circular wound about the width of my little finger.

"It looks like a puncture," Michael said. "Just like . . ."

". . . what killed Uncle Thordy's wife," I finished. My hands were trembling now. Only a short time ago Mordur and I had been sitting by the fire, talking. Now he might not ever talk again. I checked his eyes again, but there was no change. "Wake up," I whispered. "Wake up, Mordur. I'm right here." I shook him.

"Angie." Michael put his hand on my shoulder. "I don't think that's going to work."

I examined the wound again. It looked familiar. It dawned on me that it was just like the one in Grandpa's back. Is that what had been making him so sick? But if it was a similar wound, then how had Grandpa gotten it? My heart began beating even faster.

"We've got to get out of here," I said. I lifted under one of Mordur's shoulders, testing his weight.

"It's a long way home. It'll be tough to carry him back the way we came."

"What else can we do?" I asked.

"I don't know . . . we need something . . . a sled . . ."

"Why don't you build a snowmobile while you're at it?"

"Don't get snarky, I'm just trying to help."

I huffed out a breath of air. "Sorry, we . . . we just don't have time to build a sled."

"Why do you think it stuffed Mordur up there?" Michael asked.

"I don't know."

"Maybe it was like a good place to store its . . . uh . . . food. Like a meat locker. Maybe Uncle Thordy's in these rafters somewhere, too." Michael peered up. I pointed the flashlight, revealing thick cobwebs littered with dust.

I shone the light back on the butcher's bags. "They're bait, aren't they? And the way Mordur was dragged here and stuffed in the rafters, almost like he was . . ."

"Bait," Michael finished. "It's like Skoll has set a trap."

29

"We'd better go," I said. "C'mon, help me."

I shoved the flashlight in my pocket and grabbed underneath one of Mordur's shoulders, still holding the spear tight with my left hand. Michael got a hold of Mordur's other shoulder and we dragged him ahead. The door had swung partly closed.

"Did you hear that?" Michael asked.

"What?"

We stood still, listening. I couldn't see anything through the slats on the door. I opened my mouth to say something, then I heard a noise—a soft padding sound and sniffing, just outside the door. It shook gently.

"Well, this is just great," Michael said, letting go of Mordur and tightly gripping the axe.

As I lowered Mordur, his eyes flickered open, then he passed out again. I pointed the spear in front of me, my hands shaking. At least I had a weapon. One made by Mordur's father, just to hunt these wolves. These shifters. All I had to do was get one good blow.

The door rattled.

Michael and I backed up beside each other, guarding Mordur. There were two dim lights just beyond the door, flickering. Or were they blinking eyes?

"Do you see it?" Michael asked.

"No."

"It's there, crouched down just outside the door . . . waiting."

He had better vision than me. I stared at the same place, could only see a shadow within a shadow. A low growl sounded through the flimsy slats of the door, grew until it hit a howling crescendo.

The door burst open.

I brought the spear up, bracing myself for the impact.

30

There was nothing there, as if all that noise and force had come from a great gust of wind. We held our positions for a few moments, my muscles growing tight.

I lowered the tip of the spear and just then a gray blur flew through the door. It struck with the force of a cannonball, knocking us across the floor. We screamed out in terror. I dropped the spear as my face was ground across the rocky floor, getting a mouthful of old straw. I smashed my head against the wall and rolled into a ball. A snarl echoed all around me.

"Stay back!" Michael hollered. "Get away!" His axe rung off the stone floor, sparks flying everywhere.

The beast got louder and louder, a vicious sound that reverberated through the whole barn, threatening to bring the timbers down around us. Then it dived. Michael groaned, dropping the axe. He was being attacked by something that was actually smaller than him. Onni, I thought. It looks like Onni. The shifter had clamped its jaws into his arm and was shaking its head back and forth, banging him around, playing with him like he was a toy. Michael groaned in pain.

My cousin was being murdered. I staggered to my feet yelling, "Onni! Get away! Leave him alone!" My voice was not my own. It was thick and loud.

Something snapped in front of my face. Teeth. Big, yellow, bloodied teeth. In the blink of an eye Onni had crossed half the length of the barn. He raised a hand and bashed me to the floor, then grabbed my leg, jarring my ankle.

I tried to scramble away, but his grip was too tight. I jammed my hand in my jacket pocket, came out with the flashlight, flicked it on.

Onni squinted into the beam of light. Slaver dripped from his jaws, eyes glowing. Even with the snout-shaped face, I recognized him. A little boy in wolf's clothing, his breath hot and reeking of decay. Ragged, rotten pieces of meat caught between his teeth.

There was a grunting noise behind him. Michael swung the axe, striking Onni on the side of the head with a heavy thump. Onni slowly turned, unaffected by the blow. Michael looked at the axe, realized he'd hit Onni with the blunt end.

Onni let go of me, rose up on his haunches. Michael pulled back for another swing and Onni head-butted him, knocking him backwards.

I sat up. My flashlight had fallen to the ground, the light shining towards the spear. I grabbed the shaft, used it to help me get off the ground. My vision was jumbled, gray and black shapes swirled around. Onni had his back to me. I began running, spear out, balanced easily in my hand as if I had done this a hundred times before. Just as I reached him, ready to thrust the spear, Onni spun around, arms wide. He leapt. I raised the spear, caught him in midair near the side of his chest. A bluish light exploded from his flesh as he shrieked. The end of the shaft dug into the floor and the weight of his body snapped the shaft just below the spearhead. Onni fell, his sharp claws just brushing the side of my face, carving out five tiny lines of pain.

He clutched his side, howling, and twisted around, the spearhead embedded in his chest. He kept scratching at it, trying to pull it out. Sparks of light shot up and down what was left of the shaft.

Then he let out one last desperate howl.

It was answered by another long, mournful howl. Outside, and getting closer.

31

"We can't beat the larger one," Michael said. We stood, unarmed, staring through the door, out into the night. The howling outside grew louder.

"Are you alright?" I asked.

"I think my arm's broken. And I cut my back. How about you?"

"I should be hurting everywhere, but I just feel numb."

Onni was now writhing around and whimpering in front of us. Moonlight flooded through the broken door, outlining him with silver. Bubbles of saliva frothed at his mouth and he opened and closed his jaws like a fish out of water. His hands were still clasped around the shaft of the spear, but he couldn't budge it. The occasional spark appeared in his wound, making him wince.

A shadow fell across him. A hulking figure stood there, eyes glowing red. Skoll had returned.

"Simple-minded humans." The voice was so hoarse it took me a moment to understand the words. "Know nothing, understand nothing. You never change."

The shadow took another step, eyes not moving from us. Skoll's face was in shadows. He stepped into the barn.

The moonlight revealed long, gray, shoulder-length hair. And female features.

"It's Gunnvor," I whispered, shocked.

There was an odd look to her face, like it had been pulled forward and stretched. It was coated with thick hair. Her open mouth revealed long, sharp teeth behind thick lips. She knelt, placed her hand on Onni's forehead and he turned to her. "He's just a child." Her words were still hoarse, but somehow softer. "He doesn't know any better. He can't control himself."

"He was trying to kill us," Michael said.

"You are on our land," Gunnvor said, matter-of-factly. "We have been here much longer than any of you interlopers. And now you come right to my home and attack my child. We should have slain you all years ago."

"We didn't want to come here," I pleaded. "He dragged one of our friends up here."

Her eyes moved from me to Mordur. "Ah, Mordur. Thordy's little helper. Onni didn't touch him." She paused. Sniffed. Looked over at the bags of internal organs. "Lamb livers. Chicken hearts You wanted to lure my son here and kill him with your little weapon."

"Those were already here," Michael said.

Gunnvor ignored him and bent down and scooped up her son like he was a baby. He had changed slightly; his hair had shortened, making his face look younger but still wolflike. Without giving him any warning she yanked out the spearhead. He shrieked.

Gunnvor threw the spear down so that it stuck into the stone floor. Sparks arced through the air. "You came to murder my child. It has been four hundred years since I last killed one of your kind, but I will not hesitate to start again tonight." She gently set Onni down in a pile of old straw. He reached out to her, but she turned and stepped towards us.

32

I didn't move. Neither did Michael. There was no point in fighting. We had no spear. No strength. I straightened my spine and faced her. At least she'd see we came from a strong line of Icelanders.

Gunnvor was changing before our eyes. Five long claws grew out of her right hand. She raised it up slowly to strike us. Then she stopped, sniffed deeply, and sniffed again. She dropped her hand, pushed us apart, and strode by. "One of our kind," she hissed, "one of our kind is behind this." She ran from corner to corner, howling and growling, knocking against timbers so the whole building shook.

"Get out! Get out!" she yelled. "Stupid children. You bring bad luck. Little evil creatures. Get off our land. I'll find your master and kill him."

She picked up Onni, backed out of the doorway, and tramped through the thick snow towards her home. I let out a gasp. My body had been wound tight as a knot. The adrenaline in my system grew thinner. My head began to ache and my ankle tingled with pain.

"What was she talking about?" I asked.

"I don't know, but I don't want to stick around and quiz her." Michael rushed over to Mordur. I paused to pull the spearhead out of the floor. There was only a handful of the shaft attached to the point. It took a bit of a tug to get it out. I stuffed it in one of my padded pockets.

We tried to revive Mordur, whispering his name and gently slapping his face. I felt his forehead and it was burning with fever. We lifted him under his shoulders and dragged him out of the barn and into the snow. Step by step, we plodded along. My ankle was starting to throb and I found it hard to put weight on it. I glanced towards Gunnvor's house and thought I could see someone in the window.

"Hurry," I whispered. We pulled Mordur down to the edge of the plateau. The air was chilly and clear.

"The lights look miles away," Michael said, pointing at some glowing dots far below us.

I was so tired. Michael climbed to the bottom of a short rock wall. Between the two of us, we were barely able to lower Mordur down. Michael slipped and Mordur was jarred out of our grip, landing with his face partially buried by snow. We hurried over, pulled him out. I brushed snow off his cheeks.

"Sleeping Beauty didn't feel a thing," Michael said. "You need a rest yet?"

I answered by grabbing Mordur's shoulder and pulling. Michael joined me and we continued on. My ankle was getting worse, and Mordur was growing heavier, as if with every step his bones and flesh were turning to stone. For a time we were able to drag him easily thanks to the slope of the plateau.

At the bottom of the path that had taken us to Gunnvor's

was another cliff wall, a drop of some six feet, too far to lower Mordur. We pulled Mordur along it for what seemed hours, but couldn't find an easy way down. Finally, we gave up and collapsed with Mordur lying between us, looking like he was having a lovely sleep. For an absurd moment I thought it was funny.

"I can't go any farther," I admitted, "not without a good rest."

"Me either. We must be off her land by now—she won't chase us here will she?"

"I don't know, but we'll never be able to get Mordur home on our own. My ankle's sprained. We need help."

"Well, we can just wait, someone's got to be looking for us by now. They'll see our tracks."

"What if they don't? We can't leave Mordur here." I looked around. There was an overhang of rock that would protect us. "Help me move him over there; it should be warmer. You'll have to go home and bring some help. Maybe the police have arrived. Uncle Thordy probably has a sled or a toboggan we could use."

"I can't just leave you here."

"It makes the most sense. You're the one who's still got two good legs. Just help me move him."

It seemed to take forever. We finally pushed Mordur into the corner. "Now go," I said. "You can get help. Go!"

Michael gave me a quick hug, guarding his sore arm. "I'll come back soon, I promise."

I watched him disappear into the distance.

I sat cradling Mordur's head on my lap. Carrying Mordur down the cliff had taken everything I had. Now that we'd stopped moving, I could tell how much I had sweated. Perspiration had gathered on my back, soaked my clothes, and was turning into ice. I began to shiver. I hugged myself to warm up, but it wasn't enough. I kept moving my fingers in their gloves and my toes in their boots. As long as I could wiggle them, I figured they weren't frostbitten.

I worked at keeping my eyes open. I'd heard stories about a group of cross-country skiers back home who'd gotten lost. They finally sighted the ski lodge, but sat down to rest and drifted off to sleep, convinced they would wake up soon and ski the rest of the way. Instead, covered by a blanket of snow, they froze to death.

The moon was high in the sky. Stars flickered and blinked. I felt small, staring up at lights that had been moving in their own secret ways and patterns for millions of years.

Then—for a moment I thought I was hallucinating—I heard a male voice say, "Michael must be long gone now."

33

I sat straight up. Where had it come from?

"What? Who's there?" I grabbed at a chunk of rock to use as a weapon, but it was frozen to the ground.

"Don't be frightened, it's just me." A figure appeared from around the edge of the alcove. At first all I saw were two legs in torn pants. Then he knelt down and a bearded face, darkened by shadow, looked in. He was smiling.

"Uncle Thordy!" I cried out, relieved. A wave of joy swept over me. "You've found us."

He laughed. "It wasn't hard; you left a well-marked trail."

"But what happened to you? How did—" I took a good look at his clothing. It was torn into rags and he was bleeding from his side. "You're hurt."

This made him chuckle again. "It's nothing. It's healing as we speak. Soon the wound will be closed."

I didn't know what he meant. His eyes were a little glazed over. Perhaps he was in shock. "Uncle Thordy," I said, "we need to get Mordur back home before we freeze to death. Are you well enough to help me?"

"Oh no. It is *you* who will help me," he replied, a lightness in his voice like he was saying something funny. "Everything is working out fine."

"Fine? What's that mean?"

"I was waiting. Letting you two take care of the wolf boy. I was hoping you'd kill him, but wounding him was enough."

"What are you talking about? Why would you want us to go up there?"

Uncle Thordy moved ahead so the moonlight fell directly on his face. His eyes were luminous, like they were lit from inside his head.

"Uncle Thordy, what do you mean—"

"Oh, be quiet!" he snapped. "You and your repulsive little family will be rotting in hell soon enough."

I backed away from him, up against the wall. He *had* gone crazy. Or had I? His eyes were glowing now, getting brighter and narrower by the moment.

"Sorry," he said, softly, "it has been a trying time. But don't worry, it'll all be over for you in moments."

His words were icy. My heart sped up. "What do you mean?"

"I mean this." He grinned. His face changed in the light, grew elongated, morphing into a snout. He bared sharp teeth. "Gunnvor's little brat was eating *my* meat. Slaughtering *my* animals. You see, the Onni runt had been hunting on my land. The plateau is where *I* feed, where *my* father fed. That is, before your great-grandfather killed him. We shifters won't spill the blood of another of our kind. It's a pact we made, many years ago, to preserve our race. There are only twenty of us left. But I was quite happy to arrange for you to kill one."

"But . . . but you're my . . . you're Uncle Thordy, how—"

He was changing even more, hair sprouting out of the holes in his clothing. A sick, dead-meat smell wafted through my nostrils. The same smell I'd encountered in Uncle Thordy's house, only stronger.

"Thordy's dead. He died the same day as his wife. His bones are still up there, jammed into a crevice. Only ravens have found them. I assumed his shape, his croft, his life, his name. I have waited a long time to get my hands on your family. To murder two birds with one stone, as you people say."

I was stunned. "You're Skoll," I said, barely able to think. "You carried Mordur up there, didn't you? You left the butcher bags."

"Yes," he admitted, "they have a very distinct smell. Irresistible to a young shape-shifter."

"But, Gunnvor's son, he's not dead. And she's not going to go away. You failed."

"No," Skoll whispered, "not after I'm done with you. I'll limp down to the farm and tell them that Gunnvor herself came and tore you limb from limb. Michael and Sarah will believe me and your grandfather is dead, so he won't be any trouble."

The words hit me like a hammer blow. "What? You're lying."

"Oh yes, quite dead. He fought off my little pinprick for an amazingly long time. I was impressed. And he was good with an axe, too." He touched the wound at his side.

"*You* attacked him?" I said, feeling an anger spread through my veins. "You?"

"Yes," Skoll said, hissing in my face. "He would have read all the calfskins. He would have known my little secret. I had to stop him. But let's not dwell on the past. Let me tell you what will happen next. I will kill you. Others in these parts are super-stitious enough they'll band together and hunt Gunnvor and the runt down. Then this will be my hunting ground again. As for Mordur, who I dragged so far, he's of no use to me now." Skoll struck Mordur in the chest and Mordur exhaled sharply. He didn't breathe in again. "I can always find another hired man. He was as snoopy and headstrong as his father; I would have had to get rid of him soon enough."

"You smell more like yourself now," a voice said out of the darkness.

Skoll jerked his head up; the look of conceit and pride flashed from his face.

A figure appeared from around the corner, covered in hair, eyes blazing with anger. "Tried to hide your stink with perfume. Stealing the form of a human," Gunnvor accused. "You always were a pact-breaker, just like your father. The circle of elders knows about you now. About your plans. You wanted me and my child dead. We'll feed your liver to our children, that's what we'll do."

Skoll narrowed his eyes, his body shifting shape by the second. "I won't fail," he growled, then threw himself at her. Gunnvor was knocked back into the snow.

I couldn't move. I watched as they battled in the moonlight, exchanging blows. Gunnvor dodged a lunge, swiped her claws across his chest, and Skoll screamed with all his might. But he was larger than her, more powerful, and, even with his wounds, I could see he was winning.

Finally, with a great effort, he lifted Gunnvor and threw her to the ground. She landed on a boulder, her bones cracking like old branches. She lay motionless.

Skoll turned to me. "Now you," he said, wiping blood from his face with a hairy hand. "Now you."

He took a step and his leg gave out. He fell, then tried to stand. Again he fell. He pulled himself up again, moved towards me with a limp.

Finally I had the presence of mind to jump up. I took one last look at Mordur's body, then I began to run, not even sure where, my feet pounding through the snow. My ankle ached, but I ignored it. Skoll's laughter echoed behind me, a long, growling guffaw that turned to a howl.

I kept going, leaping crevice after crevice and charging along narrow paths. I barely kept my footing, winding my way down to another plateau. I couldn't see him, but I could hear him, barking angrily somewhere in the distance.

My eyes were drawn to a falling star burning through the night sky, and for a moment it seemed the heavens were splitting apart.

A light flashed again, this time just ahead of me. Maybe it was a flashlight. Or a snowmobile. I veered towards it.

My lungs were burning, my body drained of energy. Every second step I stumbled.

The light flashed once more, just over a rise in the snow. Was it a trick of the eye? Or was it Skoll's trickery?

It was getting closer now. I ran towards it, hoping for rescuers. The solid ground disappeared from beneath my feet and I fell, landing on soft snow. My breath was knocked from my chest, and my heart stopped beating for a moment. My ears filled with silence. I was lying on my stomach; my muscles refused to obey my commands. Skoll would find me here. An easy victim, even with his wounds.

I tried to breathe deeply, to stand up.

I sensed something else in the crevice with me. Something moving around.

He was here, ready to pounce.

I slowly, ever so slowly, turned my head. There, only a few feet away, was a glimmering form. Familiar, loving eyes looked down on me. A warm smile.

I reached out my hand, whispering, "Hello, Afi."

34

Grandpa Thursten was alive. Skoll had lied. Grandpa was alive!

He grinned at me, saying, *"Wake up, sleepyhead. You're not finished yet."* The cliff walls were visible through him. Stars glistened around his skin. He was dressed in his favorite sweater and tan pants.

"Whaaat?" I asked.

He drifted closer, smoothly, as if there were no snowbanks between us. His feet were bare. I still couldn't find the strength to get up.

But that was okay. Grandpa was here to save me.

He spoke again, his words sounding as if they were coming from a great distance. *"I'm not gone. Not yet. Guess I still have some things to do. So do you, Angie."*

"Grandpa, I can't move."

"Angela Laxness, stop lying around." The voice was soft, but getting clearer. *"Wake up inside."* He gestured towards the sky. *"You tell her then . . . she's not listening to me. It's the red hair that makes her that way. She's your sister, maybe she'll listen to you."*

A second, smaller glowing form appeared beside him, floated towards me. As it came closer I recognized his face.

"Andrew," I whispered. He looked the same as he had years ago.

He smiled a mischievous smile and, without a word, leaned down towards me, extending his hand. It was smooth, ivory skinned, and yet through it I could see the stars in the sky. He touched me in the center of my back and I felt a warmth spread up and down my spine. For a moment my mind held an image of Andrew, when we were young, running through the front-yard sprinkler on a hot summer day.

"*You're a good big sister,*" he said. "*You always were.*"

I was able to roll over and sit up. I stared at him, wanting to take in as much as I could. Tears began to well up in my eyes.

"*Hug Mom and Dad for me.*" Andrew faded slowly, waving at me.

Grandpa came closer. "*I don't have much time here.*" He pointed over a short wall of rocks. "*Go that way. You'll find safety. Get up, lazybones.*"

I pushed myself slowly to my feet. Grandpa was growing dimmer. His bare feet were in the snow, but he left no impression.

"Grandpa, what do I do?"

"*I don't know. I'm not meant to know. I can hear your grandmother.*" He paused. "*I've missed her for too many years. It's my time to be with her.*"

He was fading.

"Where are you going?"

"*No one gave me a travel guide. I'd love to stay around and haunt some more."* He laughed, lightly. He sounded like a voice at the end of a long valley. Far away from me. *"I've got to go, Angie. Bless."*

"Afi," I whispered, the tears coming freely now.

He blinked out like a light, like he'd never been there. I stumbled towards where he had been standing, my hands out like a sleepwalker. The air felt warmer for a moment, then it grew chill. "Not yet," I whispered. "Don't go yet."

I lowered my arms. He was gone.

The sound of howling grew louder. Skoll was charging down the hill behind me. I ran in the direction Grandpa had pointed, scrambling to the top of a steep incline.

There, leaning against the side of a mountain and glowing in the moonlight, was the church we had seen the day before.

35

There wasn't much to the church—a tiny building, maybe three times my height, with two small windows and a door latched by a flat piece of metal. I twisted it and pushed, but it wouldn't budge. When was the last time anyone had been in here?

I threw my shoulder into it. Then, feeling eyes on me, I turned to find Skoll standing just a few yards away.

"Too late, Angie," he rasped, moving slowly towards me. He was holding his side. "Too late for you."

With a final desperate shove, I banged into the door and it swung open so quickly I nearly fell over. I slammed it shut and snapped the latch down and ran into the center of the room. A large stained-glass window at the back of the church let in a dim band of light. I backed down the aisle between two short rows of wooden benches. Dust clogged my nostrils. Something brushed my neck and I almost screamed as I slapped at it. My hand discovered thick spiderwebs, caked with dust and insect wings. I was flicking the sticky mess off my fingers when the door rattled.

Grandpa had said it was safe here. I hoped that meant Skoll couldn't enter this holy place. Maybe there were invisible walls holding him out.

"You can't hide," he yelled. The latch snapped and the door swung open, almost off its hinges. He stood motionless for a moment, his glowing eyes scanning the room until they spotted me. "Why don't you just make this easy on yourself?"

"You . . . you can't come in here, Skoll. Go on. Go away." I tried to remember the Icelandic words that Sarah had used, but they wouldn't come back to me.

He stepped into the church and nothing happened. I had expected something, a cry of protest from the church itself, or the ghosts of the long-dead patrons to come straight down from the rafters like avenging angels.

I looked around for another way out, or a weapon. There weren't even any Bibles to throw at him. "I did dream about you," I said, backing farther away.

"Of course you did. I know some of your clan have a smidgen of the sight."

"In my dreams you always died at the end. Every time."

He paused. A disconcerted look crossed his face. Then anger. "You are a clever little liar, aren't you?" His canine lips turned up in a smile. "You have only been on this earth for what, fifteen years? What's that to a thousand? A hundred thousand? We have been here forever. Since before your kind crawled its way up the slopes of Europe and put your vessels in the sea. What do you really know, child? Why should I honor a pact with such weaklings? Especially when you all taste so good." He crossed the floor and started up the aisle.

For every one of my steps, he took another, coming closer.

And closer. His features were getting clearer: the slaver on his jaws, the anger in his eyes. But I could see his body was crisscrossed with deep scratch wounds from his battle with Gunnvor. And part of his left ear had been torn away. "It was my mother who died in the town square at Hvammstangi," he hissed. "She was over two thousand years old. Still so young. Killed by Thordy's father. I cannot even begin to describe the hate I have for your clan."

"We were only defending ourselves." I backed up a small set of stairs and bumped past the pulpit, an old, ornate wood structure with a cross carved on the top. I was standing in the altar.

"You're prey, nothing more. You shouldn't fight back. When your parents come to collect your body, I will kill them, too. I won't stop until every last one of your clan has been removed from this world."

Skoll stopped just past the front row of pews. He tried to budge, but it was like his feet were set in glue. He struggled.

"You can't come in here," I said, sounding ten times more confident than I felt. My voice echoed through the church. "Your kind aren't allowed."

He snarled even louder, twisting and shaking. Then with a mighty effort he lifted a foot and planted it in the pulpit area. It began to smoke, then to burn. He raised his other foot. "I'm going to tear you to shreds."

A short pole with a cross on the top was leaning up against the wall. It was the kind a priest carried during a procession; it had perhaps been there for a hundred years. Beside it was the large stained-glass window with an image of a lamb standing on a Bible, glowing white from the moon's light.

I grabbed the crucifix pole, held it in front of me. I felt a sudden rush of energy, like my ancestors were somehow lending me their strength. The pole vibrated like a lightning rod. I tightened my grip.

"That toy won't save you." Skoll grit his teeth and struggled forward, fixing me with his eyes. "I'll make you pay for every second of my pain."

The axe wound in his chest was bleeding anew, as if being inside the church had reopened it. The blood turned to smoke when it hit the floor. There *was* something magical about this place.

"You're bleeding," I said, enjoying the sight of him growing weaker. "Grandpa gets the last laugh."

He snarled and leapt. I swung the pole with all my might and a blinding flash burst across his flesh. He fell on his back with a scream.

Skoll jumped to his feet, rubbed at the burnt mass of hair on his chest. It fell away in clumps. He glared at me, a look of pure murderous intent. He leapt a second time, straight at me, and I struck him. The charge of energy nearly tore the pole from my arms. Skoll fell over, was up in the blink of an eye and after me again. This time I hit him square in the skull and the pole broke. An explosion of blinding white light surrounded us and he was blown back.

He landed in a crumpled heap, jerked about for a moment, then stopped. He looked dead; there were new gashes on his shoulder and forehead. He was shrinking back into his human form.

I dropped the shattered crucifix. My hands were black and burning with pain. I could hardly open them.

THE LOKI WOLF

Skoll lay across the steps, blocking my way out. I lifted my foot to step over him, felt him stir under me, then he grabbed my ankle and yanked me down.

36

"You little wretch," he yelled, throwing me against the wall. Even with his wounds and his power fading, he was so much stronger than I.

I used the windowsill to pull myself up and turned towards him. He was on his feet now, hunched over and clutching his ribs. One side of his face looked human, the other wolfish, as if he could no longer change into his full wolf form. He roared.

Everything slowed down. As he came at me, I reached into my coat pocket, grabbing the broken stub of wood that was still attached to the spearhead. A new strength, like I had a direct line to Grettir himself, took hold of me. Skoll leapt and I set my feet, caught him below the chest with the spear, and pushed with all my might. He yelled and hurtled past, but as he did he reached out and snatched hold of my arm. I dropped the spearhead. His claws dug into my flesh as he dragged me along. He crashed through the stained-glass window, the image of the lamb smashing into a thousand pieces and showering us both. I was yanked around and my gut slammed into the windowsill. My arm felt like it had been pulled right out of its socket. I hung there, my head and chest over the edge, looking down, the blast of cold air bringing me to life.

Skoll dangled beneath me, his claws still poking into my arm. His other hand, half claws, half fingers, gripped the window-sill, leaving grooves in the wood. Below him was a drop into darkness off the edge of a cliff.

The church was cracking and groaning like he might pull the whole building over with him. His left hand slipped from the windowsill, caught my wrist, and he latched onto my arm with both hands.

I stared down into his face. It changed so that it looked more human. Not Uncle Thordy's face at all, but younger. His hair blonde and soft.

Andrew.

"You. Must. Help me." It sounded like Andrew's voice. His eyes were narrowed, his face helpless. "I can't hold on, sister. Don't let me fall," he said helplessly, "help me. Don't let me die again."

He looked so much like Andrew. So alive. So real.

"I've got you," I said, edging slightly ahead, trying to find a better grip with my feet. I started to pull him up. My brain was getting fuzzy. There was something about his eyes that wasn't right.

I pulled him an inch higher. Then another, so he could almost grab the windowsill on his own.

"You're a good sister. Higher."

He looked down. The back of his head was all black curls and matted hair, his neck covered with fur. Not like Andrew at all.

I stopped pulling. He glanced back at me. Andrew's features

were melting away like wax. Skoll's left hand shot up, grabbing at my hair.

"I don't want to be known as the girl who was killed by the wolf," I said and I struck him. Hard.

He snarled, changing back to his wolf form, trying to get a better grip, his muscles in his arm bunching together. I pummeled him again with a fist.

He swung away from the wall, taking a clump of my hair in his hand. He was hanging on only by his grip on my useless, dislocated arm.

Then, with one final effort, I pushed and he fell like a stone, down, down, down, screaming all the way. He hit the edge of the cliff wall, flipped around a couple of times, and finally crashed into the rocks below.

37

I stared out the window for what could have been an hour. Skoll was lying far below me with his arms spread, his body outlined by the moon. Flakes of snow drifted down, lightly covering him. In time I couldn't see him at all.

I leaned against the side of the church, breathing deeply, trying to gather my wits. I shook off the numbness, found the spearhead, and put it back in my pocket. The church was getting colder and colder and I needed to get home. I wandered out through the broken door and stumbled in the direction of Uncle Thordy's yard. I had to climb down a rock wall, careful not to put too much weight on my ankle. There were moments when I wanted to stop and just lie down, but a verse kept repeating itself over and over again in my head, in time with each step: *Cattle die, kinsmen die, I myself shall die, but there is one thing I know never dies: the reputation we leave behind at our death.*

I passed the alcove and Mordur was gone. So was Gunnvor's body. It was a lifetime before I neared the farmyard. I was met by Michael and strangers in thick jackets. They looked like policemen. Two of them were carrying Mordur. The moment they got near I collapsed and they had to lift me. They wanted to know if I had seen Uncle Thordy. "He's dead, he's dead, he has to be," I whispered.

Then I passed out.

38

I awoke sweating from a fever. I was in a bed in a strange room. A shadow reached towards me and I froze, not able to move or yell out.

"It's okay, Angie," Sarah whispered, "it's just me." She dabbed my forehead with a cool facecloth, then put her hand on my cheek. A night-light shone dimly from the wall, casting her face in shadows. We were in our room at Uncle Thordy's house. "You're going to be okay."

My body wouldn't stop shaking. My joints felt like they were on fire. "I saw Grandpa. And Andrew."

I expected her to tell me I was crazy. "Good. That's so good. I feel better, knowing he was able to help us one more time."

"Where is Gunnvor? Did they find her body?"

Sarah looked at me. "No. No one found any body."

My brain tried to understand this. Maybe she'd gotten away. Wasn't dead. "Everything hurts," I whispered.

"You need another treatment. I'll get the others."

And before I could ask her who the others were, she was gone. She returned with a middle-aged man and two women.

They seemed familiar. One of them looked so much like my mom it was uncanny.

"Who are you?" I asked. My teeth were chattering.

"Don't you remember?" Sarah said. "This is Uncle Thordy's brother and sisters. You met them the last time you woke up."

The last time? How long had I been out of it?

They circled me, spoke softly in Icelandic, and made me eat all this strange garlic-tasting stuff. They washed out my wounds with a liquid that stung ten times worse than iodine and smelled like stale beer. They didn't tell me what it was, and I didn't ask, but they hummed and whispered chants while they took care of me.

"You're going to the hospital now," Sarah explained, just before I slipped back into unconsciousness.

I woke up briefly on the trip to Hvammstangi. We were inside a large jeep, heading down the road. It was light out, but of course the sun was nowhere to be seen. I was leaning against Sarah; Michael sat beside me, clutching his arm. "Hi, Angie," he said, "back from the dead, I see."

I nodded. Turned my head. Mordur was laid out in the back; the woman who looked like my mom was holding him in place. "He's okay, isn't he?" I asked.

"Yes," Sarah said softly. "Yes, of course."

Then I was gone again. The next time I came to I was on a hospital bed and a doctor was bent over me, stitching my arm. It was frozen, of course. I watched a needle going in and out of the places where Skoll's claws had torn open my flesh, sealing them up. The doctor saw I was awake and explained he wasn't sure if my left arm would ever be the same. They would have to see after the swelling went down. I'd definitely have to go to a specialist back at home. My ankle was the only other major injury. All he could do was wrap it in a bandage and tell me not to go jogging.

I was given a room in the hospital and by the next day was feeling well enough to walk around. When Sarah and Michael visited me, Michael was sporting a cast from his wrist to his elbow. "Want to sign it? I've already got a great collection of Icelandic swear words."

I did sign, using my awkward right hand. I'd have to learn how to do a lot of things with that hand now.

"After everything thaws, they're going to hunt for Uncle Thordy's body," Sarah told me, "and then give him the funeral he deserves."

Would they find anything of Skoll? I wondered. Just thinking of him made my bones ache. I pushed him out of my mind.

"Oh, by the way," Sarah said, "Merry Christmas."

"What?"

"It's Christmas eve," Michael said, "but we're going to celebrate when our parents get here."

I was stunned. I must have slept through a full day. A short while later Sarah and Michael took me to Mordur's room and left me to sit with him. He was still unconscious, had not come to at all. I held his hand and spoke to him. I found myself telling him about what my house looked like back in North Dakota, where I went to school, what my favorite classes were, and what I was hoping to get for Christmas. It all just came pouring out of me. Finally, I told him how much I missed my grandpa and my brother. I began to cry.

Still, he didn't wake up. Sarah told me they'd pulled a piece of what they thought was a claw from his neck, but it dissolved within seconds of being exposed to the air.

It was maybe the last little bit of Skoll left. The police only found ragged, torn clothes where he had fallen. There was no other clue that he had ever existed. They searched Gunnvor's property, but both she and Onni were gone.

The next morning my parents arrived, along with Sarah and Michael's mom and dad, and we began preparing for Grandpa Thursten's funeral.

39

The funeral was held in a small Lutheran church in Hvammstangi. As we arrived, I knew it was a special occasion for the people of this area; there were a lot of townspeople standing outside. Inside, the church was packed with Icelanders dressed in black suits and dresses, waiting silently for us to arrive. I'd had no idea how important Grandpa Thursten had been to all the Icelanders here. A few friends had even flown all the way from Gimli. The front pews had been left empty for us, and we were guided to them by a young altar boy.

The minister who led the service said only a few words here and there; it was mostly songs sung one after another. I didn't know what they were about, though a few sounded familiar. There was something absolutely beautiful about the voices echoing in the rafters of the church, something that was, well, heavenly.

Near the end of the service, Uncle Robert, Michael and Sarah's dad, stood and spoke. He told the story of Grandpa Thursten's life, of his marriage, and of how there had been no one like him and that truly this was a sad day on earth, but a bright day in heaven for he would be reunited with his wife. He ended the eulogy by reading a passage from the myth about how the world reacted when the god Baldur died: *"All things wept. Fire wept. Steel wept. The mountains wept. The sky, the stones, the earth wept, the trees wept, all the animals wept for him."* By the time Uncle Robert was done, most everyone in the church wept too.

After the ceremony, they carried Grandpa's coffin outdoors and into a long hearse. It was late in the afternoon and the sun had slipped below the horizon, giving us only the slightest bit of light. I would never get used to the way the sun worked here. We stood by the hearse as people came up and hugged our parents or shook their hands. Then the mourners either walked home or got into their cars and drove away, leaving us to our grief.

It was a lot different than a funeral at home. Normally everyone would come to the gravesite. Maybe they did it differently here, just let the family look after their own. We climbed into our vehicles and followed the hearse out past Hvammstangi. We stopped along the edge of the ocean. My uncles and my mother carried Grandpa's coffin and set it on a boat piled high with kindling and smelling of gas. A fishing boat, the *Akraborg*, was waiting nearby in the water.

This wasn't a normal burial, my parents had explained to me. In fact, no one did this anymore, but it was what Grandpa had wanted. Then it dawned on me that this was why the people had gone on their way. Our business was ours alone. If no one from Hvammstangi saw it, then no one would have to report anything to the authorities.

My mother and Uncle Robert lit a torch and together walked

through the snow to the side of the boat and touched an edge of the kindling. It burst into flames, circling Grandpa's coffin. The *Akraborg* pulled the funeral boat out onto the water, towards the horizon, then let it go. The flames grew higher and brighter and began to fade as the boat drifted into the distance.

We stood for a long time, watching. My mother and father held me between them and we wept.

Later, the family went to Uncle Thordy's and drank a lot of coffee, and people talked and sang and told stories about Grandpa, celebrating his life. Even we grandchildren threw in a few of the tall tales he had told us.

My mother gave me what Afi had left for me. It was a book he had carried with him his whole life, old and faded and written in Icelandic.

It was called *Grettir's Saga*.

40

The next few days were a blur of meeting other family members and seeing a little of the country. I hobbled around on my sore foot and took as many pictures as I could. There was never much light, so I was pretty sure only a handful would turn out. We did celebrate Christmas at a relative's home east of Hvammstangi. There was lots of food—most of it looked wonderful, some of it gross, but I couldn't really eat much.

On our last day, as I was laying out stuff to pack, Sarah burst into our room. "Mordur's awake," she said, "and he wants to see you."

My father drove me to town and dropped me off in front of the small hospital, saying he'd come back in a little while. I went straight to Mordur's room.

He was propped up in bed, dozing. When I sat down in the chair next to him, he slowly opened his eyes.

"Angie, I have a big hurt in my head."

I laughed. "I'm not surprised. You've been through the wringer."

"Tell me what happened."

I told him what I could remember, but I knew I'd left quite a few details out. "I'll give you the full story in a letter," I said. I handed him back his father's spearhead.

He took it from me and softly said, "Thanks. This means lots to me." He smiled. "My last real good memory is sitting by the fire, talking to you. You were going to speak all about yourself."

"I already did." I chuckled. He gave me a confused look. I explained that I had visited him while he was unconscious.

"I guess I was a good listener, I didn't interrupt you." He blinked. "You leave today, right?"

I nodded. "In a few hours."

"Thank you for letting me show you around. It was . . ." he struggled for words, ". . . it was an honor."

"No problem," I said, getting up. I felt tears in my eyes, but blinked them back. "We could have had a lot of fun. If every-thing had worked out differently." I leaned over him and kissed him on the lips. "Promise me you'll take care of yourself."

"As long as you promise to come back."

"I will."

41

Soon Iceland was far behind us and we were high in the air, the sun over one wing tip. Sarah was sitting beside me and Michael and our parents sat in front of us. The journey was quiet compared to our trip there, with Grandpa's long story about our great-grandfather.

"They never end happily, do they?" Sarah said. "The old Viking sagas. They're not like fairy tales; they don't end happily."

"No, they don't," I said. Then it struck me how one saga kept leading into the next. Story after story. "But Sarah," I said, raising an eyebrow, "when you think of it, the sagas never, ever really end."

GLOSSARY

Afi – Grandfather.

Bjúgnakrækir – A Christmas lad whose name means "sausage snatcher."

Bless – Good-bye.

Draugr – Ghost.

Fardu burt – Go away.

Flydu – Fly or flee.

Fellivetur – Slaughter winter.

Flatkökur – Hard bread charred without fat on a griddle.

Gluggagægir – A Christmas lad whose name means "window peeper."

Gódan dag – Good afternoon.

Góda nótt – Good night.

Gott kvöld – Good evening.

Gravlax – Raw salmon cured in rock salt and dill.

Hangikjöt – Smoked lamb.

Hardfiskur – Cod, haddock, halibut, or catfish that has been beaten and hung up to dry on racks.

Huldu Folk – The "hidden people," little elf-like people of Icelandic folklore.

Jólasveinar – Yuletide/Christmas lads. Thirteen imps in the

Icelandic Christmas tradition who visit, one a day, for thirteen days before Christmas eve. They leave little presents for the children in shoes that have been put on the windowsill the night before. If the children have been naughty, the imps leave a potato or a reminder that good behavior is better.

Logga – Slang, shortened version of *logreglumadur*, which means police officer.

Loup-garou – Werewolf (French).

Lupinus – Wolf (Latin).

Niflheim – A realm of freezing mist and darkness. Hel, the realm of the dead, lies within it.

Nordurleid – A bus line whose name means "North Way" or "North Route."

Pottasleikir – A Christmas lad whose name means "pot licker."

Ragnarok – The final battle between the gods and the giants in old Norse mythology.

Skyr – A butter-like spread made from milk and sour cream. Icelanders eat *skyr* as a dessert with sugar or cream or fruit.

Stúfur – A Christmas lad whose name means "itty bitty."

Svid – Singed sheep's head, sawn in two, boiled, and eaten fresh, pickled, or jellied.

Úlfr-madr – Wolf man.

Úlfslikid – Wolf-thing.

Uppvakningur – A spirit that has been awakened from the dead. Zombie.

AUTHOR'S NOTE

The question I am most often asked about the Northern Frights series is: "Where did you get your ideas?" It's a common question from teachers, students, and other readers. The ideas for the stories about Sarah, Michael, and Angie came from some wonderful, inspirational Icelandic sagas and old Norse myths. There are far too many to list, but I thought I'd mention a few of the most influential collections:

Myths of the Norsemen by Roger Lancelyn Green, published by Penguin Books. This is a fairly easy read with illustrations. There's a good selection of myths and folktales, including Sigurd's epic battle with Fafnir the dragon.

The Norse Myths by Kevin Crossley-Holland, published by Penguin Books. This is one of the most eloquent adaptations of the Norse myths about Loki, Thor, Odin, and all the other gods. It's full of poetic language and extensive notes on the text. A warning though, it is also true to the bawdy nature of the original myths.

Grettir's Saga translated by Denton Fox and Hermann Pálsson, published by University of Toronto Press. This would be tough slogging for younger readers, but you librarians and adult readers (I know you're out there) might be interested in reading this account of Grettir the Strong's life.

For anyone who wants to know more about Iceland, just visit http://www.samkoma.com. Samkoma means "meeting place," and at this site you can search for any topic under the Icelandic sun.

And finally, if you have any comments or want to know more about the Northern Frights series, or about me, just drop by http://www.arthurslade.com.

Bless,
Art